I0576968

James D Waddell

Biographical Sketch of Linton Stephens

(Late Associate Justice of the Supreme Court of Georgia)

James D Waddell

Biographical Sketch of Linton Stephens
(Late Associate Justice of the Supreme Court of Georgia)

ISBN/EAN: 9783337016289

Printed in Europe, USA, Canada, Australia, Japan

Cover: Foto ©Raphael Reischuk / pixelio.de

More available books at **www.hansebooks.com**

BIOGRAPHICAL SKETCH

OF

LINTON STEPHENS,

(Late Associate Justice of the Supreme Court of Georgia,)

CONTAINING A SELECTION OF HIS

LETTERS, SPEECHES, STATE PAPERS, ETC.

EDITED BY

JAMES D. WADDELL.

" Heu! quanto minus est cum reliquis
Versari quam tui meminisse."—SHENSTONE.

ATLANTA, GEORGIA:
DODSON & SCOTT—NO. 38 BROAD STREET.
1877.

TO

LOGAN EDWIN BLECKLEY,

(Associate Justice of the Supreme Court of Georgia,)

WHO NOW SO WORTHILY ADORNS THE SEAT ON THAT HIGH

TRIBUNAL TO WHICH

LINTON STEPHENS,

FOR A BRIEF TERM, IMPARTED SPLENDID ILLUSTRATION,

THESE UNPRETENDING PAGES ARE RESPECTFULLY

AND

Affectionately Inscribed.

THERE WOULD SEEM TO BE FITNESS, IN THIS HUMBLE WAY,

IN LINKING THE NAME OF THE ONE WITH

THE MEMORY OF THE

OTHER.

INTRODUCTION.

THE life of LINTON STEPHENS was one of character rather than of incident—more the life of a thinker than an actor upon the stage of human affairs. He chose to be a spectator of passing events, and was content to weigh their significance and watch their succession through the "loopholes of retreat," so as not "to feel the pressure of the crowd." He had little relish for the hot arena of the world-strife. The mild dignity that environs the good citizen was more beautiful and more attractive in his eyes, and more grateful to his tastes and habitudes, than "the applause of listening senates," or the victor's wreath of laurel. The blaze of public notoriety he shunned. He shrunk from all manner of self-exposition or display. Vain-glory was not among the imperfections of his nature. He was perfectly satisfied with knowing the truth of anything, or any fact, *himself*— uncaring whether the outside world appreciated his knowledge thereof or not; hence, he had no ambition to make history: he was content to study its lessons, interpret its facts, and learn wisdom from its teachings. Although it was impossible for a man of the parts he had, not to be conspicuous among men; and although his opinions upon every subject—large enough to agitate a free people—were anxiously sought after, impatiently waited for, and eagerly canvassed, yet he never held, nor—left to his own volition— ever aspired to hold, high political station. For this reason, the general reader of these pages will remark the lacking, somewhat, of that significance of events in the story of his life which imparts the chief interest, attraction, and charm to biography.

LINTON STEPHENS.

THE paternal grandfather of Linton Stephens was Alexander Stephens, an Englishman by birth. He was scarcely nineteen years of age when the affair of 1745 transpired; yet, young as he was, he ardently espoused the cause of Charles Edward, "the Young Chevalier," as he was called. When fate frowned upon the fortunes of the "Pretender's Son," the vigilance and the vengeance of exasperated power were eluded by seeking refuge in America. He at first found shelter and security among the Shawnee Indians in the colony of Pennsylvania. This was in the year 1746. How long he remained among that tribe is not definitely known—probably until near the breaking out of the Revolutionary war. Fifty years had rolled over his head, when the curtain rose upon that drama, "yet was his eye not dim, nor his natural force abated." He early and eagerly embarked in the Colonial struggle for independence. We may imagine that the memory of wrongs, real or supposed, which he had suffered in his native land, stimulated the zeal and nerved the arm of the exile in a cause which his judgment, without such incentive already approved as just. He enlisted as a private, and when Independence was achieved, his military rank was that of Captain in the Pennsylvania forces.

Captain Stephens seems to have been of the class of men—numerous enough in his day, now almost extinct—that "hate ease," are full of enterprise, fond of adventure, restless, always moving, if not always advancing. Before the close of the war, he married Catharine, daughter of Andrew Baskins, a gentleman of repute and the wealthy proprietor of what was then, and for years afterwards, known as Baskins' Ferry, at the confluence of the Susquehanna and Juniata rivers.   The marriage seems to have been displeasing to the father-in-law—for what reason we cannot conjecture, unless it was, that he looked upon his son-in-law as a "Soldier of fortune," bred, as he perhaps imagined, in the Dalgetty school, and unworthy of matrimonial alliance with a prospective heiress, who should count her possessions by so many thousands.   Be that as it may, after the consummation of the marriage, the daughter was discarded ; and Captain Stephens, some time after the war, and after all attempts at reconciliation had proved to be unavailing, emigrated to Georgia, in 1795, bringing along with him little other treasure than a wife, a large number of children, and an unbroken spirit.   He first pitched his tent in Elbert county, but finally settled in Wilkes, now Taliaferro county, where he died in 1813.   He lived to the patriarchal age of eighty-seven, and his remains lie entombed but a little way distant from the grave-yard of the old homestead.

Andrew Baskins Stephens, son of Alexander, was born in the State of Pennsylvania, in the year 1783.   He was twelve years old when his father moved to Georgia.   Facilities for academical instruction were limited and scant throughout Georgia and the Carolinas at that day.   Liberal education was the rare distinction of the children of affluence only.   Not to mention board-bills and traveling expenses, few could command means wherewith to meet the tuition fees of colleges and schools of learning in distant and more highly favored sections of the country.   Andrew, born to no patrimony, shared the common fate of other poor boys of the time and neighborhood.   The instruction doled out to him must have been essentially rudimental in kind, variety and degree. Indeed, the scholastic acquisitions of an alumnus of an institution, whose curriculum comprised reading, writing and cyphering, and which nothing but the inexorable exigence of such a state of society could create or would tolerate—the "Old Field School"—could scarcely have been grammatical, much less literary. But nature had dealt more generously with the boy than fortune. He was endowed with uncommon intellectual faculties; he had sound practical judgment; he was a safe counselor, sagacious, self-reliant, candid and courageous. He was held in high estimation as one of the "solid men" of the community—a man of inflexible integrity and great weight of character. He had large influence over the opinions and conduct of his neighbors; they counseled with him on matters of business, unbosomed their cares and vexations to him; he surveyed their lands for them; defined the metes and bounds thereof; and he was the common arbiter who settled their differences and disputes, and from his decision there was seldom any appeal. He was twice married: first in 1807 to Margaret, daughter of Aaron Grier and sister of the late Robert Grier, whose name is yet a household word throughout our Southern States.*

It is among the traditions of the neighborhood, wherein she dwelt and died, that Mrs. Stephens was a woman of capital sense and fair culture; remarkable for independence of thought; devoted to domestic pursuits; of cheerful, amiable temper, and unobtrusive, elevated piety. Three children only of this marriage survived infancy. These were a daughter, Mary, the eldest; Aaron Grier, the next, and Alexander H., the youngest, who was born February 11th, 1812. In 1814, Mr. Stephens married, in second

---

* A quarter of a century ago, "Grier's Almanac" hung beside the chimney-piece in almost every house in the Southern States, wherein a copy of the Bible could be found. The late R. C. Grier, of the Supreme Bench of the United States, was his kinsman.

nuptials, Matilda S., daughter of Colonel John Lindsay, of
Wilkes county.   He was of Scotch-Irish stock.   He bore
a conspicuous part in the struggle for Independence, rose
to the rank of Colonel in the Georgia forces, and was esteemed a gallant officer, and wary, skillful commander.   He
lost his sword-hand in battle, and in consequence of wearing a covering of silver over the stump, he acquired the
sobriquet of "Old Silver-fist."   After the war, he grew to
be rich in this world's goods, and, at one time, was the
owner of valuable landed estates on Little river, near Phillips' Bridge ; but good fortune finally forsook him ; he became involved in debt by security, and died leaving his estate very much reduced.   He had eight children, and the
patrimony, when divided among them, amounted only to
about six or seven hundred dollars to each.   He was re-
puted to be a man of strong mind, sterling honesty, un-
bending will, stormy passions ; the concurrent testimony of
all the family traditions is, that he was ardent in friendships,
implacable in hate, fond of good cheer, frank, fearless and
generous to a fault.   Some of these characteristics the
daughter, Matilda, inherited.   The basis of her intellectual
character was good sense ; the basis of her moral character
was truth ; her manners were dignified ; her disposition was
quiet and cheerful, and in all the relations of social life, she
was exemplary and amiable.   Five children were born of
the second wife, but only three lived to attain majority.
The eldest, John Lindsay Stephens, was a prominent lawyer
in the western part of the State, who died in his prime.
The next was Catharine B., now also deceased.   The
youngest was

LINTON STEPHENS,

the subject of this sketch.   He was born at the old homestead, some two miles northeast of Crawfordville, on the
first day of July, 1823.   It has been seen that English,
Irish and Scotch blood were commingled in his veins.   The

remaining narrative of his life will show that each separate
current asserted its peculiar quality and power in the con-
formation of a character which itself avouched the blended
extraction. For we shall see that he had the sturdy common sense, the iron will, the unquailing courage refined by
chivalry of Hampden; the emotional nature, the ardent affections, the unselfish devotion, the noble enthusiasm of
Grattan; the subtle discrimination, the cautious circum-
spection and metaphysical turn of the Scotch mind, as exemplified in Reid or Stewart.

His father died on the 7th of May, 1826, and his mother
died on the 14th of the same month, just seven days after,
thus leaving him a complete orphan before he was quite
three years old. At this time, the surviving children consisted of Aaron G. and Alexander H., by the first wife,
and John L., Catharine B. and Linton by the second. The
family, of course, had to be broken up. The estate went
into administration, and the children went to live with their
kin on the side of their respective mothers. Aaron G.
and Alexander H., to their uncle's, Colonel Aaron Grier,
of Warren county, who became their guardian. Linton
was committed to his grandmother and a maiden aunt on
his mother's side, where he remained for nearly four years.
The following extract from a letter to a female friend presents a touching and lively picture of the boy and his surroundings during this period.

His aunt then lived about a mile from Crawfordville:

MAY 30, 1866.

.   .   .   .

The foundation of all my ideas of friendship was laid in
the school of *solitude*. It came to me in the form of a
want, not a possession. The first recollection I have of
myself, I was an orphan at the age of three years, parcelled
out, one by myself, in the distribution of the children
among different relations at the sad breaking-up of my

father's household.   My memory goes distinctly back to
that early period of my life.   My childhood was without
companionship, and was felt to be so then.   I had my childish griefs and pains, but there was nobody to whom I could
say "I suffer;" nobody to whom I could say "I have suffered."   In the main, however, the world seemed very bright
and beautiful to me—abounding almost in enchantments.
I well remember the charms which nature used to have for
me in those days.   The woods, the streams, the skies, the
birds, the luscious fruits, the sweet-scented flowers, the
green sward in front of the door, the waving and murmuring forest of pines hard by—the whole glorious creation as
it unfolded itself to my young soul.   I remember one day
I was so full of the brightness and beauty of the world that
I ran to my aunt to know how I ever had come into it.
That thought had never got into my head before.   *That* I
could and did ask her; but it did not occur to me to tell her
how beautiful it all was to me—to ask her to share with me
in my enjoyment of it all.   But there was one short and
bright companionship which crossed my path in those days.
I was six years old then.   It came in the form of a little
girl named Cornelia Hays, who came and spent a week—a
whole week—at my aunt's.   How she happened to come
there I do not recollect; nor can I even now give a rational
conjecture on the subject; for I was the only child on the
place, and I can hardly suppose that a little girl came as a
playmate for a little boy.   However that may have been,
she *was* a playmate; and I thought a glorious one.   She
was a little older than I, and quite pretty, as I thought then,
and still think from my present recollection of her appearance.   It was in the time of the dog-woods and honey-
suckles.   How I did delight to climb the trees and bring
down these flowers, and lay them at the feet of my little
queen, or put them into her hands, and weave some of
them into her hair!   I loved to serve as her tiring-maid.
And she?   She seemed to enter into the spirit of it all.   I
remember that she particularly enjoyed a slide down a very
steep hill, which terminated at the bottom in a sand bank
bordering "the spring branch;" I found a smooth and
straight track down this descent, and conceived the idea of
running my "slide" down it.   If you don't know what a
boy's slide is, you can at least form a sufficient conception

of it from its name. It is a vehicle which moves in the manner indicated by its name. She and I, seated in this rude carriage, and with arms locked around each other for mutual support during the giddy flight, made the descent in a style which was ecstatic to such children as we were. On getting to the bottom, I would shoulder the little carriage, and toil with it back to the top again for a repetition of the glorious fun. Well, that little witch got all of my thoughts out of me in that one week. It was so delightful, so charming, to tell her everything. I do not know what has become of Cornelia Hays in the long and terrible years which have succeeded that one bright week. I have often wondered whether she lives, and remembers that week as I do. I scarcely think so, however, for such companionship was an every-day thing to her; while to me it was an oasis in a great desert.

During the year 1830, the administration of the estate of his father was wound up. The lands had been sold, and the servants apportioned among the heirs. The patrimony of each child was found to be four hundred and forty-four dollars. John W. Lindsay, his maternal uncle, now became Linton's guardian. Mr. Lindsay, who lived in Upson at the time, removed the ward and his effects to that county. The residence was not far from Union Hill. There Linton first went to school. His teacher was Master Strange—"a good English scholar"—as the phrase then was, by which is implied that he was sufficiently familiar with the elementary branches of a purely English education, and quite equal to the office of instruction therein, to wit: reading, writing, arithmetic and grammar. The school was distant two miles from the house of his uncle; the scholastic term extended through the winter months only, and having to go and return on foot, it is likely the state of the weather and roads interrupted the regularity of his attendance. In 1836, he was entered as a pupil in the academy at Culloden, whereof Mr. Ward Bullard was prin-

cipal.* There his stay was for about one year only, but
the influences over him were salutary. In the autumn of
the following year, he was transferred to the guardianship
of his brother, the Hon. Alexander H. Stephens, and took
up his abode at Crawfordville. Then and there it was "his
youth awoke first and fully to the life of the mind." Colonel
Simpson Fouche, a gentleman of ripe scholarly attainments
and accomplishments, and one of the best educators of
youth the century has produced, was at the head of a large
and excellent school at. Crawfordville. Under his tuition
young Stephens was prepared for admission to college.
The following letter from Colonel Fouche furnishes an interesting account of the deportment, progress and promise
of the pupil:

JACKSONVILLE, ALA., September 26, 1873.

MY DEAR SIR—Your letter of the 18th instant, asking
for my reminiscences of the late Judge Linton Stephens,
was received some days ago at Rome, Georgia.

I had charge of the academy at Crawfordville in the year
1838. The number of pupils in attendance was very large,
approaching very near to one hundred. Two pupils were
entered by the Hon. A. H. Stephens, one of them his
brother Linton, then a youth of some fourteen or sixteen
years of age, as nearly as I can judge. I had been engaged
in teaching for a number of years, at Washington in Wilkes
county, and at Powellton in Hancock—having generally,
especially at the latter place, a large number of pupils, and
laboring very earnestly and diligently; so that the management of the very large school at Crawfordville, with but
little assistance, was a very heavy task—particularly as the
youths of that place were pretty wild, and difficult to bring

---

* It is a feather in Mr. Bullard's cap that so many of his pupils became distinguished in after life. Among the contemporaries of Stephens
at that school were the present Governor of Georgia, James M. Smith;
United States Senator, Thomas M. Norwood, etc.; Robert P. Trippe, Associate Justice of the Supreme Court, preceded him in the academy by a
year or two only.

under proper discipline. Young Stephens was thus, at a critical age, subjected to all the seductive influences and temptations usually employed by a crowd of thoughtless associates, strongly inclined to idleness and mischief.

Yet he was regular and punctual in attendance, always blameless and manly in deportment, diligent and successful in study. Indeed, so uniformly correct and industrious was he, that I cannot now remember, nor do I believe that I ever had occasion, for the slightest reproof of him, for any error in deportment or failure in any point of duty, either in school or out of it. His progress in every branch of learning which he was then pursuing was what might have been expected from a youth of fine natural abilities, coupled with habits so exemplary. It was not only rapid, but thoroughly accurate and scholarly. If you ever taught, you can understand me when I say, that instruction to *such* a pupil is no *task*, but a positive *pleasure*. The respectful remembrance and intelligent testimonial of such a pupil are among the most grateful rewards of a faithful teacher.

During a very long career as a teacher, I can recall to mind no pupil who excelled—few who equalled—him in all the characteristics, moral and intellectual, of a thoroughly good pupil.

He was not of the number of those "born to greatness," nor yet of those who "have greatness thrust upon them," but of that better class who "achieve greatness" by their own manly efforts.

Such are my reminiscences of Judge Stephens. If you consider them of any worth, use them.

Yours, very truly,

S. FOUCHE.

In after life, when he had won his way to honorable fame— "greatness achieved"—he loved to recur to those privileged days and to hold in grateful remembrance the valuable offices of his academic mentor. But at this, the formative period of his life, there was another influence over him, stronger and greater than any other and all other extraneous ones, in giving bent to his tastes and mould to his whole character—intellectual, moral and social. It was the influence of his brother—enforced and energized alike by precept and example. Under that influence, theories of mind, of philosophy, of ethics, of religion, were discussed and embraced; the facts of history accepted; the real aims of life interpreted, and the high lessons of duty studied, learned and practiced.

In August, 1839, he was matriculated a freshman of the University of Georgia, and at the end of the full term of four years was graduated with the first honor, *solus*, in a large class of gifted competitors. Among them may be mentioned the Reverend J. L. M. Curry, D.D., LL. D., Honorable Edward H. Pottle, General L. J. Gartrell, William Lundy, Esq., the late John L. Bird*, and others who afterwards achieved honorable distinction in the various fields of labor and life.

The universal testimony is that his college-life was marked by diligent and assiduous studies, outside as well as inside of the curriculum, by exemplary deportment, by uniform civility to the Faculty of Instructors, and by respectful observance of law. The single instance of a fine having been imposed upon him, throughout the whole term of his four

---

Bird was the cousin of Stephens. He was educated by the Hon. A. H. Stephens—one of a large number, who was the favored recipient of the like benefaction from the same generous hand. Perhaps no American of the living, or of the dead, has so liberally aided indigent and deserving young men to defray their educational expenses as the "Sage of Liberty Hall;" certainly none, when his pecuniary means—competent enough for his own wants, but never affluent—are taken into account. Bird had rare genius; was full of fun and *bon-homie* and there were mixed in him the elements of a successful popular leader. He chose the profession of law, and shortly after admission to the bar, was elected to the office of State Senator. He had little relish for the *drudgery* of legislation—as little as the Arabian racer may be imagined to have for the dray—yet, he conscientiously performed the irksome work of the committee-room. On the floor, he rose to the foremost rank of debaters in the Georgia Senate, at a time "when there were giants in the land." He fell a victim of pulmonary consumption just as the auroral flush was brightening into the light of unclouded day.

years' residence at the University, was levied for the "white sin" of "playing the flute during study hours." He was a member of the Phi Kappa Society—

—— "A school wherein every principle
Tending to honor is taught, if followed."

There he won his earliest laurels ; it was the theater of his young renown ; and there he first gave earnest of the marvelous perfection which he afterwards attained in the practice of forensic debate.

Of this period of his life, the Rev. Dr. Curry writes:

RICHMOND, VA., December 21, 1873.

DEAR SIR—In fulfillment of my promise to give you some reminiscences of the college-life of Linton Stephens, I state that we entered Franklin College in August, 1839, and continued fellow-students until August, 1843, when we graduated. Having been class-mates and fellow-members of the Phi Kappa Society for four years, I had unusual opportunities for knowing him very intimately.

As a student, he was scrupulously attentive to his duties. His habits were correct, methodical, exemplary. He was too diligent to give much time to social pleasures, and, therefore, the circle of his intimate companions was not large. By uprightness, frankness, conscientiousness, and gentlemanly bearing, he secured the confidence and esteem of all his fellow-students. I cannot recall a single instance of failure in his recitations. He excelled in all departments, and the college records, if preserved, will show that he invariably received the highest marks in all his monthly reports. When the faculty, at his graduation, awarded to him the highest honor, they only gave official certainty to the unanimous verdict of the students. In the Literary Society, Linton took an active part. His speeches were the fruits of accurate reading and careful meditation, and were rather characterized by fullness of information and closeness of reasoning than by brilliancy or eloquence. To have him on a particular side of a question was, in the later days of his college-life, the earnest of victory. Sometimes, when aroused, he displayed vehemence and power. He hated sham and deception, and dealt honestly with his own mind. In the Society, he gave promise of the judicial fairness, the logical acumen, the breadth of view, and the firm adherence to principle, which so distinguished him in his brief and useful career. Widely different as were T. R. R. Cobb and Linton Stephens, I never knew two young men, whose college lives so surely gave promise of future usefulness and distinction.

Yours, truly,

J. L. M. CURRY.

I am indebted to the kindness of Judge William Lundy, another class-mate, for the following interesting reminiscences:

MACON, October 6, 1873.

DEAR COLONEL—In compliance with promise, I herewith transmit some reminiscences of the late Judge Linton Stephens, and my "impressions of the man, particularly such as cover his college-life and relate to the formative period of his character." At the outset, a remark occurs to me, which I made to a gentleman, with whom I was walking, when we met and exchanged salutations with Judge Stephens, in the city of Atlanta, some two or three years ago: "He has not changed, save that time has robbed his face a little of its freshness, and the silvery tracings are visible upon the dark locks of his hair," which then had been permitted to grow to an unusual length. It should be premised, however, that I did not know Mr. Stephens during the earlier part of his college course. I was not with him to share the troubles of the timid and often persecuted Freshman. I never witnessed any of his encounters as Sophomore, with the assumptions and arrogance of the more advanced classes—at that period when self-reliance (often miscalled self-sufficiency) begins to take deep root, and prepares the boy for the storms which await him in after life.

Leaving Mercer University, Junior, half-advanced, I matriculated at Franklin College in January, 1842. Soon after my arrival, I met an old college friend, named Bailey, who hailed from South Carolina, and who had preceded me sufficiently long to become familiar with our new surroundings. With him the following colloquy took place: "Dr. Church* informs me that you have stood your examination and found your same class? 'Yes; it is a good class; there are some splendid fellows in it.' 'Name some of the most prominent.' 'There are Tom White, of Elbert; Lafayette Lamar and Jabe Curry, of Lincoln, etc., but Linton Stephens is looked upon as the prospective first-honor man.' 'Who is Linton Stephens?' 'He is from Taliaferro, and brother of the Hon. A. H. Stephens.' I ventured to suggest that the reputation of the distinguished statesman, who even then was regarded as one of the brightest luminaries in the South, may have had undue influence in giving prominence to the younger brother, and secretly resolved to take observations and judge for myself. It was not long before I was ready to acquiesce in the frankly-expressed opinion of my Palmetto State friend. Soon, on the way to the recitation-room, I was introduced to the young man who had been the special subject of our conversation.

He was of rather stout build, with dark hair and rather heavy eyebrows, giving the eye a deep-set appearance, and conveying the impression of inflexible determination. His countenance was composed, thoughtful, and serious, almost to sadness. He wore a full suit of dark, home-made jeans; for, in those days, there was, perhaps, less said about economy than now; but there was a greater number willing to illustrate the good effects and full force of a 'philosophy which teaches by example.'

Permit me to remark, in this connection, that G. J. Orr, now our popular State School Commissioner, is inseparably associated in my memory with that old dark, long jeans frock-coat he wore so long and so well; and Ben. Hill, in those days, rejoiced in the possession of a full suit of light blue jeans, embracing a coat with a skirt of liberal length. Others of these homespun boys might be mentioned, who, let it be added for the encouragement of the young, have since fought the battle of life successfully, and become both useful and distinguished among their fellow-men.

---

* Dr. Church was at that time President of the College.

Returning from this brief digression, I shall first refer to the scholastic attainments of our deceased friend. I can state, without hesitation, that during the eighteen months I was associated with him—and we both belonged to the same division of the class—I never knew him to make a failure in the recitation-room. Ranking high in all the departments, he was peculiarly distinguished for his readiness in the solution of difficult problems in the higher branches of mathematics. During the last term of the senior year, a course of lectures was delivered on railroading, engineering, and what is now more familiarly known in the schools as 'applied sciences.' Every member of the class was required to take notes and write out each lecture—the manuscript, at the close of the course, to be bound and form a volume of valuable and useful information. Not unfrequently the notes prepared by Linton Stephens were copied and handed in by other members of the class to save themselves trouble, so implicit was their confidence in his accuracy and reliability. He was a Phi Kappa—I a Demosthenean; and, consequently, I am not so familiar as others with his performances as a debater. But I remember that on a certain occasion—perhaps immediately preceding our Junior commencement—some subject of dispute arose, which caused much excitement and provoked considerable discussion among us. A meeting of students was called in the chapel, and organized by the appointment of a presiding officer. A number of speeches were made, crimination and recrimination indulged in, with no peaceful result in prospect. At length, Linton Stephens, who had been quietly listening, arose, and, in a calm, respectful manner, made a short, lucid, well-timed speech, in which the whole subject was thoroughly analyzed. There was no assumption—no arrogance—nothing offensive, but the matter was so clearly held up to the light that it was easily comprehended. His was the last speech made, and he was sustained by the meeting, it being his good fortune, no less by cogency of reasoning than by his respectful bearing, to accomplish his purpose, and 'pour oil upon the troubled waters.'

Usually, he was rather taciturn and meditative, but not selfishly so; and often, in our evening strolls, or on the way to the boarding-house, when anecdote and fun were uppermost, he joined with the little knot of lively young fellows, whose sallies of wit and quick repartee made the 'high dome' ring with peals of joyous laughter. While endeavoring to store his mind with the treasures of learning, he was not altogether indifferent to the happy influences of a spice of mirth. As a gentleman, he was unexceptional in deportment to both students and professors. He conformed strictly with college regulations; but I will give an instance of his complicity with a practical joke, which we sometimes played upon Professor James Jackson. Glorious 'Old Major!' Peace to his ashes! 'The Major' (as he was universally called) was fond of anecdote and fun; and a lively disputation with the boys, even on politics, had for him great attraction. The history of the 'Yazoo Fraud:" its repeal, the burning of the obnoxious records on the State House square at Louisville, *with fire drawn from heaven*, and especially the honorable connection which his distinguished father had with procuring a repeal of the disgraceful act, was a topic on which the Major seemed not to know when he had said enough or heard enough. One evening, after the bell had sounded the recitation hour, it was ascertained, between Old College and the old brick laboratory, in which was his lecture and recitation-room, that only three or four of the class had studied the lesson. To avoid the mortification of so large a number answering 'not prepared,' we agreed to take advantage of the Major's pardonable weakness and 'talk against time.' A young man from Columbia county, who had remarkably fine conversational powers, (and of whom the Major was wont to say, 'Sir, if you had lived in ancient times, you certainly would have belonged to the School of Sophists, and if your tongue was a sword, sir, you would make an excellent swordsman,') was to begin. Others were to join in and lead the conversation in the direction of politics. The Major was a little restive, and not disposed to be communicative at first—perhaps not entirely unsuspicious. But when Linton Stephens, with as much gravity as he could command, asked to be informed as to some facts relative to the early history of Georgia, and more particularly the repeal of the 'Yazoo Act,' the old Professor's countenance lighted up with smiles, and he responded at length. We plied him with questions, which he answered, totally obliv-

ious of the passage of time, until the college-bell sum
moned all from recitation-rooms to the chapel and to ves-
pers.   It was with no little pleasure we heard it announced
from the chair: 'Young gentlemen, tak'n, take the same
recitation for to-morrow.'*   .   .   .   .

    I am, very truly,   WILLIAM LUNDY.

When young Stephens entered college, there began an
epistolary correspondence between himself and his brother
Alexander, which was kept up almost daily—save when
sickness, or the *living epistle*, interrupted it—for more than
thirty years.   I have had access to a large portion of that
correspondence.   Almost every topic of the passing time,
whether of general or personal concern—men, measures,
subjects of philosophy, of history, of morality, of religion,
of science, literature, and art, are therein discussed, with
that freedom, fullness and candor which the *abandon* of perfect confidence only can generate or justify.   Of those
written by the elder brother during Linton's college-life,
there is scarcely one which does not contain some word of
warning, of kindly admonition, and of encouragement in
the performance of duty; nor scarcely one wherein he does
not assert, and seek to impress still more deeply upon the
mind, his own faith in the reality of virtue, of enthusiasm,
and the progress of man.   A beautiful feature character-
izing the letters of each is the pure, fraternal affection with
which they breathe and burn.   Some conception of the influences under which the subject of this sketch was reared,
his principles confirmed, his tastes fashioned, his aspirations kindled, his whole character molded, may be formed
from the spirit and sentiment of the following letters from
that brother:

  * The students of the college, who sat under the "Old Major's" instructions, will remember that, when a little excited, with something like
a stutter, he almost invariably said, "Tak'n, take," meaning simply
"take."   He was an able and popular professor—an accomplished
scholar; and, while the kindest and most guileless of men, there was no
lack of the *fortiter in re* element in his nature.

[From A. H. S. to L. S.]

CRAWFORDVILLE, January 26, 1840.

.　.　.　　　.　.　.

The poet says:

> " A little learning is a dangerous thing :
> Drink deep, or taste not the Pierian spring."

And there is as much truth as *satire* in the couplet.　To be a *smatterer*—to learn enough only to imbibe the errors of the world, and to become puffed up or inflated with the conceitedness of self-importance—are no less ruinous to the unfortunate subject than disgustful to the whole circle of his equally unfortunate acquaintance.　To be a scholar—to place one's self above the common level—to ascend the steeps of science, and climb the rugged cliff of fame—require energy, resolution, time, self-denial, patience, and ambition.　These are not the common qualities of a fickle brain, but the higher attributes of genius.　He that possesses them by disciplining them and subjecting them to proper obedience to his own master-spirit, can control not only his own destiny, but that of others.　.　.　.　Good-bye.　Let me hear of your doing well.　Fortune is a web, and every man weaves it for himself.　Tell John howdy'e, and remember me to Lewis and Joseph LeConte, and James Green.

[From same to same.]

CRAWFORDVILLE, February 2, 1840.

DEAR BROTHER—I am in receipt of yours of the 29th ultimo, and see in it nothing that you need be ashamed of, but much that afforded me pleasure—particularly its general spirit of *frankness* and independence.　There is no virtue in the human character more noble than *candor*— plain, real, unsophisticated *candor;* it is the legitimate *off-spring* of truth, and always begets independence.　The two seldom are separated, and both should be cherished as the

2

governing principle of real nobleness of soul and all true manliness. Some parts of your letter savored a little of a morbid excitement; perhaps you have been stimulating your ambition too much, until that which should have been the embodied and living sentiment of the soul's deep *resolve* has kindled into a passion, and burns not with a healthful action, but a feverish heat. If so, this should be corrected, and that speedily, too, else the same breast that so fondly cherishes a longing restlessness for fame and distinction may come short of its wishes by falling itself a victim to its own aspirations. "Vaulting ambition," says Shakspeare, "o'erleaps itself;" or, as Byron has most beautifully expressed a similar sentiment in relation to *Kirke White*, in his satire on English Bards and Scotch Reviewers, and paraphrased to suit my present purpose, would read thus: (speaking of White's untimely death.)

> "Oh, what a noble heart was here undone,
> When *Ambition's* self destroyed her favorite son;
> Yes, she too much indulged thy fond pursuit—
> She sow'd the seeds, but death has reaped the fruit.
> 'Twas thine own spirit gave the fatal blow,
> And help'd to plant the wound that laid thee low;
> So the struck eagle, stretch'd upon the plain,
> No more through rolling clouds to soar again,
> View'd his own feather on the fatal dart,
> And wing'd the shaft that quivered in his heart.
> Keen were his pangs, but keener far to feel,
> He nurs'd the pinion which impelled the steel,
> While the same plumage that had warm'd his nest
> Drank the last life-drop of his bleeding breast."

This beautiful allusion, however, to a passion too fondly indulged in, refers more particularly to its effect on the health of the body than its reaction on the *mind itself*, while it is to this latter view more particularly I wished to direct your attention. Bulwer, who is one of the finest delineators of character I have ever read, has given many illustrations of it. Some of these you will see in the character of Warren the artist, in the thirteenth chapter of first book of "*The Disowned*," and in the character of *Talbot*, as related in the twentieth chapter of the same book. I wish you to read both these chapters soon as convenient, as well for your amusement as instruction; and many hints upon the same subject, you recollect, are to be gleaned from the character of Castruccio (*the mad poet*), in "Ernest Maltravers."

You probably judge of the opinions of others towards you from the state of your own feelings, which may have become too much excited for your own success, to be sufficiently cheerful in the company of your associates. *A man is generally treated by the world as he treats it*, and to get from others their good-will, esteem and confidence, he must generally yield the contribution of his own.

Upon the subject of *aristocracy*, to which you allude, I would say that there is one kind of *aristocracy* I with you equally despise, but another kind I greatly admire. The first is the *aristocracy* of *wealth* and fashion, etc.—a folly that is contemptible. The other is the aristocracy (the *aristos crateo*) of *honor, principle, good-breeding* and *education*—that awards distinction not to birth or to fortune, but to *merit* and *principle*, and that, in a word, which proclaims, in the language of the Muse:

> "Honor and shame from no condition rise;
> Act well *your part*—there all the honor lies."

This is the aristocracy of nature, and is *cast* by no hereditary descent, but is an impress given by Dame Fortune to her own favorite children. You should not hastily come to the conclusion, that without cause you are held in low esteem by your fellows; and if, after due reflection, such opinion or conclusion should be confirmed, why, then your own independence should cause you wholly to disregard such estimation so entertained: not by evidences of *disrespect* on your part evinced towards them in the way of retaliation—for that would prove you affected by their opinions, and not independent and superior to them—but by the appearance (which also must be genuine) of a real unfeigned disregard for themselves, their feelings, their esteem, their love or their hatred, their good-will or their prejudice; I say totally indifferent, and neither biased *one way* or the other by the show of either class of feelings. This is true *independence*, and anything short of it is a spurious affectation. To exercise it, I know, requires great self-composure, quick perception, and strength of judgment—with feelings high above all prejudice, and such as would cause a man, under such circumstances, to praise where praise was due and censure where censure was due, and to preserve, in all his intercourse with such people, the same calm indifference with which he would attend to his horse or administer to the wants of other *brutes* in the way of giving them food or affording them other relief, or even a little chastisement, if required, irrespective of any demonstration of ill-will or bad-temper that might be given during the performance of his duty. Such I know is a lofty stand for a man to take, and requires great power of superior intellect for him to maintain; but when one is able to do it, the same fellows who before were snapping and growling and barking at everything he did, will soon be seen fawning and wallowing at his feet, with all the humility and sycophancy of curs.

But as I stop, I will do so with Burns' closing stanza to his young friend:

> "In plowman phrase, 'God send you speed,'
> Still daily to grow wiser,
> And may you better reck the *rede*
> Than ever did th' adviser."

[From same to same.]

FEBRUARY 28, 1840.

. . . . In relation to the doctrines of the Universalists, you allude to in your letter, and particularly in that part wherein you request my opinion, I would barely say, without entering fully into the subject, that I do not agree with him in the belief that there is "no personal devil or fallen spirit, and that what is commonly called the devil is no more nor less than the inclination of men to do evil." What I mean by personal devil is an evil spirit—a spiritual intelligence, apostate and fallen. There are doubtless many spiritual intelligences besides the Deity. Some are pure or holy and sinless, such as we call angels; others are of natures opposite, being evil, rebellious and disobedient, such as in the Scriptures are called devils. Among all the spirits or intelligences, whether apostate or not, there are doubtless grades: some are superior and some inferior in the scale of existence. There are seraphim and cherubim, and perhaps many other grades, amongst the angels;

and as Gabriel and Michael and some others seem to stand highest with them, even so Satan seems to stand first, or archangel, amongst the fallen spirits, and is emphatically called "*the* devil." Now, there may be, and no doubt is, much error in the world about "the devil tempting men," etc. My opinion is, that the devil tempts men just as one bad man tempts another. Mind is subject to influence, and spirit acts upon spirit; and as even amongst men the associations of bad company are contaminating in their influence, so much more will it be the case with him who suffers his desires, propensities or affections to be directed to improper objects, or dwell upon improper subjects: for, in addition to his natural inclination, being himself depraved, the company of his thoughts, by the communion of spirits, will soon be courted by the *great* evil genius, who is "going about like a roaring lion seeking whom he may devour"— all upon the same law governing the association of men, except the language and such other influences as come through the medium of sense. So, you perceive, I have no doubt either of the existence of such an intelligence, personage or being, or the influence of his associations upon the minds and principles of men.

Your conclusions from my premises or principles, touching the nature of future punishments, were clearly correct. If punishment or sufferi..g be a necessary result from the laws of the soul, existence or being, in a certain state, it must continue so long as such state continues unchanged, which will be *forever*. It was certainly a very absurd idea of the preacher's about the two infinite existences, and the "*sequiter*" he deduced. But, by-the-by, to put one's self to the trouble of following such a fellow as B———, and detecting his errors and sophistries, seems to be one of those cases in which the doctrine of the maxim, "*Operæ pretium non est*," would most aptly apply. The labor would cost more than it comes to. . . . . A. H. S.

[From same to same.]

CRAWFORDVILLE, March 3, 1840.

DEAR BROTHER—I wrote you a letter which left here on last Sunday night's mail, and now send a few more lines, just because I have an opportunity. All the news since that time is that we have been disappointed in our court, in consequence of the ill-health of Judge Andrews. The court that should have been held stands adjourned till the fifth Monday in this month.

Dr. Bird has moved his quarters to this part of town, and has taken board with us—that is, with Uncle Bird. We now have quite a professional club: Mr. Cook and his lady, *teachers;* myself, Mark Johnston and Daniel Roberts, *gentlemen of the bar;* and Dr. Bird, of the *healing art.*

.   .   .   .

Mr. Baker will take up for you one of my summer coats, which, if it fits, you can wear. But be very cautious in changing your dress as the warm weather comes on. This is the most dangerous season in the year for influenza and such catarrhal affections as sometimes end in consumption. Indeed, I am disposed to think that the spring of the year has more effect upon the general health of the system than any other. It is true that its effects are not so plain and perceptible; that people then are more generally unhealthy; but that is only owing to the nature of the influence it is exerting—it is only more latent or secret; or, what may be more true, it is a kind of *seed-time* of disease— passing pleasantly by, while it sows deep the *seeds* of death, leaving summer and fall to attend to the harvest. However this may be, my experience teaches me that spring has always been the critical period with myself, and I have noticed a similar effect upon others. The same effect is also witnessed upon trees. Almost all fruit and forest trees (except pine and cedars) seem to sicken, decline, and decay and die in the spring, soon after the commencement of vegetation and the flowing of the sap—except when the death may be attributed to some direct cause, such as drought or wounds, etc. The philosophy of the thing I don't pretend to explain; but it seems that from a change in the circulation, vitality, etc., the equilibrium in the principle of life is more difficult to sustain. And so with the human system: at that time the circulation is more obstructed, and some of the organs seem to be loaded with accumulated secretions, producing dullness, while slowly and stealthily disease is making the most dangerous advances upon the constitution. But enough of this. Never grow careless of your health, nor too cautious of it. There is in this, as in all things, a *golden mean*, which should, if possible, be maintained. .   .   .   .   .

I commenced this letter on one-half sheet only, intending to send you a few lines, but some how I have spun it out so that I have called in an additional *scrap* to conclude upon. Last night, between seven and eight o'clock, we had one of the most gorgeous displays of nature I ever witnessed: it was a meteorological phenomenon, which made its appearance directly in the west. The atmosphere had been, and was dry and loaded with smoke, and during the evening it had become somewhat cloudy from the southwest. At the time of the evening mentioned, it was quite dark, and heavy thunder was heard in the distance, off to the southwest, with occasionally a gleam of lightning, brightening or lighting up the atmosphere without any apparent source of locality, when directly toward the west a faint light was at first perceived at an angle of about ten degrees with the horizon, as if reflected from some distant fire; it soon, however, grew brighter and brighter, until, within a few minutes, the whole western hemisphere was encircled in its extent, presenting just such fiery redness as you might suppose would have been the case if some large city, ten miles off, had been wrapt in flames—making, in the darkness of the night, the far-off clouds the signal of distress. Many were the spectators to the scene. Some thought Greenesboro was on fire, or some other great fire was raging, while I was fully confirmed in the opinion that it was electrical in its origin. It at last became so bright that the forest trees could be distinctly seen in its direction for a mile off, and presented the app arance of an eastern sky of a thick smoky night just before the moon's disc can be discerned above the horizon's edge. Its continuance was about ten minutes, and was in full splendor when obscured by gusts of wind and rain, with thunder and lightning, which added somewhat to the grandeur of the scene. I was at Scott's Hotel in the piazza, and was the first to observe its appearance and full developments, and I never before saw anything of the kind—not even the *aurora borealis* in 1836—to equal it in richness and splendor. It was one of nature's grandest shows; and yet, hundreds of this world's groveling crowds gazed upon it with as little thought as they would upon a huntsman's torch—so prone to earth in their cares and afflictions, they have no admiration for the beauties of the heavens—and would not be half as much affected by a similar exhibition, even doubled in magnificence, as they would be by a single glimpse at the pale and troubled light of the flickering *ignis fatuus*. But I must stop, or I shall have to call in even another *scrap* to envelop this. I write to-night as a dyspeptic eats—with a coming appetite. . . . .

Affectionately,
A. H. STEPHENS.

"The progress of the age" has frowned down the old-time custom of the younger brother donning the half-worn clothes of the elder; but the fact hardly helps to refute the theory, that there are two kinds of progress—the one *upward*, the other *downward*.

[From same to same.]
CRAWFORDVILLE, March 29, 1840.

DEAR BROTHER— . . . . I hope you are studious, and active in exercise. Don't forget or neglect your common-place book. Pen down all interesting thoughts, and don't be too choice in the selections of your interesting thoughts, for fear you will pen none. Recollect that thought is a prolific something, and one always begets another; begin with something. I should like also if you would send me a copy of your compositions. I want to see what you are doing. . . . .

[From same to same.]
CRAWFORDVILLE, April 5, 1840.

DEAR BROTHER— . . . . . . The past week has been one of great excitement and labor to me; indeed, almost greater than my strength could bear. It was our Superior Court week, you know, and the business was not got through with until Friday morning. We sent Kirkland to the penitentiary for seven years: he that procured Farmer's negro woman to poison her mistress, or to make the attempt.

I was glad to see you had taken up the "Last Days of Pompeii." It is a work of great merit, though it hardly does justice to the early Christian advocates. In that particular its greatest defect consists. I think Bulwer, in one sense, greatly Scott's superior in novel-writing; his mind is of a higher order—he is more profound and metaphysical— in a word, more Platonic—while Scott is easier, more descriptive and can deal successfully in a much greater variety of character. Scott's best characters—that is, the *best drawn* are his *lowest*—Bulwer's best are his highest. . . . .

Among the earliest and deepest impressions made upon the mind of Linton Stephens was that of reverence for the Supreme Being; he accepted the Bible as a Divine Revelation; no occasion of hilarity, in the society of wild and thoughtless spirits, ever betrayed him into profanation of things deemed sacred; and for the professors of religion, whose faith was exemplified in their walk and conversation, he ever manifested the highest respect. While at college, he became a communicant of the Presbyterian Church— then under the charge of the Rev. Nathan Hoyt, D. D. The two letters following, from his brother, relate to that subject, and exhibit a solicitude at once anxious, considerate and beautiful:

[From A. H. S. to L. S.]

CRAWFORDVILLE, May 5, 1840.

DEAR BROTHER— . . . . The subject of Religion has been one that I have seldom alluded to in my correspondence with you, either in words or by letter. The principle upon which I acted (I believe) required me to pursue such a course. Perhaps, hereafter I may dwell more at large upon the subject. Let me hear from you often. I was going to give you some advice, but fear to do so. If I were with you, I might; for then I could better judge of its propriety; but as it is, I cannot. Read your Bible—make it your text-book of faith. . . . .

CRAWFORDVILLE, June 2, 1840.

DEAR BROTHER— . . . . I cannot, however, utter to you the intensity of feeling I sustain, when I think of the temptations and dangers of your new situation. I hope your prudence and confiding reliance upon a Superior Ruling Providence, whose protection and guardianship are always extended to those who trust themselves to His grace, will preserve you harmless. I never like to be a lecturer, or to give advice, because I am so sensible of my own errors and imperfections. And this is why I have said so little to you upon subjects of religion, morality and duty. But I trust you will not think the less on them yourself, or be more remiss in your actions. If I have said nothing, it is not because I felt nothing. I do hope, therefore, that you will not even trust yourself to your judgment or caution, but ask assistance from One who is able to direct you daily. I believe in a special providence. Of all Christian virtues, cultivate humanity and meekness and a spirit of dependence upon the great Ruler of the universe—"for every good and perfect gift." . . . .

Yours, affectionately,

A. H. S.

Concerning the opinions and principles of the prominent founders of the government—their different theories and their personal and political merits—we have the following letter, evoked by one of inquiry from Linton :

[From same to same.]

CRAWFORDVILLE, August 2, 1840.

DEAR BROTHER—It is Sunday, and I send you a few lines in answer to yours of yesterday. I shall write you again by Tuesday night's mail, sending on fifty dollars, if, in the meantime, I should not get some way of sending it by private, safe hands; and that is why I now write you, that you may, on Wednesday, expect the letter. In reference to that part of your letter devoted to politics, and the opinions of Judge Dougherty about the principles of the Federalists, etc., I would barely say that, in the beginning of our government, under the new organization, in 1787–88, all who were in favor of the ratification of the Constitution, or were friendly to the compact—or *Fœdus*, as it was called—assumed the name of Federalists ; those who opposed it took the various names of anti-Federalists, or Democrats, Republicans, etc. At that time, Madison and Jefferson were known as Federalists, or friends to the Constitution. Patrick Henry, and many other noble sons of Virginia, were opposed to it. After the Constitution, however, was ratified, and the government went into operation, many measures were proposed, which some of the friends of the Constitution thought were not authorized by that instrument, and which, if carried out, would centralize all power in the General Government, to the subversion of the States. That class, of course, fell back into the ranks of the Republicans. Amongst these were Mr. Jefferson and Mr. Madison, and many others ; while Patrick Henry and others fell into the ranks of the Federal class, saying that these powers, the others were then complaining of, were granted in the Constitution, and it was too late then to raise any complaint ; that they had warned them of the danger ; had foretold these consequences, and it was now too late ; the Constitution was established, and the country had to abide by it. Many of the measures of the Federalists of that time—say from 1790 to 1800—were, no doubt, good ones, while others were truly obnoxious—particularly the one against aliens, and one upon the subject of sedition, which to this time are known as Alien and Sedition Laws. It was those measures which showed a disposition, on the part of the Federal party, to be grasping powers not delegated, that caused the overthrow of that party, in 1800, by the election of Mr. Jefferson. Mr. Jefferson, of course, did not *take his seat* until 1801, (4th March.) The canvass, however, was in 1800. But, considering the *merits* of most of the obnoxious measures of those days, apart from all party or personal character or bearing, just as you would look at the laws of ancient countries, I believe there is not a great deal more to censure in them than many of the laws we have had passed in much later times. The *patriotism*, however, of those men who were called Federalists, even at the election of Mr. Jefferson, no man can doubt. They were amongst the earliest and most devoted friends and movers of the Revolution, and were among the master-spirits that struggled for and aided in the acknowledgment of our independence. They were all, no doubt, friends to free government, but differed, as men always will, as to the best method and means of administering it. It is true that Mr. Jefferson, in his *Anas* (some notes published at the end of his works,) intimates, and clearly indicates his belief that a large party then existed in the country, favorable to a monarchy; but, for my own part, I do not believe *one word of it.*   His aim was at Hamilton; but he was, in point of mind, intellect, integrity, manly bearing, and patriotism, high above all such suspicions.   Jefferson even intimates openly, in one of his letters, that Washington was aspiring to a throne.   With Hamilton's notions of government I do not agree; but that he was in favor of changing it into a kingly government, none, I think, would pretend to believe, who knows anything of his opinions of the formation of the Constitution.   He was truly a great man, but his *theories* did not suit the genius of our institutions.   You will see a good sketch of his life in the Edinburgh Encyclopædia, under the title of his name, I think; or, maybe it is the American Encyclopædia.   For a full and accurate history of all those, and that which *I like*, I refer you to a late work called the "*Olive Branch.*" You can get it in the library.   I wish you to read it, and at this time, as your mind is now more or less directed to those periods by daily conversation, and on that account more susceptible of receiving and treasuring up a large fund of useful history and good information.   I have not seen the book since I was in college, and there I got all my knowledge (except small gleanings occasionally from other quarters) upon the subject.   I have written a great deal more than I exptcted. . . . . . .

I dreamed last night you were dead; and, while no believer in dreams, I have, nevertheless, all day been more or less under the influence of the strange phantasm.   .   .   .

Thursday I have to be at Camak at a Harrison meeting and barbecue, if I am able.   Yesterday was a great day at Raytown—a barbecue and speeches from Gamble, Foster, Sayre, Johnson, (of Greene,) and Toombs.   The weather was very unfavorable, and yet, I suppose, over two thousand people were there.

[From same to same.]

CRAWFORDVILLE, August 26, 1840.

DEAR BROTHER—I am in receipt of yours of the 23d instant. With its general character and style, I was better pleased than I have been with any received from you in sometime past. I am in hope you will get entirely over your *costive* habit of letter-writing, and become *freer* in style and fuller in matter. My "surmise," I think, is having its desired effect in spurring you up. By-the-by, it was altogether a surmise, or an inference of my own, from *data* within my own possession. I have but to converse with a man, or see the products of his brain in writing, to form a very satisfactory conclusion touching the state of his mind—whether idle or industrious, active or indolent, sprightly or sluggish—and it was from this source I derived my opinion upon the subjects of your studies during the last term. You must not suffer yourself to fall into careless and relaxed habits of thought; for you may be sure the effect of such habits will soon reach the discernment of all; and that I may still keep you on the spur, I will direct your attention to some sentences and forms of expression in your last, that, I think, could have been bettered, and this I do the more readily, as I am so much better pleased with the letter than I have been with any lately received, and because your habit of writing is now forming, and whatever kind you form now, you will be apt to conform to all your life. And at first, it is about as easy to form a good habit as a bad one, and about as easy to adopt an easy, clear and correct style as a dull, clumsy and inaccurate one. In your first sentence, then, you say: "I received your letter *only* in time to have answered it one mail sooner." The word "only" is out of its proper place; it should have been just before "one mail;" thus: "I received your letter in time to have answered it *only* one mail sooner." Again you say: "It (my letter) arrived here *much before* I took it from the office," etc. *Much before*, you perceive, is not a very suitable equivalent for *sometime*, or *several days*, etc., as you evidently intended it. Again you say: "But I think if I had have had justice, I should have got the letter from the office," etc. How do you parse "had have had?" You must make it in a kind of

plu-plus quam-perfect, not known to the common standards.
The use of this form of expression is a common error in
this country. Many persons, who know better, or ought
to know better, have fallen into it. In common *parlance*,
it is "if I had of had," or "if I had of gone," or "if I
had of seen him," etc. ; or, in common style still, it runs
thus: "If I'd a had," or "I'd a gone," or "I'd a seen
him," etc. : all wrong alike. The plu-perfect of the verb
"to have" is "had had," without the "have." If I "had
had justice," etc., "if I had gone," or "had seen him."
But again you say: "It is more than probable that my
letter to you had been opened, as it might have been supposed to have had money in it," etc. This is another form
of expression, and a use of the perfect of the infinitive
mood, instead of the present, no less common than improper. If the letter, from its appearance, had been supposed to *have had* money in it, of course it would have
been a previous matter, and there would *then* have been no
inducement to open it; or, in other words, the appearance
of its having *had* money in it would imply that it had none
in it at the time. The expression should have been: "It
is more than probable that my letter to you had been
opened, as it might have been supposed to *have* money in
it." Read Kirkham's grammar, page 193, and Murray on
the tenses.

Besides these, I would barely hint at your orthography,
which, in some instances, might be corrected. Such as
government has an *n* in it, and *manner* is not properly
spelled without two of the same nasal sounds or characters. "Mentained," also, I suppose, you meant for
"maintained." The word "reckon," I think, you are
beginning to misapply, if not misuse; it is by no means
equivalent, in signification, with "think," "suppose,"
"suspect," or "expect." Georgians misuse this word
more than the Yankees do the word "guess." I
would advise you to read over your grammar, at leisure,
cursorily. Much good information is to be got from it;
and make it a matter of daily consideration with you to
attend to the *minutiæ* of things, and to be correct (not pe-
dantic or dogmatical) in all. When *awake*, keep your mind
always *wide awake*. In your history lessons that you complain of, I think you might, with a *little system*, soon get so

as to master twenty pages at or for one recitation. The
best system is to take the whole lesson in one scope or
view. Get the mind *fixed* upon the prominent events related in it, and the order of their succession, without the
author's language; then the when, the where and the who
come in almost of their own accord. With a little close
and intense application of the mind at first, in drilling it
and bringing it by a rigid discipline to this system, you will
soon be enabled even to astonish yourself at the ease with
which you will acquire (and with accuracy, too) the details
of such recitations. It requires labor, study and close attention for awhile, but, if properly trained, a faculty of the
mind will soon develop itself, not very unlike that which,
with a little practice, is so easily acquired in looking upon
paintings, and which is so necessary to the proper appreciation of the beauties and illusions of the perspective. It
is a species of abstraction which some never attain, but
only because they do not try in the right way. Read
over your lesson first hastily; get its general import. Have
the outlines fixed deeply, as those of a map, upon your
mind. Let this be done with eyes off the book as much as
possible; and then in the same way let the details follow;
instead of marking a name with a pencil, and leaving it in
the book, transfer the whole by the process of abstraction
to the canvas of your brain, and let the impression be
made upon its tablet.

When I first commenced those "reading studies," as we
called them, they seemed the most difficult of any I had
met with. I disliked them exceedingly. But after a little
exercise in them, and when I found it was useless to attempt to know anything about a recitation in one of them
without knowing everything, I soon commenced what
seemed the *intense labor* of mastering *everything* in each
lesson by impressing the whole subject upon my own mind,
and thinking as little of the book as possible, and it was
not long until those were the easiest lessons I had. It requires a good deal of time, though, at first. The faculties
of the mind are like raw militia: they must be trained and
drilled before they can effect much, and many of your class,
you will find, never will give theirs the proper training and
drilling; and it is when you get into studies where others
fag, that you should especially exert yourself; for these are

the only points in the race where anything is to be gained. Where it requires nothing *extraordinary*, there will always be some to share the place with the first. The commonest fellow can spell "baker," as well as the ablest scholar. There must be something that requires the exercise of stronger mental powers to show the difference, and when you get into a study difficult for the class generally, that is the time to distinguish yourself. . . . .

[From Linton to A. H. S.]

Athens, March 14, 1842.

Dear Brother—Yours of yesterday was received this morning, and I take the earliest opportunity of answering it, to let you know that the money you put in it has been safely received. The conveyance of that letter seemed somewhat mysterious, though I account for it in this way: at home, yesterday, you wrote it, sealed it, and on leaving for Greenesboro carried it to the post-office with the intention of mailing it, but in the hurry and confusion of start-ing, even the fifty dollars it contained were not sufficient to quicken your memory. That you originally intended to mail it in Crawfordville is clearly indicated by the direc-tion on its back to "charge A. H. S." with postage. After writing that direction, you must have forgotten the letter, or else you changed your mind and carried it on to "Union Point," hoping to meet with a private con-veyance which would be more safe than the mail. The latter conjecture is extremely improbable, however, unless I consider that you expected to find some *acquaintance* com-ing here, in which case this service would unquestionably have been preferable to mail conveyance; but that you should have more confidence in a stripling of a stranger, than in the mails, is somewhat strange. It is also a little mysterious that when I asked for only ten dollars, you have sent me fifty—for forty of which I have no use, and if John Bird wants any, it is more than I know. . . . . The most judicious disposal I can make of it, however, will, I think, be to divide it with John, so that each of us can advance for board twenty or twenty-five dollars.

Yesterday, for the first time, I heard a sermon from Judge Longstreet. In the pulpit, to me he appeared awkward, and to come much below himself. In preaching, he sometimes used Latin phrases and terms of expression unbecoming his place. In praying, for instance, I recollect he said in a very cold, conversational manner, "Lord, we can hardly generalize our sins, much less specify them," which, though used by a very devout man, seems to be very much opposed to that earnestness and dignity with which we should address ourselves to a very Superior Being. Though his manner is not suited to the pulpit, yet I think even there he shows he has genius. Next Saturday, I think our society will adjourn for the April examination. You may expect my next circular to show me deficient in attending church. In other respects, I have been perfectly punctual. I expect to be appointed junior orator, and if I should be so fortunate, with your knowledge of my mind, would you advise me to attempt a grave and sensible speech, or one of the gentle and insinuating kind; or would you rather still advise me to be *facetious and witty?*

In giving me an answer to this question, I beseech you, above all things, to spare your sarcasm. . . . .

Yours, affectionately,

LINTON STEPHENS.

[From A. H. S. to L. S.]

CRAWFORDVILLE, March 20, 1842.

DEAR BROTHER—Yours of the 16th instant, acknowledging the receipt of the fifty dollars, was received upon my return from the Greene court. I presume you have before this received another from me sent by Judge Dougherty, together with some collars and bosoms. This morning I got a letter from John, mailed yesterday. To-night I go to Augusta, and shall not, or do not expect at least, to return before Wednesday. I regret to hear that you will probably be deficient in anything in your next circular. It is so easy to be punctual in attendance at church; a deficiency in this particular is the less excusable. I also regret to hear you speak of *Rhetoric* as being the *hardest* study you have, and my reason for regretting this is, that it leaves me with the impression that you are not properly drilled in the right way of studying it. Rhetoric, properly taught, is one of the easiest and most improving and useful studies of a col-

3 *

lege course, and to me it was the most interesting. But it requires some training to get in the right way of learning it. It is to be effected by system, method and generalization. The usefulness of the study depends mostly upon its effect upon the mind in subjecting it to system and method, and the exercises it imposes upon the memory. It should never be taught or learned by *questions and answers*. You might as well attempt to teach the beauties of a piece of painting, to a mind unacquainted with the art of catching the perspective, by a similar system of interrogatories. In the study of rhetoric usefully, the mind must be first taught to put forth its strongest faculties, and survey and scan the entire subject—that is, the lecture for any given recitation. The author's object being thoroughly understood, his manner of treating it, and his various subdivisions, soon occur easily to the mind, which naturally again suggest his ideas, and then the task is performed, and the whole lecture is indelibly impressed upon the mind like a map or chart spread out before you. In mastering a lesson in rhetoric, the author's words should never be studied; if they occur readily to the mind in reciting, they should be used, but in studying, the memory should not be taxed to retain them; the ideas and the order in which they come in the lecture should be the task of the student. The ideas he should convey in his own words. For when he understands his author, and knows what his ideas are, the student can always have words at command to communicate and make known what they are. But it is a remarkable fact, that with a little practice with this kind of study, so quick does the memory become, and so retentive of an impression, that the student will be enabled to repeat almost the identical words of his author from beginning to end. This strengthens the memory and imparts vigor to the mind, and enables the faculties to encompass a whole subject at once, and understand the whole and every part at the same time. This is exceedingly necessary for writers and public speakers. When a student, therefore, goes to recite a lesson in rhetoric, or moral philosophy, or any such studies, he should know everything in his recitation, and be able forthwith, and without hesitation, to repeat, if called on, every idea in it, just as he would tell, if called on, what he heard a man say on any particular subject on a given occasion. As, for instance: suppose the lesson is in Blair, and the subject is his lecture on "Style." At the first glance, the mind will scan his manner of treating it, commencing with general remarks about the diversity of style in authors, then the various kinds of style, and then the rules for forming a correct style. Under the first head, many smaller and subordinate ideas, where the general plan is fixed in the mind, naturally suggest themselves with little or no effect: such as, that all authors have a peculiarity of style distinctive in each, difference between Livy and Tacitus, etc., and other ideas that fill up that view; and the different kinds of style, such as concise and diffuse, then contrasted, the advantages and disadvantages of each, and the instances of authors distinguished for each, etc., which is all easily recollected and repeated—that is, the idea, but not the words—and the same of the weak and nervous, dry, plain, neat, elegant and flowery, and then on to the simple, affected and vehement: these made all distinct in their order on the mind; the filling up, or the remarks made upon each, come to the mind almost naturally; and then comes the winding up of the subject, the directions for forming a correct style, to wit: a thorough understanding of the subject, frequent composition, acquaintance with good styles, or the style of distinguished authors—not, however, running into imitation, or adaptation of the style to the subject and occasion—not to be poetical when you should reason; and, lastly, not to permit the mind to be too much "engrossed" with style to the exclusion of matter; in other words, that, however important style may be, it should always be held subordinate to ideas, and that more attention should be given to thoughts and sentiments than mere style; and with this the task is performed. And what is more easy? When once you get in the way of it, you will find it the easiest study learned. The mind will take it readily, and you will be astonished at the amount of learning you can acquire. To me, at first, it appeared very hard, because I had nobody to teach me; but when Olin became professor, and gave us a few lectures, the whole subject assumed a new appearance, and the study became delightful; and when I graduated, there was no subject in Blair, Paley, Say, Evidences of Christianity, Brown's Moral Philosophy, or Hedge's Logic, that I could not have told everything about instantly, or as fast as I could have spoken; and I could have commenced at the beginning o₁ the catalogue above named and have given substantially everything contained, from the beginning to the end, without interruption or suggestion. The same principles of system, method and analysis, I brought to the study of law; and when I was admitted, I could have rehearsed Blackstone in the same way. The whole I attributed to Olin's method of teaching, and I would not have given the advantages to myself derived from that for all my college course besides. It has been of more use to me. It called forth all the powers of the mind, and taught it to exercise its every faculty. My previous instructions were like keeping a child forever sliding and crawling. Olin made us stand up and walk. A little assistance was at first necessary, while the knees were weak, and before strength and confidence were acquired; but soon we (I mean the whole class, for there was no student in the class that did not understand the studies) began to walk without assistance, and then to run and bound, and become the perfect masters of all our faculties. I wish you to adopt the right system in these studies, and to become perfectly master of them. When a subject is mentioned, be able to give an outline of the whole, and show that you have studied your author by being able, without assistance, to go on and tell what he says.

But I can say no more to you now. In reference to the subject of your junior speech, if you should be elected orator, I can hardly undertake to give you any advice. Suppose you write several, one of each character you mention, and submit them to me. I could then give you an opinion; and, as for the trouble of writing them, it will cost you only a little time, and you will be benefited by the exercise. A subject of rather a grave character, which I think might be treated well, is a comparison between the ancients and moderns. The general feeling and sentiment is, that the people of this age—I mean in the enlightened portion of the world—are superior to enlightened men of older times. For myself, I don't believe any such thing. It is true, we have some improvements in the sciences—particularly in astronomy and chemistry; but in many things that make man truly great—that show the powers of his mind, and the boldness of his conceptions, and the high and lofty sentiments of his soul—I think the ancients were greatly our superiors. Look at their works, their buildings and temples, and various monuments of their greatness, which, after withstanding the ravages of centuries, are even still unequaled by anything that man, in subsequent time, has done or accomplished. Why, even the public roads leading from the city, constructed and made before the Julian day, are now better and more substantial than any in the United States, or perhaps in England or France. A part of a bridge is yet standing over the Danube, which was built soon after the time of the Cæsars. What a people must they have been to leave such vestiges behind them! Why, if this country should be overrun by savages, as others have been, what have we that would remain one thousand years to tell that such a race as ours ever existed? But Rome is only a small part: Greece, Persia, Egypt and Assyria, all come in for their portion of reflection. What design and architectural skill must it have required to erect such lasting monuments! And the philosophy of Cato, Cicero, Cæsar, Seneca, Tacitus, Xenophon, Solon, Plato, Socrates and Solomon, has never been excelled. I should not have omitted Aristotle. I have said nothing of their generals. The whole subject presents a wide field, and, if properly treated, might make an interesting topic; but I can only now suggest, and must conclude by saying that I believe the people in those days were literally *giants* to what they are now.

I write in great haste, and do not know whether you will be able to read all or not. . . . . . . Write often, and with more pains. Try to improve your hand-writing.

Those who have seen the hand-writing of Mr. A. H. Stephens will smile at the last injunction. Then, as now, it was a task to the unpracticed eye to decipher his manuscript. It has, however, the merit of uniformity—*uniformly illegible*.

[From same to same.]

CRAWFORDVILLE, June 2, 1842.

DEAR BROTHER—Your letter of the 27th ultimo was received this morning. I was absent yesterday and the day before, at Warrenton, attending the trial of a negro, charged with the offense of assault and battery, with intent to murder, on a white man. I defended him, and he was acquitted. But what I meant, in commencing, was to say that, in consequence of the absence, your letter was not received until it had been here nearly two days. In reference to your speaking at commencement, I can only say that you must not suffer yourself to vacillate one moment between *speaking* and getting yourself *excused*. You *must* speak—that is, if you are chosen (and, by-the-by, you did not state whether this was the case or not)—and you better set right out in good earnest to writing. There is nothing that a student is more apt to do than to postpone the duty of composition, and no intellectual habit is more injurious when one such is once acquired. The mind should be active and industrious, and never be suffered to grow slothful and indolent; and it is much easier in one's business to keep *ahead* of time than it is to keep anything like *up with* its rapid march when once thrown ever so little in the rear. You will lose nothing by having your speech well committed, even a month before commencement, and it should be a rule of your life, established now, in this your first appearance before the public, *never to appear* unless you *appear well*, and also *always* to *appear* whenever you can. "The kingdom of heaven suffereth violence," saith the Scripture, "and the *violent* take it by force." So it is with the world. The most resolute and inflexible bear off the palms and crowns in both. A man's character, standing, reputation, fame and distinction, are the works of his own hands, and the industrious, active, vigilant and energetic, build to themselves great names; while the lazy, careless and indolent live but to die, and, without hope or care ever to be known hereafter, permit the meed of fame to be seized by the more eager and violent, and, in their own obscured littleness, soon pass away in one general, common oblivion. Let not this be the character of your ambition; but in contests for honorable distinction, ever be found amongst the first of the foremost. "*Nihil arduum est ipse volentibus, sed, nihil potest fieri illis invitis.*" In the selection of a subject for an oration, or an address, upon any occasion, you should pursue the rules laid down in Blair; and, in the first place, make choice of one suited to the occasion, the time, the audience, etc.; and, in the second place, such a one as will allow as much of method as possible in its treatment—that is, which will require styles and manner of speaking in its different parts or branches, such as the negative, descriptive, argumentative, and, as Blair has it, the *pathetic* or sublime. Every discourse should have some part devoted exclusively to the excitement or the passions and emotions. This is the work of fancy and the imagination, and the subject chosen should furnish the material for the occasional flights or colorings. The error of most young men is trying to make their orations *abound* with eloquence, and nothing else, and hence, high-sounding words and animated descriptions from beginning to end. The consequence is, in trying to be eloquent in everything, they are eloquent in nothing. I can hardly, at this time, suggest any subject to you; I am in too great haste. "Time" is a good subject; the measure of existence—its origin, or its eternity—its history—the creation and destruction of worlds other than this—the changes or revolutions it has traced on earth—its passing events, destinies, duration, etc.: thoughts growing out of all these views might be presented in an interesting garb. The greatest objection to it is that it savors too much of the "all eloquent" order. . . . .

In my travels this Spring, I have in different sections found the woods alive with the singing locusts; they were in some parts of Wilkes and Lincoln, and throughout the western counties from Morgan, millions of millions. It is said they appear every fourteen years. . . . .

Affectionately, A. H. S.

[From same to same.]

CRAWFORDVILLE, June 5, 1842.

DEAR BROTHER— . . . . In reference to the riot, I did not exactly understand from your letter whether John Bird was amongst those on the evening of the disturbance of the temperance lecture, who fired the pistol, and went back in pursuit of the officers, etc., or whether he barely left the church at the same time with others who went into the excesses. I should be utterly astonished to learn that he was in company with and countenancing men engaged in acts and proceedings so utterly disgraceful. But more on this subject, in reference to him, I will not say

to you.   I will write him a letter.   It seems strange to me
to think in what way the vision will become warped sometimes in its observation of men and things, and how, from
familiar association, or some other cause, conduct the most
improper, ungentlemanly, disreputable, and even base and
criminal, can be looked upon as common-place, and very
little out of the way.   Now, I would not have a student to
denounce, or even make mention of the conduct of a fellow-
student, however low and contemptible it might be; for
it is none of his business; it is even dishonorable to do
it; but, at the same time, from the very bottom of his
soul should he *loathe* and detest a mean deed, or anything
that savors of disreputable or dishonorable conduct.   A
man of correct principles moves on in his own sphere, and
permits others to take the same course; and while his leads
to elevation and refinement, he lets them (pursuing theirs)
wallow in the dirt and mire if they choose.   It is true, that
philanthropy will dictate and urge him to relieve all the
misery he can, and by example, persuasion and advice,
(when it can be properly given) to prevent as much suffering, and misery, and degradation, as possible; but never
will such a man be brought to bend and stoop to infamy.
It is certainly a difficult matter, since so few people accomplish it, to pursue the even tenor of one's way in this life,
commingling with men amidst all their vanities, and contra-
dictions, and excesses, and improprieties in conduct and
character, without giving improper offense to any, and securing the esteem of all, and, at the same time, to maintain
stern, fixed and inflexible principles of honor and integrity;
and yet, it is not only possible, but easy; and in this consists not only the secret of life, but the first principles of
politeness and gentility, and the very soul of benevolence
and philanthropy.   A man should study it.   It is the lever
by which the moral world is raised.   Some men have no
talent for this thing.   Indeed, most have not; and hence,
you see them arrayed class against class, each hating the
other with a moral enmity.   One is guilty of some impropriety; the more righteous, in his own estimation, cuts
his acquaintance—denounces him—and would as soon be
caught with a leper as found in his company; now, this is
wrong and foolish.   No man is so bad that he has no good
qualities, and even from the thistle, tansy and rue, and

hoar-hound, honey is extracted: so, even from the worst man, some good thing can be drawn out; but the difficulty lies in the difference between being *set* against a man and his improper act. and necessarily denouncing or censuring any one guilty of such an act.   It is the difference between being utterly adverse to becoming a leper and a disposition to *kick* any one who is so unfortunate as to be one.   Now, I hold that a man might almost sooner die than be a leper; and yet, be so far from injuring one that is as that he would do all in his power to relieve, assist and comfort the sufferer; and so with morals and intercourse with mankind.   A man may, from his very soul, abhor a principle, and sooner die than possess it, or encourage, or countenance it in others, and yet, treat with civility and kindness the most miserable and wretched victims of its development.   Now, that you may understand me fully upon this subject, I would remark, that when I speak of the "disgraceful conduct" of those engaged in the riot, I speak of it as I would of a "loathsome leper"—not that I would shun, or scorn, or condemn, or because I think myself better, but because it is a most disagreeable and fatal malady; and as I would be kind and urbane to the bodily sufferer, so I would, in the other instance, to him whom I should consider as destitute of principle more necessary for honorable action, than all that is lost in the life is necessary for good and vigorous health.   I should be kind and agreeable, and associate with such companions—or, in other words, be not distant, or morose, or Pharisaical; and while I would pass the individuals themselves this way, and without the slightest duplicity, I would have the most perfect contempt and detestation of the principles that could induce any one to be guilty of such conduct.   This is what I hold to be regard for one's character—stern and inflexible honor.   Now, what could a set of young men imagine more disgraceful to themselves than whooping and hallooing in the streets of a town like a set of savages in a forest?   What is there more unbecoming and ungentlemanly? Particularly in those who are reaping the advantages of the best school in the country—to improve their minds as well as morals—and to make themselves better, or better qualified for business in life, than the great mass of their contemporaries? Young men, whose ambition it should be to be-

4*

come the exemplars for their fellows, and for future men to follow? And then, as for blowing horns, getting drunk in the square, or old field, and throwing rocks at the venerable preceptor, to whom they are paying so much to be taught, besides the loss of their time, etc., how utterly little and low, and beneath a man whose mind is as great as a mustard-seed! *Worse* conduct could not be expected from a set of negroes—*as mean*, I never knew any of these guilty of; and shall a young gentleman, a collegian, have no better principles instilled into him than those by which the meanest of slaves are actuated? Is this the effect of education—this the refinement of the schools—this the perfection of intellectual training—this the end for which so much time is lost and money spent? Oh, shame! that boys are not better taught—that they have no better minds to think and reason with themselves, and see the gross impropriety of such conduct! But it needs not thought or reason: it seems to me that brute instinct would almost be sufficient to restrain them from such conduct. But the whole, I suspect, is excused on the ground of the insult— the threat of the citizens to prosecute if certain improprieties were repeated. This was a kind of censure of previous conduct that could not be borne, and hence the row. Well, all that is just of the same character. The first disorder was either censurable, or not. If censurable, of course a repetition, with great excesses, was no way to make the proper *amende*. If they were not censurable—if they had behaved like honorable gentlemen—it was certainly a very bad way of proving it by perpetrating such very dishonorable acts. If the first disturbance was from momentary feeling, and without any intentional or concerted disorder, after it was known that their conduct was misconstrued, they should rather have felt mortified at so dishonorable an action being imputed to them, and their endeavor should have been to show that it was wrong, and this should have been done by their exemplary and good conduct. That is the way to purge a man's self from a charge of dishonor. But I think this *narration* has also run out far enough. . .

The preceding letter was evoked by a memorable disturbance which occurred between some of the citizens of Athens and a portion of the Faculty on the one side, and a portion of the students of the college on the other. It threatened for a while to become quite serious, and was a matter of painful concern to the friends of the institution throughout the State. As usual in like cases, neither party was wholly right nor wholly wrong. Young Stephens attached himself with neither: he maintained the interests of law and good order, and contributed largely, by example and counsel, to restore the peace.

[From same to same.]

CRAWFORDVILLE, August 7, 1842.

. . . . Your circulars have not come to hand yet; when you find out, I wish to know who got better, or as good circulars as you. Let me know this without fail. I will send you the books by the first opportunity. You must continue to apply yourself *laboriously*. You have but one step now to take to place you in the world amongst men, and you have much to learn yet to fit you for that place. Pay strict attention to your writing, and learn within the next twelve months, if you live, to write a good hand. You will never have time or chance to form your hand after that. Tell John to pay more attention to his writing. He had better write from a copy every day. Remember me to Dr. Church, and Professors Hull and Waddell, and tell them I stood the travel very well, except the heat, which was oppressive for a short time.

[From same to same.]

CRAWFORDVILLE, August 16, 1842.

. . . . I am up to-day. Sunday I was confined to my room in consequence of a blister. I stay at home, however, and attend to no business, except writing letters, and giving or joining in some consultation about the business of the office. I will keep you advised of my situation, and I want you, by all means, not to permit yourself to grow or become uneasy. I don't feel so myself, and do not want anybody to feel so on my account. Life and death, and everything, should be

considered and regarded philosophically.   We have all got
to die.   The end of all of us will come in due season.   .
. . . . . .   Then, why should we suffer any uneasiness
from any indication of the immediate approach of death,
when we know it must come in due season?   Philosophy
teaches us to be looking forward to this event throughout
life, and to direct all of our pursuits and pleasures in reference to this ultimate end.   This consummation of earthly
existence, and with life thus spent, to die is but to take a
journey.   Those who are left behind will soon follow, and
in reference to my particular friends and relations, I hardly
know whether it would be more agreeable to me to take
my turn in advance, or to go after.   Be, therefore, not disturbed, because, in the first place, I think there is no immediate cause for it, and perhaps none will occur ; and, sec-
ondly, it is wrong in principle.

. . . .

[From same to same.]

CRAWFORDVILLE, January 21, 1843.

. . . .

It is a general feeling in most of our writers to pay too
little attention to style—to the selection and arrangement
of their words, and the structure of their sentences.   And
it is a failing the more considerable, because it can be so
easily avoided.   It would require only a little more labor,
and perhaps at first, or in the formation and acquisition of
style, a little more time.   But what are these when compared with the additional beauty and usefulness of their
compositions, imparted by such a finishing touch.   The
application or moral (as the preachers say) of this episode
is, that you should pay great attention to your composition,
and learn to write, as you would move or walk, neither
clumsily, lazily, nor awkwardly, but with ease, grace and
elegance.   . . . .

[From same to same.]

CRAWFORDVILLE, June 14, 1843.

DEAR BROTHER—Your two letters of the 10th, and the
other of the 12th instant, were both received by me this
morning, and I send you an answer *now*, as I shall have no

other opportunity of doing so before my return from Milledgeville, for I expect to start there to-morrow. My object in going down so early is to attend to the granting of
some lands for a number of friends before the meeting of
the convention, as I fear there will be too great a press of
that kind of business in the offices, after the general assemblage of that body, to have it attended to with order and
promptness. I shall be absent some six or seven days.
This, therefore, in all probability, will be the last letter I
shall write to you until after your final examination, and
your college course—at least, so far as its studies are concerned—will have been brought to a close. The occasion,
I need not add, to me, is one not without its interests, and
the associations which the reflection awakens fail not to en-
hance that interest. It seems like a short time since the
memorable night I bade you and John adieu, as you took
your leave to enter upon that adventurous scene from which
you are now about to so shortly return. To *me* the term
of four years in prospect then seemed long—and no doubt
much longer to you—but now they are passed ; the whole
is as quickly counted as the incidents of yesterday—that is,
if we consult our conciousness only of their transit ; but
if we reflect and consider awhile, and look about at the
great changes effected around us and in us, our thoughts
and actions, and in the relations of individuals, families,
communities, and the country at large, or even in the surface of the earth itself, the period magnifies, the field of
contemplation enlarges, and it seems strange that so much
could have been wrought in so short a time. You were
then young, inexperienced, fatherless, motherless, and
almost friendless. Well do I recollect with what solicitude
and intensity of feeling, known only to myself, I fitted you
out for your departure for college, and then, when all things
were ready, the hour arrived, and the last words were
spoken, and, in a few moments, when the whirling car
rushed recklessly on in the darkness, and I returned lonely
to my room ; how I committed you and your fortunes into
the hands of that kind and mysterious Providence, who
governs the hearts of men and rules the destiny of nations—
hardly permitting myself at that time, owing to great fee-
bleness of health, to indulge the hope of ever living to see
the time of your graduation. But now your course is

nearly ended, and that period has almost arrived. In a few short weeks, if you should live, your academic education will be finished, and you must take your stand among men. Have you ever seriously considered, and fully realized in thought, how near you are to so important a crisis in life? If not, it is time the subject, with all its gravity and responsibility, was kept constantly in view. Would that I had time and space to present it in its various shapes. The past has been pleasant: the future is active. You have been agreeably entertained in looking on the world at a distance, and as a stranger, a disinterested person, philosophizing, perhaps, upon its various characters, its pursuits, its inconsistencies, its passions, strifes, struggles, and teachings; but your position is now to be changed, and all these have to be encountered. Some liken a college-life, which you are just finishing, to the world in miniature, and the illustration is not without some aptness; but it is the miniature of the smooth sailing upon the unruffled surface of the broad river, or the still, widening bay just before it issues from its restricted channel, and the protecting embrace of its contiguous banks and lofty capes, into the wide expanse of waters just ahead, compared with the breasting and weathering the heaving waves and surging billows that ever heave, and roll, and surge on the ocean's bosom. Life's passage is over a tempestuous sea, and well-constructed, well-manned, and well-piloted is the gallant barque that safely makes the voyage. Many spread their sails joyously to the courting breeze, but few reach the wished for haven. Be not inattentive, then, at the present moment. It is an important period of your life. You never did, and never will stand in more need of cool thought, sober reflection, and good judgment, than at present. Let no passion get the sway or control of your feelings. Life is just before you, and the part you act in it has now to be chosen, and the character you wish to sustain is to be formed. . . . .

[From same to same.]

CRAWFORDVILLE, July 2, 1843.

DEAR BROTHER—Your letter by John Bird was duly received, and I should have answered it before now, but for my absence, first to Washington and then to Augusta. I was indeed gratified to learn that you had received the *first honor* in your class—not that I attach the least importance to the mere show or *eclat* of such a distinction—on the contrary, there are great evils attending it—but gratified to have this evidence, that you had not misspent your time, and that during the four years of your absence, you had not been unmindful of the first of all duties—your duty to yourself in the cultivation of your mind and your morals, and in fitting yourself for usefulness in those scenes of life upon which you are now about so soon to enter. With these reflections, I hope you will look upon your distinction with the same views as I do. In rendering yourself worthy of it, you have but done what you ought to have done, and deserve the same commendation due to all people who pursue a similar course of conduct, and nothing more. From a want of a correct way of viewing such things, many young men, who otherwise, doubtless, would have succeeded well in life, have been utterly ruined by being the favored subjects upon whom such distinctions have been bestowed. Their judgments are not good. The nature of true honor by them is not understood. . . . . I say that cool and collected forethought, which dwells upon all these things in such persons, is entirely wanting. I need hardly add, therefore, that you should by no means suffer yourself to grow the least inflated; and if such feelings at any time rise, you have nothing to do to repress them but to look to the future. Your work has just begun. The first step has just been reached; the whole mountain of life has yet to be ascended. . . . .

Idleness is the sure path—yea, the highway—to ruin, and bad associations and companions grow around and overpower one as imperceptibly, and as irresistibly, as the glow and full force of passion itself. I think it possible I may be in Athens during the coming or ensuing week; in the meantime, write me immediately on the reception of this; or you may wait until after the show of the Fourth is over, and let me know how it passed off, and on what subject you intend to write your commencement speech. . . . . I have never read Gibbon regularly through—for want of time only. I have found it necessary to consult him upon particularly points, and have been pleased with him as an author. His style is good, though labored. He had great bitterness of feeling towards the religionists of his day, which shows itself very prominently in several parts of his writings. Affectionately, A. H. S.

In December, 1843, Linton Stephens visited Washington City, and spent the winter there with his brother, Hon. A. H. Stephens, who was then in Congress. He watched, with interest and instruction, the proceedings of the Congress and of the Supreme Court, and formed acquaintance with many of the illustrious of the land. It may be questioned whether any period of his life, of equal duration, was more privileged or more profitably spent. In 1844, he began the study of the law under the tuition of Robert Toombs, Esq., at Washington, Georgia. Mr. Toombs had then scarcely passed his third decade; but he stood at the head of the profession in the State, both as a jurist and an advocate. Linton remained there, prosecuting his legal studies, with occasional interruptions, nearly a year. In December, 1844, he was entered as a student of the Law-school of the University of Virginia. That department of the University had been in high celebrity, under the supervision of the late Henry St. George Tucker. At first, Judge Tucker does not seem to have impressed young Stephens very favorably, either as an able and profound lawyer, or as a person of uncommon preceptorial gifts; nor was he slow or stint in expressing his disappointment—dissatisfaction—almost disgust. Longer observation and better acquaintance, however, seemed to greatly modify, if not entirely eradicate, his earlier unfavorable impressions of Judge Tucker's juridical ability and attainments, and of his fitness for the office of instruction.

Anterior to his matriculation, the Presidential campaign of 1844 transpired. The following letters may not be uninteresting to the reader who can recall the high party excitement of that day:

[From A. H. S. to L. S.]

HOUSE OF REPRESENTATIVES, May 4, 1844.

DEAR BROTHER—I barely have time to say to you that I
am well, and that I am in receipt of yours, acknowledging
the reception of my two letters, that seem to have met
with some extraordinary delay in their passage. I was
glad to hear from, and to know that you were well. I got
back from Baltimore yesterday. Berrien, Dawson, T. B.
King, General Clinch, Colonel Joseph H. Lumpkin, Colonel Sayre, Colonel Joshua Hill, Toombs, Harris (a young
man of Elbert) and myself were the Georgia delegation in
the nomination. Chappell was chosen to fill Kenan's vacancy, but *declined* to act. An immense concourse of people were assembled on the second, the day of the convention for ratification. The like was never before seen in this
country. The Harrison ratification convention, in the same
place, in 1840, was not to be compared to it; nor the great
gathering at Bunker Hill last summer, as I am assured by
those who witnessed each of them. It is impossible to
give any adequate or correct estimate of the number present; the nearest approximation to truth, I think, is to say
that there was ''a great multitude that no man could number;'' not less than thirty thousand, I think, were in the
procession, and they were not missed from the crowd when
they left. They were not a drop in the bucket, and the
best reflection is, that but one feeling, one spirit, and one
hope, animated and actuated every breast in the ''count-
less thousands.'' You will learn before you get this that
Clay and Frelinghuysen were nominated for President and
Vice-President, etc. . . . The debate on the tariff is
still going on in the House. Cobb and Chappell, of our
State, have spoken; none of the rest yet. Not much said
now about Texas. The treaty will get but few votes in the
Senate. I have no time to say more. I must tell you,
however, a good anecdote on our friend Cobb. You know
''Mr. McFadden'' is a pet name with him, which he has
made famous, and you know that *hack-drivers* always know
everybody in town—that is, ask them if they will drive you to
such or such a place, they always say, ''Yes—yes, sir,'' etc.
Well, Cobb, in the usual way, walked up to a company of
hack-drivers, asked them if any of them could drive him

5 *

to Mr. McFadden's. All sang out, "Yes, sir—yes, sir;" and Cobb hopped into one of them—the finest one—and was soon closed in, and off rolled the hack. After a while, the hackman asked, "Where was it you wanted to go to?" Answered Cobb, "To Mr. McFadden's." "What street does he live on?" asked the hackman. "I don't know," said Cobb; "you told me you could carry me there, and you *must.*" So round about town he got a good ride, looking out for Mr. McFadden's. . . . .

[From L. S. to A. H. S.]

WASHINGTON, GA., May 11, 1844.

DEAR BROTHER—I was truly rejoiced to get a letter from you yesterday morning; it was like a green spot in a desert. But I find again that my long failure to hear from you has been owing more to the mails than to you; (your letter was dated fourth instant), so hereafter, whenever I get in a dearth of letters, I will not complain, but suffer in silence. I have read several descriptions of the Baltimore Convention. I suppose it was a grand show. But neither you nor the papers have said anything about any speech of yourself or Toombs. Mrs. Toombs has written home that the latter made a speech at Baltimore—at what time I didn't hear. The people here expected to hear from both of you. I didn't regard it as certain, but thought it probable, that you would give the crowd a specimen of Georgia eloquence. But in that immense multitude, I suppose you were a small fish, and remained unseen. Reese is very extravagant in praise of Webster's speech. It was undoubtedly a good confession of faith; but the sketch in the papers doesn't show it to have been anything else. The prodigal has returned, and of course the fatted calf must be slain. Already they begin to call it his *great* speech. I have no time to write more. It is nearly twelve o'clock, and as I am going home this evening, I must begin to make a little preparation. I go up to see that all your law books are carefully started to brother John. He has written that you had consented to let him have them, and I go, at his request, to pack them up and send them to Madison, whence they will be carried by wagon. So no more at present.

Yours, affectionately,   LINTON STEPHENS.

P. S.—Your account of Cobb's trick upon the hackman, I read in Vickers' piazza, to the great amusement of the crowd.

The allusion to Mr. Webster as "The Prodigal" was perhaps generated of the fact that he remained in Mr. Tyler's Cabinet after his defection from the party that elected him to the Vice-Presidency; the great body of the Whigs condemned Mr. Webster's conduct at the time; now there is but one opinion as to the propriety and patriotism of his course.

[From A. H. S. to L. S.]

WASHINGTON, D. C., May 14, 1844.

DEAR BROTHER—I wrote you a letter yesterday and dated it the fourteenth, as I did all my other letters of the same day, which I suppose only shows that I am beginning to live *too fast* in this city of "Treaties." Yours of the eleventh instant has just come to hand, and I now send you a few lines by way of acknowledgment for it, if the mail will ever be so kind or *safe* as to carry it—or I cannot understand how it is that you hear so seldom from me. I write sometimes every day, and at no time omit to write more than three or four days at a spell. There must be something wrong somewhere. I wrote you yesterday that Van Buren stock was a little on the *rise*, and I think the tendency this morning is still upwards. Cass' letter has been received, and it is not *satisfactory;* but this, I believe, I mentioned yesterday. His *revised* opinion has not yet come to hand—so says *private rumor*. And I "guess" it is true. There is now some disposition amongst the Southern Democrats to take up Tyler. But he cannot get the nomination of the convention. I have not heard from Toombs lately. I expect him back here in a day or two. The last I heard of him, he was speaking at Newark, where he gained many laurels for himself, and much distinction for his State. Lumpkin and Dawson were also with him, but he seemed to outshine the whole grand constellation in that exhibition. My health is as good as usual. The House has been engaged all this week in the business relating to this District.

But nothing has yet been done of any importance—not even the passage of the bill to *pave* the avenue to prevent the accumulation of dust, etc. The Senate sometime ago passed a resolution to adjourn on the twenty-seventh instant. Yesterday, we amended that resolution by fixing it on the seventeenth proximo. To-day, that body laid the whole matter on the table. It is now thought that we will not get away before July. But I expect the Baltimore *doings*, to come off Monday week, will render the time of the adjournment less doubtful than it now is. The Democrats do not intend to quit here until they see some prospect of land ahead, even though it should be some of the points of Texas. . . . . .

[From L. S. to A. H. S.]

WASHINGTON, GA., June 1, 1844.

DEAR BROTHER—Yesterday morning, I received your letter of the twenty-sixth ultimo, together with the scraps of poetry, and the sketches of Adams and Choate from the ladies' gallery. As you said nothing further of your health, I inferred you were in a measure restored. The poetry was very good. The photographic sketches were, I suppose, the work of your friend Edwards—at least, they are just such as I would expect him to perpetrate. The account of your speech on the back of the sketches, I had seen before in the papers, and I am now getting very anxious to see the speech itself. There is nothing new here, except the prospect of fair weather—or I might almost say fair itself—and also that Vickers, the hotel-keeper at Washington, in favor of somebody, or some event or other, has made a deviation from his custom and killed a pig on Tuesday instead of Saturday. Whether the premature fall of that one, however, shall inure to the benefit of his brethren, and save the accustomed victim this evening, remains yet to be seen. The best, however, is to be hoped for. We have got no news here yet from the Baltimore Convention. Democratic news don't move like that of the Whigs. The zeal is wanting to disseminate it. Judge Andrews, his brother, the doctor, and Captain Brown are *Texas* men. They, however, with a few Democrats, whom probably you do not know, (the Moons for instance,)

form the only exceptions to a determined opposition to
Texas in this place. I forgot to tell you that Tom Simmons is a *Tyler-Texas* man, and that Bob Burch is for immediate annexation, "in spite of h—l." His zeal for Clay,
however, is unabated. Dr. Alfriend, too, was flying away
on Texas, but Clay's letter clipped his wings, and has restored him to the earth and to his senses again. His difficulty arose from the *necessity of giving an opinion* before he
knew the position of his party. Many, no doubt, would
have obtained a similar relief—or rather have avoided the
difficulty already, from an earlier publication of their
leader's sentiments. The Whigs about Crawfordville were
not really disposed to attach any importance to the Texas
question, and were inclined to regard it as a humbug; but
some of them, through fear of *seeming to wait for an opinion*, prematurely betrayed themselves into a false position.
Old Parson Wilson is a most determined opponent of the
Texas clique, and is actually on the point of falling out
with Mr. Calhoun. . . . . . .

The following letter, describing a diplomatic dinner at
Washington a quarter of a century ago, derives additional
interest from the distinguished characters of the persons
present, as well as the well-known tastes of the writer:

[From A. H. S. to L. S.]

WASHINGTON, D. C., June 11, 1844.

DEAR BROTHER—It is twelve o'clock at night, and I have
just got home from the first "diplomatic dinner" I have
attended during the session—or I may say, I ever attended;
and as I do not feel disposed to sleep, I have thought I
would give you hastily a "sketch of the scene," as I know
I shall not have the time to-morrow. The dinner was given
by Messrs. Archer and Berrien, who have moved to the hill,
and have quarters just on the opposite side of the public
grounds from where I am situated. A. and B., you know,
are "sort of chums" and live together. Mrs. B. has been
here since April. That you may know the particulars in full,
I enclose my invitation card, that you may "begin at the
beginning," as Benton said in his speech upon Texas. The

hour, you perceive, was half-past six o'clock.   I was there
to the minute—not one minute too soon or too late.   I
found Mr. Barrow, Senator from Louisiana, and the Belgian Charge, the only company assembled.   But in a few
minutes, all the guests were present, to wit: The British Minister, the French Minister, the Belgian Charge, and
Mr. Thompson, our late Minister to Mexico, Mr. Barrow
of the Senate, and Mr. J. R. Ingersoll, Daniel D. Barnard,
R. C. Winthrop, Hamilton Fish, Gales, and Seaton, Evans
of Maine, Mangum of North Carolina, the Brazilian Charge
and myself.   Mr. A. sat at one end of the table and
Mr. B. at the other.   Mrs. B. (the only lady present)
sat in the middle of the table with the French Minister
on her right, and the British Minister on her left, and
M———— directly opposite, between the *Charges* from
Brazil and Belgium.   I sat on M————'s right, and Evans
to me on the right, and Ingersoll fronting me, with Barnard on his left, while Thompson and Gales filled up
the line on towards Barrow's right, and Winthrop, Seaton and Fish on the other side, on the left.   We were
seated at the table in about fifteen minutes of the appointed time for dinner; that is quarter to seven.   The
table was decorated with flowers, etc., and filled with glass,
but nothing eatable was to be seen, except some jellies and
strawberries.   Everything was handed round by servants.
First soup—then fish, then beef, then something else, I
know not what; then sweet-breads, then chicken, then birds,
then beans and asparagus, then strawberries, then *Charlotte
de Russe*, with jellies, then ice cream, then cherries and
apples.   A change of plates took place at each of these
courses—six wine-glasses were placed near each plate, and
in them we first had Sherry, immediately after soup, then
Madeira, Claret, Champagne, Brandy, etc., with Hock, and
just what each wanted at all times.   I forgot to mention
Henderson, the late Texas Plenipotentiary, as one of the
company; and I forgot to say also that the last course was
a *snuff-box* handed all around.   The candles were lighted as
dark came on, and we left the table at half-past ten, and
repaired to the drawing-room, where coffee was served in
the handing order.   The whole passed off very well, and
nobody got drunk.   The whole company was jovial and the
conversation spirited.   All sorts of subjects were talked

about, and I was much pleased with Mangum. The servants who handed meats, etc., were called *waiters;* those who served wine were called *butlers.* They were all colored but *one,* who was a *French cook,* who figured largely, and all wore silk gloves and had on aprons. Packenham was decidedly the best-looking man in the crowd. He is a man of fine countenance and manly form—does not look to be over thirty-five or forty—wore a white vest with upright collar, dark coat with shining metal buttons. The French Minister, whose name I do not know how to spell, is a pleasant fellow. The Brazilian Charge is small, dark and *sprightly—* tries to show off like a *fice* in company. The Belgian Charge is an angular-looking, sober-minded man of reflection and practical life; he is, I should think, fifty. As for H——, he went from North Carolina, and is about like five hundred other men you might see on Tar River anywhere. Mrs. B. is a good-looking woman, affects nothing extra; she seemed to entertain the two ministers about her very well. But I can say no more; and this I have said to you, only to write for a few moments before going to bed. I will state this, however, which surprised me: When I was here in 1838, General Thompson was then a member of Congress from South Carolina, and I was introduced to him, etc., and immediately on coming in the room, he came up and recognized me. I had not seen him since 1838. He is a thorough *anti-annexation* man, and has promised me to be at the mass-meeting in Madison on the 31st of July. Tell Cotting of this; I mean tell him that Thompson, late Minister to Mexico, will be there. . . . . . . I don't write such stuff as this for anybody but yourself. .

. . . .

From Charlottesville, Virginia, Linton writes to his brother, in December, 1844:

[From L. S. to A. H. S.]

DEAR BROTHER—After we parted, the Charlottesville train waited at the "Junction" until the arrival of the Southern train, and then went on without accident to Gordonsville. We arrived there about two o'clock, and got a dinner which fully realized my ideal of Virginian cooking.

When I left the dinner-house, I felt a good deal like I was
leaving home—the house was so warm and cheerful, the
landlady so neat and accommodating; but, above all, they
fed me so well that I felt a very lively regret at leaving;
(a dog will take up where he is well fed.) From Gordonsville, the conveyance was by stage, over a road which, for
the difficulty of traveling it, can't be equaled by any I have
ever seen.   It was bad—not from want of attention, but
from the face of the country and the character of the soil,
which in wet weather becomes muddy and lets a wheel sink
very deep.   Upon getting into the stage, the first question
of a passenger, who afterwards proved to be very well acquainted with the country, was, if the road was *deep*—and
deep it proved to be.   The stage arrived here about eight
o'clock.   The Montreal man—who, you may remember,
stood outside of the car, and said he was going to Charlottesville—proved to be quite a genius in his way.   He had
no humor, and, I think, not the slightest ambition to raise
a laugh; and yet, to laugh was almost the natural consequence of his opening his lips.   There was an indescrib-
able oddity about him that made you laugh without being
able to tell why.   Montreal is his home now; but he went
from this State thither, and when he got to this place, and
stood about the bar sometime, one of the waiters recognized him, and went up to him and called him *Mars*, (something that I did not understand.)   He shook the negro by
the hand and said, "Why, how do you do, Jim?   D—n
it! I'm glad to see you!"   He then went on talking to Jim
with as much zest as you would if you were to meet Ben
or Bob in Egypt, or as I would if I were to see one of them
here now.   The last of the conversation I heard was an inquiry from Jim about "Mars John, away yonder!"

   The first thing I did this morning, after breakfast, was to
walk out about a mile to the university, and present myself
to Judge Tucker.   About his third remark to me was
the question, "Have you ever seen *my Commentaries?*"
I learned from him that he had two classes of law-
students, Juniors and Seniors.   The Juniors are now on the
subject of "Things Real," in Blackstone, and the Seniors
on the subject of "Personalty," in the same book.   The
Juniors, he says, will graduate in two years, and the Seniors in one.   He says if I will join the Seniors, and will be

diligent, and should *prove intelligent*, I can graduate at the same time—that is, the fourth of July next. Then, after making a few remarks about the advantages which he "could but flatter himself" (was the expression) "were to be derived from *his Commentaries*," he told me the *proctor* would give me all necessary information. I thereupon quit him and went to see the proctor. I learned from him that I would have to pay $70.00 professor's fee, $15.00 for the use of public rooms, deposit $10,00 as a contingent fund to meet my share of damages, etc., (the surplus, if any, to be returned at the end of session,) and if I was twenty-one years old, I could have my choice of boarding in or out of the college. The price of board in the college hotels (of which there are two or three in the campus) is $110.00 for the session, and you will have to pay $16.00 rent for dormitory. I am told by Hunt, of Wilkes county, whom I found here, and is an old acquaintance, that board in town can be had for about the same cost. Board, in and out of college, must be paid quarterly, in advance. All these sums have to be paid *before I can enter;* so if (I tell you I don't like the *appearances*) you want me to enter, you can tell how much money I will need. I now have $78.93. No more room and dark. Yours, affectionately,

LINTON STEPHENS.

[From L. S. to A. H. S.]

UNIVERSITY OF VIRGINIA, December, 1844.

DEAR BROTHER—Your letter enclosing the half-bills, I received this morning, and the money came all safely, but was delayed one mail from some cause or other. I believe I shall, to-morrow, offer the proctor one of my half-bills as a pledge for the payment of my tuition-money, etc. If I wait for the counterparts before I begin to attend lectures, it will probably be Friday before I can commence. To deposit the half-bill would be evidence of my honest intention to pay, and make it my interest to pay what might be due, for, of course, the remaining half, without the one deposited, could have no value. My only objection to doing so is, not the fear of refusal, but the appearance it would carry of doubting any man's confidence in my honor. That men will distrust a stranger's honor is inevitable, but to confess

6*

his consciousness of their distrust is rather unpleasant. I believe, on the whole, this consideration will deter me from the step and make me content to sit in my room and read one week longer. I should not have said *longer*, for what I have already read scarcely deserves the name of a commencement. The reason I have not read has been the want of books, and the reason I didn't buy books sooner was, my expectation that the course of study would be controlled by the lectures of the professor. I understand now, though, that his lectures are very scanty, and that the chief part of the course is to be found in the "Commentaries." I don't know what change the old fellow may work in my opinions, but, with my *present* knowledge of him, and his system of teaching, I never should have come here. The students here, too, generally, are *mean*—right down mean— *they look like it*; they are generally a set of *striplings*—very few *men* amongst them—and they have a foolish way of passing a man—always without the least notice of him, unless they have gone through the formality of an introduction. The assumption of such airs has just disgusted me with the whole concern, and I have resolved to have nothing to do with them. Reese is wrong in a great many of his prejudices, but he is perfectly right in his contempt for a *college-student*. The Athens students had traits pervading the whole that seemed to be derived from the very air they breathed, and to infect everything within the college walls; but here those same traits are immensely magnified; and the most prominent of them is *self-conceit*. . .

I have a constant inclination to the past. I take a gloomy pleasure in viewing it. I can't look to the future with any hope, and I often wonder how anybody else can. Death and decay are impressed upon everything. What motive is there to do anything in this life? Work to acquire honor and avoid disgrace? Sixty years will cover both. Work to do good to mankind? If you could shower down blessings upon the whole generation that now covers the earth, how long could they last? They must perish with the subjects that receive them. And how short is life? Sixty years will bury all the good you can do, too, and when the sixty years have expired, what will it matter whether you have done good or evil? Some men have left discoveries, and inventions, and thoughts, behind them which may long survive, and continue to others the benefits we now derive from them; but who can hope to be of that fortunate number? And how many centuries will be required to entomb both great and small alike in one common oblivion? And when those centuries shall have been numbered, what will distinguish a Newton from the thousand worms or ants that he daily crushed in his path? . . . . . .

Yours, affectionately,

LINTON STEPHENS.

The compliment paid to Dr. Olin in the following letter will not be deemed extravagant by those who had the good fortune to hear that superlative pulpit orator. It is "*Laudari a viro laudato:*"

[From A. H. S. to L. S.]

WASHINGTON, D. C., 1844.

DEAR BROTHER— . . . . . I attended church at the Chapel, and heard Dr. Olin, of whom you have often heard me speak. He looks much broken since I saw him last, twelve years ago, and also appeared in very bad health; but he preached a very good sermon—an eloquent one—the best one I have heard in a long time; and perhaps I should except this particular from the dull routine of the day's incidents; for it rarely occurs that I am so well pleased at church as I was to-day; and it rarely occurs to any man to hear a better sermon at any time. He had a large audience, and gave great satisfaction. Of course, I *bragged* on him as being a Georgian, my instructor, etc. Judges McLean and McKinley were out to hear him. The Chief Justice and Judge Story missed the treat. Toombs and Cranston were at the capitol.

Some of the letters which follow will show that devotion to Themis did not occupy all Linton's time and engross all his attention while at Charlottesville. He offered sacrifice upon the altars of some other divinities as well:

[From L. S. to A. H. S.]

UNIVERSITY OF VIRGINIA, December, 1844.

DEAR BROTHER—This morning, I received from you five papers—one of which, the *Miscellany*, ought to have come yesterday; but, what I should have valued more than all the rest, no letter. Yesterday, besides the letter I then answered, I got a copy of the *Huntress*. I read everything in it, from Henry Clay down to the advertisements, and among them I saw many names which I remembered: one was Winters, the man who sold you cigars last session. I wish you would send me the next *Huntress* also; for in that the old lady promises to conclude a tale which has interested me enough to make me wish to know how it ends. By-the-way, did you notice this sentence in the copy you sent me: "Little Georgian, (in capitals) don't give up the paper." It is a solitary, disconnected piece, and I cannot imagine any meaning for it, unless *you* have been threatening to stop the old lady's paper, (because she won't describe you,) and she intends *that* sentence as an exhortation to you "to hold on and you'll get the blessing in due season." That you may be better able to interpret it, I cut it out, together with the piece immediately preceding it, and enclose it to you; the preceding piece is to show its want of connection with anything else. The *Miscellany* I devoured even with more avidity than the *Huntress*. One piece in it—"The Departed One"—is very humorous, and for its strain of consolation is elegantly suited to the present condition of the poor Whigs. It was very generous, too, of a *Loco* (Neal, the author of "Charcoal Sketches,") to be so considerate of his opponents in the hour of their affliction. If Clay could just see it, he would almost congratulate himself upon his defeat—the leisure of a beaten candidate is painted in such charming colors. And then, too, Mr. Clay has what that piece considers an indispensable for turning a beating into a pleasant thing—"*he's used to it!*"

DECEMBER 11.—This much I wrote yesterday, but (it being late in the evening when I was writing) was prevented from finishing my letter by the entrance of the man who came to set up my *clock*. He detained me some half-hour, and didn't leave me time to finish my letter and mail it by dark; so having nothing to write of interest any way,

I deferred it until to-day. It is now nearly eleven o'clock, and my clock hasn't *made a blunder.* I think it is quite a sure-footed animal, and will, in all probability, *hold up* to the end of the track—that is, to the end of the present session here. But whether it does or not, I have got it warranted anyhow. Am I not a perfect *Moses Primrose?* I believe he had his gross (a whole gross) of spectacles warranted, too—didn't he? I shall make my fortune at trade if I stay here long. A clock for $27, and a clock out of pure economy! Campbell, the blind phrenologist, told me some years ago that my *head* indicated *mercantile talent,* and notwithstanding the limited field which my genius has had for display in that line, I am likely to establish both the truth of the science and his claims to an understanding of it. The Message which you started for me has not arrived yet; suppose you send me another, if you have a copy by you, as I should take some pleasue in reading even the lucubrations of "The Captain,"* when they derive some importance from the position he occupies. I have already, though, some hints of its contents, both from your own account and the papers you have sent me. In the *Globe* you sent me, I sat and read the correspondence upon the subject of annexation. Mexico is certainly pretty belligerent, at least, in language, and I presume it was that feature in the correspondence which (as you say in a letter of Sunday's date, and which I received this morning) has somewhat abated the hopes of annexationists. But as I am no politican, and you recommend me to continue so, I will say no more upon annexation. I will mention, however, that Calhoun advanced a new idea (to me) to prove the independence of Texas—that feature of the Mexican Constitution authorizing Texas, or any other of the Confederated States, to erect an independent government after attaining to a certain degree of population. The idea is not conclusive, but certainly has more plausibility than some I heard from the stump in Georgia upon the same point. And speaking of Georgia: the piece you sent me this morning, upon "Abolition in Georgia," is, as Greeley calls it, "truly a gem." . . . . . .

The commencement of the rain at Crawfordville corresponds to the time of its commencement when I was on the road, and though we had no *pour,* yet for the next two days

* President Tyler was called "The Captain."

the rain was nearly continuous.   My zeal "to make a pil-
grimage to Monticello" will never make me encounter such
weather as they have in winter: so I believe I shall defer
it until Spring.   I wonder Cobb didn't come over to pay
his adorations, in his holidays, particularly, as he started in
this direction.   If it just was "Old Hickory's" place of repose, wouldn't he bow to it?   His devotions would do
honor to a Catholic.   .   .   .   .   .   .

[From A. H. S. to L. S.]

WASHINGTON, D. C., December, 1844.

DEAR BROTHER—   .   .   .   .   .   .   We had an interesting time in the House to-day, in some skirmishing between Dromgoole, Rhett, et al.   But principally between
those two.   For myself, I think it was the most interesting
debate I have witnessed upon the floor of the House since
I have been a member.   There was no noise—no confusion.
The House was attentive and the speaking was good.
Rhett made decidedly the best speech I ever heard made
in the House.   It was short, as well as all the rest of them,
(and such are generally the most interesting—set-speeches
I detest,) and the latter part highly impassioned.   I do not
know how it will appear in the report, or even how it will read,
if written just as it was delivered, but it was first-rate to
hear; and I have long since been of the opinion that eloquence depends mainly upon *action* and *manner*.   I will
send you the papers of to-morrow, that you may see the
proceedings.   They were, upon the whole, the most interesting we have had.   The subject was Dr. Duncan's bill
relating to the election of President.   .   .   .   .

[From A. H. S. to L. S.]

WASHINGTON, D. C., December, 1844.

DEAR BROTHER—   .   .   .   .   .   .   I have put up for you
the *Globe* of last night, which contains the report of the
debate yesterday in the House, which I mentioned in my
last night's letter; but, just as I expected, it seems like a
poor affair in the report, and the *meanest* speeches—such as
were not listened to at all, for instance, quite as good as
those which produced such sensation in the House.   I be-

lieve I mentioned that Judge Story always has his bottle
of brandy at dinner; he is one of the most incessant talkers
you ever heard, and, moreover, always talks good sense.
I am much pleased with him. He just seems and talks to
the company as if he had always been acquainted with each
one. He came into my room yesterday to borrow the
New York *Tribune*. He says we ought not "to work too
hard," or try to do too much; but when the day is spent,
we ought to go home and sit down, *and look in the fire*. . .

It is said that the best spoken speeches rarely read well;
vice versa. One of Charles James Fox's sayings was: "Did
the speech read well when reported? If so, it was a bad
one."

[From L. S. to A. H. S.]

UNIVERSITY OF VIRGINIA, December, 1844.

DEAR BROTHER—I this morning received from you a
number of papers (13)—so many that I presume they were
not all started at once—and had letters, one enclosing one
from John Bird, and the other inquiring certain names.
That poor postmaster this morning certainly had his triumph converted into chagrin and dismay; his patriotism
by now must have reached the fusing point; its high temperature *may melt* your sealing-wax. In the letter enclosing John's, and bearing date of the 12th instant, you said
you had already written to me that evening; that letter has
not reached me yet, but I shall expect it to-morrow morning—that is, if, after inquiring, I find the office will be open
on Sunday; very probably it will not, and if so, I shall go
up to-night when the mail comes. But, no doubt, you are
getting uneasy at my silence about old Mr. Barlow. The
old fellow's name, as it appears on his sign, is "R. Barlow." I remember, as you and I were driving on after
him down to his house, just before we got to him, you said
his name was "Billy Barlow;" that fact made me examine
the sign to see how it appeared there, and I remember very
distinctly that it was R. Barlow, which I mentioned to you,
and you interpreted it to stand for "Bobuel." The name of
"the boy at the grocery," as you uncourteously style him,

is *Leroy;* but as you will have to content yourself with the
"old man's initials," it would be good policy to curtail
"the boy at the grocery's" name to the same dimensions,
in order to give the appearance of not taking the old
fellow's name from the sign, but by knowing it from reputation.   Let your address, then, be "R. & L. Barlow."   I
am sorry that I have forgotten the man who wanted you to
send him a document to Wrightsboro or Raytown ; it seems
to me it is something like Briscom, or Perry, and I am not
altogether certain that I ever knew it ; he put me in mind
of Threewitt, of Warrenton, but upon what principle of association, I have also forgotten—perhaps from the similarity of names—but I believe it was from some business
allusion he made to Threewitt.   Now, again, his name
seems to be Bryant, and still again he somehow or other
reminds me of Hugh Ward, and he contrived to revive in
my mind the memory of Daniel Watkins, of Elbert.   If all
these materials can be of service to your correspondence, you
are welcome to them, and I hope they may prove more
profitable in your hands than they have thus far proved in
mine.

I attended another lecture to-day, (the Seniors attend
Juniors' lectures,) and have yet found little cause to change
my opinion of Judge Tucker.   He is a very clever old
fellow, and, I will admit, shows more sense than his first
appearance promised.   Aylett—*Allet*, as they pronounce
it—that I mentioned yesterday as having the reputation
of standing well, is of the Juniors, and, perhaps, does
answer best of his class ; but Gregg, of the Seniors, is
far superior to him in an understanding of the author.
Gregg boards at my house, and, I think, is quite a smart
fellow.   He has a green look, but also seems both conscious
and *careless* as to its effect.   He has a big head, long, light
hair, and usually has a half-reckless, half-swaggering, half
good-natured (if a thing can have *three halves*) smile upon
his face.   There is in my class one man from Georgia—his
name is ———.   I presume he is a relative of ———.   I
could determine a man's locality by "that air" as readily
as you could his origin by "taken"—the Taliaferro provin-
cialism—for I have never yet seen it in a *North Carliny
nigger.*

I see Jones* has changed you from the Committee of

Claims to that on the District. How do you like the change? Less laborious, no doubt, and perhaps less *honorable* also.

It is getting late in the evening, and as I want a walk, I will go down town and mail this letter, which I must now close from want of time, room and matter.

Yours, affectionately,

LINTON STEPHENS.

[From A. H. S. to L. S.]

WASHINGTON, D. C., December, 1844.

DEAR BROTHER— . . . .

. . . . I intend to send you a small book upon " Etiquette," which I want you to read; the style is pretty good, and it is quite instructive. I commend it the more to your attention, inasmuch as General Clinch, the other day, in his inquiries after you, said that you had "paid more attention to the cultivation of your mind than you had to your manners, and that you ought to devote more attention to the latter than you had done." I only give you the substance of the old General's remarks. They were made in "all kindness," after a free and full conversation about young men, their prospects, etc., and after giving instances by way of illustration. I did not know that he had hardly noticed you, much less that he had paid any attention to your appearance. He, by-the-by, has a high opinion of your ability, but says "a man, to be useful, must, in the present state of society, pay some attention to the graces." That was his language. . . .

[From L. S. to A. H. S.]

UNIVERSITY OF VIRGINIA, December 10, 1844.

DEAR BROTHER—Yesterday I delayed writing to you until nearly dark, through negligence; this evening I have done the same thing through the necessity of entertaining a consummate *bore*. And if a short letter to you is less entertaining than a long one, why, then, the consequences will very properly fall upon the shoulders that ought to bear them; for you are the cause of the brevity that must characterize this epistle. You may be at a loss to know how you, at the distance of one hundred and seventy miles, could interfere with my writing here, but many things are true that can't be explained. In this case, however, though you may not imagine the explanation, yet I have the key to the mystery; and—to turn the key and throw back the bolt immediately, without any ceremonies at the door—I am indebted to you for the visit of the gentleman who has just left me, and whom I have used the freedom to denominate a *bore*. He is a Mississippian, and has not lived beyond the reach of your notoriety, (I might have said *fame*, mightn't I?) He knows you as a politician, and takes it for granted that I must be also infected with a love of politics, (Hunt, I suppose, having told him I was your brother.) He has a brother-in-law who is a *big politician*, and he himself certainly is infected with a love of politics—though I do not come to my conclusion upon his system of reasoning; nor do I undertake to say that the infection was caught from his brother-in-law. The fact of its existence, however, is certain; nor do I go beyond himself for the evidence of it. Accordingly, the relish for politics which he imparted to me has acted like a charm, and drawn him towards me by the irresistible laws of sympathy. I judge of the motive of his visit by the theme of his conversation; and though I may have misjudged the one, I certainly shall never forget the other, for *misery* makes a deep impression. But after I have told you that your name received its share of his notice, I am afraid I might exhaust all my evidence and all my spleen without converting you to my opinion of his agreeability. I shall, therefore, not make the attempt, but content myself with giving you his name to be blended with whatever impression you have already taken of the man, and also the name of his big brother-in-law, who "has been called the *Father of the Whigs* in Mississippi." The name of my acquaintance is ———, and the name of the "Father of the Whigs" is General ———." Do you know him? I have seen his name in some newspaper sometime during the canvass just over.

So free, and full, and frequent was the correspondence between the brothers, that almost every incident of the day, every good story, every new anecdote, etc., was communicated.

The life of a Congressman at Washington, thirty years ago, was a busier one than now, perhaps, if we take the following description of one as ensample of all.   Surely the office should be a *sinecure* at no time:

[From A. H. S. to L. S.]

WASHINGTON, D. C., December 20, 1844.

DEAR BROTHER—I was cut rather short in my letter last night by the arrival of Henry to carry my mail to the office sooner than I expected.   Indeed, I had not been conscious of the lapse of time, or how long I had been engaged in my other correspondence; for you must know—or if you do not, I will tell you—that I have almost as many letters to write this winter as I had last, of all kinds and characters, except congratulatory ones, and I may also except "buckets," for in the midst of general depression, I have been spared that mortification.   Most letters now received are expostulations for intercession in behalf of honest postmasters, who are about to be put under the "law of proscription."   What will our country come to?   ———, of Athens, poor fellow, is about to be made to walk the plank—is at the head of it. He and I, however, have got along thus far remarkably well.   ——— is more distant, but social upon passing. Cobb and Lumpkin board at the next door, you know, and we see each other much more frequently.   I never was so destitute of leisure hours in my life.   I am now living completely by the clock, and each day is but the routine of the succeeding one.   I arise exactly at half-past eight, and get ready for breakfast in just twenty minutes; the next ten I spend in sitting by the fire in a large arm-chair—not a rocker, (though I have one on the other side of my table,) but a great big cushioned, calico-covered affair, which almost hides me—looking over the morning papers just to see if there is anything new to talk about at breakfast, which is announced at nine precisely.   After breakfast, I smoke a cigar—or rather, two or three—finish the papers, and then read miscellaneous matter (I am now upon the debates in the Virginia Convention that adopted the Federal Constitution) until twelve.   I then go to the House and remain during the session, which generally continues until

about three.   I then return and commence writing letters,
and keep at that until dinner, at four o'clock, which lasts
generally about an hour.   I then resume writing until tea
at six, where I remain about five minutes, and then return
to close my correspondence by seven, when the mail closes.
I then read until twelve o'clock, after which I know but
little until half-past eight next day; and these are my daily
habits.   I have not yet been to one of the departments—attending to all business there by correspondence; nor have
I yet attended a meeting of our committee.   It has not yet
been called together.   Upon the whole, I am quite *agrec-
ably* situated. . . . . .

    We had an interesting debate in the House to-day upon
the bill to renew the Sub-treasury, which Dromgoole
brought up.   The speakers were Adams, Dromgoole, Smith
of Indiana, (Caleb B.), Kennedy of the same State, and
Schenck, which kept the House in session until past four
o'clock, when Yancey got the floor, and there was an adjournment until to-morrow, when the same subject, I presume, will be taken up.   I expect the bill will be passed
to-morrow.   I can then say, "I told you so," to my worthy
constituents.   Hereafter, I believe I shall send you no
paper but the *Globe*, and *Intelligencer*, and the Georgia
papers, for I suspect, judging from myself, that it is too
great a draft upon your time to look over all the trash that
is printed; and, in speaking of your time, how is it you say
nothing of moot-courts?   Do you have none in the university?   I should also like to know how you answer in your
class, compared with others.   Have you taken a respectable stand or not?   You have not yet told me whether you
joined the Senior or Junior class.   The letter I got from
you last night mentioned the note enclosed in a previous
one, which came duly to hand.   All your letters have been
received, but I have not got them of a night until about
half an hour after our mail closes.   I sent you last night
one sent from brother John the night before, and to-night
I send you another which came to hand last night.   But I
have not time to say more. . . . . .

                    Affectionately,
                              A. H. STEPHENS.

[From A. H. S. to L. S.]

WASHINGTON, D. C., December 20, 1844.

DEAR BROTHER— . . . . . We had an agreeable dinner-party. General Clinch told the best anecdote of any, and a good one it was. It was that of two Georgians— one up-countryman and a low-countryman—meeting at St. Mary's during the last war. The up-countryman had never seen tide-water, and said it was a "strange river that runs both ways." The low-countryman had never seen any but tide-rivers, and said, "Why, you d—d fool! who ever saw a river that didn't run both ways? Why, don't you know if the river always runs the same way, it *would run out.*" . . . .

[From L. S. to A. H. S.]

UNIVERSITY OF VIRGINIA, December 22, 1844.

DEAR BROTHER—Your letter of the 20th instant, and those you sent me from brother John and John Bird at the same time, together with the President's message, all arrived here by last night's mail, and I received them and read them this morning, (it being now quarter-past ten A. M.) As your letter reminded me of some omissions I have made in my account of the law-school, my stand in the class, etc., I will, before I forget them again, (I have several times, but always at the wrong time, thought of giving them,) proceed to supply the omissions. As to *moot-courts:* such a thing is not dreamed of here. I expected the exercises of such courts to be the chief advantage of coming here, and accordingly, one of my first inquiries was, how *often* they were held, and how managed? To my surprise, the answer was that there was no such thing known in the concern. The class, however—or rather, the two classes of law-students—have formed a contemptible *Law Club*, (I don't think clubs are efficient instruments—witness the defeat of Clay, backed by a nation of them,) which meets once a week *at night*, and with which Judge Tucker has no more concern than you have. You may well imagine, the discussions in it are none of the most edifying, nor long in continuance. In fact, I don't think there has been a meeting of the thing since I have been here. I shall make an effort to get into it next Wednesday night, the regular time of meeting. I have not informed you of my stand in the class, and cannot do so now, for the simple reason that I have none at all. I haven't answered a single question yet. I am making great progress, ain't I? But there are many others who do very little better; and then, the difference between them and me is, that they *try* and I *never do.* They have questions *asked* them; I never have—not *one yet.* Judge Tucker said he would not question me for "sometime," because, I suppose, he took me to be a fool, and didn't wish to expose me until I might reconcile myself to my fate by witnessing that of others; at any rate, that's what he said; (I don't mean that's the reason he gave.) And I don't much regret the course he pursues in excepting me, for his examinations are not close at all, and could, therefore, operate as no incentive nor help to study; and as to *display,* I am as indifferent to it as to a dish of *collards.* There is considerable curiosity, however, in the class to hear me questioned. They don't at all understand my exemption, and sometimes ask me why the Judge doesn't call on me to answer. I never tell them, but leave them in their wonder. By-the-way, they consider me a *queer chicken* here. I don't wear *straps* to my pants; and then, too, the want of *boots* completes the oddity of my costume. You may think I am unduly suspicious, but it is a fact as I tell you. I have not been in the company of one who didn't cast a sly glance at my *feet;* (perhaps, after all, their *size* was the only wonder.) To all this, of course, I'm perfectly indifferent—rather enjoy it. Another strange and inexplicable thing is, that any mortal man should get as many letters as I do; (each morning a list of all the letters in the office is put upon the door, and in that way they see how many I get.) They say I get letters enough to break a common man, and to keep the devil (it's their phrase, not mine) from study, if he answered them all. Then comes the question, "Look here: do you in earnest, though, have to pay postage on 'em all?" "No." "Is it paid at home, or are they franked?" "Franked." "Well, who the devil franks so many?" That's rather a rude question, but still I answer, "A brother." "Your brother's a member from Georgia, then, is he?" "Yes." And by just that series of questions and answers is the only way *these Virginians,* or any of them (Virginians) know that there ever was such a man as Stephens in Georgia. (Great fools, ain't they?) The Alabamians, however, and Mississippians, and South Carolinians, seem to be pretty familiar with your name. . .

But speaking of the Tuckers reminds me to tell you that the Judge is a half-brother to John Randolph. He told it himself, the other day, in the recitation-room. By way of quarreling with the English rule, excluding half-bloods from the inheritance, he said he "could have loved no man more than Mr. John Randolph, who was only his half-brother." After leaving the room, I heard a very strong *reason* for his love: The Judge, in his young days, went to Kentucky to settle himself. When he had got there, Randolph wrote him that he was unwilling for him to settle over there, and that if he would return, he himself would give him an estate here. . . . .

[From A. H. S. to L. S.]

WASHINGTON, D. C., December 22, 1844.

DEAR BROTHER— . . . . . . Judge Story says he never told but one anecdote, and he used to tell that on all occasions, until Webster stole it from him, and had the impudence once to tell it in his presence; and after that he had forsworn anecdotes. This he related with a good deal of humor at the table this morning—but, of course, it was all *fudge*, for he is always telling anecdotes, or indulging in jokes. etc. Ewing is a great hand at *puns*, and is constantly indulging in them. For instance: this morning at the table, in speaking of the abilities of the lawyers and judges of England, Story was running down Kenyon and holding up for Buller. McLean and Taney were descanting upon the merits of others—and amongst them Scarlett, who, you know, is one of the great men of that country. Ewing remarked that he was certainly the deepest *red* (read) man of any of them. And in speaking of the attack of the *Huntress* upon the judiciary, which you will see in the papers of this week, the partiality of Mrs. Royall was commented upon. For the truth in that matter was, when Mrs. Royall came in, Judge McLean was the only man that got up and cut out, and yet she compliments him. Some one mentioned the fact of how Judge McLean had passed by her as she came in at the door.   Ewing remarked that he supposed she thought the "Judge *did passing well.*"   Judge Story takes it all in fun, however, and says he must send Mrs. Royall his card with apology, etc., and that there is as much truth in that narration as in any history, etc.

If so, I pity the world; for to tell you the truth, there is not one word of truth in it hardly.   I was at the table and saw the whole show.*

Yours, affectionately,

A. H. Stephens.

[From L. S. to A. H. S.]

University of Virginia, December 23, 1844.

Dear Brother—After filling a sheet and a half yesterday, I found I had omitted to tell you which class I had joined, and also to ask your opinion of offering for graduation.   I have entered the Senior class, which, in the regular course, graduate next July.   A student, however, can pursue the studies he likes without *offering* for graduation. The only advantage that I know of in a diploma is, that it operates as a license to practice law in this State.   The disadvantage to a student from any other State is, that to get a diploma, he would have to devote a great deal of attention to *Virginia* law, that might be more profitably employed in other reading.   The fact is, I can read just what I please, and be excused from what I please by asking the indulgence of departing from the usual course.   Judge Tucker is just one of those old gentlemen who will let you do anything.   I don't think you have any idea of the time I am throwing away here upon Virginia law.   Those interminable "Commentaries" are to be the text for a long time yet, and I think it would be too liberal an estimate to allow *half* their contents to be *common law* doctrine.   The largest portion of them is devoted to *Virginia* statutes and discussions, many of the latter taken from his own practice.

.   .   .   .

I am glad, for the sake of your reputation, that the Subtreasury bill has passed the House; but your prediction is

---

*This incident recalls the late General Benning's definition of history: "History," said he, "is *true in general, and false in every particular.*"

not yet fully fulfilled, for I think you risked your reputation before the Raytown people, at least, upon the sub-treasury's becoming *one of the measures of Polk's administration*, if he should be elected. But I suppose, however, even under this construction of your predictions, there was a plain understanding that both branches of Congress should have administration majorities—and, yet again, I suppose the Senate of the next Congress will be Democratic, and therefore, as I said at first, the prediction is not yet fulfilled, but is only in process of fulfillment. It must be confessed, however, that it is fairly "under way" and sailing beautifully, with 123 to 65. That measure seems to be decidedly even more Democratic than the repeal of the 21st rule. These two acts combined must certainly throw some confusion into the Southern wing of the Democracy. They will no doubt, though, take great consolation from the proportion of Whig and Democratic votes upon *rescinding the 21st rule*, and on that *hook*, it must be confessed, they may shuffle off some of the blame on the shoulders of "Federalism," as old Blair persists in denominating Whiggery. But this will do for this time—so good evening for to-day.

[From L. S. to A. H. S.]

UNIVERSITY OF VIRGINIA, December 24, 1844.

DEAR BROTHER—It seems, at present, that the elements intend to smile upon this Christmas; for you will seldom see a more charming day than we have here now, or a finer prospect for a continuance of the fine weather, until the great "natal day" itself shall have been ushered in, and numbered among the many that have preceded it. Christmas, however, seems to be a day of very small importance with the people here, if you judge from the preparation to celebrate its return. Everybody, it is true, speaks of observing the day itself, but don't think of paying any attention to that glorious festive week beyond, which is emphatically called "Christmas Holidays," and which in other places, and even in old Georgia, is devoted to joy (perhaps not a very reasonable joy) over our passage through the toils of another year, and feasting upon the good things it has yielded to the labors of man and beast. . . . .

I have read the debate upon the revival of the sub-treas-

ury, and found it very badly reported in the *Globe*. In the
Intelligencer, the report was, if not more faithful, at least
much more sensible—particularly with respect to the
speeches of Adams, Dromgoole, etc.; but as that report
stopped about mid-way in the debate, I suppose I have got
a very imperfect idea of how the whole passed off. I
thought Adams raised a strong objection to the first clause
of the bill. Dromgoole attempted to ward off the old
man's attack upon the *first* clause by interposing the
eleventh to support it. But the distinction which, for the
purpose of his argument, he drew between *transferring* and
disbursing, certainly has no foundation in the eleventh
clause, which makes it obligatory upon *sub*-treasuries to obey
the orders of "the treasury," *either* for transferring or disbursing moneys. There seems to be some difference in
opinion as to what issues were decided in the late canvass.
Tyler says "Annexation" was the issue, Dromgoole, the
"Sub-treasury," and Caleb B. Smith says broad, unmeaning
"Democracy." "How this world is given to lying."

But speaking of Congress: didn't Foster make a fine
Democratic speech on the bill to reduce the duty on railroad
iron. Chappell must have congratulated his sagacity in dis-
covering the *allies of the South*, and applauded his patriotism for throwing himself into their arms. I noticed your
name recorded *against* laying that bill on the table—how
is that? Did you want to still hold it up, and encourage
and persuade the vandals to lay their ruthless hands upon
the "great Whig tariff of '42"—that source of so many
blessings? or, would you really like some "modification of
detail," but so much as "not to disturb the equilibrium of
the bill?" Are you suiting your remedies to the condition
of your patient? You certainly have very carefully examined the *pulse* of poor sick old Georgia, and perhaps have
concluded that the medicine heretofore has been given in
too large doses, and, like any humane physician would, have
determined to diminish the prescription and administer it in
broken doses. The next stump-speech I hear you make, I
shouldn't be surprised to find something after the following:

"*Fellow-citizens*—I always said the tariff of '42 was not a
perfect measure; it is beyond human ability to attain per
fection in anything, much less in adjusting the difficult
subject of a tariff, and the burthens of government press

equally upon every nerve (you are fond of medical figures) of this vast and extended people. Our fathers themselves (then you'll wax eloquent) foresaw the necessity of making changes even in the Constitution itself, and one of the wisest features in the instrument is the power which it lodges in posterity of, suiting it to their condition—so in all other things, there are imperfections which cannot be developed nor remedied but by the lapse of time and the test of experience. I have been governed by these views (very explicit) in casting my vote, which is now arraigned before the bar of your judgment, and, as a faithful servant, I lay my work before you, and commit my fate to the decision of an honest constituency. The duty on iron weren't right 'nohow,' and it ought to have been repealed. I always told *you just that same*," etc. But I have been long enough upon foolishness, and having nothing else to add, I'll "just enclose" for to-night.

[From A. H. S. to L. S.]

WASHINGTON, D. C., December 25, 1844.

DEAR BROTHER— . . . .
I think, upon the whole, that it is best for you not to set for graduation if you have to devote too much of your time to the study of the statute-law of Virginia. But if, with a little additional exertion, you could do it, it would be of great advantage hereafter. Becoming acquainted with the statute-laws of any one of the States, to a lawyer, is a little like acquiring our language to the linguist—all others come much easier—and crossing such studies does great good. It gives new ideas upon law, and leads to nice discrimination of principles; and moreover, if you should go to the West, a knowledge of Virginia law will be essential, for almost all their laws are taken from that source. I want you to make the best of your time until July; you can, notwithstanding the character of your instructor, learn a great deal at the University, with proper application, and doubtless your club will hold something like moot-courts, or have discussions upon questions of law. And in all this, if there be such, do not be backward in taking part, nor do you be too indifferent to display.

. . . .

[From L. S. to A. H. S.]

UNIVERSITY OF VIRGINIA, January 9, 1845.

DEAR BROTHER— . . . . . . But as I am not at all disposed to moralize this evening, I will proceed to answer your other question, which was, whether I retained my hearing that "come to" on the Weldon Railroad. Now, all the "clearance," though perceptible at the time, was only temporary, and has been succeeded by the usual deafness. You once told me that you thought my mind had been affected by the rupture, or whatever derangement it is in my head. I think so, too. That supposition accounts for one of the most (perhaps, the most) prominent defects in my mental constitution, the one which you have so often attributed to me, but which nobody else ever has, (perhaps because all who would take the liberty had the same fault, and consequently didn't see it in me)—I mean the want of attention and observation. You see I can *hear* only on one side, (though on that side as well as others) and the difficulty of hearing naturally made me careless as to what was said—especially after experience had so often told me that what I heard was no compensation for the increased *effort* of listening. People generally say so little that is worth hearing, that it is rather a wonder that men with *good ears* should not become negligent of hearing what gives them so little pleasure or information when understood. And thus, what was begun in indifference has long since ripened into a habit, and has now become a source of real mortification to me. I try constantly to stem the current of habit, and shake off a dreamy listlessness which I sometimes feel stealing over me, and which, though it has of late yielded somewhat to changes of scene and a rising sense of the responsibilities of life, I must confess is still one of the most *pleasing* enchantments of my mind.   .

The defect in hearing through the right ear was never cured. The inconvenience was a source of occasional embarrassment to him; he once laughingly said, he could turn his head to catch a sound, quicker than most men could wink the eye, if he was curious to hear the sound.

UNIVERSITY OF VIRGINIA, January 12, 1845.

DEAR BROTHER—There was a failure of the Northern mail last night, (owing, perhaps, to the snow) and consequently, as you have often had occasion to complain in your own case, I have nothing to reply to this evening. Yesterday morning, when I awoke, the ground was covered with snow, (the second time this year) but before night it had almost entirely disappeared. The ground was pretty damp from previous light rains, which, I believe, I have faithfully chronicled as they fell, and the melting of the snow, therefore, was very rapid; there was, however, not much to melt; for it was at first not deeper than an inch; so there are no remains of it now, except on the mountains, which always retain it much longer than the level. They, however, still lift their heads, crowned in snow, and will probably for some days yet to come. None fell during the day yesterday, but the whole fall was during the previous night. To-day the clouds are broken up, but not dispersed; they still float about, and, before they are completely disbanded, may yet rally their forces and make another discharge upon shivering mortals beneath; but I will not risk my pretensions to being "weather-wise" by predicting such a result. If such *should* be the result, however, my hint of the probability will of course justify me in claiming the merit of having *foreseen* it, and I shall then say, "I told you so," with as much complacency as you can assume when you shall congratulate your *constituents* upon *your foresight* in predicting the repeal of the 21st rule, the revival of the sub-treasury, etc. But if there should be *no* such result, why, then I will be just as *mute* as you possibly could have been, had fortune been less propitious than she has been in fulfilling your prophecies. This has been a dull day to me, and apathy is still so strong upon me that I have very little expectation of getting to the end of the sheet this time. Again to-day, I have failed to go to church, and for the same reason that detained me last Sunday—the trouble of shaving and dressing after breakfast. But you "needn't to say nothing about it" in your answer, for "*I won't do so no more.*" Experience has so fully shown me the evil; I shall hereafter avoid it for self-defense, if for no other reason. Indeed, all punishments seem admirably designed to remind us of departure from duty by appearing in immediate succession to the transgression. I have expressed the idea, as "the preacher" would probably do, but not, I believe, exactly according to the truth, for I doubt whether punishments are *designed at all*, and should rather say they are *necessary evils*. Life is a machine, and the Maker of it, fully comprehending its operations, benevolently gave man *directions for managing it*, and those directions have emanated from perfect knowledge: any departure from them results in disorder, (which we call pain or unhappiness) as the clock must stop when the weight runs down, or a cog is broken in the wheel; and the stopping of the clock from such a derangement is as little the result, the design, as the punishments that follow in the wake of our sins. The machine was not contrived to run *under such circumstances*. The design and expectation of the Maker was, that it should run only so long as all the parts perform their allotted functions, and when that performance fails, the contrivance is no longer adequate to answer the design, (till after restoration) and disorder and confusion are the consequence. Or, another illustration of the idea is to suppose life a difficult journey, and that God, with perfect knowledge of the way, has given man, the pilgrim, a chart on which is marked out the way, and all the dangers which beset it, clearly: whenever the pilgrim disregards its directions, he must inevitably wander from the path and encounter the dangers that hedge it about at every step; yet, his troubles and perils are by no means designed by the benevolent Director. The design is, that the pilgrim shall arrive at his home which awaits him at the terminus of the path, and the misfortunes he experiences on the way, so far from being designed, are the result only of his failure to consult the Chart, or his disregard of his directions. But how many a poor fellow in the world *can't read the Chart!* The great book of nature and of revelation has no directions for him, and his only reliance is upon the original impressions which Nature stamps upon his heart at the beginning of the journey; and how liable are these, too, to be obliterated by the malice or ignorance of those who are wayfarers upon the same great route, or even by his own passions, which discover and pursue beauties that float before him to lure him to his ruin!

But when I began, I had no idea of preaching a sermon; (and I doubt whether the doctrine be orthodox) and, indeed, I didn't know what I would say. But since I have been delivered, you mustn't make any sly allusions to "Combe's Constitution of Man;" (like I did yesterday to Byron) there may be a similarity in our ideas; (ahem!) yet, I have not drawn them from him; and, moreover, if they are similar, they are not identical, for I have the authority of Sir Edward Coke for saying, "*Quad simile est, non est idem.*" . . . .

[From A. H. S. to L. S.]

WASHINGTON, D. C., January 12, 1845.

DEAR BROTHER— . . . . . You need not have cautioned me against intimating a coincidence between your views and Combe's. If I am not mistaken, your plagiarism is from a source or quarter which I watch with much more sensitiveness than I do the rights of Combe, or of anybody else. I think you got them from me, and, therefore, will not charge you with taking them from any higher authority. But I have no leisure to vindicate my rights at this time, and will let it pass for the present.

There was an amusing spat kept up between them for sometime as to the "plagiarism," so called; but so far as I can judge, it must have been a drawn battle.

[From L. S. to A. H. S.]

UNIVERSITY OF VIRGINIA, January 14, 1845.

DEAR BROTHER— . . . . . This morning, I read the *Intelligencer's* report of Yancey's speech in reply to Clingman and others—having previously read Clingman's speech. To judge from the report, I should imagine that Yancey was quite eloquent—especially when I associate the remarks with my recollection of his appearance. I thought he had a fine eye and a prepossessing person; and in his speech, he soared immeasurably above the whole tribe of the whining Democracy, who speak for nobody but their constituents. You needn't imagine, however, that I was at all carried away by his eloquence, for I found very little to approve of after all; and yet, again, I thought he told some truth—particularly in his charge of a spirit of disunion upon Massachusetts—and he might have added other States, too. Massachusetts either wants to break up the Union, or, by a little blustering, to scare others into making it a little more agreeable with her views. But really, it seems to me, she hasn't much attachment for the Union; and I should say that she and South Carolina have less than any others—the feeling, in the one instance, springing from the ambition of maintaining a reputation for "chivalry," without any real chivalry entering into the motive, and the other from pure Yankee contrariness and dogged obstinacy. But because this might have been true, it by no means justified Yancey in declaring it to be so. Such a declaration—especially when accompanied by Yancey's impassioned manner—can, I should suppose, have no tendency for good, but, on the contrary, may do much harm by widening the breach at the same time it was exposed to view. Therefore, I say, I found very little to approve of in his speech. His attack upon Clingman was certainly not justified—though, to confess the truth, Clingman deserved a castigation. Yancey, however, I thought, proceeded to an entirely unjustifiable extent. I said he soared above the whiners to their constituents—not, however, that I think Yancey's constituents were by any means out of his mind, but for the most part he appealed to their pride and endeavored to rouse their indignation; while the puppy tribe, of which I have spoken, addressed themselves only to the pockets of their constituents by a perpetual *cant* for retrenchment, and to their vanity by the most unbounded assertions of their "sovereignty." I discovered no instance of such a littleness in Yancey's speech; he maintained throughout a respect for himself; and though he may have had an eye upon his constituents, yet I think the ruling motive was to make a fine speech—one which should *tell* upon the House and put him in the papers; in short, that his aim was to acquire the reputation of an orator. . . . . . .

And speaking of yourself and speeches reminds me of "one big lie" that I heard my friend ——— tell upon you last night: he told me that, in your discussion at Dahlonega last summer, when you rose in reply to his father, several of the Democrats left the crowd, and that thereupon you shouted out, "There go those rascally Democrats, and d—n 'em, let 'em go!" He said he was present at the discussion; but when he saw me smile rather dubiously, he stopped short and said, "But does your brother swear?" I told him I had never heard you swear; whereupon, he faced about and said he reckoned he must have been mistaken, but that he thought you used "some such expression." . . . . .

I am very much interested in the "Federalist," and am becoming a great admirer of Hamilton, by whom most of the numbers I have read were written. Well might Judge Tucker say, "He was every inch a statesman." He reasoned admirably, and predicted almost as well. . .

[From L. S. to A. H. S.]

UNIVERSITY OF VIRGINIA, January 21, 1845.

. . . .

Daniel asked me if he could propose me as a member of the club. I told him he could. He said he would do so, but forgot it at their last meeting; at the second, however, (which was two weeks ago last night,) he did propose me, and at the third, I attended, as already said. Of course, however, it would not do so well to speak at my first attendance, and I accordingly reserved myself for last night. I went up swelling with a speech against universal suffrage; (they don't discuss law.) Hunt asked me, beforehand, if I intended to speak, and when I told him "yes," he said he was going to carry out a crowd to hear my *debut*, and that I must be on my "p's" and "q's." There was, accordingly, a pretty good crowd; but I am sorry to confess that I was not the chief object of attraction. That honor belonged to Colonel ———, of Tennessee, from "Mr. Polk's own district." He is a common jest; and whenever he promises to give a speech, (as he did last night,) he is always able to command an audience. He is a member of the law-class, (Senior,) but has not, I think, given a correct answer to a single question since I have attended recitations. He certainly is thus far a very remarkable parallel to Chancellor Kent, who, you remember, Jim Jones said, read Blackstone through without getting an idea. Colonel J——— has not yet, it is true, read through, but so far as

8*

he has read, it may be safely asserted that he has gathered
no idea.   In so great demand is his oratory, that he has
been appointed by the club to deliver a public oration, on
the 22d of February, in celebration of the anniversary of
Washington's birth-day.   But he has not the least suspicion
that he is made a *butt* of—rather sets down his promotions
as the sincerest evidence of respect for himself and admiration for his genius.   If he should hereafter "astonish the
nation," and prove himself another Kent indeed, then his
college honors will doubtless be recounted by some faithful
biographer, as the repeated testimonials of his associates,
to his brilliant parts, and as indices of that genius which in
mature years burst forth with such splendor upon the "profession."   I have never seen but one parallel to the Colonel,
(whatever similarity there may be between him and Chancellor Kent,) and that one is Travis Lindsay; he said once,
"if his father would give him five hundred dollars, he would
study medicine under Dr. B———,* and make a man of
himself."   I say, "*par nobile fratrum!*"   But as I really
feel very little like writing, and have written more for *regularity* than because I had anything to say, I believe I will
bring my lucubrations to a close, trusting to-morrow evening will find me in a more willing mood; so, good-bye for
this time.

Affectionately,   LINTON.

[From L. S. to A. H. S.]

UNIVERSITY OF VIRGINIA, February 9, 1845.

DEAR BROTHER—I was glad to get a letter again from
you this morning, after an interval of two days between it
and your last; and I was also glad to find from its date
(6th) that the failure turned out to be owing to some fault
in the mail, and not, as I began to fear, to your being too
unwell to write.   You were sick last winter just after you
made your speech on your right to a seat, and the same
happening again, seems to indicate that *Congressional* speaking doesn't agree with you, while *stump*-speaking, instead of
hurting you, seems to act like excitement does on old man

---

* Dr. B. belonged to that class of the disciples of Galen, commonly
known as "*Root-doctors.*"

Adams—fattens you. Are you sufficiently skilled in the philosophy of the human frame to assign a cause for the difference? or do you admit that a difference exists? Your letter of this morning enclosed another from John, mentioning the death of Tom Simmons. Poor Tom! Though his was a small sphere in life, and even there, he was a quiet citizen; yet who, for some time to come, can fill the vacancy his absence makes in his own little town? To think of Crawfordville without Tom Simmons in it, seems strange indeed. I can scarcely think of a man there who would be missed more. I can scarcely recall a single little scene there, but he, with some of his odd sayings, and his dry, quiet laugh, seems a principal figure in the group. It is hard for me to realize that he is gone; and it seems strange, too, that a man's misfortunes should put him out of reach of the very sympathy that should soothe it: the only hope of befriending the dead is, to remember and soothe those he would have cherished if alive. Tom's little Emily is now an orphan girl; and well do I remember the feeling it used to produce upon me, to be told that I was an "orphan boy." Though I had never known a father or mother, yet nothing broke my spirit like being told that I was without them. It seemed to make me an object of pity in the eyes of other people, and that, in turn, made me *humble* in my own. The negroes and the neighbors used to speak to me of myself as an "orphan boy," and I never heard it applied without feeling *subdued* within myself, and lonely in the world. That was the *tendency;* and though I may not seem humble or subdued now, or might not have seemed so even years ago, yet what I appeared, could be no measure of the cause at work, and it could be estimated only by what I would have been without it; and if I had been brought up entirely free from the sense of dependence, and unconscious of being pitied, I verily believe I should have been one of the wildest wretches on earth. Gleams of such a feeling shoot across me even now, but they are only gleams, and sink and fade ere they have assumed shape and taken direction.

[From L. S. to A. H. S.]

UNIVERSITY OF VIRGINIA, February, 14, 1845.

DEAR BROTHER— . . . . . . He is altogether a rare chap, and I cultivate his acquaintance, or permit him to cultivate mine, that I may have the double pleasure of hearing him spin his *yarns*, (which, true to his sailor's education, he takes great delight in,) and then of *proving* them to be *lies*, as I did the other night, for instance. He was entertaining a crowd with an account of the wonders of Antwerp, (which he visited in some of his sea-faring wanderings,) and, among other things, mentioned the steeple on the cathedral there, which, he said, was about three hundred feet high, and was ascended by a flight of steps eleven hundred in number, and each a *foot* in *thickness*. When he brought that out, I broke into one of the biggest kind of laughs (which the crowd did also, though I believe in my heart they saw nothing ludicrous, save in the stupendous dimensions of that steeple) and asked him if he didn't mean eleven hundred instead of three hundred only, or else that there were only three hundred *steps* instead of eleven hundred, each a foot thick. He at first boldly defended himself by indorsing his first version, and he immediately brought the crowd to a *stand*, and (my remarks had by this time pointed out to them the true cause of my laughter) reduced them to the unpleasant predicament of not knowing on whom to throw the laugh; fearing that they would prove themselves fools by laughing on the wrong side, and equally fearing they would produce the same result by not laughing at all, since a blunder was evidently committed on one side or the other, and not to laugh would be not to *perceive* or to *appreciate* it—so they were brought to a *stand;* but I by no means permitted things to remain on so critical a balance, but immediately put off all my mirth, and by a very few words satisfied every one of them that eleven hundred steps, each a foot thick would (let them *wind* as much as they might) inevitably reach eleven hundred feet high; and I then again immediately relapsed into my former fit of laughter, in which I was again followed by the crowd and by ———— himself as heartily as the rest.   .   . . .

The person, at whose expense the laugh was created, had just entered the law-school as a student. He attempted to complete his academic education at three different colleges *in vain*. Dismissed from each, he tried a sea-faring life. A few months' experience disgusted him with that—so he, as a *dernier ressort*, betook himself to the law.

[From A. H. S. to L. S.]

HOUSE OF REPRESENTATIVES, January 19, 1845.

DEAR BROTHER— . . . . . . Last night, Mr.
Clay made a show on the colonization question—and such
a show I never saw before! People were here from Baltimore, Philadelphia and New York, to say nothing of
Alexandria and this city. The House of Representatives
and galleries were jammed and crammed before five
o'clock. The Colonization Society were to meet at 7. I
came over at half-past 6, but found I could not get in at the
door below, much less to get up the steps leading to the
House. The people were wedged in as tight as they could
be squeezed, from outside the door all the way up the steps,
and the current could neither move up nor down. There
were several thousands still outside. I availed myself of my
knowledge of the meanderings of an intricate, narrow passage under the rotunda, and round by the Supreme Court-
room, into the alley from the clerk's room, into the House
at the side-door by the House post-office, and through this
Cobb and I, with Robinson, of Indiana, wound our way,
finding it unobstructed, until we got to the door, where the
crowd was as tight as human bodies could be jammed; but
we drove through the solid mass and got in and passed on
the space by the fire to the left of the Speaker's chair,
where, by looking over the screen, we could see the chair.
When we got to this place, what a sight was before our
eyes! The great new chandelier, lighted up with gas, was
brilliant and splendid indeed; and then, what a sea of heads
and faces! Every nook and corner on the floor below, and
the galleries above, the aisles, the area, the steps on the
Speaker's rostrum, were running over. The crowd was
pushed over the railing, and men were standing on the outside cornice, all around, and they were hanging on the old
clock and the figure of time. Such a sight you never saw;
none in the Hall could turn; women fainted and had to
be carried out over the solid mass. At about seven, Clay
came, but could hardly be got in. The crowd, however,
after a while, was opened, while the dome resounded with
uninterrupted, continuous "huzza! huzza! huzza!" and
when he got to the chair, one fellow *hollowed* "three cheers
for Henry Clay," which were given in the loudest burst

you ever heard; and when he got through, some fellow
"hollowed" out, "three more," and again the welkin
rang. When this burst was over, altogether cried out,
"three more," and so they kept it up. You never saw
such a scene! After a while, order was restored; the business of the Society was transacted. Dayton, of New Jer-
sey, offered a resolution and commenced speaking; but one
fellow cried, "Clay! Clay!" the cry became general, and soon
also became general with "put him down!" "put him out!"
"pitch him out the window!" but Dayton held out, kept
speaking until he was literally drowned with "down! down!
down! hush! hush! Clay! Clay! Clay," etc., and then the old
hero rose. Three more cheers for Henry Clay were suggested, and quickly did they come; three more! and they,
too, came; three more! and they came; *three more!* and
they came quicker and louder than any of the others. At
length, still and quiet reigned, as if no breath stirred from
any bosom: Clay commenced speaking, and all were silent.
Of his speech, I say nothing. He was easy, fluent, bold,
commanding, but, in my opinion, not *eloquent.* At about
nine, an adjournment was announced. Cobb and I made
good our retreat through the same narrow passage, and got
out in a few moments. I suppose the great mass did not
get out in an hour. I understand that *whole acres* of people had to go away without getting in at all. Shepperd,
of North Carolina, whom you know as being more *Whigish*
than *Clayish,* rather snappishly remarked, when we got to
our mess-quarters, that he (Clay) could get more men to
run after him to hear him speak, and fewer to vote for him,
than any man in America.

[From A. H. S. to L. S.]

WASHINGTON, D. C., February 23, 1845.

DEAR BROTHER— . . . . . . I dined with Hunt
at Coleman's. He had a large party, and we had a fine time
of it. The best joke we had was upon General Clinch, who
was also present. . . . . . . Sometime ago, upon
a call of the House, the General was not present at first, but
came in (having been sent for) just as he heard his name
called by the Clerk; and all vexed and mad, and puffing,
and blowing, and sweating, replied or answered to his name,

at the top of his voice, "*No*," instead of "*Here*," as is usual in such cases. This caused general notice in the House, when I said to him, "General, say 'Here;' it is a call of the House;" to which here plied, "Oh, d—n it, I don't care; I am against all they do anyhow," loud enough for all to hear, which caused a great laugh; and it caused a loud burst, I assure you, at the table. The old General took it finely, and we had some fun. Crittenden told, however, what affected me most. He said that he had just got a letter from a friend in Lexington, who, in giving him the news, etc., remarked that Mr. Clay came that morning to his office as usual, (you know he has gone to hard work in earnest,) when some stranger being present, remarked, "Why, Mr. Clay, have you come from home this morning?—it is early." The old Roman replied, "Yes, sir, and walked at that;" and, pulling out his watch, told how many minutes he had been walking the distance, which was a very short time. When his friend, who seemed to be himself surprised at it, remarked, "Why, indeed! I believe I will enter you in the great foot-race to come off on Long Island next month." "Oh, no—you needn't," replied Clay, "for if I were to win it, they would contrive some way to cheat me out of it." A noble old fellow, isn't he?   .   .   .   .

[From A. H. S. to L. S.]

CRAWFORDVILLE, May 29, 1845.

DEAR BROTHER—I wrote to you yesterday, informing you of my safe arrival home, etc., and enclosed you fifty dollars, giving, at the same time, some suggestions touching your return, etc. Since then, I have been reflecting upon a subject that I had before thought a little upon, and have concluded to mention it to you, and that is the propriety of your going on to Cambridge and spending the ensuing fall at that school. The additional expense would not be an object, I think, compared with the advantages to be derived. I am more inclined to this opinion, from the fact stated in one of your previous letters, that you had not taken up the subject of Evidence at all in your present course, which is so soon to come to a close. Nothing is so important to a lawyer as a thorough knowledge of the law of evidence. At Cambridge, I understand, you can pursue whatever study or branch of the law you wish, and I think it very advisable for you to take a course upon Evidence and Equity practice. Those subjects are well taught there. You could govern your studies according to circumstances after your arrival. The moot-courts there also would be of great advantage. If you were now to return, you would not get any practice immediately. You, perhaps, had better be improving your mind there, with more facilities than you possibly could at home, though it might and would be at an increased expense. You would have an opportunity of seeing the large Eastern cities—Philadelphia, New York, Boston, etc.—with an opportunity of seeing something of Yankee character. You would, of course, go directly to Boston. . . . The commencement at Cambridge is in September, and by that time, you can see how you like the place, and by November, or the meeting of Congress, you can determine whether it would be worth while to continue during the winter; if not, you could then return, spend a few weeks in Washington, see Congress again in session, and come on and set out "your shingle" at the beginning of next year. What think you of it? I make the suggestion, and advise you to take that course, believing it to be best. .   .   .   .

[From A. H. S. to L. S.]

CRAWFORDVILLE, June 11, 1845.

DEAR BROTHER—Yours of the 4th instant came to hand this evening, and I was glad to hear that you had concluded to go to Cambridge; for there, I think, you will have superior advantages to those at the University of Virginia—though I do not think your time at that place has been misspent. You have made acquaintances—learned something of the world, if not much of the law—and your reading there will render you more capable of improvement at the other place. But I suppose I need not venture the opinion that you will find everything entirely different, and you will soon discover that you know nothing of law. This, perhaps, you will discover sufficiently early. I will, however, barely suggest to you, in order to put you on your guard: your having graduated at the Law School of the

Old Dominion, will cause attention to be somewhat directed to you, and something will be expected of you, and you will not be disappointed in finding that to maintain a stand, you will have to study, and *study hard*. Nothing but close application will do there. It is for this reason I wished you to go. Your last six months, I take it, have been a sort of holiday; you must now go to work. The Yankees are a different people from the Virginians. You will find everything different—the school, the habits and manners of the students, as well as the system of instruction. You must accommodate yourself to the new state of things in which you are placed; and, above all, you must recollect that you go to learn—to gain information—to acquaint yourself with the principles and practice of law. Let these be your absorbing thoughts. You will find no card-playing, horse-racing, and cigar-smoking there. You must, therefore, drop your Virginia habits, and bend yourself to work. I would advise you to attend to Evidence and Equity practice mainly, and never neglect the *moot-court*. . . .

He received the diploma of Bachelor of Laws from the University of Virginia, in July, 1845. Immediately after graduation, adopting the suggestion of his brother, as well as attracted thither by the splendid reputation which the genius and learning of the late Joseph Story—*clarum et venerabile nomen*—had contributed so largely to give to that nursery of legal science, he repaired to the Law School at Cambridge, Massachusetts.*

* Judge Story, at that time Associate Justice of the Supreme Court of the United States, was, during the sessions, one of "The Mess" at Washington City, whereof Chief Justice Taney, Judge McLean, Judge McKinley, of the Supreme Bench; Mr. A. H. Stephens, Mr. Jacob Callamer, of the House of Representatives, and others scarcely less distinguished in the juridical or political history of the country, were members. He was the central figure of the board—the soul of social hilarity and mirth. When weightier cares did not forbid, the "Attic nights"—their social gatherings reproduced—recall the club-meetings at Wills', or "The Monks of the Screw"—

—— "Nights spent not in toys, or lust, or wine,
But search of deep philosophy,
Wit, eloquence and poesy—
Arts which all loved."

9*

[From A. H. S. to L. S.]

HAMILTON, GA., June 22, 1845.

DEAR BROTHER— . . . . I was very much amused at your account of the first interview with Judge Story, and the more so from my knowledge of the man, and correct idea of just how the scene passed off. He is one of the jolliest old men I ever saw, and is always in a fine humor and great flow of spirits. But you must be somewhat on your guard with him—that is, you must be very careful in the observance of certain rules of propriety and decorum. Don't suffer yourself to imagine that he has no sense of dignity, and that respect which his age and character are entitled to from his inferiors. He is free and easy, and intimate even with inferiors, if they pursue the proper course on their part. You must, therefore, always keep your *distance*. You may be free and easy, and laugh at his anecdotes, but never assume an air of equality or familiarity. Forwardness in a young man is extremely disagreeable to Judge Story, and *modesty* with him is a great virtue. Your conduct, therefore, must be exceedingly circumspect. A high sense of honor he quickly perceives and greatly appreciates, and nothing touches or kindles his dislike sooner than the discovery of a principle of lawlessness, or recklessness, or disorder, or insubordination, or even that *impertinence* which characterizes so many of our young men of the South. Be careful, therefore, of your actions, and always endeavor to show yourself orderly, attentive, studious, courteous and decorous in all your deportment; for you may depend upon it, he is a close observer, however little you might, on first acquaintance, suppose him to be. . . .

. . . .

There Linton Stephens first formed the personal acquaintance of Judge Story. It ripened into the warmest friendship—to be dissolved, alas! too soon, by death! Judge Story died in September, 1845. *En passant*, I heard a gentleman—now deceased, then a leader at the bar, and prominent in politics, and who was generally very accurate in his statements of fact—say that it was Judge Story's influence over Mr. Webster that made him a Federalist. The truth is, Judge Story never was a Federalist. He was brutally beaten by a mob, in the streets of Salem, in 1812, because he supported Mr. Madison and the friends of the last war with Great Britain—he maintaining that the war was necessary and just.

After completing his course of legal studies at Cambridge, he returned home; and at the March term, 1846, of Taliaferro Superior Court, was licensed to practice law in all the courts of Georgia, except the Supreme Court. He opened an office at Crawfordville, and at once entered into an extensive and lucrative practice. Perhaps no young man in the State ever rose so rapidly and so deservedly to the head of the profession as he—unless the solitary exceptions be found in the instances of his brother Alexander and the late Thomas R. R. Cobb, a gentleman of great gifts, great industry and ripe culture—who gave the first years of his manhood unremittingly and exclusively to the "jealous science of the law." Young Stephens' first fee was in a case which fell within the jurisdiction of the Inferior Court. Before that *august* tribunal, he lost his case. It was carried to the Superior Court by writ of *certiorari;* there again he lost it. Nothing daunted, and contrary to the opinions of gentlemen of the profession, whom he consulted, and who were agreed as to the legal accuracy of the judgments rendered, he appealed to the Supreme Court, and his case was there sustained. How many young lawyers any where would, *under such circumstances,* have manifested so much steadfastness of purpose, so much persistence of conduct, and so much faith in the truth of his own convictions! The incident is important only, and is introduced here only, because it mirrors forth one of the capital features of his character—SELF-RELIANCE—and *that* unmixed with arrogance.

The following letter must have been a stimulant to the ambition of the youthful aspirant for a fair renown, and gratifying to a pardonable pride:

[From A. H. S. to L. S.]

WASHINGTON, D. C., February 3, 1846.

DEAR BROTHER—Your letter, written the day after your return from LaGrange, came to hand last night, and I was glad to hear once more from you; for it had begun to seem long. I suppose you are now preparing yourself for admission to the bar, and you must keep yourself closely at study. You ought to review Blackstone thoroughly, and make yourself familiar with the statutes of the State—particularly on Attachments, Garnishments, Civil Process, Bail, etc.; indeed, you ought to know well *all the statutes*. To do this, and keep up your other studies, your time is short. You ought to recollect that you will have some reputation at hazard in your examination; for not only in La-Grange are you considered a great man, but all your acquaintances, and those not your acquaintances, will look for something extraordinary from one who has enjoyed so many extra advantages. Moreover, the impression has got out, by some means, that you are a very *smart fellow*—a splendid young man—a great deal smarter than "Ellie"— and you must not disappoint that impression; for recollect, when I was admitted, Colonel Lumpkin and Judge Crawford said I stood the best examination they ever heard. Joseph Sturges told me, the other day, that he saw somebody who told him that you "were a splendid young man"— far above ordinary. Some Virginian asked Howell Cobb, the other day, about you. He said you had a great deal better mind than I had; so you see something very *great* is expected of you, and, to come up to expectation, you must "eat but little idle bread."   .   .   .   .   .

Shortly after his admission to the bar, young Stephens formed a co-partnership, in the practice, with his cousin and class-mate, Bird, of whom mention has been made in preceding pages. It is no mean proof of the high estimation in which each was held by their fellow-citizens, that professional partners in a business which makes, however unjustly, personal foes, living in the same village, of consanguine relationship, of common opinions, feelings, affinities, should have been simultaneously, by a common constituency, elected to political station at so early an age. Stephens was chosen Representative, for Taliaferro, in 1849, and re-elected successively to the same office, until he changed his residence to the county of Hancock. Bird was chosen Senator, for Taliaferro and Warren, in 1851, and was re-elected to the same office in 1852 and 1853, but died in October, 1853, and never took his seat under his last election.

[From A. H. S. to L. S.]

WASHINGTON, D. C., January 13, 1847.

DEAR BROTHER— . . . . I must tell you a good thing Toombs said in reply to Burt the other day; and first, by way of explanation, I must premise that Burt is anxious to get up an excitement upon the slave question. He wanted Toombs to speak upon that subject, and upon Wilmot's Proviso, etc., and, amongst other things, told him to "peel old Ritchie." Toombs was listening to all his lecture, as if agreeing with him, until he came to the last— that is, Burt's injunction to him to "peel old Ritchie." Here Toombs broke by saying: "Now, by George! skin your own skunk! for I'll be d—d if I am going to hunt any such game!" . . . .

Mr. Stephens was an ardent Whig. His individual preference for President of the United States, in 1848, was Mr. Clay, as it had been in 1844; but, believing that General Taylor could be elected, and that another defeat would follow the nomination of his favorite, and that a change in the administration was necessary, he advocated the nomination of General Taylor on the ground of availability only. The canvass was an exciting one, and marked perhaps by more of personal acrimony in Georgia than in any other State of the Union. Stephens entered into the canvass with great zeal and ardor; in it he "won his spurs," and took his place among the knights of the political arena.

The General Assembly of 1849–50, in either branch, was unusually distinguished for talent and ability. The roll of the Senate was illustrated by the names of Andrew J. Miller, Joseph E. Brown, Richard H. Clark, Charles Murphy,

David J. Baily, John Jones, Edward D. Chisolm, William
W. Clayton and others; in the House were A. H. Kenan,
J. N. Ramsey, R. P. Trippe, L. J. Gartrell, J. A. Jones,
A. C. Walker, W. T. Wofford, A. T. McIntyre, Y. L. G.
Harris, Alex. McDougald, T. C. Howard, A. J. Lane, and
others, then or since distinguished in the history of the
State. Conspicuous among the foremost in the bright gal-
axy was Linton Stephens. When he rose to speak, no
person commanded more considerate and respectful attention, and none better repaid it. An assiduous course of
mental discipline had made him master of his faculties; he
could call up to his aid, at any moment, all his resources of
knowledge, logic, illustration, wit, satire—indeed, every
weapon of his intellectual armory he kept bright, polished
and ever ready for use; and, like the sword of Fitz James,
the weapon employed was equally formidable for assault
or defense. It was this power—conjoined with an emotional nature and earnest convictions, animated by the in-
spiration which deep feeling can alone breathe into spoken
thought—that made Charles James Fox the most accomplished debater that ever appeared upon the theater of public
affairs in any age of the world. There are many features
of mental and *cordal* resemblance between Stephens and
Fox. In one respect, there was no similitude; Stephens '
did *not* "speak to every question."

[From A. H. S. to L. S.]

WASHINGTON, D. C., January 2, 1850.

DEAR BROTHER— . . . . . . I send you with
this a copy of the address drawn up by a committee from
the Memphis Convention. Read it. Mills, whose name
is to it, is that same Charles C. Mills, of whom you have
heard me speak, and who, at one time in my life, gave an
important turn to my destiny. He is now here. He has
entertained me with strange incidents in his life. Amongst
others, the other night, in speaking of the nearest distance

to San Francisco, he got off upon the idea of the nearest route from any two points on the same latitude, being on that line of latitude. I told him it was not necessarily so, and attempted to explain by an apple on my table. He saw that, but thought it would not apply to so large a body as the earth; and then went on to say that he had no doubt that just such a mistake occasioned the loss of the steamship, *President*, in 1841. He said he went to Europe in 1839, and had Captain Roberts, I believe it was, in command; that Captain Roberts told him the same thing, and that he thought he could go to Liverpool much nearer than the usually traveled route or course; that in 1841 he started to go to Europe again; got to New York, went on board the *President* to start; there met the same Captain Roberts, who recognized him, and told him that he was going to make the shortest trip ever made between this country and England; showed him the course he was going to run. Just before the ship started or sailed, he concluded not to go; had his baggage put off; stood upon the wharf and saw the steamer leave the harbor amidst the shouts of thousands. The *President* has never been heard of since. He says the captain ran up into the icebergs to find a *near passage*. But enough of this. I was entertained at the incident in his life. I asked him what induced him to leave the ship. He said, nothing in the world, but a *whim* entered his mind that he could do his business as well by correspondence—though he had gone from Alabama to go out in that steamer and had got aboard. He had a large amount of cotton in Liverpool. You know that I am a believer in special Providence: hence this made an impression upon my mind. . . . . .

All who have visited "Liberty Hall" know Harry, the faithful body-servant of Mr. Stephens; frequent visitors there know Eliza, his wife. Linton Stephens had in life no friends, white or black, more sincerely devoted to him, and few mourned him dead with deeper sorrow, than these faithful and devoted servants. The subjoined letter relates to the marriage of the couple. Shortly after the event, Mr. Stephens purchased Harry.

[From A. H. S. to L. S.]

WASHINGTON, D. C., March 14, 1850.

DEAR BROTHER—In my letter written at the House to-day, I forgot to reply to the request of Googer's Harry to take Eliza for his wife. Say to him that I have no objection. And tell Eliza to go to Solomon & Henry's and get her a wedding dress, including a pair of fine shoes, etc., and to have a decent wedding of it. Let them cook a supper, and have such of their friends as they wish. Tell them to get some "parson man" and be married like "Christian folks." Let the wedding come off some time when you are at home, so that you may keep order amongst them. Buy a pig, and let them have a good supper. Let Eliza bake some pound-cake, and set a good wedding-supper.

Yours, affectionately,

ALEXANDER H. STEPHENS.

[From A. H. S. to L. S.]

WASHINGTON, D. C., March 23, 1850.

DEAR BROTHER—Your two letters of the 18th instant (one enclosing copy of your *expose*) were received last night. In a letter I wrote to you yesterday, I gave you my views upon that matter. I think the piece well written. Indeed, to tell you the truth, it is better written than I thought you capable of, if you will pardon this awkward expression. A little more concentration would have made it a *powerful* paper. I noticed in the *Southern Recorder*, at the time of the disorganization, a short statement by some anonymous writer, which struck me with its force and vim. But it lacked the substance. It was the mere thunder without the lightning. If your argument had been clothed up in the same style, or hurled forth with the same energy, it would have been a paper of unusual ability. In reference to Mr. Toombs' opinion, I will barely say, that the day after I read the piece, I casually, or "artfully," if you please, asked if he had seen the "Whig exposition, or the address of the members of our Legislature in justification of their course in withdrawing from the House." He replied that he had, and it was a fine paper, or some words of that import. I told him that I had received a letter

from you stating that you had written it. He replied,
" Ah, indeed! Well, it is a good paper; I was struck with it,
and well pleased with it." This is about the substance of
his remarks. Jones has not published it, and I doubt if he
noticed it in the *Recorder*, for I did not; I saw it in the
Journal. . . . .

I fear we shall have some weeks now of cold weather.
It keeps me in-doors. As to my health, I am *in statu quo*—
perfectly well, except that disease which Alfriend calls urti-
caria, and which Hall calls *exema*, and which I call the
mange. I feel about as I did yesterday after taking a sulphur vapor bath. The itching is not as aggravating as it
has been.

[From A. H. S. to L. S.]

WASHINGTON, D. C., April 15, 1850.

DEAR BROTHER—I send you to-day two slips from the
Baltimore *Sun*—one giving an account of a fire in our vi-
cinity yesterday, and the other giving an account of the
flare-up in the court here Saturday. It was quite a scene,
I understand. I am a May man in the controversy. This
is the third or fourth time, I hear, the court has undertaken
to set aside verdicts rendered in his favor, on in favor of his
clients, when the grounds were not thought by impartial
judges to be sufficient. On Saturday, he gave the court a
raking which they will never forget, and perhaps if he had
given them a slight touch of the same character before, he
might have been spared the unpleasant duty of laying on
so hard at this late date. I detest a court that acts partially,
or from prejudice, on the bench. May is a young man—
Bradley is of long standing. May is struggling his way up
against adverse fortunes; Bradley is at the head of the
"*elite.*" May stood it as long as he could, and when he
did break loose he hurled his thunders with the potency of
a young Jove. Now, in my opinion, no court ought to
allow any lawyer to make such a remark at the bar, as
Bradley did, about the verdict of a jury, without a repri-
mand. A jury may act wrongly—they may act foolishly—
they may render an absurd verdict; but it is rare they act
corruptly: and they should be treated with respect.

The House adjourned to-day immediately after meeting.
The death of Campbell, the Clerk, was announced by the

Speaker. Gentry then made some remarks, accompanied with resolutions, and the House adjourned. What is to be done, touching the election of a successor, I have no idea. I remained in the Hall but a few minutes, and interchanged views with nobody upon the subject. I expect we shall have a renewal of the scenes we had at the organization—that is, we shall probably ballot or vote several days before an election is made. Steele, formerly of Milledgeville, was Campbell's Chief Clerk, and I suppose he will act in the *interim*. I feel less interest in politics than I ever did in my life. I don't think, if I should live many a year to come, that I should ever again feel any deep interest in the success of any ticket upon mere party considerations. The *principles* in issue, and not the men before me combined, shall always hereafter control my vote upon all elections. All parties are corrupt, and all party organizations are kept up by bad men for corrupt purposes. I shall hereafter treat all alike. I am out of party. I have been very much pained lately at seeing the course of men that I once thought so well of, and for whose elevation to office I strove so hard. My only consolation is the consciousness of the integrity of my motives. I was for good government; I looked to nothing but the common good and prosperity of the country. I was *green* enough to suppose that there was such a thing as *disinterested* patriotism. I thought those to whom I have alluded were actuated by that principle. I find I was mistaken, and I feel mortified at my disappointment; but I bear my mortification as I do a bruise or a sprain I sometimes get by my own negligence or blunder. I shall endeavor to avoid such accidents for the future. The men to whom I now allude are P——— and ———. These men, I think, I had put in the cabinet; I know I contributed to it; I am inclined to think that the responsibility rests upon me; and I would not have you understand me as saying anything against them, farther than that I have been disappointed in the course of policy they pursue. ——— is clever, friendly, honest, and free, I think, from all intrigue, but he is wholly unfit for his present place. He takes no interest in public affairs. He consults nobody as to the propriety of his appointments; he makes great blunders in these. He has formed no acquaintance with members of Congress, has no complacency

of manner, but is rigid, grum and austere in his intercourse.
He manifests no concern in what is done in cabinet, or in
the public policy of the administration. He has none of
the elements of a statesman about him. And as for
P———, I am much worse disappointed in him; for I find
he is a scheming, intriguing politician. He was elated and
transformed by his mere position. He was put into a new
and higher sphere; with this change, "a change came over
the spirit of his dreams." He is not the man now that he
was two years ago—his opinions have changed—his views
are different. He was then looking to his district; he is
now looking to the wide horizon of the whole country—not
to what will contribute to the peace, quiet, honor, renown,
and prosperity of all, but to the miserable, petty party feelings and prejudices of the different sections, and not even
with the view of correcting these, but with the purpose of
courting popular applause by pandering to popular favor
and feeling. He is a theorist and an enthusiast. He takes
up an idea and adheres to it with the pertinacity of a dog-
matist. He has done more to ruin this administration, I
think, than all the other members of the cabinet together.
He has *Taylor's* confidence; he has more influence with him
than any other man. Taylor is pure and honest; his im-
pulses are right, but he suffers his own judgment to be
controlled by that of others, and by no one so much as
P———. The blunder he made was in suffering himself to
be influenced and duped by Seward. I allude to P———
now. I have no doubt an alliance was formed between
them before Congress met. The extent of the implied
understanding, to call it nothing else, I do not know; but
the anti-slavery men of the North were to be brought to
the support of *Taylor* by Seward—not by the surrender of
the sentiment, but by making Taylor the head of the party—
not as an abolitionist, but as a liberal man of the South,
opposed to the extension of slavery, and willing for the
majority of the North to carry out any measure they might
think proper. The Whig party, in other words, was to
absorb the Free-soil party at the North, and become the
great Anti-slavery party of the nineteenth century. The
Democrats of the North would be put down by their affil-
iation with slavery—the whole North would be Whig—
Taylor would be re-elected, and then Seward would suc-

ceed, and a long list of successions doubtless loomed up in
the opening vista.   These are the illusions which, I think,
broke upon the vision of the Secretary as he began to open
his eyes after his transfer to his new sphere of action.   In
plain English, I believe he formed an alliance with the Free-
soilers; and I believe he is now exerting his utmost power,
and all the influence of the government, to prevent an adjustment of the slave question upon the plan of Clay's resolutions,
McClernand's bill and Webster's speech.   I am not with him;
I am done with him; I have no further use for him; I have
had no unpleasant words with him; I have told him can-
didly and distinctly, that his policy will ruin *General Taylor.*
It will break down the administration North and South.
It will leave him with a smaller party than Tyler had.   I
have been for months doing all I could to get P—— to
look at this matter rightly.   I never gave him up as hopeless till last week; and I will here remark, that, if you remember last fall when I first came here, I told you Taylor,
in my opinion, would sign the proviso.   You may now
understand why I thought so.   That point alone would not
have caused me to break with the Whig party, but I soon
saw that the expectation was that Winthrop was to be
elected by a coalition of the Southern Whigs with the Free-
soilers, and the Whig party was to be the Anti-slavery
party.   Against that I kicked—I detested the idea.   I
would not act for a moment with a party that had the remotest hope of accomplishing such a result by my co-operation with them.   We made a point upon the Whigs; we
got up a great row; we shook the country from one end to
the other.   The disorganization of the House aroused public sentiment; the feeling of the North began to give way;
we soon learned that the *proviso* would be vetoed, if passed;
of this I informed you.   But the storm was then up, and
it could not be calmed.   The Northern Whigs, feeling the
great pressure from home, and fearing they would be compelled to yield their sentiments, and come to a full and final
settlement of the question, caved in and let Cobb be elected
Speaker.   Mr. Clay, who came here a Wilmot Proviso man,
seeing the state of feeling, seized upon the occasion and
brought forward his compromise; Webster followed, and
twenty Northern Whigs, perhaps forty, in the House, were
ready to follow, and settle the whole question.   But P——,

(jealous of Clay, and not willing that his movement should succeed—that is, that territorial bills without the proviso should pass, which would always be as good as Clay's compromise,) set his head against it. I worked with him, hoping he would yield, but he set all his powers against it, and has got General Taylor dead against it; and, if we carry General McClernand's bill, we shall do it over and against the whole power of the government, and the Whig party will be defunct. Now, you see why I say I am disappointed in P——. As for ——, he is with us in this matter, but he is not worth a stiver, or he never would have let P—— got so wrong himself before we came here, and he never would have let him got such unlimited control of Taylor. He never would have suffered the whole patronage of the government at the North to go, as it has gone, to sustain the Free-soilers and Seward men. But enough. Good-bye.

Yours, affectionately,

A. H. STEPHENS.

[From A. H. S. to L. S.]

WASHINGTON, D. C., April 19, 1850.

DEAR BROTHER— . . . . To be present and hear continuous debates for four hours—to watch every turn that even a word or an expression may give to the winding current of great national events which will soon be historical—is a source of peculiar gratification; but to rise in the morning after, and see the whole spread out in a broad sheet for dissemination to the remotest parts of the world, is a matter which excites, or should excite, something higher than gratification. It is true, we have got so used to it that we think no more of it than the air we breathe; and perhaps the same may be said of them at a distance, who are mostly benefited by it. What a wonder would such a state of things have been in England one hundred years ago! The first debates of Parliament, I believe, that were ever published were written by Dr. Johnson, and published in the *Gentleman's Magazine* in 1740. He barely got notes of the speeches in the gallery, and wrote them out in his garret. I have been entertained lately in reading some of these debates. Johnson did not give the names of the speakers. The whole was kept up as a fictitious report of proceedings in the legislative councils of the Island of Lilliput.   The questions were stated with such an analogy that no one could mistake the caricature, and they were read with avidity all over England.

That was the commencement of Parliamentary reports; and it is a striking fact that the great speech of Pitt, that overthrew the Walpole Ministry in 1740, which is treasured up as one of the brightest ornaments of British eloquence, was written by Johnson in his garret, and never seen by him, who was afterwards Earl of Chatham—I mean it was never seen by him until after it was published.   Johnson disclosed this fact himself, and in rather an interesting and *interested* way.   The speech was highly lauded at a table where Johnson and others were.   The old rascal could not act the part of Junius and remain *sub umbra*, but his vanity was so great that he said: "I wrote that speech in a garret."   This was some years after its publication, and it led to a disclosure that the whole debates at that period were written by Johnson, as above stated; and the old Tory-dog said he always took care that the Whigs should not get the better of the argument.   But he missed it in Pitt's speech; for whatever he might have thought, the *people* were of the opinion that Pitt carried his point.   Perhaps Johnson was partial to him, individually.   But now, if you please, just think for a moment what we and our ancestors were as late as one hundred years ago, and what we and they are now— I mean what the people of this country and England, from whom they sprang, were one hundred years ago, and what both peoples are now, in commerce, trade, facility of travel, transmission of intelligence, and everything that marks and distinguishes civilization from barbarism!   Why, just in this thing of printing, I suppose I am within the bounds of truth when I say that, in one night after the adjournment of Congress, before the morning session begins, the *Globe*-office will throw off more printed matter than all London could have done, one hundred years ago, in *one month*.   It is astonishing to step into that office and see the magic genius at work!   The ideas and thoughts of men, as uttered on the respective floors of the two Houses of Congress, are caught in their airy sounds and fixed in strange marks or ciphers; then transformed into English manuscript; then handed to divers compositors, who transform them into a new language of types, which are bound fast and then put under steam, which throws off five or six hundred impressions while one hand would be copying a few sentences, and in a few hours, fifty or a hundred thousand, as the demand requires, are ready for delivery. The steam-engine is a wonderful invention. We are in the habit of paying this compliment to it when we think of its power on the railroad, the river and the ocean; but when I have lately noticed its wonderful agency in the diffusion of news and intelligence by the press, I am disposed to think that its real powers are as strikingly observable there as when driving the iron-horse at his most powerful speed, or forcing the massive ship against the elements of wind and water. But what is this compared to the telegraph? It may seem strange to us to be told that one printing-office can to-day do more work in twelve hours than any one in London could have done in one whole month a hundred years ago; but how small a matter is that, in contrasting the present with the past, when we realize the fact, that now we can send, in ten minutes, intelligence from Maine to Louisiana, a distance of two thousand miles, which, one hundred years ago, would have required almost a month by the swiftest couriers known, with relays arranged previously for the purpose. We are certainly making great and rapid strides in making the laws of nature subservient to the uses and purposes of man; and in this, I think, consists all useful knowledge and science. Whoever contributes a new idea on this subject is a pioneer in knowledge; and whoever devises or contrives any scheme, by which any of the elements about us can be turned into a useful purpose, is a benefactor of his race. Science—true science—is nothing but the knowledge of the laws of nature, and is useful only in so far as it enables mind to get the mastery of matter. Now, what shall we be one hundred years to come? This is a most interesting question. Shall we go on, or shall we retrograde? This depends, in my opinion, very much upon the course of political events. Politics and government, in my opinion, have in the main, since the formation of human society, been at war with the best interests of man. Government, place and power have always been the prize which those have sought and struggled for, who have strong passions and mean propensities—those in whom the ani-

mal and brutal qualities of our nature triumph over the refined and intellectual. Hence, those who contend for the
prize of government resort to all sorts of means to arouse
the worst and basest animal passions of the low and vulgar,
to get them, as ministering devils or demons, to accomplish
their purposes. The good of the people—the elevation, or
even comfort, to say nothing of the happiness, of the masses
of mankind—seldom enter into the minds of those who am-
bitiously aspire to rule. They look upon the low, the ignorant and the humble as fit only to be the tools of their ambition. This, I think, the history of the world shows. Hence,
in the records of the past, we read of little but the wars of
kings and princes, the intrigues of courts, and the change
of dynasties; and hence, the history of our race, as we find
it in books, is but a melancholy record of blood and carnage. There is very little consolatory, much less useful,
knowledge to be gleaned from it. What a great pity the
majority of mankind cannot see their error! The only history of the world, that the great mass of men have any interest in, is that which gives them the beginning, the origin,
the progress, and advancement of the useful arts and sciences. The authors of these have been the real benefactors
of mankind. From this list, it is true, I would not exclude
a few of the statesmen who have, at long intervals, dotted
the annals of the past—men who breasted the storm of tyranny, and upheld, with heroic virtue, the standard of truth
and the rights of their fellows.

But if I were to write a history, ancient or modern, I should
allow the name of no mere politician and trickster, who
pandered to the baser passions for power, to have a place
therein—unless it were to hold it up for scorn and hatred—
as some more daring pirate that might figure at a particular
time. My word for it, *politicians* are enemies of mankind.
I speak of them as a class. They corrupt, debase and degrade the people, instead of improving, elevating and fitting
them, as they should, for further advancement in knowledge, refinement and civilization. All the influences of
government, therefore, are at war with the improvements
of the age. These have sprung up in time of peace in spite
of opposing influences. They are the fruits of an active,
inquiring, untrammeled intellect. For free inquiry, we may
be said to be indebted to government. That may be true

in one sense, but not in the sense in which I speak of government; for this very liberality of government was never conceded until extorted by the people, whose interests were at war with the real principles of most governments. Free inquiry, freedom of debate and opinion, were never the foster-offspring of unlimited government; and the only hope I have for the future is in the virtue of the great mass of the people, in our own country particularly, in resisting the temptations of those who would deceive, cheat, degrade and destroy them for their own individual, political purposes. I am beginning to suspect and to detest all political parties, clubs and combinations. I look upon them as dangerous to the great and permanent interests of the people. The people, in government, should have but one object, and that object—good laws—I might add, with a faithful execution of them. It is a matter of no sort of consequence with them who may make them, or who may execute them, provided their agents in their behalf be honest, capable and faithful. Integrity is the most *essential* requisite in a public officer.

But I am wandering from my question. What shall the people of this country be one hundred years to come? Have they now reached the *maximum* of discovery and improvement allotted to men, or shall future efforts of genius elevate them to new and unexplored regions of science? Shall a wider horizon, and even new spheres, yet be opened to their visions? Shall their progress still be onward? Shall those who fill our places a century hereafter contrast their condition with ours, as I now contrast ours with that of our ancestors in the days of Pitt? This, in my opinion, depends upon the government—and the government depends upon the virtue, intelligence and patriotism of the people. If the people are true to themselves, our progress shall be onward and upward. If we remain at peace with ourselves, and cultivate the arts of peace, a bright and glorious future is before us; but if demagogues triumph—if civil strife is once ripened into civil war—our course will soon be ended, and we shall add another chapter to the great Book of Chronicles, in which are registered the deeds of warriors, the glory of battle-fields, the wily tricks of courtiers and courtezans, and the splendid *fetes* of emperors and kings. . . . .

The year 1850 is memorable in the annals of the United States for the passage by Congress of the "Compromise Measures"—so-called—which led to the first serious disruption of old party-ties, upon purely sectional issues.   Mr. Stephens joined in with the friends of those measures, and supported the action of Congress and Government in giving, as it was then hoped for, a finality to agitation in the Federal Councils, upon the subject of African slavery.   He saw nothing in those measures to endanger the safety of the South or Southern institutions.   He was one of the founders of what was known in Georgia as the "Constitutional Union Party," which swept the State by a very large popular majority in the selection of delegates to the Convention of 1850, and which framed the celebrated "Georgia Platform" of that year.

In 1851, Mr. Stephens warmly supported the election of Howell Cobb, the nominee of the Constitutional Union party for Governor, against Charles J. McDonald, the nominee of the Southern Rights, or Resistance party.   Governor Cobb was elected by a larger majority of votes than any candidate for that office had up to that time received.

In the Presidential campaign of 1852, both the great National parties accepted in their platforms the principles of adjustment set forth in the compromise measures of 1850.   General Pierce, the nominee of the Democratic party, in his letter of acceptance, unequivocally indorsed those measures in letter and spirit; General Scott, the nominee of the Whig party, in his letter of acceptance, did not; he accepted the nomination *cum onere*.   Southern Whigs, who were dissatisfied with the position of General Scott, and who could not exactly approve *all* the doctrines laid down in the Democratic platform, brought forward for the Presidency, Daniel Webster, of Massachusetts, and for the Vice-Presidency, Charles J. Jenkins, of Georgia.   Prominent among the leaders of this movement were Toombs,

A. H. Stephens, Brooke, of Mississippi, Gentry, of Tennessee, etc. Linton Stephens supported the Webster-Jenkins ticket. The death of Mr. Webster, a few days before the election, frustrated their hopes, if, indeed, any that were sanguine of success ever existed.

Among the visitors at Milledgeville, during the sessions of the Legislature of 1851-2, was a lady with whom this sketch has interesting relation. She was a young, accomplished, blooming widow—Mrs. Emmeline Bell, daughter of the Hon. James Thomas, of Hancock—"a gentleman of the old school," a large and successful planter, and an able lawyer. He presided with ability and acceptance as Judge over the Superior Courts of the Northern Circuit for several years. The daughter, richly endowed with all the gentle attractions of her sex—modest, amiable, affectionate, intellectual—made an easy conquest of the legislator's heart—a heart, hitherto, not overly susceptible to female charms. The result was the solemnization of their nuptials in January, 1852, at the residence of the bride's father, amid a large throng of delighted relatives and friends.

This congenial alliance was one of the many felicitous fortunes in Mr. Stephens' life. Nothing can be more beautiful than the pure, ardent, reciprocal affection which characterized and illustrated their conjugal relations: she idolized him, while his devotion to her "glowed with an ardor that might almost be called romantic."

Shortly after the marriage, Mr. Stephens became a citizen of Hancock, and opened a law office in the village of Sparta. He formed a partnership in the practice with Colonel Richard M. Johnston—one of his earliest and most cherished friends. Certainly, the unbounded confidence indicated by a correspondence, which covers many years, discloses a rare degree of mutual personal attachment. Their professional relationship was kept up until Colonel Johnston accepted the Professorship of Belles-Lettres and Oratory, in the University of Georgia, in 1857.

Mr. Stephens determined to devote himself exclusively to the business of his profession after his removal to Sparta. He took his place at once at the head of a Bar, distinguished, perhaps, before any other in the State for juridical ability and forensic power. Toombs, A. H. Stephens, Cone, Dawson, Meriwether, Johnson, Saffold, Sayre, Thomas, Cobb, Reese, Foster, Billups, Hill, Miller, Kenan, Harris, Pottle, King, Lewis, are some of the names that imparted celebrity and illustration to the courts of Middle Georgia at that day; and he was abreast with any of these, in the forum, whether standing before the Judge, or the Twelve. Before entering into the law partnership with Johnston, their relations were those of the closest personal intimacy. They were congenial spirits. They frequently interchanged letters; some of them will appear in these pages. The two following are characteristic of the men and illustrative of their personal relations:

[L. S. to R. M. Johnston.]

CRAWFORDVILLE, February 25, 1851.

DEAR DICK—Yesterday I received a letter from E. C. Williamson, (the doctor, I presume—is it not?) stating that you had informed him, you had turned over to me his case in Hancock, against B. R. Gardner, and requesting me to make out interrogatories for Drs. Haynes, Smith and Stone, but not giving me one Christian name for either of these gentlemen of that learned fraternity. Nor does he state what sort of a case it is, farther than that his drift seems to be to prove that *"she* was unsound." Now, whether *"she"* be a filly, a *nigger gal* or a Durham heifer, is to my mind *res vexata.* I, however, being a man much averse to *extremes,* incline to the (not golden, but ebon) *mean,* and planting myself upon a certain dignity of learning, which restrains its votaries from exercising its mysteries on the races afflicted with glanders and murrains, are enabled to pronounce with some confidence in favor of the *nigger.*

The shrewdest inferences I can draw, from remote and doubtful premises, have led me to the conclusion that Edward, Edmond or Erasmus C. Williamson now has pending in Hancock Superior Court, against B. R. (known to me as Burton R.) Gardner, an action for breach of warranty of soundness on the sale of a certain *nigger gal*. Acting upon the best lights before me, I have accordingly drawn up interrogatories for the three learned gentlemen, surnamed Hayes, Smith and Stone, leaving' blanks to be filled by your superior knowledge, in such places where my own conjectures are wholly at fault, and particularly trusting that you will prefix to the learned witnesses those Christian appellations which are thought to preserve fame from confusion and error among the names of the great. I have thought, too, that the depositions of one Robert Maxwell might not be amiss; and, therefore, I have added a set of interrogatories for him, experiencing in his case many difficulties common to the cases of his more erudite compeers. In each set, you must be careful to supply Edward, Edmund or Erasmus, (as the case may be) and to insert Dinah, Mahaly or Phillis, according to the truth of the matter. When all this has been done, will you then please have commissions attached and have them sent to the plaintiff? All that your information may not compass can doubtless be supplied by Erasmus himself; and when all this is done, why, then just sit down and write me how far I have missed the mark—what sort of case I have to deal with. If you have ever said one word to me about it, it has wholly slipped my memory. . . . .

Yours, truly,
LINTON STEPHENS.

[L. S. to R. M. Johnston.]

CRAWFORDVILLE, May 12, 1851.

DEAR DICK—When I got your letter, stating you had not fixed the day for your examination, but would fix it *about* the first of June, I thought of requesting you not to have it earlier than the fourth, in order to allow me to attend our Superior Court here on the 28th, and go over on the 30th. I have concluded, however, that it might give you some inconvenience; and in case your appointment should conflict with the aforesaid court, I could leave my business with John and go over anyhow. At that time, however, I had but one case (trover for a negro) of much importance in the Superior Court, and on that case I knew there would be an appeal. Now, the case stands differently. To-day one fellow has instituted proceedings against another fellow for establishing the freedom of several of the last named fellow's negroes. This same last named fellow has employed me to defend his rights, and the case is to be tried at our next Inferior Court—first Monday, and second day of June. It is a very important case, and I *must* stay and attend to it. If you have not, therefore, fixed the day of your examination, and if a matter of a few days will work no particular derangement of your plans, why, don't have it before the fifth of June, allowing me *two* days for court (and it may be possible that it will last that long) and one more day to go over. If you have fixed the day, or if compliance with my suggestion will incommode you in the least, why, to confess the truth, I should feel, in the escape from the rash promise I have made, a satisfaction almost equal to, and counter-poising the disappointment of not seeing you, and—but anon. Dick, this is a dilemma which I could not foresee, and I know you will perceive the obligation upon me. It gives me the less concern, too, because it can involve no serious disappointment to you or your patrons; for speech or no speech, on the occasion, is just a matter as it may turn up—very well in its place, if it only be well placed, and not missed, if it only be not out of place. Write me forthwith and let me know whether I am to take the steam off my speech factory, or whether I shall pile on more fuel. The wear and tear of machinery is too considerable to be incurred for nothing. It would be like running a saw-mill without stocks, or a grist-mill without grain.

Give my love to all "enquiring friends," and remember me particularly to Mrs. Johnston.

Yours, very truly,

LINTON STEPHENS.

He made the speech, and had the "satisfaction" of seeing "D'ck" and —— her, who was to be his wife.

But Mr. Stephens was not allowed to gratify his own

wishes by remaining in private life. The people of Hancock elected him to the State Senate in 1853. In the gubernatorial election of that year, he supported Hon. Charles J. Jenkins. It was the closest contest of the kind ever known in the State. Governor Herschel V. Johnson was elected by 510 majority out of a popular vote of about one hundred thousand cast.

The resolution he offered in the Senate on the Nebraska question—and it was resolved on by himself before he had consulted any one—foreshadowed the position he occupied, subsequently, when the principles asserted in the Kansas-Nebraska Bill were absorbing issues in the politics of the country.

On the 18th of December, 1853, he writes to his brother from Milledgeville:

"Cooley's speech, which you said in a letter I got several days ago you had sent me, has just come to hand to-day. I have read it through. He's a pretty Judge, isn't he? It is a right strong speech, but the author of it is as bad as Brownlow. These Northern fellows are a nice set; but to say the truth, we are all—North and South—a nice set. Cooley seems to talk like an honest man who meant something, and the excuse for his epithets is to be charged, I suppose, to the account of provocation. This is a most rascally administration, beyond all doubt. Cobb is here, McDonald is here, Warner is here, and Jack Jones is here. What it all means is yet to be seen. Our Democratic allies, on the question of bringing on the election of United States Senator, all are *firm, they say*—they tell our people so, and I think they are in earnest. It is said here that Cobb has *denounced* them. It is also said that he is to address the Democracy to-morrow night. Cobb has been asked what brought him here: he said he came here to get two bills passed—one giving the election of town marshal to the people, and another creating a new county around Athens, with Athens as county site. . . . .

[From L. S. to A. H. S.]

SPARTA, February 24, 1854.

DEAR BROTHER—I have seen a report of your speech in the *Herald*, and a short synopsis of it in the *Chronicle and Sentinel*, taken from the *Intelligencer*. I was much pleased with it, and I was particularly pleased to see that you put yourself on the same ground which I had taken before.

How do you like my Nebraska resolution, which I introduced into the Legislature? I suppose you have seen it before now in the papers. It was in these words: " Resolved, etc., That opposition to the principles of the Nebraska Bill, in relation to the subject of slavery, is regarded by the people of Georgia as hostility to the rights of the South, and that all persons who partake in such opposition are unfit to be recognized as component parts of any party not hostile to the South." It passed unanimously; but notwithstanding that, I called the yeas and nays. Stell, the President, asked leave to vote, and he stands recorded among the yeas. It also passed the House unanimously, but the yeas and nays were not called there. I voted against Cochran's resolutions on Nebraska (which you have doubtless seen) for several reasons: In the first place, because there was no substantive idea in them, unless they meant to assert that our confidence " in the great body of the North " had been greatly strengthened by the fact that the Nebraska Bill had been *introduced* into Congress—a declaration which I was not prepared to make. To make such a declaration would require a little too much of that spirit which expresses great thanks for very small favors. When the "great body of the North" *vote for* the bill, then I may feel that I can give the great body of the North a vote of confidence, but not until then. In the next place, I looked upon the resolution as a hobbling attempt to bolster up the administration. In the third place, it asserted the right of instruction. There was no chance to debate it, for they put the previous question on it at the first hop; our men generally voted for it; indeed, there were only five nays in the Senate and none in the House. I have seen a statement in several papers that it passed both branches unanimously. That is a mistake. The yeas and nays were taken in the Senate, and five nays stand recorded against it.

I don't think the administration can take much comfort from it in connection with *mine*. Do you? Nor do I think our Southern rights, fire-eating contemporaries can take much comfort from it for themselves. Don't you think that they have clearly and unequivocally voted that their own conduct and positions, in 1850–51, were "hostile" to the rights of the South, and that they themselves, upon the measures of past merit, are "unfit" to be recognized as component parts of any party which is not "hostile" to the South? What will men do! I offered another resolution, declaring that the measures of 1850 were "wise, liberal and just," etc., but some of our own friends were tender on that point, and I did not press it to a vote. Our friend ———— would have been in some trouble—not more, to be sure, than from the one which was passed; but still some did not seem to *see* it in that same light. Indeed, the Democracy never suspected, for an instant, that my Nebraska resolution contained anything that could be construed into a reflection upon their own past course, nor upon the purity and propriety of their present alliance. . . . .

The life of no professional man is more barren of incidents of general interest than that of the lawyer; for it is a short radius that sweeps in judges, juries and clients only. The year 1854 found Mr. Stephens diligently engaged in the practice of his profession; and as his reputation grew and spread, the emoluments he reaped were large and rich. The letters following relate to his domestic life and pursuits, and bring out to view some of the gentler and more amiable features of his character:

[From L. S. to A. H. S.]

SPARTA, June 28, 1854.

DEAR BROTHER— . . . . I had heard of the death of poor cousin Sabra before I got your letter announcing it. John Stewart (Billy Harrison's son-in-law) was over here and told me of it. I have known her so long and well—have spent so many cheerful, happy moments in her company—that her image mingles, at almost every turn

11 *

and corner, with all the many other figures that flit in
throngs, varying and changing through all the scenes which
memory wakes.   To strike out her existence from the face
of the earth—I cannot realize it!   It seems strange and incredible to me that it should be so!   Her days had not
been very many, and yet they had indeed been full of
trouble.   She bore a cheerful spirit through every trial, and
evinced in every emergency more of the spirit of true philosophy than anybody I ever knew, who was a woman, and
had no greater share of intellectual endowment. . . . .

[From L. S. to A. H. S.]

SPARTA, June 29, 1854.

DEAR BROTHER— . . . . Before
getting your letter, I had mailed one to you, in which I had
spoken of the same subject in a manner which struck me
as bearing a singular resemblance to the train of thought
suggested to you by the same occasion.   Since I have heard
of her death, she is constantly in my thoughts, awaking associations with brother, with Billy, and with my school-boy
days, that have not been so vividly presented to my memory in many years.   It all impresses me *painfully* with a
sense of how they have passed away *forever* from earth, and
how we are *rapidly* passing away likewise.   Life, with its
longest continuance, with all its joys, with all its sorrows,
with all its associations, with thousands of other existences,
seems but a flash—blazing but for an instant, and then sinking again into impenetrable darkness—a mere point, un-
marked, in the vastness of that *immeasurable Eternity* which
lies behind it and before it. . . . .

The succeeding letter was written on occasion of the
death of an infant but a few months old.   He was devotedly
attached to all his children, as this narrative will abundantly
show; but his yearning tenderness seemed ever to run out
most fondly for the latest-born, because the youngest and
most helpless.   It was but the exemplification, in another
form, of one strong element of his nature:

[From L. S. to A. H. S.]

SPARTA, August 24, 1854.

DEAR BROTHER—The struggle is over, and little Kate is no more in life. She went out as quietly and beautifully as the day dies away into the twilight and darkness. She is lying robed in white, in her crib. They have scattered flowers around her tiny form, and she holds a white rose-bud in one of her little hands. She seems to be in a sweet sleep. I had not thought it possible for me to feel so keenly the death of one so young. Strange to say, she now has—*as* she never had struck me strongly *as* having before—a likeness to you. It was pointed out to me by Emm, and I had *thought* I had observed it before, but had not mentioned it. She died at 6½ o'clock this morning. She will dwell on my memory as she appeared in the beauty of health, but I shall not regret to mingle with that bright image the little pale, sweet face that now sleeps in its last mortal array. One comfort I have, even in this first burst of grief: I feel that, while I am deeply touched and smitten, I might have been desolated and blasted. Good-bye.

Affectionately,   LINTON.

Addison, of all the English fine writers of prose, was the favorite of Mr. Stephens. It was not the unequaled style of the author that attracted him only, but the soul and sentiment that animate his pages as well.

[From L. S. to A. H. S.]

SPARTA, January 1, 1855.

DEAR BROTHER— . . . . Addison is to me, of all men, the most pious, rational and entertaining upon subjects of a religious bearing. Another very pretty, and to me novel, speculation of his is upon the subject of the Jews as a people. Upon such subjects he is full of piety and free from superstition—so abounding in fine philosophy, and so exempt from fine-spun theories, so fruitful of profound suggestions, and so joyous in the healthful hope of a cheerful spirit, that to read his religious speculations is food equally for the reason, the imagination and

the heart.   I know of no writings having so fine a tendency
as his to cultivate a sound and cheerful piety.   I don't wonder that the man had friends of so much devotion to him;
for he clearly possessed just that sort of sense, and flowing
charitableness and pleasantry, which are so well qualified
to inspire attachments amounting to personal devotion.
But you don't agree with me about Addison; and I verily
believe it is because you are not acquainted with him.   His
fine veins are somewhat rare, but they are rich.   A man
may be able to say that he has read many of his pieces, and
yet no man can appreciate him unless he has read them
all. . . . .

The nomination of General Scott, in 1852, by the Na
tional Whig Convention, for the Presidency, disrupted the
party.   A majority, perhaps, of the Old-Line Whigs went
into the Know-Nothing organization—or, as it was afterwards called, the American party—which loomed up so
suddenly and so formidably in the summer and autumn of
1854.   The history of American politics furnishes no in
stance—with exception, perhaps, of the Anti-Masonic
party in 1832—of a political party, which sprang up with
such surprising quickness, having such thorough organization, numerically so powerful, and whose existence was so
ephemeral, as the Know-Nothing, or American party.   It
swept the country—North, and West, and East—with a
tide of unbroken success, until the current was first rolled
back and lashed into spray as it dashed against the Gibral-
tar of the Virginian Democracy.   Mr. Stephens was among
its earliest opponents in Georgia.   He, along with probably twenty thousand Whigs in Georgia, locked shields with
the Democrats to defeat it in 1855.

[From L. S. to A. H. S.]

SPARTA, January 17, 1855.

DEAR BROTHER— . . . . The Know-Nothings
here are holding up their heads high at the news from Phila-

delphia about the adoption of the platform, and the secession of the fifty-three Northern members. There is just one remark I have to make now in the hurry of the present moment, concerning that same platform, illustrating the great gulf between that and the fourth resolution of the Georgia platform: A man is about to strike me; I announce to him that if he does, I shall shoot him. Another man, a by-stander, says to that man, he is *wrong* to strike me, but says no more. He *fails* to say I will be right in resisting by shooting. Does that by-stander back my position? By no means; he condemns my adversary, it is true; but he fails to *justify* me. He is silent as to the *extent* of the wrong, and as to the measure of resistance. This Philadelphia platform contains *no fighting line*. It announces a principle, but fails to announce at what hazard it ought to be maintained, or what ought to be the consequences of its violation. It does not place anybody, North or South, upon a platform of resistance. It declares it is wrong for people to spit in our faces. You may not see the force of my criticism; but I tell you, it is just, and I can make you comprehend it when I see you. There was no fighting line, I know, in either of the late Baltimore platforms; but its omission left an immeasurable distance between them and the Georgia platform. You may be inclined to suggest that a fighting National platform (one adopted by the people in all sections) would be inappropriate and out of place. I would not have the North to declare that they would themselves fight in our cause precisely, but I *would* have them *affix a value* to our rights by announcing a conviction that their violation would justify resistance and separation. Such a recognition would be of vast importance to us whenever the separation might come. Under it we would stand justified in doing what we have said at home we will do when the emergency arises. . . . .

[From L. S. to A. H. S.]

SPARTA, January 18, 1855.

DEAR BROTHER—Still no letter from you. What is the matter? I have had none from you since those I found on my return from Savannah last Saturday, now nearly a week ago. Have you made a speech and been busy writing it out? If you have been taken up with that matter during the whole interval between your letters, you surely have been playing it *a la* Campbell—writing what you *didn't speak*. I observed that you had the floor for Friday; but I found this morning that neither House of Congress sat on that day, in consequence of the death of Senator Norris. So, I suppose, you delivered your speech Saturday, unless that be, as I think it used to be, private-bill day. But what were you doing all the week before? Monday, the eighth, is the last date I have from you—ten days ago—or have you only been trying the virtue of that forbidden law, the *lex talionis?* or, in English words, giving me *tit for tat?* It is true, I did not write to you any time during my several days' absence at Savannah; and it is also true, that just before leaving home, I said I would write from Savannah; but you would excuse the failure if you knew how poor the chance was there for writing with comfort or convenience. My interpretation of the whole thing throws the *onus* on the mails. . . . . The Know-Nothings are a great power in the State just now—greater than you may have imagined in Georgia. They aim at an *evil* no doubt; but they are on the opposite extreme. The result may be great good to the country; but the man who desires to do right, and to be found in the right *always*, would desire to be found on neither *extreme*, but on the ground of *sound doctrine*.   Affectionately,   LINTON.

The two next letters show his opinion of the celebrated speech of Mr. A. H. Stephens, in reply to that of Mr. L. D. Campbell, wherein the resources of Georgia and Ohio were contrasted.

[From L. S. to A. H. S.]

SPARTA, January 24, 1855.

DEAR BROTHER— . . . . Henry has brought up my mail since our return, and, among other things, I got two copies of your late speech in reply to Campbell. Both copies are in the *Globe*, and came under your frank. I have already read more than half of your speech, but have laid it down in order to have a few lines for you in the mail of to-day. I will write you what I think of the speech after I have read it all. I will, however, give you notice now, after reading a part only, that I intend to perform a very friendly office towards it, according to your own estimate of what is friendly and useful *criticism*—that is to say, I am going to find some *fault* with it. I will say, however, that as yet I have no faults of matter to charge, but one or two purely of *manner*. The gravest one is more properly, yet a fault of *taste*. But for the present, you must be patient, and wait for the whole at once. I never did like to *take* a bad thing in broken doses, and in *administering* one, I will be equally considerate. . .

[From L. S. to A. H. S.]

SPARTA, January 24, 1855.

DEAR BROTHER—To-day I wrote you a letter, not very short or very long, which has gone, or ought to have gone, by to-day's mail. It is night now, and I have read over your speech twice—though, when I wrote to-day, I had read only a part once. I promised you to-day to do a friendly office for your speech by finding fault with it. I confess that my feeling of fault-finding was stronger then than it is now. From reading the whole speech, I more perfectly caught and appreciated the spirit of the whole, or I became more *biased*. But I still adhere to my original impression, that part of the speech is not in keeping with the best taste. That part which occurs early in the speech, and which alludes to your record as one that had not been made for an hour, or an electioneering campaign, but for all time, and by which you are willing to abide, living and dead, is somewhat *Bentonian* in its tone, and, even considered by itself, is to be regarded by *good* judges as out of taste. *That*, however, by itself, might be regarded, not only as free from blemish, but as a noble expression at once of defiance to your own generation, and of appeal to posterity; but when you spoke of your "tables" as something that would do "to keep," and that you meant "to keep" the likeness of "old Bullion," became too palpable to be quite agreeable to a delicate sense of modesty. But after reading the whole speech, I could not precisely find it in my heart to say that you had transcended the provocation.

Without commenting further upon the manner, which I took up first as being of the least importance, I proceed to speak of the *matter;* and upon that point, I suspect (from the speech itself) that you will be astonished when I say that it is the *greatest speech* you ever made, and a speech, marking more distinctly than any other in American history, the commencement of a *new era.* I do not believe, from the speech itself, and from the manner in which you have put it up, that you regard it in the high light in which I hold it. Your speech in reply to Mace foreshadows, and this speech clearly and distinctly reveals, *a new idea;* and that is, the comparative effects of free and slave labor upon all the developments, and consequently upon the prosperity, of a country. I can truly say, that while to *me* your general idea is not a new one, yet, that your manner of illustrating it is wholly new, and very striking. Allow me to give you another idea which bears upon the *philanthropic* view, and which, though obvious, has never been hinted at, by anybody whomsoever, within my knowledge. The office performed by the African—menial services and manual labor—is one which, on *universal confession,* must be performed in *every country* by *somebody:* now, in the view of the *philanthropist,* who looks to the interest of *mankind,* is there any difference between confining these offices to a *class* of men defined by *blood,* or diffusing them through a *class* marked by *poverty?* The same *amount* of that *kind* of labor is necessary to be performed for a given community; and is it any misfortune that it should all (even) be performed by the black man, *unless* there be *some superiority* of the black man over the white? But, on the contrary, are there not several *strong* reasons for throwing it upon the black man rather than the white? I will allude only to the great line of demarkation arising out of color, and to the known superior docility of the black race. As a question of *humanity,* we inquire obviously into the numbers only, and not into the color, of those engaged in pursuits of inferior rank or dignity. This, in my opinion, is the *germ* of a new and untouched view of slavery, as a social, and particularly as a *humane* institution. I could enlarge upon it to a great extent; indeed, I have for a good while been thinking of presenting it, in some amplitude, in the shape of an article for some review. I only throw it out, however, as a thought

to you, and as a most powerful forerunner and auxiliary to
the train of thought pursued in your last speech. This
idea of mine, when fully comprehended, reduces the whole
discussion to two simple considerations—the effect of slavery
upon the *master* in regard to physical, moral, and intellectual development and progress, and its effect upon the
slave, or upon that *class*, which answers to the condition
and offices of the slave, in the same particulars. Upon the
latter branch of the inquiry, your argument beams with
new light and overwhelming power. The first branch you
leave untouched. The views presented by you really per-
tain to the most *practical* branch of the subject; and they
are likely to produce (in my judgment) most practical fruits
upon the great Yankee nation, who are emphatically a
practical, and money-making, and money-saving people. I
merely throw out the hint. If you comprehend my full
meaning, I think you may use it to great effect; and nothing
would give me greater pleasure than the reflection of having furnished you with a hint, which might be worked by
you into an argument so magnificent and statesman-like,
and which, thus treated, might result in fruits so grand and
so just. But I will conclude with saying your speech, in
view of its novelty and its probable effects, is the greatest
and grandest of your life, and is not surpassed by any in
American history. I am not extravagant—I *may* be mistaken.

Affectionately,   LINTON.

[From L. S. to A. H. S.]

SPARTA, February 2, 1855.

DEAR BROTHER— . . . . I don't think you
exactly caught the idea, which I intended to convey, concerning a certain view which would have put a finishing
stone upon your speech. The natural adaptation of the
negro race to slavery is the least part of it, and, indeed,
hardly a part of it at all, though it does come directly in
aid of it. I was in a great hurry when I wrote the last part
of my *critique* upon your speech, and did not succeed, I
imagine, in expressing precisely what I meant; and now I
have just got a call, summoning me to town, and I must go,
and must finish my letter before I go. I can now only say,

12*

in the most general terms, that my idea was, that, as a question of *humanity*, it is obviously indifferent whether the services performed for us by slaves be performed by white men, or black men, so far as the good of the greatest number is concerned; the only question is, the nature of the service, and the necessary number engaged in it. What is done by our negroes must be done by *somebody*, and the only real question, therefore, in point of humanity, is, whether anybody else could perform the same service and be in a *better* condition. If not, the tears of humanity are shed in vain over the woes of the negro, and ought to be shed over the imperfections of nature, which require *men* to perform such services. The abolitionist would simply *substitute* the white man in place of the black. He would not make the bed *easier*, but only give it a different *occupant;* and *humanity* is concerned only at what befalls man as such, and not for the fate of one particular man, or class of men, rather than another, when the fate is *inevitable* to *some* man, or *some class.* . . . .

Fanaticism is blind, and never stops to reason. It has no capacity to reason. "Menial services and manual labor" are, for the most part, still performed at the South by emancipated slaves, and with poorer reward than in *ante-bellum* days.

Governor Herschel V. Johnson appointed Mr. Stephens counsel to represent the State of Georgia in the controversy with Alabama. The following letter relates to that subject:

[From L. S. to A. H. S.]

SPARTA, February 7, 1855.

DEAR BROTHER—To-day I got your letter of the 3d instant, saying that Mr. Phillips had inquired of you about the Answer in the case of Alabama *vs.* Georgia. I sat down and drew about half of the Answer, but was interrupted, and have not since had a good opportunity to finish it. This week, I shall be obliged to attend to other matters; but after that, I will finish it and get the signatures of the Governor, the Attorney-General, and of O. C. Gibson, my associate counsel, and send it to you to be filed. I shall not go to Washington this winter, but I want the Answer filed. . . . .

[From L. S. to A. H. S.]

SPARTA, March 8, 1855.

DEAR BROTHER—I got your letter this morning, announcing the painful news of the death of Lou Toombs. The announcement did not greatly surprise me; for it was not altogether unexpected; and yet it shocked me. It fills me with a feeling too near akin to grief to be called by any other name. I almost loved her as a sister. She was so good, so intelligent, so artless, so innocently gay and cheerful of spirit, that it was impossible to know her well without being touched with a tender and most kindly regard for her. She had the blended virtues of her father and mother, and added a chaplet of gracefulness and quietness, all her own. Poor Lou! poor Lou! . . . .

In 1855, Mr. Stephens was nominated, by the Democratic and Anti-Know-Nothing party, for Congress, to represent the Seventh District of the State. His repugnance to again entering the turbulent field of politics was pronounced and extreme. Indeed, he never had relish for that sort of life. There was a spell about *home* that he owned and loved ever; and now, all which lends to it most of attraction and charm—wife, children, affluence, good neighborhood, the society of cherished friends, "the sweet hours of elegant leisure spent in the library"—were his in full fruition. He, however, yielded a reluctant consent to the wishes of the party, authoritatively expressed; and after a heated canvass—albeit characterized by nothing of personal bitterness—his competitor, the late Nathaniel Greene Foster, was elected by a small majority. No one regretted the result less than Mr. Stephens. He did not rejoice over his defeat, as it is related of the old Grecian patriot, when no shell bore his name for a seat in the Amphictyonic Council; but his purely personal feelings were far from being ruffled, or his hopes in the least disappointed. The satisfaction he derived from the re-election of Governor Johnson, whom, two years before, he had opposed on other issues, and the overthrow of the Know-Nothing party in Georgia, was ample compensation for any unrealized dreams of ambition his candidature may have inspired.

In the Presidential race of 1856, Mr. Stephens supported, with his wonted ardor, the Buchanan-Breckinridge nomination. He was a delegate to the Cincinnati Convention of that year, and was tendered a place upon the Electoral ticket. That position the exacting cares of a large and laborious practice compelled him to decline. He, nevertheless, rendered efficient service to the party with his tongue and his pen.

I heard him relate, with great glee, an anecdote connected with the mission to Cincinnati, which I have never seen in print. The Georgia delegates to the nominating convention took Washington City in their way, and remained a day or so at the Federal City. Congress was in session. General Toombs, from Georgia, complimented the delegation with a dinner, inviting several other distinguished Democrats. Many of the aspirants for nomination to the Presidency were present—invited guests. Late in the evening, when wit and wine had pretty well performed their office, and the company were about to disperse, Colonel James Gardner, the Chairman of the Georgia Delegation, full of the kindliest feeling, filled his glass, and, surrounded by Cass, Douglas, Cobb, Toombs, Breckinridge, and others, who *would not* have declined a nomination, if tendered, offered as a toast: "Gentlemen, may you *all* live to be President of the United States!" Douglas, standing close by Cobb, nudged him at the elbow and said: "Well, Cobb, here's a *long* life to *you!*"

[From L. S. to A. H. S.]

SPARTA, June 18, 1856.

DEAR BROTHER— . . . . The Know-Nothings here look chap-fallen; but they intend to fight. We are to have a meeting Saturday to send delegates to the Fourth-of-July Convention at Milledgeville, and I am to make them a speech. A speech on the right string, at this time—or rather, at that time—(for all the candidates will be out then) may do much good in this county. G—— told me that M—— and J—— had declared for Buchanan. I don't believe it; but he said so. The nomination is received well by our friends everywhere, so far as I know, or have heard. Jim Jones is raving like a madman. In his paper, which I got this morning, he invites all lovers of the country to avert the disgrace of electing Buchanan by mounting the "broad platform of Fillmore"—a platform consisting of the "leading principles" of another platform, (or the same,) which Jones, only a few weeks ago, pronounced unfit for a Southern latitude. "*Quem Deus vult perdere*," etc., is a maxim which gives me great comfort under present circumstances. I am glad that Stringfellow brings such good tidings from Kansas. The indications inspire me with the hope that we shall make a complete rout of the enemy. . . . .

The year 1857 was the saddest in the life of Mr. Stephens. In January, his wife died. The event, for a time, quite unmanned him: he was prostrated by the blow. The insatiate archer's arrow penetrated his very soul, and produced an anguish—an agony of grief—such as the tenderest hearts only can feel, and the stoutest withstand. For years succeeding, his letters are laden with expressions of sorrow for his loss—deep, boding, eloquent—and with testimonials of her worth, and tributes to her memory, of surpassing tenderness and beauty. The precincts of private grief are too sacred to be invaded by stranger-step. But this sketch would fail to present a faithful portraiture of Linton Stephens, and do injustice to his memory, if the evidences of his devotion to her—recorded in an epistolary correspondence, at once the saddest and most beautiful I ever read—were altogether omitted. He exemplified, in his domestic life, all the virtues that make *Home* sweet and holy.

[From A. H. S. to L. S.]

CRAWFORDVILLE, March 14, 1857.

DEAR BROTHER—The day is fast waning towards evening twilight. Since you left, I have written eighteen letters—this is the nineteenth—my fingers are tired, but I could not close my labors without saying a word to you. You are before this time at home, I suppose—safely there, I trust. Long did I watch the carriage to-day as it slowly bore you away. I thought of the muddy roads and chill air you had to encounter, and then the sad scenes you would meet at your journey's end. With a fervent prayer that you might be sustained by that Power above, that rules and shapes our destinies, and that with resignation and fortitude you would bear up against whatever sorrows or griefs may ever betide you, I watched your progress. When no longer you were in sight, still my heart's yearnings pursued you, and though I betook myself to the duties of life, and for a time had my mind absorbed in business, in attending to the demands and wishes of men of various kinds, scattered all over the country; yet, after it is all over, my mind is with you. You, above anything else or anybody else, are the object of my solicitude, anxiety and love. I feel for you in your grief—I mourn with you in your sorrow—I weep with you in your distress. I would fain soothe your pangs if I could; but, after all, human consolation can avail nothing. Look to a Power higher and abler. But do not despair—do not let your strength fail you. Bear with fortitude and resignation whatever afflictions may befall you. Don't indulge in despondent feelings; rise early—take bodily exercise; devote your mind to some engaging subject; don't be much alone; don't brood over the subject of your grief; above all, don't let your mind be absorbed in thought after you retire at night; seek repose and sleep. Exercise will conduce to this. Be as cheerful as you can; cultivate the feeling; read such books and seek such company as will conduce to it. Be master of your passions, appetites and weaknesses, whatever they may be, and may God bless and sustain you, now and forever.

Yours, affectionately,

A. H. STEPHENS.

He was again nominated this year for Congress. The American party was known to have a decided majority in the district; but it was believed that a vigorous canvass on his part, and his great personal popularity, would overcome it. The Hon. Joshua Hill was the nominee of the American party—undoubtedly their strongest man. The canvass promised to be a spirited one—for, the opposing candidates were the idols of their parties, and deservedly so—but it had scarcely opened before Mr. Stephens met with an injury by being thrown from a stage-coach—returning from the burial of his sister, Catharine—which so far disabled him that he could not meet his competitor upon the hustings. His right knee received a hurt from which he never entirely recovered. Mr. Hill was elected by a small majority.

Mr. Stephens attended the Democratic Gubernatorial Convention which first nominated Governor Joseph E. Brown for the office which he filled for nearly eight years.

[From L. S. to A. H. S.]

SPARTA, June 29, 1857.

DEAR BROTHER— . . . . I intend going over to see you and stay with you a day or two; but I write, lest something should prevent me. I was well pleased with the action of the convention. The Kansas part of the platform was drawn by me. . . . . Brown is a man that I know to have decided ability; as a debater, he is far superior to any of those who were before the convention. Indeed, without being an orator, he is a very effective stump-speaker. He is quick, clear-headed, and a close reasoner, with considerable turn for sharp, witty remark. He was a firm Southern-rights man, and one of the most prudent among them. Besides all this, he is a man of fine personal character, and self-made. He was poor, but borrowed money and graduated at Yale College. He stands high in the up-country, and deserves it. I served in the Legislature with him in the sessions of 1849 and 1850. The man, and the section from which he comes, are also an excellent lick for Toombs. I have written to Mr. Cobb to-day, urging him to have Walker recalled. I don't know, nor care much, (as far as I am concerned) what they do. Colonel Foster told, at a party-meeting in Madison the other day, (so Carlos writes) that they need not nominate him, unless they wanted him to take a *beating*. If they concluded that they needed a candidate for a beating, he would not run off for fear of defeat, etc.

[From L. S. to A. H. S.]

SPARTA, July 4, 1857.

DEAR BROTHER— . . . . I got a letter this morning from Nisbet, of the *Federal Union*, saying that the Democratic party will not go as far, in relation to Walker and Kansas, as the convention went. He says they will not make Walker's removal a *sine qua non;* and that he has received numerous letters from friends requesting him to write to me, and request me to withhold my letter of acceptance for the present. This is exactly the substance of the letter—introduced and closed with great assurances of friendship, etc. I don't know what I shall do yet. I intend, however, to wait and see what the Know-Nothing concern may do next week, and then decide on my course. I am at times disposed to run anyhow, on my own platform, with defiance to everybody who is against it, and calling upon all men, of all parties, to back me in defense of our own section. But the prevailing disposition with me is to set forth my opinions on the present state of affairs, and my reasons for them, and then leave the turf, and all the scramblers for office, and party slaves, to take care of themselves. This is what I think I shall do. I had begun to feel some interest in the subject, and had begun to occupy myself with it as a *divertisement;* but now I don't care anything about it. . . . .

[From L. S. to A. H. S.]

SPARTA, December 10, 1857.

DEAR BROTHER— . . . . I am sorry
to hear that Douglas is against the Kansas Constitution. I
don't suppose his objection can be that of Forney—that
the whole Constitution is not submitted—for he himself, in
his Springfield speech, held that no submission at all was
necessary. If the convention had power to complete their
work without submitting it at all, or to submit it if they
chose, assuredly they might finish one part themselves, and
submit another, covering the main topic of difference. I
scarcely suppose he can object to the class of voters; for
certainly the convention had the power to prescribe them,
and in exercising it, they have not exhibited partiality by
excluding anybody. Nor can there be any valid objection
to the test-oath, requiring each voter, if challenged, to swear
to support the Constitution as adopted; for any one, who
would refuse to take such an oath, would be an enemy to
government in the proper sense of the term. Such a man
could intend to submit to government, only in the event
of government going his *own way*—that is, only provided
he could govern *himself and other people, too.* Such a man
is hostile to the compact on which all government rests; he
is an outlaw, and ought to be excluded from all participation in the general action. He should not be allowed the
chance of getting his own way over other people, while he
stands with the defiant declaration that he will not allow
other people to have their way over him. Is his objection
founded on the provision that the present laws shall remain
of force until repealed by the Legislature under the new
Constitution? They surely had the *legal* power to make
that provision; for, out of their sovereign power to establish a Constitution, they might have instituted a new government, entirely cutting off the existing one, and enacting
what laws they pleased. To be sure, there is a difference, in
this respect, between a *State* convention and a *Territorial*
convention; and, on this difference, I can well imagine that
difference of views might arise; but if you do not already
see the solution, I think I can give it so clearly that there
can be no answer to it; but, lest the difference may not
have presented itself to you, let me first state it, and then

13*

show that the difference cannot legitimately affect the mat
ter in hand—that is, the legal power of the Kansas Con
vention to do precisely what they did.

A State convention (assuming always that it is assem
bled in pursuance of the existing Constitution, so as to avoid
revolution) would be sovereign, not only in degree, but in
time also; for they might immediately inaugurate the new
state of things and wipe out the old—they could *dissolve an
existing Legislature*. A Territorial convention, on the con
trary, is sovereign in degree only, and not in time. Per
haps it is a better phrase to say, that the power of the State
convention would be complete without awaiting action by
anybody else; while the power of the Territorial conven
tion is only *inchoate*, and needs the admission of the new
State, by Congress, to set it in motion. The difference
may be illustrated by the departure of a ship out of port:
In one case, the captain can sail where he pleases; in an
other case, he must await permission of some one else; but
in both cases, suppose him to have power to take aboard
what *freight* he pleases: then my idea is illustrated. The
State convention can start when they please, and carry what
they please. On the other hand, the Territorial convention
can start only when Congress speaks the *fiat*; but, then,
their power is as great as that of the State convention over
the *freight*. The Constitution, formed by a Territorial con
vention, is like Adam was when his body was formed—com
plete, but still waiting for the breath of life. It can have
no operation until the new State is admitted. How, then,
it may be asked, (and I say it may be asked, because the
question occurred to my own mind,) can the Kansas Con
vention enact that existing laws shall continue in force until
repealed by a Legislature under the new Constitution?
How can they supersede the existing Legislature, or put
restraints upon its power, before their own power has had
vitality put into it? This question may have given to
other minds, as it did, at first presentation, give me, some
difficulty. The Constitution which they have formed (if
our papers have given a correct synopsis of it) seems, on its
face, to *attempt* to hamper the present Legislature by an
nulling their authority to alter, amend or repeal existing
laws. The language of the second section is: "All laws
now of force in the Territory of Kansas, which are not re

pugnant to this Constitution, shall continue and be of force until altered, amended or repealed by a Legislature assembled by the provisions of this Constitution." And then the seventeenth section declares: "This Constitution shall *take effect*, and be in *force*, from and after its ratification by the people, as hereinbefore provided." Now, in my judgment, this will not interfere, nor was it intended to interfere, (but whether so intended or not, in point of fact, cannot legally interfere,) with the intermediate powers of the existing Legislature. Although it is declared that the Constitution shall take effect, and be in full force, from the time of its ratification, yet this, by legal intendment, *must* be applied to the great, and indeed *only end in view*—the formation of a Constitution to be *presented to Congress*, and to govern the country after the State shall be admitted into the Union. The whole work of the convention (and of the people jointly, it being partly submitted for their ratification) was, if you please, to build the ship and rig her off, furnished for sailing, and then turn her over to Congress, who must *launch* her; and they have simply declared that their work shall not be complete—that the ship shall not be pronounced *sea-worthy* and turned over to Congress—*until* the people shall put on the finishing rope by ratifying, or rejecting, the slavery clause. After she is *launched*, then she passes out, free from all action by Congress, and rigged and freighted just as she was offered at the wharf. Then, and not until then, will the laws existing in Kansas, when the *convention adjourned*, *begin* to be in force, (so far as any validity is imparted by the Constitution to them,) and continue to be in force until repealed by the State Legislature. In other words, these second and seventeenth sections are only a declaration of the *status* on which the new State will start. Nor could the convention have meant anything else, because the Constitution expressly provides the manner of its own presentation to Congress, and, therefore, could not have intended that it should go into *action*, as a government, before Congress should have admitted the new State. Nor would any *unfair* consequences result to the anti-slavery men there, if the people should reject slavery from the present laws protecting slave property, being included as a part of the new statutes; for they would *not be so included*, except so far as to protect existing slave property; because,

if the people reject slavery, then would all laws protecting
prospective slavery be repugnant to the Constitution, and
only those are to be "continued in force" which are not
repugnant to the Constitution.   Such would be repugnant,
because the Constitution expressly declares, that if there
shall be a majority of votes for the Constitution, without
slavery, then shall the pro-slavery clause be stricken out,
and it is declared that *slavery shall not exist;* and let me
further remark, what I was about to omit, that, in the other
event, of slavery being ratified by the people, then a *status*
of laws protecting slave property would be of the utmost
consequence to slave-holders; for, otherwise, this present
Black Republican Legislature might, by repealing all such
existing laws, start the new State off with slave property un-
protected, *although* the people should have solemnly decided in favor of slavery; so that this provision is a *fair* one
and an important one to the pro-slavery men, and just such
as cannot possibly impose any unfair disadvantage upon the
other side.   Indeed, the *absence* of it would be absolutely
unfair to our side.   I am afraid I have wearied you, and I
will quit.   It may be that I have only been fighting men of
straw; but, at any rate, this sketch will serve to give you
my general analysis of the Kansas Constitution, and my notions of its defense.   I would like for you to write me how
far you agree with me, and also whether or not I have
struck any of the points of difficulty; and yet, there is one
other view I must present in relation to the matter of *fairness:* The convention was *fairly elected,* and was largely
pro-slavery, and was under no legal obligation to submit
their work to the people.   We had won *the trick,* and we
are entitled to it.   But, again, when we had it in our hands,
and might have kept it simply by holding on, isn't it hard
that we should be charged with *unfairness,* when we voluntarily yielded it up, and gave our opponents another chance
at it?   But enough.

[From L. S. to A. H. S.]

SPARTA, December 13, 1857.

DEAR BROTHER—I am just about to start to Milledgeville.
Thomas W. Thomas is here, and is going with me.   He
came over from there, day before yesterday, on his way to

Washington City. The Governor appointed him and Ward as counsel in the case of Alabama *vs.* Georgia. Brown was served with process lately; and as Johnson had been served with a copy of the bill two years ago, they all concluded then, that this last was a *new* case; but they were not satisfied; so Thomas came by to see me. When I explained it, he decided to go back. He says he will not retain his appointment, because it was made under a mistake. Obadiah Gibson was appointed associate counsel with me, by Governor Johnson, on the 30th of October last. . . . .

[From L. S. to A. H. S.]

SPARTA, December 29, 1857.

DEAR BROTHER—It is night again, and again I am about to close a night of work with a letter to you—not that I have anything of consequence to say, but merely because, while I am at it, it comes easier. The *vis inertiæ* is a prevailing law of nature, controlling matter and mind. It is a powerful law with me. I can continue, when tired, more easily than I can commence, when dull or indisposed. Resistance to change seems to be stamped upon all things, animate and inanimate; and yet, alas! the great tide of change sweeps all things, good and bad, beautiful and loathsome, lovely and horrible, along its own ceaseless and resistless course. All things instinctively oppose it; yet all things are inevitably its victims. It is but the struggling of the fly in the spider's web, or the fluttering of the poor bird under the serpent's charm. It is a hard thing to move and a hard thing to stop; and yet it is true, that we are forever moving and eternally stopping. What wonder, then, that, in the conflict, there should be a very severing of the joints and the marrow! The universe is but a vast mass of contending elements in travail. What wonder, then, that the births should be woe! woe! woe! or, it is true that *light* was indeed stricken out of the darkness of chaos? When does it shine but to make visible the torture and misery which before lay unseen and unfelt in the repose of dark nonentity? Who is the great Intelligence, or what the unknowing Cause that ever, *eternally* drives the crushing and relentless wheels of Necessity? But I had no idea of running into such an unavailing train; such thoughts were not in my mind when I commenced to write to you. . . . .

Mr. Stephens, from early manhood, was often applied to, by almost all classes of people, in emergency, for pecuniary aid. Hardly any one of his acquaintance, needing the benefaction, felt delicacy or showed hesitancy in approaching *him*. No worthy applicant was ever turned away empty, if compliance were a possibility; and while he dispensed many charities, whereof it was impossible the world could be ignorant, he also bestowed uncounted thousands, which will not be known until the common Father shall say: "Inasmuch as ye have done it unto one of the least of these my brethren, ye have done it unto me."

[From L. S. to A. H. S.]

SPARTA, January 3, 1858.

DEAR BROTHER— . . . . For the want of something else to do, I will tell you of some applications which I have lately had for money in charity. ———— (whom I took to be a son of ————, and who wrote me a very good letter) asked me to send him to school this year. I agreed to do so, and am to see his board and tuition paid at the end of the year. ————, (a grandson of old ————,) asked of me the same favor, and I granted that, too, after passing several letters—and, at last, with considerable reluctance. I did not like the way he wrote, and I gave him some very plain talk. His last letter was in much better taste; but I was afraid the improvement arose from a *desire to succeed* with his application, rather than any real amendment of his views. But I hope for the best. ———— (————) wrote me, a few days ago, that he must have eighty dollars soon, and called on me to furnish it. I simply replied that it was not convenient for me to do so. About the same time, ———— sent me a letter, asking the loan of twenty-five dollars for three months, saying he was going to clerk for somebody in ————, and had "*no close*," and promising, faithfully, to pay me at end of three months. He concluded with a peroration that would have done honor to a finished rhetorician: "*I am poor, but honest!*" My reply to him was, that he must call on ———— for my answer, and at the same time I wrote to ————telling him what ——— had written to me, and requesting him to let me know if it was true that ——— was going into a clerking business, etc. I authorized him, if it was true, to buy clothes for him to the amount of twenty-five dollars, and that I would pay for them the first time I might go to Crawfordville. I explained to him that I doubted ———'s story, and suspected it might be a mere trick to "*make a rise,*" and gave him the history of how ——— fooled you about the horse. I reckon it would have been better if I had merely refused the application, as I have just refused ———'s; but I really desired to help him, if it would indeed be true help; and so I took the risk of offending ———. I tried, however, to put it as kindly as possible. I have heard nothing from him, though sufficient time has elapsed for him to have written. Another application was from ———, of ———, for me to give her one hundred dollars, which she desired to use in restoring her health (if possible) by a trip to Florida. She said she had consumption. I declined to do so in a short answer expressed in as civil terms as I could command. Besides these, there have been divers others in the county here at home. I have refused most of them, for they were simply bold cases to attempt to sponge and rob. By the way, ——— told me that ——— had made a similar application to him, (though not for any specific amount,) and that he sent her fifty dollars. . . . .

[From L. S. to A. H. S.]

SPARTA, January 13, 1858.

DEAR BROTHER— . . . . January 18. This letter was commenced at the date it bears, but was cut short at the time by an interruption of some of the servants, and has since lain as you find it. I have received your letter about young ———, and I am truly sorry I did not get it sooner. I suppose he is at school before this time. I think to educate such a fellow is only to augment the power of a rascal—a bad deed instead of a good one. I have never yet heard farther from ——— nor from ———. It was clearly a trick of ———.

I am glad to see the stand you and Mr. Toombs have taken on the Central-American question; and I am glad to see that Douglas is with you. I noticed the few words between you and the man who laughed at me for eating *ground-peas*, about instructions to his committee. It was my turn to laugh when I saw it; but indeed I did not use my just privilege, even to the extent of a silent smile. I felt sorry for him. He is manifestly affected with that infirmity which the Irishman said was worse than being a knave—that is, being a fool—because, as Paddy had it, he could quit being a knave, but could not quit being a fool. What effect do you think your course on the Central-American question will have on the administration in regard to the Kansas question? *I* think it will *scare* them, and tend, at least, to make them stand up. If they have got any sense at all, (?) they must see that they are in danger of losing the whole South, and that they can't afford any shuffling on the Kansas question. I discover, from the indications in the Senate, that the Southern Know-Nothings intend to take sides with the administration on the Central-American question. Is it not so? What did Josh Hill mean by voting for Henry Winter Davis for Speaker? . . . . Dick Johnston has gone to Athens. I am almost literally alone in the world. But sometimes I get along pretty well. The return of good weather has helped me. I don't think I shall go to Washington this winter, but I do not *yet* so decide positively. I should like very much to be with you, but I should be very uneasy about the children. Little Emm has been sick, but is now about well again. She is very fond of me, and so indeed are Becky and Claude. They are about me nearly all the time when I am at the house. Last night, just at twelve o'clock, Becky got out of her bed in the nursery (the folding, or rather *drawing* doors being open) and came to me at the fire in my room where I was reading, and said she wanted me to go to bed. Everybody else, children and servants, were in profound slumber. I asked her what made her wake? She said because she wanted me to go to bed. I told her I would put her to bed, but she said she wanted *me* to go, and she would go with me. So I quit my reading and took her to bed with me. I thought it was a singular thing in her. She did not seem to be *scared*, or at all seeking protection from her fears, but it was just simply a freak that she wanted to see me go to bed, and for her offer to sleep with me was an *inducement.* That was the spirit of the whole action. But I really fear that I weary you with such details of simple, childish things. I am free to own that such, in anybody else's children, would be of little interest to me. But these little passages with my little ones and me are really the greatest comforts I have, and sometimes I grow tedious on them, no doubt. But it does me a little good to write them, and you can skip them, and I will never inquire about it, nor care about it. . . . . Mr. Thomas staid with me the greater part of last week, and is coming back to-morrow to stay the remainder of this week. He went home yesterday evening with a spell of the headache on him; but Bill was in town to-day and told me he had got over it. He was here professedly on business, and he really had business, but did little of it, and is coming back. I thought he wanted *company.* He is just the man to consider it a weakness to feel such a want, or rather to allow the feeling to take him away from business. For my own part, I think the true philosophy is, that the best business is to be happy, so far as that is attainable in life, consistently with innocence, and therefore with happiness hereafter. . . . . But I have no idea of going off into an account of my feelings or griefs, or its variations. At this time, at least, I prefer to write in a pleasant vein, if I *can* do it, and I will not allow myself to-night to call upon you for sympathy, which grieves you, and can scarce assuage a pang for me. So again, good night, and may you be as happy as possible.

Yours, most affectionately,

LINTON STEPHENS.

[From L. S. to A. H. S.]

SPARTA, February 9, 1858.

DEAR BROTHER— . . . . I read Mr. Toombs' speech to-day, on the message of the President accompanying the Lecompton Constitution. It is very powerful. I am getting sick and tired of the manner in which the subject of slavery is treated by Northern men— Democrats and all. If Kansas is not admitted—or rather, if she is refused admission—I am for dissolution. I would not acknowledge allegiance to a government which sets upon me and my section a brand of sin, and infamy, and degradation. Douglas, and h's Black Republican backers, may smile, and split hairs, and swear that they are honest until they turn black in the face, and I shall not believe one word of it. If Kansas is rejected, it will be simply and purely because she is considered unfit to keep company with the "Holy Willies" of the canting, Pharisaical North; and when that test of association is made, I am for leaving the company that makes it. The bonds of my attachment to the Union are powerfully loosened, and if Kansas is rejected, they will be broken. We scarcely know the Union now, except through its burthens, and I am not willing to pocket its insults. They should not evade the issue by a pretext. The true issue is, and Congress ought to be held to it, and it ought to be so proclaimed to them with a united defiance, whether a State with slavery is fit to be admitted into the Union. If it be decided against us, honor leaves but one course, and that is, for all the slave States to walk out of the Union, and fling their defiance behind them; and if no other will, I hope Georgia will do it, "solitary and alone." I do trust that, at the right time, you will give them fire and thunder. Read the Georgia platform to them; and tell them it shall not be evaded by a miserable pretext. Let the hunters of the Presidency know that there will be no Presidency left to be hunted for. I say, if the South submits to the rejection of Kansas, she is a craven, and deserves her fate. She is ready for a master, and if she could be left the poor privilege of *choosing* one, I should prefer to see her take *one*, rather than fifteen millions of a lawless mob. A pure Democracy, in a small State of homogeneous interests, is tolerable, but in a State divided into two permanent antagonisms, with a large numerical majority on one side, is the most despotic of all governments. A mob, when unrestrained by interest, is terrific in its utter irresponsibilty. If Kansas is rejected, our government becomes a pure Democracy; the only law is that of superior numbers; the only power is that of an irresponsible mob, and that mob hostile to us. We have got to fight it, or deter it, or succumb to it. I am for the first, whenever it is necessary, for the second if it can avail, but for the last, *never, never!* . . . .

[From L. S. to A. H. S.]

SPARTA, February 11, 1858.

DEAR BROTHER—I write to-night with the single design to mark the day as it passes; to let you know that I am not unmindful of your having this day arrived at one more mile-post on the short road of life. I was about to say that I send you birth-day greetings; but, alas! I have no greetings to send—if greetings are to imply joy or congratulation. But in their stead, I can, and do send you the heart-warm good wishes of your affectionate

BROTHER.

P. S.—It is a sad thing that such a superscription as the above should be so specific—without a name, and yet a perfect identification of my individuality.

[From L. S. to A. H. S.]

SPARTA, February 13, 1858.

DEAR BROTHER— . . . . I have written a letter to-night to Josh Hill, and I wish you would contrive to get a chance to read it, so as to give me your opinion of it in point of *taste*. Considering to whom it is written, I am very doubtful about the good taste of the vein in which it is written. I mean, however, to send it. The part which gives me doubt is *intended* in pure fun, and I suppose he will take it so. The other part of it, I hope, may produce good, wholesome fruit. I gave him a message for you in the letter as an *introduction* of the subject: so you may ask him what I wrote, and so see the letter, unless he is resolved not to let you see it. . . . .

] From L. S. to A. H. S.]

SPARTA, February 17, 1858.

DEAR BROTHER— . . . . I have been very busy of late, and have not had time to finish the Answer of Georgia. I cannot do it now during the term of court. I read your remarks on Campbell's motion for a continuance with a great deal of satisfaction. I only regret that you did not tell them plainly what object the "pretext" was designed to accomplish, so as to show in vivid light the aid and comfort our enemy was receiving from the poor, cowardly dodging of small Southern men. . . . .

MARCH 2, 1858.

DEAR BROTHER— . . . . Let me tell you an incident that occurred to Becky and Rio just before she was sick. She had got to taking Rio through his manual (of tricks) occasionally, by the aid of a piece of meat, which she would hold up for him as a reward of obedience. On the occasion to which I particularly refer, she made him "sit up" and "turn over," and then got him stretched out to be dead. After waiting a little while, she gave him the signal to rise; but, somehow or other, Rio had become oblivious as to the master (or mistress) of ceremonies, and all her "that'll do's" were of no avail to raise him from his death-like posture. She became very energetic at last, and urgent with her "that'll do," but still Rio lay immovable. Becky looked uneasy, and I took occasion to play on her. Said I: "There now! what have you done? You've killed uncle Eckly's dog! Shall I write to him about it?" At this, the servants (it was just as we had risen from the breakfast-table) all broke out in a laugh, and poor Becky looked like the picture of despair; but she didn't remain long inactive: she looked at me, as if to read my face, (which was solemn as I could make it,) and then suddenly she jumped at Rio (who, a grand villain, seemed to be enjoying the scene) and shook him pretty roughly. His reply to that salute was a very audible *groan*. Instantly, triumph was in Becky's eye. She stepped a pace backward, having Rio between her and myself, and, with the air and emphasis of a tragedy-queen, demanded of me, "Do you call *that* dead?" The effect was irresistible to me, and I exploded, and so did the servants, and so did *Rio*; for the scoundrel clearly perceived that the game was up, and he did not hesitate to throw off the *sham*, and, in the most marked manner, express his appreciation of the sport. Poor Rio! he is at Crawfordville, and he was very loth to stay behind. . . . .

I do not know what else I can write, unless I tell you I am sad and sorrowful; but I do not wish to give you my thoughts about that; so I will say, good-bye.

ELBERTON, March 13, 1858.

DEAR BROTHER— . . . . You say I have never said what I thought of your speech in Walker and Paulding. I saw that speech in due season, and wrote you my opinion of it immediately. I expressed myself as greatly pleased with its doctrine and its style. I thought it was an able exposition of the true doctrine, unanswerable, and passing, as the debate showed, with many allusions to it, but without any attempt to answer it. . . . . . .

I made one jury speech, at Madison court, in defense of a man who was charged with an assault with intent to murder. Thomas prosecuted him. He was acquitted—very much contrary to everybody's expectations. The State introduced two witnesses, and I got up a conflict between them; introduced no evidence; had the conclusion; and Nash says I will forever be known in Madison as the "Susannah man." I was appointed by the court. The fellow's name was Stephens. That was the second occasion on which I saved the *name*. The other was the poor fellow in Warren. . . . . I have defended one of Thomas' friends here, and acquitted him on a technical point. Thomas did not defend the case at all. I had no fee, nor did Thomas. . . . .

[From L. S. to A. H. S.]

SPARTA, March 29, 1858.

DEAR BROTHER— . . . . Have you made no speech on the Lecompton Constitution? I have seen none from you. Did you ever get a letter from me, saying what I thought the South ought to do in case Kansas shall be rejected? I wrote it long ago, but you have never attended to it. I said we ought to break up the Union. I don't allude to it for the purpose of going into the matter at all at this time, but merely by way of identifying the letter. I think but little about it. Indeed, I am sorry and distressed to see from your letters that you allow yourself to be made so unhappy about it. It is not worth the trouble. Fame is a poor thing—a miserably poor thing! Life is a poor thing—patriotism is a poor thing—all the things of this world are poor, beggarly elements—ashes and emptiness! Almost all men *talk* in this strain sometimes; but I think he is a poor, deluded man who does not *feel* it always.

A messenger has just come from my plantation for a doctor to go and see a negro who is taken suddenly very ill—so goes the world.   Again, good-night.

[L. S. to R. M. Johnston.]

SPARTA, March 30, 1858.

DEAR DICK—I returned home last Friday, after an absence of five weeks at Taliaferro, Madison, Elbert, Hart and Wilkes courts.   I found nothing, on my return, from you.   Will you not be at Hancock court?   Are you all well?   How are you pleased now, and how are you all pleased with your new home since you have all got together again?   But is it home?   How would you feel in reading an instrument, under seal, opening in this wise: "This indenture, made this, the first day of April, in the year eighteen hundred and fifty-eight, between Richard M. Johnston, *of the county of Clarke*, of the one part?" etc.   Wouldn't it, in fact, have the appearance of a transaction, dated with great fitness, on the first day of April?   Wouldn't it be a fooling piece of business?   In short, I want you to inform me—distinctly inform me—whether or not you consider yourself suable in the county of Clarke. . . . . . I did not see the five chapters in the *Constitutionalist* until the matter was called to my attention, by members of the bar, while I was out last.   It was a subject of much talk, and *favorable* talk.   Nobody knew the author, or seemed to suspect him; but, to confess the truth, after hearing them talk about it, I couldn't help telling them who he was; and I *rather* pulled my shirt-collar up, too, when I did it—as much as to say, "My old partner, gentlemen—mine intimate friend—ahem!"   Let me tell you a good joke about it: Huff, of Warrenton, said the scene was laid in Warren county, and that Judge Roberts was well acquainted with the characters that figure in it.   Now, I protest that, in all my attempts to connect myself with the honors of this new author, I have confined myself to the truth; but you now perceive that others have been too strongly tempted to be "delivered from evil;" but in plain, sober narrative, I have heard the piece much praised, and have been greatly delighted; and now, with my warmest good wishes for your happiness here and hereafter, I remain, as ever,

Yours, most truly,   LINTON STEPHENS.

The last paragraph has reference to some amusing papers which Colonel Johnston furnished to the Augusta *Constitutionalist*, and which were subsequently published in book-form. They were in the vein of the "Georgia Scenes," and were very popular, and greatly admired by those who have a relish for what is ludicrous in incident or in character. "Philemon Perch" is immortal in the realms of funny fiction.

[From L. S. to A. H. S.]

WASHINGTON, GA., March 31, 1858.

DEAR BROTHER— . . . . Mr. Thomas was at my house very sick with headache. I was up with him, and afterwards wrote ten letters. I slept in the cars this evening and dreamed all the way. My dreams were of home, sweet, happy home, as it used to be, and the loved One who use to bless it, but shall never bless it more—no more, forever, except in dreams and in memories! These memories are sometimes sweet, and yet always painful— often overwhelming. Often, very often, do I cry out, "Oh! had I wings, I'd fly away and be at rest." It's a weary, weary life to me. When I die, one weary head and worn-out heart will be at *rest*. Good-night.

Affectionately, LINTON.

[From L. S. to A. H. S.]

WARRENTON, April 5, 1858.

DEAR BROTHER— . . . . Mr. Toombs went on to Washington City yesterday evening; I parted with him at Camak. The court here will probably be a short one, on account of the absence of him, yourself and Thomas, though no case has been continued yet for the absence of any one of you. I am afraid something is the matter with Thomas, or some of his family. You will hear through Mr. Toombs all the news. . . . . You have sent me no instructions about your cases here, nor anywhere else. I will get all continued *here* if I can; for I shall certainly, if possible, avoid the putting of my *Warren luck* upon you. I have succeeded everywhere else this riding; but I have *never* succeeded here, and I don't expect to now.

April 6th. This morning, before I got out of bed, in came Dick, (Thomas' man) with a letter to me from Thomas, saying his wife was very ill, and he could not leave home. . . . . Poor Thomas—I pity him deeply, and fervently do I hope that the cup may pass from him. I also got a letter this morning from Tom Cobb, saying he cannot come to this court on account of a religious revival which is going on in Athens. Tom has got to be very much of a religious *zealot*. But, withal, he is uncommonly modest, and unobtrusive, and sincere in his religion. Poor fellow! He, too, has been a great sufferer.* . . . . .

[From L. S. to A. II. S.]

WARRENTON, April 8, 1858.

DEAR BROTHER— . . . . Saving a very few objects of affection, life has little that can add to, or take from, the small sum of happiness now left to me. My children, my poor children! I do deeply pity *them*. But enough of this, too. I have a great propensity to talk, or to write of my griefs and my sufferings; but I cannot help feeling that the ear of the warmest friend is growing dull, and constantly more dull, to the oft-repeated story. No man has a right to make himself disagreeable; and human nature will not pardon disagreeableness long. The man who inflicts his griefs and complaints upon his friends must soon lose his friends. Yet, it is hard to speak otherwise than out of the abundance of the heart. The consequence with me is, that I have but little to say. Silence and soli tude are my most constant and congenial companions. I have talked and written of the thoughts that possess me, to you more than I have presumed to do to anybody else. And now, good-night. . . . .

Affectionately,   LINTON.

[From L. S. to A. II. S.]

SPARTA, April 13, 1858.

DEAR BROTHER—The last letter I got from you was dated the 7th instant, and was received on the 10th, on my return

---

* Mr. Cobb had at that time recently lost a lovely daughter, Lucy, just blooming into womanhood. "The Lucy Cobb Institute," at Athens, was named for her.

home from Warren court Saturday night. Jack Smith tells me he saw you on the 8th, and that is the last news I have had of you. I think my letters to you, while I was on the circuit, were pretty frequent, considering that I was away from home, in crowds at night, and often busy at night. I am sorry yours to me have become so much less frequent. I wrote you from Warren court, that Thomas had not got there on account of the illness of his wife. He afterwards came, and then came on home with the Judge and me in our conveyance. He and I went to church here on Sunday. Monday night, a messenger came to tell him that his wife was worse. He started off home that night. Daniel took him in my buggy to Double Wells. He got Dr. Alfriend to go, too. Alfriend got back here on Wednesday morning, and reported that he and Thomas had arrived at Elberton about two o'clock the day before, and found Thomas' wife *dead*. She had been dead about twenty-four hours, having died about ten o'clock Monday morning. She was dead when the messenger got here. Thomas did not hear of the fact till he had got half way from his back gate to his wife's room. They buried her the same evening of their arrival, and Alfriend left that night. When Thomas left home, his doctor had pronounced her out of danger, and she had urged him to go to his courts. Little did either of them dream that they were parting to meet no more. They observed no change for the worse until Saturday, and did not regard the change as serious until Sunday, when they started the messenger for Thomas. Oh! what a terrible stroke it was to poor Thomas! I think of him every hour in the day, and pity him with a pity that few can comprehend. Poor Thomas! poor Thomas! But he has one great stay and comfort in having a mother left to him. My own greatest sense of bereavement has been in the loss of that *one single being* on whom I leaned in every trouble. It has often seemed to me that I could bear any other affliction as heavy as the loss of her, (if it were possible for any other to be as heavy) if I could only have *her* help me bear it. But *she* being gone, all is desolation! There is no comfort, and nothing but despair. But I imagine and trust that it is not so with Thomas. It is a great calamity to be dependent on any one being, as I was upon my wife. I was aware of it to a great extent while she was in life; but I had not compre-

15

hended it all. I had often trembled at the prospect of our
separation; but still had cherished a hope, which was a
blessed and blissful one, that we should glide gently along
through many happy years, and then sink to rest *together.*
Often, often, did we express to each other the fervent as-
piration that we might not be separated in our deaths.
Oh, God! it seems to me I am crazy! So keen and so sudden does the sense of my loss strike me at many times, as
to deprive me of all sense, and transport me in a twinkling
into a world of confusion and doubt. I often doubt whether
I exist. It is so curious, because it is so sudden and con-
founding. I am so overwhelmed by a sudden sense of what
I miss, that I cannot realize that I am alive. This is a feeling that is very frequent with me. I never had anything
like it before, and my description of it is but weak. I doubt
whether you can imagine what it is. . . . . I intended to
give you the result of our court here when I commenced to
write, but I have not interest enough in it now to do so. I
will write more in the morning. I have not gone to Oglethorpe court, because from Thomas' absence, and Tom
Cobb's absence on account of the religious revival at
Athens, it is certain that nothing will be done. I wanted
a little rest, but I have not had it yet.

Old Mr. Prescott, the hotel-keeper in Warrenton, died
the night after we left there. He was stricken down with
apoplexy the day before we left. Poor old man! The
family seemed in great distress. May God have mercy on
us all! . . . .

[From L. S. to A. H. S.]

SPARTA, May 9, 1858.

DEAR BROTHER— . . . . I yesterday got
and read the debate between you and Winter Davis. In
reading his speech, I could easily perceive that he was
really replying, or at least shaping his words to meet a
speech which *followed* him. I think I should easily have
detected that without any previous intimation that it was so.
Your complaint of the report of his speech is a most just
one. I can well conceive that if he had spoken the speech
which is printed, your reply would have been differently
turned, and, in many places, differently worded; but I do

really think it is bad enough on him as it is; and yet, I felt so indignant that he should at all escape. I cannot draw a full and clear conception from so mutilated a history as the *Globe* gives; but I could still very satisfactorily perceive that he was badly *threshed*, in the opinion of the House, and in his own opinion. But I must close. I am sorry you did not come home as soon as the Kansas Bill was passed. You need rest. You ought to come. I like the Conference Bill, after comparing it with the others, better than I do the Senate's original bill; but I did not like it a bit when I first read it. I thought it had gone off on a new and manufactured issue, and was nothing but a *dodge*. I felt outraged, to tell you the truth; but I held my peace. I did not then understand the Senate Bill. I perceive the issue was an *original* one, and a *meritorious* one. I like the Conference Bill a good deal better than the other, since I have come to understand both. Good-bye.

Affectionately,   LINTON STEPHENS.

[From L. S. to A. H. S.]

SPARTA, May 10, 1858.

DEAR BROTHER— . . . . I have found several of our friends who did not like the "Conference Bill," and I think many, very many, are lukewarm towards it; but I have not met with one who did not change his mind upon being correctly informed as to the comparative merits of that and the original Senate Bill. The truth is, the Conference Bill is not what I wished to see. I wanted the naked issue of admission or rejection, under the Lecompton Constitution, decided by Congress. The Conference Bill does this theoretically, but not practically. It declares it, and, therefore, recognizes the right and the principle, but it leaves to a future vote the decision of the result. While this is true, I still have no quarrel with that bill. It accomplishes all that could have been accomplished by any bill. The issue which I desired was not decided, because it was not presented. It came in company with another issue, which complicated it, and which was obliged to be separated from it, unless you had submitted to be swindled out of the public lands. That the true issue was not practically and finally decided by Congress is the fault, not of

Congress—for they have done all that could be done—but it is the fault of the Constitutional Convention of Kansas, who presented that issue on terms that were wholly unallowable. The only course, therefore, was to do what you have done—decide the issue and leave them to reform their terms. It is not Congress who fixes a condition, but it was Kansas herself who offered a very unreasonable condition. You have told her all that you could tell her—that you admit her into the Union if she will remodel her Constitution and make it reasonable. There is no further action needed on your part. You have placed her in a position from which she puts herself into the Union as soon as she comes to reason. Indeed, the legal effect of the Conference Bill is so clear and decided that I am amazed that any Northern man could support it, who had voted against the other bill *because* it failed to submit the Constitution. The Conference Bill does not submit the Constitution; nor does it even submit the question *whether they will come into the Union under the Lecompton Constitution.* It doesn't submit the Constitution; for it says expressly that this is your *legal, valid* act, and if you don't come in under *this Constitution*, the offer of *grace* is withdrawn from you, and you are remitted to the general rule, which requires more population than you have got; nor does it submit the question whether they will come into the Union under the Lecompton Constitution. I know there are in it some words that seem to bear that import; but, in my judgment, they do not admit of it. There are other words following in the same sentence which control the first. The effect of the whole sentence is this: a vote against the proposition submitted shall be deemed an expression of unwillingness to come into the Union *on the terms proposed.* The real question—the exact, precise question which is submitted is, whether Kansas will consent to come into the Union *with less land than she has demanded.* I could still further illustrate my analysis of this bill, but I must close. . . . .

[From L. S. to A. H. S.]

SPARTA, May 29, 1858.

DEAR BROTHER— . . . . The last letter I got from you was yesterday, on my return home. It an

nounced the result of the Ohio contested election.   I am
truly glad that Vallandigham got his seat.   I had two cases
at the Supreme Court, and was plaintiff in error in both
cases.   I gained one, but lost the other.   Thomas lost the
one I gained, and he was pretty mad about it.   Reese and
I were together in it.   It was the case of Nolan's will, from
Wilkes.   Mr. Toombs was of counsel with Reese and myself.   If you happen to think of it when you are with him,
I wish you would tell him we gained the case. . . . . .

[From L. S. to A. H. S.]

SPARTA, June 3, 1858.

DEAR BROTHER— . . . . I have neglected for some weeks to write you what I intended to write
immediately upon its occurrence.   Lamar, of Newton,
wrote to me, inquiring whether I desired to be a candidate
for Congress next time, and saying that the friends of Harper desired to bring him forward for the race if I should
not be in the field.   He said that his inquiry was not
prompted by a wish for me to decline; for, he said, there
was no man in the State whom he would prefer to see in
Congress rather than myself; but he said his object was
solely to be informed what my intention was, so that the
friends of Harper might govern their course accordingly.
He assured me that, under no circumstances, would Harper, or his friends, interfere with me; for, he said, Harper's
friends were my friends.   I replied to him, immediately,
that I should not run the race any more; and that I should
be gratified to see the choice of the party and the district
settle on Harper.   I consulted nobody about it; I needed
no consultation; for none could have changed my decision;
that decision had long been made up, irrevocably.   It was
a painful thing to me to express, among those who had all
been warm friends to me, a preference for any one; but I
never did like neutral people.   Harper is a noble fellow,
and he ought to be the man.   His qualifications, and the
complexion of the district, alike point to him as the man,
and I felt that it would be a selfish regard for my own comfort and pleasant relations to refrain from saying so; and so
I said it.

   I agree with you entirely in the view you express about

our proper course towards the British ships which have outraged our rights. We ought to catch them, or sink them,
and be ourselves the party to render an explanation, instead
of demanding one; and the explanation should be a very
short and pointed one: simply that we had punished indignity and insolence as they deserved: that could give no
offense to anybody, except to those who back and defend
the indignity and insolence; an offense to *such* people, I
should not regard. I think the defect in our national administration is a want of clear views of courage. I think
they are quite as good as any we have had since Polk's
time; but that is not saying much. Don't understand me
as expressing admiration of Polk's administration; but he
had a policy and a will, and he carried both out with stead-
iness and ability. . . . .

[From L. S. to A. H. S.]

SPARTA, June 7, 1858.

DEAR BROTHER— . . . . Among other
things, Mr. Thomas talked about the British aggressions on
our ships. He had seen Mr. Toombs' position announced,
about seizing or sinking. He said he thought that right.
He went on to say that he thought we ought to seize the
offenders and keep them until their government disavowed
their acts or backed them. If a disavowal should be the
result, he said we ought to punish them; if an indorsement
should come, we ought to *turn them loose*, and then declare
war against England. I asked him why we should *turn
them loose*, and then declare war? I asked him what he
would do after declaring war, and after he had turned them
loose, except to go right straight to trying to catch them
again? And I asked him if he did turn them loose, how
much start he would give them? The old gentleman smiled
and gave it up by a severe silence. The rest all laughed,
and I went on with somewhat of a war harangue. It does
seem to me to be a very clear case, that we ought to capture the offending ships. Of course, if England disavows
their acts, she cannot claim to screen them from our just
punishment; and if she backs them, it is only to declare
that she had already thrust a state of war upon us. As a
peace question, it is a clear one; for we are only punishing

individual breaches of the peace. As a war question, it is equally clear; for, in that case, we would seize not only the offending vessels, but all *other British vessels* that we could catch. What can be a more legitimate act of war than to capture the enemy's vessels? That is one main aim of warfare. The only question, then, is, shall our enemy be entitled to an advantage by making war covertly? If she had declared it, of course, our plain duty is to capture all her vessels that we can. Shall we be restrained from capturing them because she has done acts of war without declaring war? If there is no war, we seize and punish; if there is open war, we seize; and shall we lose the right to seize by reason of secret or covert war? It does seem to me, however, that, after seizing the offending vessels, we ought to detain them, *without punishment*, until we know whether they are to be treated as malefactors, or as prisoners or prizes of war—not to let them loose to go to doing us all the harm they may be able to do, but to detain them as prisoners of war, or to punish them as offenders.

But I believe I shall cease to tax you on the war question, which you doubtless understand too well to be entertained by anything I can say on it. I think Mr. Toombs' recent debates on the internal improvement question are crushingly powerful. I have been delighted with his speeches on that subject. In my humble judgment, nobody in this country, now or formerly, has ever understood that subject so well as he does. He, himself, gets better on it the longer his mind runs on it. It looks like a Herculean labor—and so it is—but I do believe the power of his arguments will burst up the abominable system. It seems to me that the error is obliged to fall under the terrible battery he has opened upon it. He is fighting it alone, and I love to see him stand as the solitary champion. He is more than a match for them all. . . . . .

[From L. S. to A. H. S.]

SPARTA, June 8, 1858.

DEAR BROTHER— . . . . Dickenson (my overseer) is very ill indeed. I wrote you yesterday that I had him brought up to my house to take care of him. He was delirious all night, last night, and is still so. He has no rationality about him. While I am writing, I have Travis with him to keep him from tearing off a blister which is drawing over his stomach and bowels. I have somebody with him all the while; but nobody can control him, when I am away, but Travis. Poor fellow! He is constantly talking about his crop, and wanting his hat and clothes to go to business. He is a very worthy young man, I think, and I am very sorry for him. I sent for his father this morning. He lives ten or twelve miles distant.

Affectionately,   LINTON STEPHENS.

[From L. S. to A. H. S.]

SPARTA, June 11, 1858.

DEAR BROTHER—Dickenson, poor fellow, is dead. He died last night a little after 10 o'clock. For more than sixty hours, he had lain without any rational connection in his thoughts, and he so continued to the last. He is to be buried thirteen or fourteen miles from here, and I am going to the burial. I want to return this evening, and go to my plantation to-morrow. I have seven or eight cases of fever there, but none bad. I think poor Dickenson killed him self by keeping up so long after he was attacked. I don't think that any of my negroes will have to encounter that difficulty. Under these circumstances, it will be out of my power to meet you at Crawfordville on your return home. I trust you will come over here immediately. I have al ready written you that we are to have an adjourned court here, next Monday, to try cases of Mr. Thomas', wherein you are interested. . . . .

[From L. S. to A. H. S.]

SPARTA, July 2, 1858.

DEAR BROTHER—Yesterday, I was thirty-five years old— just the half-way house in the road allotted to life. Many break down long before they reach the goal, and very many before they attain the half-way house. How much longer I shall endure on the route, I cannot know. . . . .

In the summer of 1868, the two brothers took a recrea- tive journey to the Northwest, passing by and stopping at

Chattanooga, Lookout Mountain, Nashville, Mammoth Cave, Louisville, Lexington, Ashland, where they were the guests of the Hon. James B. Clay, the son of the great statesman; thence to Cincinnati, North Bend, Indianapolis, Terre Haute and Chicago, returning by the Illinois Central to Cairo, where they took steamer down the Mississippi to Memphis; thence they returned home by the Memphis & Charleston Railroad, etc. They were absent four or five weeks. This was the first travel, for recreation only, the elder brother had ever taken. The following letter refers, in part, to that travel:

[From L. S. to R. M. Johnston.]

SPARTA, September 3, 1858.

MY DEAR DICK—Again I am about to leave home; and one of the last things I shall do, before getting off, is to send you a word of remembrance and farewell. I have just finished a long letter to Cosby—the first one I have written him since he went up the country. He has written to me none at all. He had promised to write to me, and I had resolved not to write to him until he had fulfilled his promise, but I have heard that the old fellow has been sick, and my heart softens towards him. He and John DeWitt are now both at Dr. Connell's, and are both convalescent, as I hear. But I mustn't run off the handle at the start; for I haven't time to afford it; so I must, at once, answer some points in your last letter. I mentioned to Ellic the subject of his "speech," at Athens, the first time I saw him after getting your account of it. He professed to be very well satisfied with it: neither elated, as with a triumph, nor depressed under a sense of failure. He seemed to think that he had got over a hard place in very good order; and further seemed to think that it was *rather* a sharp thing to do *that*. He insisted on my telling him what *you* had written me about the speech, and I rallied him on his *anxiety* about your report, as an evidence that his own complacency on the subject was *assumed*. He protested that it was a decent, respectable speech—though not exactly to be called a "hit"—and still insisted on hearing your account of it.

I put him off by telling him I would read it to him the first time he should be at my house. He has been here once since, but did not call for the letter; and so it now stands. You ask me about our Northwestern trip, and about Douglas and his prospects. The trip was a pleasant one, and a very remarkable one in one respect: We travelled about twenty-five hundred miles, and never had an accident, never lost a connection between routes, and were not delayed one hour beyond the usual time of arrival at any place whatever. I may have made the same remark to you in my last letter; for it is a thing that has rather dwelt on my mind. As for Douglas, we did not see him. We were ten days in Chicago, while Healy was painting our pictures, but Douglas was off in distant parts of the State, stumping for dear life. I rather thought he would succeed; but, really, I formed no satisfactory opinion on the subject. I was very clear, however, that he *ought* to succeed in the fight he has *now* on his hands. I certainly disapprove of his course on Lecompton as much as anybody does; but I do not like the mode of expressing my disapprobation of one act, by electing over his head another man who backed him to the fullest extent in that act—besides his many other damning sins from which Douglas is free. To beat him with a *worse* man is rebuking him, not for doing badly, but for not doing bad enough. Douglas is this day making a bold, gallant and manly fight against the Black Republican heresies of his opponent; and how any Southern man can wish to see his defiant plume go down in the conflict is passing strange to me! He has my hearty sympathies in *this* fight. . . . . I think some of the newspapers—Democratic as well as American—have made asses of themselves about Ellic's visit to Illinois. It had no more to do with Douglas' election than it had to do with the moon; he talked about the election, and talked very freely, too, while he was there; and so the moon shone on him while he was there, too; but he went there to talk about the election, just as much as he went there for the moon to shine on him, and no more. It is a great outrage on decency and comfort, that a gentleman cannot be permitted to make a visit of recreation and pleasure without being dogged by the imputation of unworthy motives from *friends* as well as foes. It is a shame. But it is of no consequence; for nothing that has been said about it has given him the least uneasiness. He took it as coolly as a duck takes a shower.

. . . .

I treated cases of typhoid fever among my negroes, and last night the third death occurred. All three who died were young and grown. There are two more very ill indeed. I have taken such thorough precautions that I hope there will be no more cases. They have suffered greatly from disease and from alarm, and I do feel most deeply for them, and particularly for poor old Abram and Charlotte, who have lost two children, and now have another at death's door. The fatality in that particular family is strange; for no two of them, who have *died*, resided in the same house, and one of them lived at Mr. Thomas', where no other case of the disease has occurred. He was striker in the blacksmith-shop, and only went home once a week to see his parents and brothers and sisters. Your old friend, Isaac, of the same family, has recovered from a hard spell. Kindest remembrance to your wife and all the children. Can't say now when I can be at Athens.

As ever, most truly yours, LINTON STEPHENS.

The speech referred to in the foregoing letter, concerning the merits of which Mr. A. H. Stephens was curious to ascertain the opinion of Professor Johnston, was that delivered before the Sophomore declaimers, at Athens, on accasion of presenting the prizes to the successful competitors.

The canvass which Judge Douglas was then making—"stumping for dear life"—was the celebrated one in Illinois, between himself and Abraham Lincoln, for the United States Senatorship. The result was the election of a Democratic Legislature and the return of Douglas to the United States Senate.

[From L. S. to R. M. Johnston.]

SPARTA, October 26, 1858.

MY DEAR DICK—"Auld lang syne," when you and I were boys, some ill-natured person put out a report on my old uncle Bird, that he had said that baptism with *sand* would do as well as baptism with water. The old fellow heard of it, and denounced the report as false; indeed, he went, in the glow of his honest wrath, so far as to declare that it was a "d—d lie." Years afterwards, I asked him whether he had used the terrible epithet which I have just quoted. I shall never forget the grandeur of the old man as he rose and replied, "Yes, I did; and, cousin Linton, it *was* a d—d lie—it was so monstrous a lie that God Almighty condemned it as soon as it was uttered." Now, I have brought up this incident in the life of a good man, not for the sake of any parallel between it and anything which I am going to say, but *simply* as an authority for a little bit of "cussin," which I am about to perpetrate, and which, I think, I can explain away as effectually, at least, as he explained away his. The remark which I had in contemplation to make, and which I do now utter, is simply this: You are a *damned* man. The oft-quoted, ever-to-be-admired and immortal Shakspeare said (through the mouth of a character, to be sure, but still Shakspeare said it):

> "Lay on, McDuff;
> And *damn'd* be him that first cries, 'Hold, enough!'"

Now, you and I have been for sometime "laying on" in scribbling to one another, and you have been the "first" to cry, "Hold, enough!" So, on the authority of the immortal bard, you *are* "damned;" and, on the authority of a great man in Israel, I am authorized to pronounce you so. I do remember me, that, in some of my hasty effusions, I dropped an indiscreet intimation, to the effect that I did not expect you, in this the season of your business pressure, to answer all my scribblings; but surely you didn't take me to be in *earnest*, did you? I thought you were too well acquainted with that vile old sinner, Human Vanity, not to know that he has a favorite trick of covering himself with divers transparent pretensions to modesty and humility. Besides, I said I did not expect you to answer *all* my scribblings, and you have *presumed* upon this to answer *none*. Why, you are worse than Lorenzo Dow said the Calvinists were. The Scriptures say, "Come unto me *all* that are weary," etc.; but he said the Calvinists construed this to mean, "Come unto me a *part* of ye," etc.; and hence, his

common designation of them was, "The, A—double l—a—
part people." I said you needn't answer *all*, and you have
construed it to mean that you needn't answer *one*; hence,
you are an "A—double l—" *one* now; and so you are
worse than the Calvinists, inasmuch as a part may embrace
more than "one;" and you have, therefore, detracted
more than they did from the natural fullness and glory of
A—double l—*all*." So you see what a bad fellow you are,
and how fully justified I am in following old uncle Bird's
example in dealing with your case. So readeth a part of
the first chapter of the book of "Cussin," according to
Bird, Shakspeare and Dow. Look out for the rest of it,
unless you mend your ways.

I sat down with the intention to give you a sketch of an
amusing scene which I witnessed a few days ago between
two of our lady friends; but the Dow part of my discourse
was not anticipated at the start, and has run it to too great
a length to leave room for anything else; besides, as I have
written so long a letter, with absolutely nothing in it, I have
a fancy to keep it undefiled, even to the end, by a single
semblance of anything which might mar the beauty of uniformity. The only exception which I shall allow is in sub-
scribing myself,

Yours, most truly, LINTON STEPHENS.

[From L. S. to A. H. S.]

SPARTA, November 15, 1858.

DEAR BROTHER— . . . . I shall probably
not return home from Glasscock before going to Athens.
I have seven cases to represent at the Supreme Court, if
Gibson should give me the brief in your Burkhalter case;
and I am defendant in error in all, except one from Hart—
yes: there is another (making the eighth) from this county,
tried by Judge Cabaniss, where I am for plaintiff in error.
I am also under a sort of promise to Tom Daniel to help
him argue the Pierce Bailey case; but I think I shall not do
it. I did not promise, but said I might do it, or something
to that effect. I don't know anybody for whom hanging
would be so good as for old P———, and the temptation
is very strong to put in against him. It seems to me that
I am obliged to gain *all* the cases, except the one from

Hart; and as that was not my case until the present stage
of it, I believe I should not argue it but for one consideration: it would be too bad a thing for the court to allow one
man to gain *all* his cases, having so many; and I am rather
glad, therefore, of one *bad* one for them to throw off on.
That one, I trust, will prove a safety-valve. My next
weakest case is a new-trial case, from Warren. The Judge
granted it; but I am afraid they may reverse him. If that
were my only case, I should be very confident of their sus-
taining him; but Pottle is against me in it, and he is against
me in several others, which I am obliged to gain and he to
lose. It is, therefore, dangerous. They will want to throw
him a *bone*, and I am afraid they may make that bone out
of my case. . . . .

[From L. S. to A. H. S.]

SPARTA, December 4, 1858.

DEAR BROTHER— . . . . Your letter in
relation to Harry, and the list of your notes, I have laid
away with your will. Should it be the fortune of our lives
for Harry to fall to my care, your injunctions shall be observed in regard to him, because they are your injunctions,
and because my own estimate of Harry is not below yours.
I sympathize most deeply in the vein of sadness which pervades your letter. My heart was very full when I left your
house, and I felt that it was nearly running over. I was
almost on the point of telling you, as we lay in bed the
night before, that I felt as if it were the last night we would
ever spend together. I did feel so; but I knew you were
sad, and I forebore to say one word to make you more so.
If I had given way at all, the dam would have burst and
the flood swept through. . . . .

[From L. S. to A. H. S.]

SPARTA, December 5, 1858.

DEAR BROTHER— . . . . I have often
told you of my observation about things going in streaks or
schools. I had rather a striking instance of it the day I left
you. I bought a horse once, and lent him to Jimmy Cox,
at his request, and since then, I don't think I have ever had

an application of exactly that kind until Mary ———— made hers. Well, I gave her fifty dollars towards buying her a horse, the morning I left you. Before I got home, I met N—— P————, and he wanted me to buy him a horse; and when I got home, I found a letter from B—— B————, wanting me to buy him a horse. Wasn't that a streak of applications, for one day, in the single article of horses? B—— B———— I flatly refused. I had already bought a tract of land and put him on it, and I was satisfied that he simply wanted me to maintain him in idleness. I signified as much to him in my answer—though not in the same words I have used about it now—and told him plainly that I had done quite as much as I intended to do. As for N————, he assured me that what he wanted with a horse was to *move him to Florida*, and I consented to oblige him upon the idea that it would be a *good investment*. He is to have the horse on the express condition that if he does not go to Florida, (I will, however, give him the full benefit of substituting any other place as far off,) the horse is to be taken back. In this adventure, Mr. Thomas and I are co-partners, entitled to equal profits, and bound to bear equal losses. Mr. Thomas says he knows that N———— intends to get the horse, and then have something to happen to him, so he can't get off; and it was he who insisted on the condition about returning the horse. He long ago declared that N———— should never have another cent out of him; but when I proposed the horse-scheme, he said I had come at him in a shape that was irresistible, and he immediately bethought him that he himself had an old *mule* that would precisely answer the purpose. The reason why I proposed the matter to Mr. Thomas was, that N———— had already done so, as he informed me, and his request, as expressed to me, was, that Mr. Thomas and I jointly should furnish the horse. He assured me that if we would, *just for this one time, overlook* his wrong-doing towards us, (and he freely admitted it had been manifold and grievous,) he would go "clean off," and never be any further trouble to any of us. So I confidently expect soon to see N———— strike for the "Land of Flowers," drawn by a mule. I did not have the heart to ask him about the efficacy of his remedy for fits. Poor fellow! He is incapable of taking care of himself, and he has just capacity enough to prevent anybody else from taking care of him. He has an idea that he is a badly used man, because people don't divide their estates with him; and if it were done, he would come again in two years for another division. There are a great many very close approximations to poor N———, in this world; but he is, on the whole, about the poorest specimen of his class that I have ever encountered.   .   .   .   .

[From L. S. to A. H. S.]

SPARTA, December 14, 1858.

DEAR BROTHER—Whoop! I am out of the woods—my Answer is finished—a long explanatory letter to Obadiah Gibson is finished—another to the Governor, and another to the Attorney-General, are all, all finished, and now lying before me, in three packages, ready for the mail; and I have done it all in one day, sure enough, as I said I would, if I could get a fair lick at it; and it is a very small day's work at that. The Answer contains only six pages of this same sized paper on which I am now writing. I think I have packed it pretty well; and my Answer almost presents the argument. I don't mean to say that I think much of it, for I do not. It is up to the case, but the case *ain't much*. When I got to the close of the last sentence above, except two, they called me to supper, and while I was at supper, Alfriend came. He has just gone, and it is now 9 o'clock. I have a notion of going to bed sooner to-night than usual, but how it may turn out is very doubtful. It is strange how I do hate to go to bed, and how little I do sleep! Last night, the clock struck one before I got to sleep, and I had then been in bed half an hour. I woke just after three, and lay awake until I heard it strike six. After that, I got the most of my sleep. Last night was a pretty fair sample of the rest. The children also woke last night while I was restless and wakeful; but, supposing that everybody else was buried in profoundest slumber, little Emm suddenly struck up a *song*. I never heard her sing before, and I thought it was Claude, who is quite a singer. So I called Claude, but there was no answer; the little one turned into calling her, too—"Cordy," (so she calls her,) "papa call you, Cordy!" and she soon had Claude, and Becky, too, awake with her. No light was struck, how

ever, and they all soon again subsided into silence and
sleep. Not so I. What more shall I write? I know not,
unless I pursue the present theme by giving you some of
the annoyances which keep me from sleep, or wake me
from it. I am reminded of them by Sport's *squealing* at this
moment, and in the saloon. He literally *squeals;* it comes
a sudden, sharp, piercing squeal, which would infallibly
wake me, though it doesn't seem to affect other people so.
The cause of it is pains in his ear. It is very annoying to
me, but my pity always predominates over my vexation.
I am truly sorry for the poor dog, and he often leads me to
remember poor Rio, too, in sorrow and pity. Another of
my evil genii is William's snoring. I can sleep under one
of his cannonades about as well as I could if a saw-mill was
making planks out of my body; but my main one is sleep-
lessness. Oh, the miserable, wakeful hours I have spent in
trying to drop the burden of the day, and get rid of thought
in the blessed oblivion of sleep! And then, when nature
can maintain the struggle no longer, and at last takes refuge
in slumber, how brief the respite often is! Dreams come,
and sometimes take up and carry on the weary thoughts of
the day, or introduce strange vagaries of their own, which
are often not less tormenting; but, after all, the dreams
have a balancing in them; for some of them are far sweeter
than sights or sounds that greet me during the day; some,
too, are so strange as to entertain me afterwards with their
unaccountable whimsicalness. I dreamed, for instance, a
few nights ago, that you and I were dining with Judge
Story—nobody else present. He brought a bottle (which
I thought was wine, of course) and said, "Here is a bottle
of first-rate *dondy*," (that's the word, "dondy,") and I
thought, what is "dondy?" but you immediately said,
"Linton, I have often told you of *dondy*, and now you must
drink some." I thought it very curious that you should
say you had often told me of what I had never heard mentioned before in my life; and, still thinking it was some
kind of wine or spirits, I thought it was no less strange that
you should urge me (as your manner did) to drink it. I
tasted it, and said it tasted like apple-jelly; whereupon, you
and the Judge laughed very heartily. Why you laughed,
I never knew; and, to this hour, I am utterly unenlight-
ened, by dreams or other agency, as to what "dondy" is.

Such was that dream—pointless vagary—and yet, it woke
me; and long was it before I again fell to sleep. Life is a
weary, weary thing to me! But I am going to bed soon
to-night; and so good-bye.

Affectionately,   LINTON STEPHENS.

In January, 1859, Mr. Stephens went on to Washington
City to argue the case of Alabama *vs.* Georgia, then pend
ing in the Supreme Court of the United States. From
that city, he writes to his friend Johnston:

WASHINGTON, D. C., January 13, 1859.

MY DEAR DICK—Your letter of the 8th instant was received to-day, saying that you expected to return to Athens
the following Monday. Already, no doubt, you have gone
from Sparta. At my distance from both places, it might
seem that it would be a matter of indifference with me at
which place you may be, but it is not so. It is a sad thing
to think you have gone away from the place that knew you
so well. . . . . Has the obituary notice of
your mother yet appeared in the *Christian Index?* I suppose it appeared in the paper which ought to have come to
Sparta the day before I left home, but which had not come
when I left. I expected it to appear in the paper of the
week before, as it had time to do, but it did not. . . . . .
The case which I came here to try cannot be heard until
the second Monday in February, and may not be heard
then. The opposite side have proposed to me *that* as their
earliest time, and it will be accepted by our side, if Gibson
consents. He is not here, and has given me no intimation
of an intention to come. I find that the time of hearing
cases of original jurisdiction (in which only States and
public ministers are parties, you know) is fixed by *consent*,
out of deference to the dignity of the parties concerned;
and I, of course, do not feel at liberty to agree to any time
without consulting my associate. I am almost tempted to
say that I will not argue it until the second Monday in next
December, and go straight home. I shall remain here a few
days longer to make up my mind on that point, and in the
hope of getting some money from home wherewith to buy
some books. Speaking of books: I have not bought either of

the two novels which you commended to me. I inquired in all the book-stores here for "Debit and Credit," but none of them had it. For the life of me, I could not think of the name of the other one; and so, as yet, I don't know whether they have Wilhelm Meister's "Apprenticeship" or not. When I finish this letter, and one or two more to those at home, I shall take another excursion among the book-stores to find out—being now refreshed, as to the name, by your letter. I delivered your message to Ellie about your expectation, founded on a parting promise, that he would write to you. He said he had a distinct recollection of the parting interview between him and you, and that *his* understanding was that *you* were to write first. I simply replied, that when a fellow is caught in a scrape from his own remissness, there is nothing more natural than for him to try to at least divide the blame with somebody else by getting up a *squabble*—at which he laughed—and so it passed off with an additional remark from him, that he had thought of writing to you very often, and had wondered why he had not heard from you. Your letter was my first news of Fed Brooking's death. Poor old fellow! There is more and more desolation. Most deeply do I feel for his poor old mother; she is now ruined and forlorn. Life is despoiled of all its beauty, and her little remnant of existence is but a mockery of life. Her poor, tottering frame will linger among us yet a little while, but her heart is not here. "Her heart is awa'! her heart is awa'!" May God have mercy upon the stricken hearts everywhere that will mourn, and will not be comforted! . . . . . . If I had been elected to Congress the first race, I should have liked it, I have but little doubt; but I am now satisfied that it would not have suited me since then, nor ever will suit me again. Good-bye. . . . .

Yours, most truly,   LINTON STEPHENS.

[From L. S. to R. M. Johnston.]

WASHINGTON, D. C., January 22, 1859.

MY DEAR DICK—I am glad that you had decided to send to this place your answer to my last letter; for, sure enough, I was still here this morning to receive and welcome it. It did me much good, because it breathes such strong and friendly interest in my welfare. . . . . Without an accident, I shall start home Monday night next. Yesterday, we took an order of court, setting our case down for a hearing on the second Monday of next December. I should have started home last night but for the prospect of spending Sunday at the dull little place, called Kingsville, in South Carolina. The weather also is bad for traveling just now. There was a great fall of rain here yesterday; and, in consequence of it, brother expresses some apprehensions about the safety of the railroads. It will, however, have to be very extraordinary weather which detains me longer than Monday night—this being Saturday—so your next must be sent to Sparta—sent home. I got a letter, last night, telling me that my children were well. I have been disappointed in the pleasure of my sojourn here, and yet, I am loth to leave. Night before last, I heard the famous *Piccolomini*. She is a good singer, but her chief charms are outside of her singing: it is her beauty and her *acting*. The latter is admirable. She sang a little English song—"I Dreamt I dwelt in Marble Halls," etc.—and her acting in it was irresistible—coquettish and winning in a high degree. Her pouting was capital. I was pleased with her far beyond my expectations, and beyond the pleasure I ever received from any other musical wonder. I have been to see Mrs. Craig twice since I have been here. She is staying at the President's. I saw Miss Lane both times. I like her very much. She is sensible, modest, and, I should think, very amiable. . . . .

In May, 1859, Judge Charles J. McDonald, in consequence of advancing age and infirmity, resigned the position he occupied and adorned on the Supreme Bench of Georgia. Governor Brown appointed Linton Stephens to fill the vacancy thereby occasioned. He was the youngest man that ever sat upon the bench of that court in Georgia— he had not completed his thirty-sixth year; he was the youngest lawyer—he had been at the Bar but little over thirteen years; and, in the opinion of many, competent to pronounce upon the subject, the ablest Judge: high encomium; yet, I believe, severely just. His published decisions are models of logic—cogent, compact, Attic—the perfection of judicial eloquence. But his claim and title to the character of a great judge have been portrayed by a pen—dipped in the "Well of old English, undefiled"—of one whose intimate knowledge of the subject he handles—perfect candor, sharp, critical acumen, and rare fitness, in all respects, for such a performance—will relieve the tedium of my narrative: I gladly avail myself of the obliging kindness of the Hon. Logan E. Bleckley, long the learned head of the Atlanta Bar—now Associate Justice of the Supreme Court of Georgia—for the following:

ESTIMATE OF HON. LINTON STEPHENS AS A JUDGE, FOUNDED ON HIS JUDICIAL OPINIONS, PUBLISHED IN THE GEORGIA REPORTS. VOLS. 28, 29 AND 30:

It was not the lot of Judge Stephens to occupy the bench at a time when exceptionably great questions were presented to the Supreme Court for adjudication. Indeed, it may be doubted whether the points that came before him, taken in the aggregate, were of average magnitude or moment. He delivered not a single opinion on the principles of Constitutional law. Only three times did he have occasion even to mention the Constitution—twice in discussing the agreement of statutes with their titles, and once in the still more narrow inquiry as to what term of the court, with reference to the return of writs of error, was to be regarded as the first term, and the effect of failure to make return in due season. The cases with which he dealt were such only as make their appearance in ordinary times, and represent the ordinary current of judicial business, touching contracts, wills, crimes, the practice of the courts, and the duty of officers. He was thus without the advantage of great public questions upon which to found a reputation. Neither was he long enough in office to add anything to his judicial stature by the mere force of experience and continued service. He presided, altogether, but a little more than one year, having come in with May term, 1859, and gone out with June term, 1860. What mark he made as a judge was due, therefore, to what he was when he came to the bench—

to his learning as a lawyer, and his sheer fitness for judicial functions—not, in any degree, to the materials on which he wrought, or to long-continuance in labor.   His early opinions are quite as good as his later ones—the first as good as the last.   Indeed, he was ripe and ready for the bench at his first sitting, and needed no judicial education.   He was not a pupil, but a master.

In the second month of his service, a case was decided by a majority of the court contrary to his views of the law; and his dissenting opinion (the only one which he ever had occasion to deliver) is a model of strength and clearness. The case was that of Hill *vs.* The State, reported in 28 Ga. R., 604; and the rule for which he contended was, that on an indictment for murder, charging the prisoner with the offense as principal in the first degree, it was not competent to convict him if, in fact, he was guilty as a principal in the second degree.   He insisted that there is a substantial difference, under our penal code, between being the actual perpetrator of the crime, and being present, aiding and abetting in its commission by another.   The reasons for his dissent from the judgment of his learned colleagues are so forcible in themselves, and stated by him with such overwhelming power, that they have exerted a controlling influence over subsequent decisions of the court.   See 36 Ga. R., 222; 40 Ga. R., 120.   It is, perhaps, not going too far to say that the majority opinion, in so far as it conflicts with his, stands virtually overruled, and that the principle of his opinion is now established as law.   In announcing his conclusion, that the verdict ought to be set aside, there is a degree of pith and point in his language quite characteristic: "The verdict is not the *truth*.   I do not know what more can be said against any verdict."   Another able opinion, which he delivered in the same month, was upon the question, whether a deed to land, made in the face of adverse possession, was void?   On this point, there had been early decisions in the affirmative, and later ones in the negative—the former on the line of Judge Lumpkin's opinion, and the latter on the line of Judge Benning's. Judge Stephens agreed with Judge Lumpkin, and thus restored the early rule; but he placed his judgment entirely on the common law, and not at all on the adoption of the statute of 32 Henry VIII.   He was not the first judge to suggest the application of the common law to the question, but was the first to turn the statute of Henry out of the dispute. The unanswerable argument of Judge Benning against the application of that statute to the condition and circumstances of our Colonial population, commanded his concurrence and frank acknowledgment; but he contended, nevertheless, that conveyances made by a claimant, out of possession, while an adverse claimant was in possession, were void by a rule of the common law, and that the rule (not as modified by the statute, but the naked rule itself) came over with our ancestors, and was applicable to their situation. In a few pointed sentences, he demonstrated the policy of discouraging, in a new country, trade in occupied lands, under circumstances where immediate possession could not be given to the purchaser, and of inducing purchasers to push out into vacant territory and get land itself, instead of the mere chance for it at the end of a protracted and expensive litigation. See 29 Ga. R., 121.

Judge Benning, who was so well prepared on the statute of Henry, took time to consider before settling down into a final position on this theory in reference to the common law. After examination, he hurled at it his powerful dissenting opinion, in Gresham vs. Webb and Williams, 29 Ga. R., 320; but the doctrine stood as established, until changed by act of the Legislature. From the time of this last case until the present, it has never been made a question before the Supreme Court, whether, prior to the new statute, a deed executed, pending an adverse holding, was or was not void. From this circumstance, the inference may be drawn that the argument of Judge Stephens was convincing to the professional mind of the State, and that even the great ability of Judge Benning failed to supply the logic and learning requisite for successful reply.

In January, 1860, was decided the case of Jones vs. The State, 29 Ga. R., 594—the case, of all others, which will probably be the longest associated with the name and fame of Judge Stephens. The main question was, as to the meaning of the rule that drunkenness is no excuse for crime; and Judge Stephens, in the splendid opinion which he delivered for a majority of the court, (himself and Judge Lumpkin,) undertook to show how and why drunkenness, as a fact, may be allowed to avail the accused, even upon

the question of malice, without trenching, in the least, upon
that rule, properly understood. That drunkenness might
be urged to disprove the physical constituents of crime, was
probably never doubted; but with reference to the mental
constituents, the distinction between *ascertaining* them and
excusing them has not always been discerned. It was the
great achievement of Judge Stephens, in this opinion, to
bring out that distinction, and display it in the broadest
legal daylight. Until there is a case of crime *ascertained* in
all its elements—mental as well as physical—there is nothing to excuse; and so long as the process is one of investigation, and not of palliation, the drunkenness of the accused, just as any other fact, may be relevant on either
branch, or on both branches, of the alleged criminal action.
Not to screen the accused from responsibility for what he
has done, but to find out exactly what his deed was, and
how to grade it in the scale of legal offenses, which scale is
precisely the same for all, whether drunk or sober, is the
purpose for which drunkenness is to be considered. Whatever demerit there is in drunkenness, it is not to be stripped
of the protection which everything in God's universe is entitled to claim—the protection of *truth*. If, in very truth,
there was a crime, notwithstanding the drunkenness, then
should drunkenness count as nothing; but if the fact of
drunkenness shows there was no crime, or would have been
none if the same mental and physical elements had coin-
cided without the drunkenness, then should the drunkenness, as evidence, though not as excuse, furnish a ground
of acquittal.

Without reading carefully the opinion of Judge Stephens
in this case, it is quite impossible for any person to take
his full measure as a judge. It may be doubted whether
half a dozen of his contemporaries on the bench could have
written that opinion.

Two classes of persons are, however, liable to misunder-
stand it, and misconceive its whole scope and bearing:
these are the very inattentive and the very timid. If it is
not read with attention, it will break into fragments; and,
to be comprehended, being a connected argument, its connections must be preserved. So, if it be read by one in a
nervous state of apprehension, as to the danger of tenderness to drunken men, it will probably fail of its due effect,

through seeming, to a mind in such a state, more tender to them than it really is.

The capacity of Judge Stephens to construe conveyances, and apply the dry law of estates, may be seen by reference to the following cases: Brown *vs.* Weaver, 28 Ga. R., 377; Adams *vs.* Guerrard, 29 Ga. R., 651; Mason *vs.* Deese, 30 Ga. R., 308; Burton *vs.* Black, *id* 638; Tennille *vs.* Ford, *id* 707; and Springer *vs.* Congleton, *id* 976. The opinion in Burton *vs.* Black is especially able, and, both in substance and in style, would have satisfied Lord Coke himself. There is reason to think that, in the estimation of Judge Stephens, that opinion ranked above any other which he ever delivered—not excepting even the one in Jones *vs.* The State. An example of an interesting question, well treated, in less than two pages, is seen in Springer *vs.* Congleton. Very many of the minor opinions are well worthy of notice, though but few of them can be commented on here. Striking sentences occur in several, not to quote some of which would be to omit touches essential to accuracy in drawing the portrait which this paper is designed to reflect. In one case, he says: "We think there was a capital judge, but no law." 29 Ga., 56. In another: "Argumentativeness may be a good objection against an answer, but it will scarcely serve against a speech;" and "He who has reasons for his judgment is, at least, as good a witness as he who has none." *Id* 82. In another: "Communications between husband and wife are protected *forever.* This is necessary to the preservation of that perfect confidence and trust which should characterize and bless the relation of man and wife. Each must feel that the other is a safe and sacred depository of all secrets; and the protection which the law holds over the dead is the very source of greatest security to all the living."[*] *Id* 470. In another: "Estates, like everything else in life, are generally better off in the hands of their friends than in the hands of their enemies." *Id* 519.

[*] This sentence occurs in the judgment of the court, pronounced in the case of Lingo *vs.* The State; he was indicted for murder. Those present when it was delivered can never forget how Judge Stephens thrilled the audience, by the awful grandeur of his manner, when he uttered the words: "Thank God! there is no *running* law in Georgia!" The sentence does not appear in the printed decision.—ED.

In another: "The law does allow the owner, overseer or employer of the slave to furnish him such quantity as the *owner, overseer* or *employer* may deem beneficial to the slave's health; but the law has not done so foolish a thing as to put this same discretion in him who sells the spirits, nor can it be put there by delegation from him who has it.   If it were placed there, the quantity supplied would generally depend much less upon its reasonableness or healthfulness than upon the amount of money the slave might happen to have.   How many vendors would consider that a purchaser was transcending the limits of reason, or health, so long as he was paying for all he got?" *Id* 522.   In another: "It was said that any girl, with or without an estate, has a right to get relieved of a toothache, and make her guardian pay for it.   If this doctrine is conceded in favor of gallantry, (and it can hardly be conceded on any other score,) still, some care must be taken not to make the guardian pay for anything but relieving the toothache.   Now, it is very possible that the toothache, in this young lady's case, could have been relieved, as the toothache of her grandmother had no doubt often been relieved, by a plug of cotton with a little laudanum on it, instead of fine plugs of gold." 30 Ga., 35.   In another: "Surely there ought to be some compensation for the suffering endured.   The pain from the wounds must have been great, and the dread of the approaching collision between the two engines, though brief, must have been terrible.   Mental agony has been known to turn a head gray in a night, and gray hairs are often but the effervescence of some great mental anguish." *Id* 146. In another: "Proof of hand-writing is, in its nature, the identification of an acquaintance." *Id* 476.   In another: "What more verity is there in a gesture, or exclamation of surprise, than in plain words, expressing the same emotion? It would be exceedingly difficult to distinguish this from the case of spoken language; it is acted language—the one being quite as voluntary as the other." 29 Ga., 285.   In another: "A privy in estate is a successor to the *same estate*—not to a different estate in the same property." *Id* 374.   In another: "The question I ask is, whether all *promises* on which the parties rely must not be in the writing—I do not mean *representations?*   These last relate to the truth of existing or past facts, and not to engagements in the future—but promises, if they are to have any efficacy, must have it in the future." *Id* 461. In another: "The penalty falls not on him who shoots and kills, but on him who shoots and misses. Its penalty, therefore, seems to be leveled at *bad shooting*." 28 Ga., 395. In another: "But it was said they had *ceased* to be counsel when they were served. The reply is, that under the statute prescribing service on attorneys, for the purpose of receiving service, they *couldn't* cease." 29 Ga., 29.

The opinion in Bowie *vs.* Maddox and Goldsmith, 29 Ga., 285, deserves attention as a specimen of carving all the law in the case, as it were, into slices, with a few strokes of the knife, and making an end of the matter at once. Three points are not only ruled, but reasoned out exhaustively, in less than a page and a quarter. Roddy and Wife *vs.* Cox, *id* 298, shows how the body of a case can be squeezed until the points protrude like broken bones. Prince and Stafford *vs.* The State, 30 Ga., 27, shows as tight a grip—not used for exposing points, but for deciding: "It may be that a riot was brewing; but, if so, Prince spoiled the riot by an assault and battery." *Id.*

Among the most excellent opinions is that in Lively *vs.* Harwell, 29 Ga., 509, touching the revocation and probate of wills. In stating the views of himself and Judge Benning, on a point not directly in judgment—namely, whether the simple revocation of a subsequent will revives a prior revoked one—he makes a presentation of the reason for holding the negative, that ought to settle the question for all time in all parts of the world. Nothing can possibly be more conclusive.

Though he delivered but one dissenting opinion, proper, he differed with a majority of the court upon one of the points in another case—that of Ector *vs.* Welsh and Ector. 29 Ga., 443. The point was one of practice, and turned on the construction of a statute which declared that, unless exceptions to interrogatories and the answers of witnesses, examined under commission, were taken and determined before submitting the case to the jury, the testimony should be received, subject only to objections for *irrelevancy*. He contended that hearsay was to be treated as irrelevant testimony, and was open to objection at any time on that ground. The argument which he made on this line, drawn from the object and purpose of the statute, is very cogent, and, in the absence of anything to countervail it, from the other members of the court, seems absolutely convincing.

In still another case—Mason *vs.* Deese, 30 Ga., 308—each one of the judges had his separate views, and the judgment was formed by Judge Stephens yielding to the course favored by Judge Lumpkin, which was a kind of middle ground. The question was on the construction of a marriage settlement, and related to the exclusion of the husband from the property after the wife's death. Judge Stephens thought he was excluded; Judge Lyon thought he was not; and Judge Lumpkin thought it was not clear either way, on the face of the instrument, and that the paper should be referred to a jury for construction in the light of the surrounding circumstances. This was done. In all other instances of a divided court, the concurring judges were Stephens and Lumpkin—the dissenting judge, Benning or Lyon.

The whole number of opinions delivered by Judge Stephens is one hundred and fifty-three; and, assuming that his colleagues each delivered as many, the cases in which he presided would number about four hundred and fifty. One hundred and thirty of his opinions contain no citation of authority. Those citing authority refer chiefly to the Georgia Reports; Blackstone is cited three times; Jarman on Wills, twice; Story on Agency, twice; Adams on Ejectment, once; and an English Common Law Report, once. He respected authority, but the use he had for it was as a guide to principles—not as a prop on which to rest his judgments. When the principles were found, he rested his judgment on *them*, and not on the authorities that had led to their discovery. When he could render a legal reason, he preferred to state the reason itself rather than cite the volumes and pages from which he had drawn it. He thus gratified his taste for brevity and directness; for he had the power of condensing the substance of many authorities into a few sentences; and, I doubt not, he was averse to that appearance of judicial pedantry which belongs to parading books and cases in long strings of citation. I am tempted to think that he must have prescribed to himself some very rigid rule on the subject; for there is nothing more striking than the extreme rareness of his direct appeals to authority; yet, he made calls for it more than once, not satisfied with what had been produced. See 29 Ga., 310, 449, 465, 469, 470. His precise position with reference to precedents may be understood by quoting from his opinions. In one case, he says: "I thought, and still think, that the case is not within that statute, upon a sound and safe construction of it; but my colleagues informed me that a different construction had prevailed in the courts for a great number of years, and with entire uniformity, to the extent of their knowledge on the subject. I was not prepared to dispute it, and, therefore, acquiesced in what seemed to be established by authority." 30 Ga., 8. In another case, in refusing to interfere with a former decision of the court, he says: "Without considering its original propriety, the decision ought to be maintained *now*. It was made nine years ago, and attracted the universal attention of the profession at the time. The Legislature, with full knowledge of the decision for nine years, not having changed the law declared by it, may fairly be considered as having acquiesced in it. The great body of the common law derives its authority from the decisions of courts and legislative acquiescence in them." *Id* 232. In another case: "Whether the rule be a reasonable one or not is not the question; it is too firmly fixed in the law to be disturbed by courts. It is a case for the Legislature only." *Id* 280. But, in his estimation, there were two classes of precedents—one of them strong and the other very feeble. On page 104, of the 29th Georgia Reports, he says: "A decision, pronounced upon full argument and consideration, is justly entitled to great weight—indeed, to a controlling influence on subsequent decisions; but such decisions as this court, from the nature of its organization, is sometimes obliged to render, without argument and on short consideration, ought, in my judgment, to carry but slight authority for subsequent decisions." His view of the relation of principle to precedent is admirably stated in the same volume on page 515: "Where a principle is *sound*, it ought to be carried to all strictly analogous cases, unless stringent authority forbids; but if the principle be *unsound*, analogy ought not to be allowed to carry it to a single case beyond the imperative demands of authority—the cases in which it has been already planted by decisions."

The legal force and literary excellence of his opinions are so interwoven that they strike the attention in almost equal degree. He had the grace, as well as the power, of logic; his strength was chaste and elegant. Never ornate, but always correct, he makes the impression of an artist who is so masterly in drawing that he has no use for colors. He simply engraves—never paints. That his mind was sharp without being narrow, and broad without being blunt, constituted, I think, his great intellectual characteristic. When he concentrated, he did not contract; and when he expanded, he did not become vague. His thoughts moved, with equal vigor and accuracy, inward to the very center, or outward to the very circumference. He could both grasp and pierce; he seized his logical prey, and then slaughtered it. However extended the outlines of his subject, he reached out to them in all directions, and penetrated every inward part. Even his briefest opinions are exhaustive. The beginning and the end may be ever so close, but you feel that what lies between them is all that should have been interposed—that greater fullness would have been artificial cramming, and not natural growth. There is a staid relevancy in all he writes—no straying into sentiment, and no swelling into passion. You would not know, from anything he has recorded, that he had any hopes or fears, any pity, any anger, any indignation—or that he knew of any abuses to correct, or any reforms to introduce. He champions no cause, no class, and attacks nothing but error in the record. The prominent moral trait which he discloses to us is love of *truth*, evincing, in himself, perfect truthfulness of character. He was *genuine*, through and through—no counterfeit—no pretender—no humbug.

Such a man was fit and worthy to preside in any court; and had he made judicial administration the chief labor of his life, he would have gone down to posterity as a very illustrious judge.

L. E. BLECKLEY.

When Mr. Stephens was appointed to the office of Justice of the Supreme Court, one partisan gazette in the State expressed strong dissatisfaction thereat; the burthen of complaint and criticism was "the atrocious crime of being a young man," as the elder Pitt said in his reply to Walpole.

One person of the legal profession, commenting on the appointment and the appointee, said, in language he deemed, doubtless, classical, but which "Cosby" certainly considered coarse: "Stephens is a leather-headed fop."

Professor Johnston furnished to another newspaper, in vindication of the prudence and propriety of Governor Brown's action, "the piece" alluded to in the following letter:

SPARTA, June 4, 1859.

DEAR DICK—The date at which I am actually writing is the 10th; but I preserve the caption, which I truly dated the 4th, in order that you may see the beginning of a good intention, which broke down sadly early on the road. I wrote "Dear Dick," supposing that I had plenty to say, but in truth not a word could I summon to my aid. I was lazy—incontinently lazy, as the malicious world would say—but I, understanding the matter much better than the world, only choose to say that I was dull, heavy and stupid; and, to confess the truth, I am not much better off now. . . .

Dick, your piece about me is very kind and very handsome; but I do believe there is hardly more than one or two other men in the world who would have laid it on *so thick*. It was just like you; but I am perfectly, unaffectedly sincere in saying that I believe you said more for me than I deserve. I think you are in a woful minority in your opinions of me—I mean, in the extent to which you go. Everybody knows who wrote it. The initials, of course, give a ready clue to the authorship; but I do believe, Dick, that it has stronger ear-marks than the initials—and everybody would have known it anyhow. One thing surprised me a little: and that was the exactness with which you stated facts in my history. I didn't suppose that some of the things you mention had made any abiding impression on the mind of anybody. Your facts will do; but when it comes to your opinions and judgments, let me say, that if you are ever called on to make affidavit to them, I beg you to qualify, very decidedly, with the legal phrase, "Accord-

ing to the best of my knowledge and belief," and especially
your "belief;" for truly, I believe, in this case, your *faith*
is very superior to your *knowledge*.   I feel as if you had
stuck a false label on me; and I feel very much like a pretender, unless I proclaim, as I go along, that *you* have done
it, and that I am not responsible for it, and don't believe in
it.   But, by the way, was ever Wirt a judge?   I think
not; but I may be mistaken.   I see that Gaskill, of the
Atlanta *Intelligencer*, gives the piece his indorsement very
heartily, from his knowledge of *you*; and I see, also, that
he says the Opposition Griffin paper "has been pitching
into me in a very uncalled-for and unkind manner."   I don't
mind that; for I don't know the fellow, and the best part
of it is, he doesn't know me.   He said he understood that
Judge H———, when the news of my appointment reached
Newnan, said I was a "leather-headed fop."   Cosby was
mighty mad about it.   The fact is, the old fellow turned
pale when he told me about it.   He seemed in much better
spirits, and took a new and brighter view of the subject
when he saw me laugh and make merry over it.   If the
Judge had contented himself with the "leather-headed," he
might have hurt me; but when he stuck on the "fop," the
thing became preposterous.   That showed malice; and I
know he was speaking not from knowledge, but from envy.
Malice, like ambition, often, and most generally, overleaps
itself.   A moderate thrust might have gone home; but the
very fury of the blow carried it over my head.   When he
calls me a "leather-headed fop," I laugh at him; but if he
had simply called me "leather-headed," I suspect I should
feel inclined to *knock* him.   You remember the anecdote of
Mr. Petigru: When a fellow called him a liar, he passed it
by as a thing nobody would believe; but when the fellow
said he was a "d—d old Federalist," he knocked him down;
for he said he didn't know but what some people might be
d—d enough fools to believe it. . . . .

The following reminiscences, furnished by Professor Johnston, give an insight into the milder features of Mr. Stephens'
character: his pure and hearty domestic affections; his true
and rare social virtues; his high and delicate appreciation
of the offices of friendship, and of the more sacred relations
and duties, whereof *Home* is the endeared exemplification:

PEN LUCY, WAVERLY, MD., October 17, 1873.

My DEAR COLONEL.—I have been thinking of your request that I should send you some "reminiscences" of our departed friend, Linton Stephens. I hardly know where to begin, and what are the things most suitable to speak about in the case of such a man as Linton Stephens. If I could be with you, and we could have time for a long talk, I have no doubt that I could interest you with many anecdotes of his private life, and then you might afterwards so frame them as to make them interesting to the public in your forthcoming memoir. I can scarcely hope to do so in the limited time at my disposal for this purpose.

But I conclude to send you a short sketch as I knew him *at home*. I do this more readily, because, with all my admiration for the position which he held in public, it was while he was *at home* that I admired him most. Nor was this great admiration due only, or mostly, to our long intimate, and never-broken, and never-interrupted friendship. Such a friendship, indeed, gave me opportunities superior to those of most men, even among his neighbors, of seeing and knowing what he was in private; but had I been less intimate with him, I could not have failed, while living so long in his neighborhood, to see and know enough of the life which he led there to fully justify the preference which I have expressed. Though he and I were born in a few miles of each other, yet, from the fact of our having been sent to different schools and colleges, we did not become acquainted until after we had grown up and come to the bar. Being a year or two younger than myself, he came in a little later. When he first began to attend our Hancock courts, at Sparta, I was then a partner of the late Judge James Thomas, whose only daughter, Mrs. Bell, Linton married in the year 1852. He then made Sparta, as you know, his home, and ever afterwards resided there. Before this time, however, our intimacy had begun, and with it the love and admiration on my part, both of which steadily increased to the last. I well remember how I was first impressed by his manners, and that I little expected to be ever so related to him as I afterwards became. His sternness of countenance, with his usual taciturnity, and his apparent entire disregard of the value of making a good impression on the minds of others when he spoke at all, induced me to regard him as misanthropical, and to suspect him to be incapable of forming strong attachments to persons or things; but I soon discovered I had made a mistake; that under that grave exterior, and accompanying, harmoniously, the thoughtfulness often descending to melancholy, which had formed it so, there was an abundance of that sort of tenderness which led him to love deeply, to pity cordially, and a humor which, in genuineness and richness, I have seldom seen equaled.

The people of Hancock cordially received him; and, being a member of the political party which had a majority in the county, (Whig,) he was sent to the Legislature at the next session after his removal. Though a Democrat myself, I had already formed so strong an attachment for him, and so admired his genius, that I could but be pleased to see him thus have opportunities of making the reputation which I knew was in store for him. Even those Democrats who were most strictly party men' were led to console themselves in defeat, that the new leader of their opponents was a man of real genius, and a thoroughly honest gentleman.

And now, this last word reminds me afresh what a *gentleman* was Linton Stephens! Sure I am that in his whole life, whatever may have been the objects of his desire, he not only did never swerve from the straight line of honorable pursuit of them; but, as I fully believe, he was never tempted to do so.

In his practice at the bar, in his conduct of a political campaign, in his business dealings with his neighbors, he was entirely incapable of the employment of a trick, and would have scorned to have any object, however desirable, that he could not fairly win; for he prized his own honor above all possible human possessions, even to the love of those who were the objects of his best love. It was this exalted sense of honor that made him sometimes so terrible in debate; for the slightest deflection from honorable conduct, and even the suspicion of it, aroused his indignation.

Such a man must exert great influence in his neighborhood. He had not been long a resident of Hancock before he became its leading citizen. His character, not at all less than his intellect, made him such. He was never a flatterer of the people—and, indeed, was not often among them. A visit from him to other than his kinsmen was extremely rare. He did not often go to his office, and when he did go, he usually staid but a short time, and then returned to his home; but when he met the people, whether one or two of them, upon the streets, or in assembled crowds at the court-house, or the hustings, he so spoke and acted that they continually grew in their respect and their love for him.

I said that he would often return home during office-hours. Of all men whom I have ever known, I think he was the most averse to leaving home. The love of home, with him, far outweighed the desire for professional or political success. But for his conviction that such a course would have been an unjustifiable employment of his talents, I am confident that he would have retired from the law and from politics long before his death. Many a struggle has he had on mornings, when he was to start upon the circuit, between the reluctance to leave home and a sense of duty to go. It was only two weeks before his death, when I was at his house, and he had a short respite from the State prosecutions in Atlanta, that he spoke of his repugnance to going back to them, and of a desire, amounting to longing, to retire from all public life, and be always afterwards with his family.

Yet, when he went to the courts, this home-feeling did not interfere with his attention to his cases, and at recesses, especially in the evenings at the hotels, when he had such company as he liked, he could fully enjoy social reunions, and there was no lawyer who was more quick to notice the funny things which used to occur in the circuit-ridings, or rehearse them better, or enjoy their rehearsal more keenly than he. Yet, while he would never dispatch business too hurriedly for the sake of getting home, when he did get there, no man could more fully have enjoyed the return.

At home! It was here that Linton Stephens was at *his* best. The singleness of heart that made him so just and straightforward among men made him as honorable a husband as ever lived in this world, I do believe. He had married from pure love. He could not have married but from pure love. Otherwise, he would have been most unhappy in marriage. The longer his married life continued, the more he loved the woman who had blessed it and the children she had borne to him. He was not only loving,

but he was attentive and tender—a continual companion in
all seasons, and almost the best of nurses in the seasons of
sickness.   Five years after his marriage, his wife died.   I
never witnessed greater anguish than he suffered from this
affliction.   It continued through many years, and until he
met the lady who became his second wife.   You will have
noticed in some of the letters which I have sent to you,
written long after, how he dwelt upon this loss.

Time, however, healed the wounds of this grief, and,
having again most fortunately married, as before, he loved
as he loved before, and was as happy with his noble second
wife as he had been with the first.

It was during the ten years of his widowerhood, from
1857 to 1867, that our friend, as it seemed to me, exhibited
the rarest qualities of head and heart.

He was left with three little girls.   There was no female
relative who stood in such near relationship to him as would
make it practicable for her to undertake their guidance during these years.   His wife had been the only child of Judge
Thomas, and her mother had died before her.   Linton's
only sister resided in a remote part of the State, and had a
considerable family of her own.   But in the household there
were some faithful and well-trained servants.   With these,
therefore, he undertook to bring up these little girls.   It
would have touched the heart of any man, however little
acquainted with him and his condition, to see how assidu-
ously he labored to compensate these children for the
loss which they had suffered—how he strove to be both
father and mother to them, and how, when sometimes he
would feel that he must, and did come short of this responsibility, he lapsed almost into despair.

But here the tenderness which was one of his most striking qualities came to his aid, and was sufficient for his and
their needs.   He took upon himself the care and education
of these children, and those of us who knew him best
saw with pleasure how he adapted himself to this delicate
and most difficult task.   To me, he seemed to have succeeded in making himself again a child—so fully did his
heart learn to accord with theirs in the love and appreciation of things which are intended and generally seem to be
fitted only for childhood.

Patiently he **taught** them the principles of learning, and his old love of childish literature came again to him, as, with his little ones around him, he read the old stories, and his and their tears flowed together. I have often gone to his house and found him with his little charge. But he usually dismissed them, after I entered, to their nurse, and though most generally we went to the consideration of other things, yet, he would sometimes linger upon a subject that their last lessons had suggested, and fondly tell of some of their sayings and doings. There was one story, in particular, of the old days, which he and I often referred to, and pleasingly remembered how, when very young children, we had wept over it. The book containing it had long been out of print, but I found it once at an administrator's sale and bought it. I told him of it, and mentioned that I had not read it again, and had hesitated to do so in the fear that I might not feel the old emotion. He asked me to send it to him. I did so; and not long afterwards, he said to me: "Dick, you need not be afraid that you won't cry from reading Little Jack. I have read it to the children. They cried as if their hearts would break, and I cried about as much as they did."

It was this tenderness in his nature which, more than anything else, enabled him to bring on these little girls in the sort of education which it was best for them to have. Not only his natural love, but his sympathy for them, his commiseration even for their very unconsciousness of the loss they had suffered, made him the more easily become sometimes like them in tastes, feelings and emotions. It would have put to shame most fathers, and those with greatly less capacity than his for the enjoyment and pursuit of greater things, to notice how thoroughly he had learned these children's various characters, and how he delighted in employing the means of giving them suitable development.

Sometime during the war, Mr. Cosby Connel, an unmarried gentleman, about ten years his senior, an intelligent man of ordinary education, and of great probity of character, went to live with him, and so continued until his death in the year 1868.

A very ardent personal friendship grew up between these two men. Mr. Connel was a man of decided likings, and, being of domestic habits, rendered invaluable aid in the management of household affairs. The children became strongly attached to him, and he to them. He watched over them with the care and affection of a father, and Linton was greatly relieved of his anxiety, in his absence, when he knew they were under the charge of Mr. Connel.

And now, what shall I say about what it was to visit at that house in those times? The absence of women did away with much ceremonious entrance. The door was ever open, and his friends seldom paused to knock. Advancing through the spacious hall, they entered into his library, where he literally lived. He might be reading to his children, or reading for his own entertainment, or writing, or playing at solitaire, or simply musing while he smoked his cigar. The open box was on the mantel, and the visitor would light up and read a newspaper, picking up one of a dozen from the floor, or take a hand at cards, or sit and smoke, and wait for talk to begin. Cosby Connel would just have been in, or would soon come in from the garden, in which he took great pride, and we might begin on him until Linton would turn from his table and join in. We might talk of politics, or a law case, or of Cosby's peas, and cabbage, and potatoes. The presence of friends would unbend him from his studies, and make him seem to forget his grief and solitude. I never expect to enjoy again such raciness of talk as we used to have in that library when we would all get warmed well in contact. His humor was only the more genuine and flowing from the melancholy, which, natural to him, had been mellowed by affliction. There was many a character, both in Hancock and the adjoining counties, whose oddities he and I well knew, and the rehearsal of their doings and sayings would be followed by shouts of laughter that it would be glorious to hear and to utter. But later in the day, I may have lingered longer than the rest. After dinner, Cosby might be out at his work, or taking his evening nap on the sofa. As the day would wane, we would lapse into serious conversation, which might lead to his own condition, the prospects of his children and his own; on these he would converse with me as freely, I believe, as he did with his own heart. When, at last, the day would end, and I must go, we would shake hands without other words than "good-bye;" yet, he would know, and I am sure it comforted him in some degree to know, that I loved and sympathized with him more and more from every additional interview.

Alluding to the merry times we sometimes had, I am reminded that I have observed that his appreciation of humorous things was not as generally known as it was by those who were his intimate friends. Added to an uncommonly serious exterior, he had, beyond any one I have ever known, the faculty of postponing the enjoyment of a ridiculous occurrence, if a postponement was proper or desirable. He could witness, without a change in his face, the funniest things, and then store them away, even the smallest bits of them, and afterwards, when a fit opportunity occurred, bring them forth, and they would have lost none of their freshness. I well remember his first visit to me after I had removed to Athens, and when he came there as Judge of the Supreme Court. One afternoon, we had taken a long walk into the country, and were returning down the hill near Governor Lumpkin's. He had been telling me some good things about several of our old acquaintances, and we had gotten into a vein of uncontrollable laughter. He then told me several anecdotes of Gabe Nash, Esq.; one, especially, about the municipal ordinances of the new town of Hartwell, under one of which Gabe was fined a dollar for loud talking in the streets. We were both so convulsed by this that we became uproarious in our bursts of laughter, and had to lean upon each other to keep from falling. We had not noticed a carriage that was coming up the hill. It contained some of my lady acquaintances. We bowed in some confusion as they passed, and they afterwards said to me that they had made the driver linger a while at the foot of the hill in the apprehension that a couple of escaped lunatics were in their way.

We were both extremely fond of his father-in-law, the late Judge James Thomas. The Judge, a capital lawyer, and otherwise an excellent man, had many eccentricities. These manifested themselves most frequently in his seasons of sickness, and unfortunately the latter occurred very often. Whenever one of these came on, Linton would go to his house and remain with him until he was well again. I have already said that the latter was one of the best of nurses, and the Judge, having lost his wife, and having no female relative in the house, needed the nursing that Linton knew how to bestow. Another reason for this necessity was, that the Judge had the greatest confidence in his own medical skill, and none whatever in that of any physician. It was only Linton who could restrain him from employing whatever remedies his whimsy might suggest—remedies which often were the most unsuitable possible for his condition. It was always an extremely difficult matter to control him in such cases. Only Linton, with his coolness and firmness, could hold him in check. The old gentleman doted on his son-in-law, and always his most potent reason with him in yielding his point would be the apprehension that he might not be sufficiently considerate of Linton's feelings if he should persist in his course. Still, he would argue every point, and sometimes Linton would be driven to put his hand upon the potion that he had resolved to take, and gently withdraw it from his grasp. At such times, there had to be a compromise of some sort, for nothing could get him to take the prescription of the physician. The highest compliment he had ever been known to pay to any physician was when he said of Dr. Edward Alfriend, his family physician and very dear friend, that he really did believe that Alfriend killed fewer patients than any doctor he knew.

After such a sojourn with the Judge at Lancaster (his country-seat), Linton would return home. When we could get a fair opportunity for such a purpose, and had gotten fully rested from his long watching, he would take out of his pocket, as it were, scores of the funniest things imaginable that had occurred at Lancaster, tell them over to me, and, for the first time, would laugh and laugh until the tears would run out of his eyes.

I have spoken thus freely of his humor, because I am sure the public generally were not aware how abundant and hearty it was. While his elegant culture enabled him to see at a glance and to fully appreciate the most delicate playfulness of the best literary humorists, yet his simplicity, and broadness of understanding and heart, allowed him to take in all humorous things, from the most sparkling sallies of genius to the droll gambols of even the lower animals. When we would be going on the circuit together, in a buggy, while much of our conversation would be on serious subjects, and very often upon our own, and especially his domestic afflictions, yet he would often be diverted to making charades and conundrums, and other sportive suggestions. Occasionally, these speculations would imperceptibly lapse into a vein of sentiment, and even of melancholy, that would be most delicate and most touching. The shadow that his great affliction had cast upon him was ever there, but the humor that was a part of his nature must assert itself sometimes, and I am sure it became the richer from the pathos which went along with it. To one who shed so many tears in secret, a laugh was sometimes as refreshing as food to the hungry, and he enjoyed it the more because it seldom came, and came irresistibly.

The intercourse that he had with his clients was interesting. No lawyer was ever more free from the habit of either encouraging litigation, or flattering clients by giving too favorable opinions. Thoroughly sincere in all things, he counselled exactly as he thought. Whenever an attempt was made to arbitrate, he was one of the few, who could see and feel the strong points in the adversary's right, equally with those of his client, no matter how long he had been connected with his case. He was almost a perfect lawyer, and the thorough control he exerted over his intellect made such a task easy. It was thus he could win suits without appealing to the prejudices of juries, or too hastily assailing his adversary, preferring and feeling safe to rely upon the strength of his case and his power to establish it. Aside from the eloquence that comes from an ardent and vigorous understanding that had received great culture, there was a perspicuity in his spoken language, and a facility of simplifying contested questions, that I never saw surpassed at the bar.

Counting the work that he did, he ought to have amassed a fortune by his practice. But his charges were almost uniformly below the average of the profession, and often, very often, he would lower the fee after the termination of a great case, and lower it again and again, upon the representation (not always sincere) of his client that he could not afford to pay it. This was particularly the case in his own county. The poor had their little cases attended to with as little cost as the poor anywhere, certainly, and, by his prudent counsels, he kept out of the courts a greater number of litigants than he ever carried there. There is no calculating the blessing that such a lawyer is to a community.

After the war, when almost every man became reduced to poverty, he did an immense amount of such work—not excepting the destitute negroes from his charitable counsels and aid. He was constantly making their little settlements, and adjusting their disputes, and counselling them generally, and without reward.

Such devotion had its legitimate results. Of course, there was some ingratitude in his experience, as in that of every generous man. But he was as much beloved in that county as any public man could be anywhere, and when he died, all, as well the poor as those who had been able to recover from pecuniary disasters, as well the black man as the white, mourned as if they had lost their best friend. The little village of colored people, built in the suburbs of Sparta since the war, was draped with crape.

As his children grew older, his friends hoped he might again marry, they being all girls. I do not doubt that his grief for the loss of his wife was the deeper and the harder to be subdued, as he contemplated daily the increasing loss which her death had brought to them. But it was not until 1865 that the idea of a second marriage was permitted to enter his mind. It was in the fall of this year, while on a visit to his brother, then a prisoner at Fort Warren, that he became acquainted with Miss Mary W. Salter, of Boston. This acquaintance ripened into most devoted affection, and led to his second marriage, which took place in 1867. This marriage was most happy in its results. In this new sharer of his after fortunes, he and his children found every quality becoming the character of wife and mother. Never was man, so sorely afflicted for years, more eminently blessed in the end. Three other children were born; and I have never known a house in which it would have been more difficult to notice in all, parents and children, that there was any difference in their relative positions among one another. Even now, since the father has been removed from them, the only alteration that death has seemed to cause has been to bind that blended circle the closer together in reciprocal duties and affections.

I scarcely know how even to begin to speak of Linton as a friend. He was so unspeakably dear to me, that I feel like saying more than would perhaps be becoming in such a letter. While he was so generally beloved in his neighborhood, he was on strictly and entirely confidential terms of friendship with a limited number. Without much constraint in his associations with his neighbors, his deepest and most secret thoughts and feelings were imparted to very few; and to them, they were imparted without the slightest reserve. The tenderness of which I have before spoken gushed out, abundant and free, to the friends he loved. For his friendship was pure love. He had grown to be warmly attached to Mr. Cosby Connel. In the summer of 1868, he and Mrs. Stephens went on a visit to her parents in Boston, and left this gentleman and the older children behind. During their absence, Mr. Connel died. I regret much that I have mislaid the letter Linton wrote me from Boston when he heard by telegraph of this event. But he wept and wept! I saw from the letter, what I knew before I received and read it, that his very soul was pouring itself out in sorrow for the friend of his love.

I know you will be touched when you read the letters he wrote to me about the sickness and death of his servant woman, Mary, the wife of Travis, his coachman; for *there* was another friend, though a slave. That great, loving heart recognized its dues to the lowly as well as the high, and paid them all fully out of its allowance. I have frequently remarked that, though he was ever kind and considerate to negroes generally, yet he seemed to have a feeling akin to friendship for all belonging to his special friends. My old house-servants liked him very much for his friendly notice, and he and they usually shook hands on meeting and parting at my house.

It was always beautiful to me to observe the relations between him and his brother, Alexander. I suspect that no two brothers ever stood in the relation to each other of greater love and sympathy. While they were never partners in the law, yet they would never appear in court on opposing sides. Their love was such that each, I believe, could not endure the thought of attempting, or even wishing for things different or adverse among themselves. It was for sometime unfavorable to the growth of Linton's reputation, that the general public delayed to give him full credit for independence in his political opinions. The truth is, that their thorough intimacy and their mutual fondness had induced a similarity of thinking upon most subjects;

and though living in different counties, they often, and indeed generally, would form instantaneously the same judgments upon questions that had newly arisen, and upon which they had not had time to confer. I have noticed, sometimes, the pleasure each has felt in such a case.

The brothers sympathized always and entirely. The joy and the grief of one were the joy and the grief of the other. This was most especially the case with the elder brother. To Linton he had been both brother and father. He had educated him with almost unequaled care, and, I am sure, that his greatest happiness, aside from the consciousness of performing his own duties, consisted in seeing Linton successful and happy. Their love for each other was perfect in its kind. The death of Linton would have broken the heart of the survivor, but for his religious faith, and his sense of obligation to hold out to the last in the work which he had yet to do.

In conclusion, I say to you frankly, that I feel like saying something more, if I could find what was becoming to say, about Linton as my friend. But I fear I have already alluded too often to myself in this letter. But I knew him best, when he and I were together, alone. We had been friends from the first to the last. In those twenty years, through what varied scenes we passed together! We have rejoiced together, and we have mourned together. He had domestic afflictions—so had I. In those twenty years, he and I several times were in alternate relations of wailer and consoler. Deeply and long as he could bewail his own griefs, so tenderly and considerately could he be a consoler of mine. I have never known a man who understood, as well as he, the blessed art of searching into the breast of a sorrowing friend, and applying healing balm unto its sorest wounds. In all of his moods, whether sad or gay, he was ever the same to me, trusted and loved; and, I do not hesitate to say, trusting and loving. When I heard that he was no more, few things that might have happened could have impressed me more deeply with thoughts of what havoc death can make with the happiness which comes from indulgence in human affections.

Very truly, your friend,

R. M. JOHNSTON.

I insert here a few additional letters, without regard to chronological order, which avouch the accuracy of Professor Johnston's judgment of the beauty and tenderness of his domestic and social virtues.

From the White Sulphur Springs, Virginia, whither he repaired for health, in 1868, he wrote this letter to his three eldest daughters—Rebecca, Claude and Emm:

WHITE SULPHUR SPRINGS, September 1, 1868.

MY PRECIOUS DARLINGS—The main purpose which your poor, old, gruffy, morose, petulant, melancholy Papa has in writing to you at this late day is to *apologize* for not having written to you sooner. The penalty of duty neglected is always, in the end, humiliation in some way or other; and the offender gets off very lightly when the humiliation comes in no worse form than confession—especially, when the confession has the reactionary effect of procuring pardon or absolution, and thus setting him on his legs again with a relieved conscience and undaunted brow. I have made the confession; it depends upon you to grant the absolution. Will you do it at once, and thus set poor Papa up all right again, or will you prolong his punishment by withholding your forgiveness? If the latter, I shall not complain, for I richly deserve it; but if the former, I shall be very happy in having one more proof that you are the sweetest and best children in the world. To forgive neglect of ourselves, on the part of others, is one of the very highest exercises of unselfish love, and therefore one of the highest and brightest elements of excellence, since there is nothing which exceeds neglect in its tendency to wound our self-love. To subordinate self-love to our love for another is as beautiful as it is difficult and heroic. If, therefore, you shall exhibit the beauty of heroism, I shall have the felicity of forgiveness. I shall cease to regret my sin, because it will be taken away from me and converted into the exaltation and glory of my children. Can my sweet darlings now refuse to forgive poor old Papa? No. I am sure they will eagerly contest the point among themselves, which of them will be the *first* to spring into his arms and tell him he is forgiven. Do you know, by the way, that the enormity of

my delinquencies obliges me sometimes to incur the humiliation of apologizing to so *small* a personage as Baby?*
Just think of it! a grave, gray-headed man like me, asking
pardon of a little frowning monkey like her; and yet, my
petulant humors or irreverent speeches are sometimes
resented by her little ladyship in a way which brings the
repentant old father right down on his knees.   But bless
her bright, sweet, loving little soul! she never fails to forgive her " Papy " whenever he asks her forgiveness in the
proper handsome manner.   I am indeed blessed in my
children—in *all* my children, from the greatest even unto
the least   You will understand, however, that in estimat-
ing which is greatest and which is least, I shall be guided,
not by the size and beauty of their bodies, but by the size
and beauty of their souls.   Do you want to know *which* of
your four souls Papa regards as the biggest and most beautiful?   Ah! well, that is Papa's *secret*.   He defies any and
all of you to find it out.   You need not try to worm it out
of Mama, for I do not intend to let her any deeper into it
than the rest of you.   I give all of you, including her, full
leave to form an alliance against me, and to use all your
art.   I shall not be cajoled or surprised into a revelation.
I will, however, give you a *clue* to guide your guesses from
time to time.   I say from time to time, because the size
and beauty of the soul are things of *growth*, and the soul
that excels at one time is often overtaken and surpassed by
the more rapid growth of an inferior one.   Yes, my darlings, the soul is even more capable of growth than the
body is; for, unlike the body, it has no *limitation* upon its
growth, neither in time nor eternity.   It may forever and
forever expand in capacity and beauty—finding forever a
new happiness in its very sense of *expansion*.   Is not this
a very sweet and *encouraging* thought?   To know our capacities of happiness is the opening of the gate which
leads to its attainment.   The sight of the splendid prize, as
a possession which *can* be made our own, is a most powerful
incentive to struggle for its appropriation.   This sight comes
to the soul by the eye of faith, founded on reason, just as
images of beauty in the material world sink sweetly and
lovingly into the chambers of the material eye, if it will

Little Nora, then not much over a year old.

only open its doors and let in the light. But I said I would give you a *clue*. Well, here it is: I shall be very apt to *think* that soul the biggest and most beautiful which *is* the biggest and most beautiful; and you will, therefore, be most likely to get at my secret opinion by forming for yourselves the most candid judgment of your own comparative characters. Aha! you think now I have betrayed my secret. Not a bit—I hope and believe all of you will exhibit such an equal growth—each resolved not to be surpassed by any other—that the difference shall ever remain a contested point and a doubtful matter. Do you suppose, from what I have said, that I would have you to look upon one and another as rivals? No, not rivals—not even in greatness and beauty of soul—for rivalry implies a certain sort of selfishness, even when the contest is pursued for the noblest prizes; while real greatness and beauty of soul consist in nothing more certainly and luminously than in the negation of self and devotion to others—preferring one another in honor, even in the *honor* of *goodness*. Lest all this may seem incomprehensible to your young minds, as it equally seems to many, very many older ones, I will express it in a different form, which I think is clearer, and, at the same time, more accurate. I begin by saying that my idea must not be understood as excluding all selfishness from the pale of greatness and beauty; on the contrary, there is one sort of selfishness which forms the necessary basis of rational character, whether rational or insane—everything does and *must* act with a view to his *own* happiness. Do you suggest that very few people seem to act from that motive— that many seem to be pursuing their own misery instead of happiness? Well, this is only a seeming—not a reality. It is too true that very few persons pursue their happiness in a *wise way*, or with wisdom equal to their knowledge; but it is still equally true that every person is always impelled by some view of his own happiness as a motive-power. It is often a most *mistaken* view—so obviously mistaken that it would be readily corrected by his own stock of knowledge, if his knowledge were only realized and applied to the case. The difficulty is, that knowledge is *not* realized, and *not* applied in the case. It is not realized, because there is not the necessary reflection to bring home, as a present reality, its logical conclusions which lie in the future. There is nothing so difficult for human nature as to preserve a just relative estimate of the present and the future, the short, evanescent, but ever-presiding present, and the future which has not yet come in contact with the soul. The future, although it may be known in the sense of being open to reflection, if reflection could only be made to bear upon it, and *accept* it as an *inevitable experience*, loses its just weight in the balance. The present always asserts itself, and never allows itself to be overlooked or depreciated. The poor, unreflecting human soul often indulges in a *small present* gratification, from which it would shrink appalled if it would but realize and appreciate, as a present experience, the miserable consequences which lie in the yet unreached future; but still, in the very act of present indulgence, the soul is moved by that view of its own happiness which is then predominant. The present reigns triumphant because the future is *shut out*. Thus you see how it is, as I have said, that a certain sort of selfishness forms the necessary basis of every character, and is the spring of all human action. But there is an immeasurable difference between *two kinds* of selfishness, and in this difference lies the secret of greatness and beauty of soul. One kind of selfishness is solitary—the other is social. One finds its happiness or gratification in the indulgence of its every passion and desire, without regard to the happiness or misery of others, and even sometimes *in* the misery of others. The other kind finds its pleasure in seeing, and still more in creating, the happiness of others. *This* kind cannot have a real happiness unless it is shared by loved ones. Neither of these two kinds exists in its perfection in any one person; but the two kinds are mixed in every person, yet in very different degrees in different persons. The solitary kind is despicable; the social kind is noble, and beautiful, and lovely. Greatness and beauty of soul are best cultivated by cultivating that noble selfishness which finds its happiness in the happiness of others. All of this, which I have taken so much space to explain, is embodied in the command to love God with your whole heart, and your neighbor as *yourself*. The selfishness which I call the noble kind is but another exposition for the law of love. It is the fountain of the purest, sweetest, and most abundant happiness. But I must hurry to a close. I am, perhaps, a little better in health than when I came here. In a few days, your uncle Ellic and I expect to go to another spring about sixteen miles from this one. It is called the Sweet Chalybeate spring. Send your next letter to Boston. I have received three letters from Claude, two from Rebecca, and one from Emm. Emm's letter I got this evening. It bears date of the 25th of August. I think you have *all* improved very much in letter-writing. I think Claude has improved the most, and I expect it is because she has written the most letters, and taken the most pains to write them. Your uncle was quite sick day before yesterday. He seemed quite well again yesterday, but to-day again he is quite unwell. His affliction is of the nature of cholera-morbus. He thinks it was produced by some frozen custard which he ate for dinner the day before his attack, but I suspect it came from the water here. Before that attack, he had greatly improved in strength and health. I think now, my darlings, that we shall not get back home before the middle of October. I don't want you to go to school while the sun is very hot. Take care of your *health* by all means. We may get home sooner than the time I have mentioned, but you needn't expect us sooner. I don't know how long I may stay at the other spring—as long as I may get benefit from it. And now, good-bye, my darlings, and may God bless you.

Your loving   FATHER.

[From L. S. to A. H. S.]

SPARTA, August 19, 1869.

DEAR BROTHER— . . . . . . I got your letter of yesterday, and the *Constitutionalist* containing your reply to Greeley. I think this reply is one of the very best things you ever wrote. Indeed, I think it the *best*. It is vigorous, luminous and crushing. I have sent the paper to Ben Harris, at his request. He promised to take care of it and return it. I was down town a while this morning, and spoke of the piece in a way which caused him to ask for the paper. While I write, Claude has Baby on the sofa, showing her the pictures in a large illustrated Bible. She has the passion for pictures stronger than I ever saw it in a child of her age. She has a "Mother Goose" which she pretty

18*

generally carries around with her, annoying people to death with begging to have the pictures explained. She decidedly prefers me as expositor, because I render them to her in dramatic style. You can't imagine how intense an attention she gives to these representatives, nor what a Babel of gibberish she sometimes delivers in response to them. She remembers, too, a great deal of what I tell her about the pictures, and universally selects for comment those which have before been most highly dramatized.

[From L. S. to A. H. S.]

SPARTA, February 5, 1860.

DEAR BROTHER—I am now about to do what I have no recollection of ever having done before—*re-write* a letter to *you;* or, to express the truth more nearly, I am about to write you a new letter, because I have become dissatisfied with the one on hand, and have discovered it. I was about to say, discovered it midway, but I don't know whether it was midway, or one-tenth, or one-twentieth of the way to its end, for one of the main reasons I had for dropping it was, that I could see no symptoms of its coming to an end at all. I was like a novice trying to dispatch an oyster, and feeling the thing grow bigger and bigger in his mouth instead of becoming prepared for the passage down his gullet. So I have just taken the unmanageable morsel out of my mouth, and laid it gently down, in the spirit of Martin Crawford's man, who took the hot pudding out of his mouth at the grand dinner and laid it down with the complacent, self-gratulatory remark, "A damned fool would have swallowed it." I tell you I had got the thing into a terrible tangle, and I am very much disposed to compliment my own ingenuity in getting rid of it. There are not many men who would have done it. Now I am ready to go on. . . . . Yesterday, I got your letter of the day before, written at home, saying that you expected to go back to Augusta yesterday evening, and telling me also what an escape you had from being burnt out.

There was one thing in your account of the burning that made me *laugh*, though I have not the slightest idea that you meant or expected it to have that effect. It was the grand moral you drew from the affair: "I do *abominate* this

way of carrying *pipes* about." Now, that a fellow, after
giving an account of his being so near a burning from a
careless pipe, should wind it up with a grand flourish that
he abominated this way of carrying pipes about, struck me
as being *superfluous* in an irresistibly ludicrous degree. It
communicated to me just about the same amount of *information* as Walter Shandy got from his brother Toby's remark when Toby informed Corporal Trim, in the hearing
of Walter, that he believed the *auxiliaries* with which he
and Trim were acquainted, and those auxiliaries about which
his "brother Shandy" had been speaking, were *different*
things; and if I had been by you when you said it, I
should certainly have given you "brother Shandy's" identical reply—"You do?" That passage in "Tristram" is
not exceeded in humor by anything that I ever heard or
read, and the whole humor of it lies in Shandy's state of
mind, produced by the extreme superfluity of Toby's remark. I insist, therefore, that *if you had had Shandy for
an auditor* when you said you "did abominate this way of
carrying pipes about," it would have been as funny a scene
as the one just referred to between the Shandy brothers.
Did you ever try to analyze the fun of that passage? It is
worth the trouble. Toby's palpable and patient superfluity
is a funny thing in itself, in the first place; and so is *yours*.
In the next place, his mode of expression *implies*, that however the idea might have been in his mind before that time,
in a vague, chaotic form, it had come to development but
very lately before it was formally announced; and so does
yours. So far, the parallel is complete—not one whit against
you. But the cream of the joke in Toby's instance could
not be matched in yours, unless you had had Shandy for an
auditor, for it consists in the very peculiar state of mind
induced in him. Toby had just said a most ludicrous thing;
but the moral is, that it did not strike his brother in a ludicrous light. His reply, "You do!" is exceedingly suggestive of a state of mind which he had rapidly passed
through, as well as the one at which he had then arrived.
The first feeling excited in his mind evidently had been
contempt for Toby's slowness in coming so late to an idea
which Shandy certainly believed had been in his own mind
ever since he was born, and this first feeling had been
quickly tempered by pity, which instantly cast a glance

into the future, and saw no hope of *amendment for Toby*
there; then it was that despair entered into his mind and
he softly said, "You do?" . . . .

[From L. S. to A. H. S.]

SPARTA, February 27, 1860.

DEAR BROTHER—This is another memorable anniversary
with me. To-day, eight years ago, I was married. That
was a brilliant day and brilliant night—the most brilliant, I
have often thought, that I ever saw; and it seems to me
that its annual returns are apt to be of like character. Such
is to-day. I will not write about the thoughts which crowd
upon me with a peculiar force at this time, for they would
only sadden you to read them, and their expression can do
me no good. . . . . . . But it occurs to me at this moment that I will write you a piece of news. We have got
a vigilance committee here. Yesterday they tried a fellow
for uttering abolition sentiments. The culprit was a native
of this county, by the name of Pool. He is a young man,
26 or 28 years old, the son of old Pool, the *shingle-getter*.
He is a poor, ignorant fellow, whose lot in life has rendered
virtue almost an impossibility, and his vices almost a necessity. The proof against him—as I heard the witness, Long,
Mr. Thomas' overseer, detail it to me and two or three
others yesterday in an outside, informal way—was this:
Long met Pool one day going home from Sparta, and asked
him the news in town. Pool replied that he heard Mr.
Edwards read a piece from a newspaper that day about the
abolitionists forming a band to go and turn old John Brown
out of jail, and he had heard that the "Hancock Volunteers" were going to Milledgeville and get arms and "go
on" to help prevent it. He then went on to say that he
thought we were going to have *a war*, and that he thought
that Brown's side would be the strong side, because there
were so many more negroes than there were white folks,
and that when the "war" came, he was going to *take care
of himself by joining the strong side*. He added that he
wished "there weren't no niggers, nohow," for then he
could get more for his work. Long asked him how he
could get to Brown's men when he should undertake to
join them. He said he would *black himself and go to them*

where they were. "Mark you this, sir: he would *black himself.*" This was the proof. Poor Pool denied every bit of it, most bitterly, and swore he was as good a friend to the South as any man who owned a hundred niggers. His denial was as emphatic as old Peter's was, and made, no doubt, for the same reason—to save himself from being hung. Jack Smith, who is one of the "Vigilants," came to me, where I was sitting in the street on a goods box, taking the sun, and talking to Cosby and two or three others, and asked my advice about what was the best to be done with Pool. Whereupon, I gave him my advice, with such a prelude as I hoped might secure its adoption. I told him, for my part, I was not in favor of Lynch-law, but I couldn't help feeling glad whenever I heard of a straggling abolitionist being sent back on his own side of the line *with our mark on him;* that I was perfectly willing to see the rascals fed out of their own spoon by rendering the slavery question a *practical test* to them as they were rendering it to us; and hence, whenever I heard of a strolling Yankee of this class sent back home with a little token to keep us fresh in his memory, and the memory of his friends, I felt that a good work was going on; but that there could be no good accomplished by harshness towards a poor, simple native like Pool. There was nobody to be *annoyed* or corrected by it, except a few other simple people of his own class, whose sympathies would only be increased by a martyr in their own class, however their tongues might be stilled by the terror of the example; that such fellows as he were to be watched and taken care of when a conflict might be thrust upon us by a far different class of men; but that he never could *produce* the conflict, nor start the first ripple towards the first move; that he certainly was not a *dangerous* man, whatever his wishes might be; for there wasn't a negro in the county with so little sense as to be fooled into trouble by such a fellow as Pool. The conclusion to which I came from all this was, that it would have been best, perhaps, to have said nothing about it in the first instance; but as they had noticed it *officially*, the best thing now was to *lecture* him, and turn him loose on good behavior. Jack went off to rejoin his associates with an evident intent, as I thought, to advocate the course I had advised. John B——, who had been standing in ear-shot, came up as soon as Jack had left, and in a tone of remonstrance against the advice I had given, said: "Well, I tell you what it is, when they get so far along as to talk about *blacking themselves*, sir, I'll tell you, sir, something ought to be done with them." I laughed and Cosby laughed. The result of Pool's case was that he was lectured and turned loose. I believe the lecturing was done by Jack Smith. Cosby was not pleased with my views about strolling Yankees. He is an extreme conservative, and undertook to argue the question with me. He said my position—that I myself would not administer Lynch-law—was an acknowledgment that Lynch-law was wrong. I told him, in the first place, I had only said I was not in favor of Lynch-law—that is, that I was not its advocate; but while I was not prepared to say that I would myself administer it in any case whatever, I was equally unprepared to say that I would not administer it in any conceivable case; on the contrary, I was inclined to think there might be cases in which it would be right, and in which I would myself administer it; but that my rejoicing to hear of its administration, in a temperate style upon strolling Yankees sometimes, was independent of the question of whether it was right or wrong in the person who administers it; that my rejoicing might be right while their act might be wrong. He said he couldn't understand that morality; and as you may have a similar difficulty, allow me to lengthen out this letter, already too long, to justify my position. You may find me wandering into some curious abstractions, but you must be patient. I prefer that you should read them and set them right if they should be wrong, rather than throw them aside because they are wrong. Did you ever read Bulwer's "Eugene Aram?" If so, you of course remember the splendid sophistry by which Aram satisfied himself that he might justifiably kill the old miser in order to get his money and make a good use of it. It is, as I have called it, truly a sophistry, but it contained much truth, and is logically separated from the conclusion at which it arrives, only by a single fallacy, at the very last link of the chain. I speak from memory, unrefreshed within twenty years or more; but I think every link in the chain is a good one, except the last. According to all human apprehension, it would have been a good thing for the money

to get out of the hands of the miser, where it did no good
to himself nor anybody else, into the hands of the benefi-
cent Aram, whose large charity was withheld from its mission of blessings, and his genius restrained from its career
of usefulness, only by penury. It would have been a good
thing for him to get the money, but it was not right for
him, as he concluded it was, to kill the old miser and take
it. If the old fellow had died in the course of nature, and
left his money to Aram, everybody would have said that a
good thing had happened, and everybody would have been
glad to *hear that the old man was dead*, if it had been known
beforehand that he had a will in Aram's favor—glad to
hear that he *was dead*, but glad not *because* he was dead, but
because Aram would get the money. So, if the old fellow,
with such a will on hand, had been *killed* by some great
scoundrel who had missed being hung long before, from
want of evidence, and not want of dues, the people would
have still rejoiced to hear that he was dead, (however, a
thrill of horror might have passed over them,) not *because*
he was dead, but still because Aram would get the money,
and a great scoundrel, besides, would get his long-delayed
deserts. They would all have said the great scoundrel had
done a great crime, and they would have hung him for it,
and there would have been regrets and pity for the poor
murdered old man ; but the whole drama, when played out,
would have caused more pity than sorrow, and anybody
who *could have foreseen the end* would have felt the joy as
soon as the curtain was raised. A good man would have
given his voice for hanging the murderer who opened the
drama, and yet would have rejoiced that it was opened *because* of the results which he could foresee would necessarily come as a consequence of the opening. Now, you may
begin to perceive why I may rejoice when I hear of a
strolling Yankee being sent across Mason and Dixon's
Line in a coat of tar and feathers. I rejoice, not in the
poor fellow's pain, whether he be guilty or innocent, but
because I foresee that his treatment will either bring his
deluded friends to a sense of justice, by showing them that
justice to us and their own interests are one and the same
thing, or will madden them into the disruption of a government which has become an instrument of our annoyance and torture, instead of our security and protection. I

might even condemn the men who play such fantastic tricks, and yet be glad the tricks are played. I might not be willing to do the deed myself, because I might feel that it was wrong, and yet be glad that it was done, because I foresee that its fruit will be good. The philosophy of the idea is about this: there is in the world plenty of dirty work which needs to be done, and which is well done, provided it be done by dirty fellows. About the same philosophy is taught by that Scripture which declares (in substance) that "offenses must needs come, but woe unto him by whom they come!" . . . .

[From L. S. to A. H. S.]

LANCASTER, January 29, 1860.

DEAR BROTHER—Soon after finishing my letter to you day before yesterday, I went for Becky according to expectation. I stopped here on my way to see Mr. Thomas, and found him quite ill. I went on, however, and got Becky, and Mollie, and Genie. Mr. Thomas got worse in my absence, and sent Bill to hurry me back; when I met Bill, I hurried on there as fast as I could, and on getting here found Mr. Thomas in great pain with his head—not sick headache, but a headache, resulting, I think, from nervous prostration. I sent for Alfriend, who soon came. He staid until after dinner yesterday, and then went home and sent his brother, who staid until early this morning. Mr. Thomas is now greatly better. Of course, I did not go home, and the children and I have been here ever since we came from the school. My opinion of Mr. Thomas' case is, that it is the result of the sudden withdrawal of the stimulant to which his system had become accustomed. He has been suffering more or less in the same way ever since the first attack about which I wrote you soon after his return from the Southwest. What sustained him during the trip was, I think, the excitement of travel and looking after his lands. He also passed safely through the period of our adjourned court here, borne up, as he doubtless was, by the excitement of court and the company he saw. When that excitement was withdrawn, the collapse came; such is my theory. I told him so to-day, but he expressed his dissent from it. My own judgment is decided on the point; hence my prescription was different from the doctors. They, as usual, put him on starvation. I recommended a generous diet, in moderate quantities, and he has accordingly been on oysters since yesterday evening. He says the oysters are curing him. He is certainly greatly relieved. I have also recommended nitric acid as a tonic, and he is going to try it. The doctors have now come very fully into my line of treatment, and have made an addition to it this morning in the form of a nervine stimulant composed of ammonia and valerian. To me, the case seems to involve nothing but plain sailing; the system ought to be built up by tonics and generous diet, carefully and moderately used. The mind, too, needs to be doctored, even more than the body. I have managed him with a skill that greatly pleased me, because it has worked good results, and has worked them in the precise way I anticipated. I have contrived to get him mounted on the *oyster* sensation, with a most confident faith in its virtue. He is now riding the oyster *hobby* beautifully; in fact, he needs a little watching to keep him from jading the animal. I go along with him to regulate his paces, and he allows me to do so without any resistance. One great point in my programme is to keep the doctors *well abused*. Last night I got my mail, and in it three, yes four, letters from you. I now have got all that you addressed to me at Macon. . . . .

What was there to make you *laugh* in the editorial on you from the Louisville *Journal?* I don't understand your *laughing*. Was it the artful use the fellow made of circumstances to guild his notions about you in the lines of probability? I suppose so, but I am in doubt. This editorial doesn't very well support Dr. Bush's declaration, which I read to-day in a letter from him to Mr. Thomas, to the effect that the editor of the *Journal* is for you for the Presidency. Bush declares himself to be for you, and says you would be exceedingly acceptable to Kentucky. He says he wants Georgia to press you before the Charleston Convention.

. . . .
The meeting between me and Becky, the other day, was quite an event for both of us; she met me 300 yards before I got to the house, and was almost out of breath. I do not remember to have felt such a gush of real, bounding, childish joy at any time within twenty years, as I did when

19*

she sprang into my arms. Her own joy was irresistibly infectious. The very first words she uttered were these, between her puffing and panting for exhaustion: "Papa, I'm (puff) learning (puff) fast." "Bless the darling" was my response as I enfolded her again in my arms, and almost squeezed out of her what breath she had left. You may think I *cried*, but I didn't; I was *too* glad to cry. I desired very much to see the meeting between her and her little sisters, but I missed it. The day was so cold and windy that I put her in the carriage instead of the buggy with me, and after meeting Bill, I made such haste as to leave the carriage far behind. So I was in Mr. Thomas' room when the carriage arrived here, and the children had got together before I was aware of its arrival. They were very, very glad to see each other; but from what I heard, the meeting between them was not so demonstrative as I had expected it to be. I think Becky's meeting with me had taken off somewhat of the edge of her joy. After that, there was something approaching a sort of collapse. I think that the new associations of the school have already had a very visible improving effect upon her. I would give you divers instances of things I have heard her say, to make good the proof of my assertion, but I have got sense enough to know that I am a fool, and so keep my folly to myself. . . . . This letter has been written without any fire; and though the weather has greatly moderated in a day or two, still it is cold enough to render it desirable to hunt a fire, after so long sitting without one; so I will hasten to an end.

I have just heard to-day of a place in Jefferson county, which I think will suit me, and I am going on Tuesday (if nothing happens unforeseen to prevent) to look at it It is about eight or nine miles from Louisville, on the road from the Shoals (of Ogechee) to Louisville, on Rocky Comfort creek. It is known as the old Cobb place, and is now owned by Bob Phinizy, of Augusta. There are four thousand acres of it, and his price is four dollars per acre. I hear that it is capital land; if so, this is even a better bargain than Simpson's purchase of the Fitz-Simmons place. I am obliged to have another place. I do not need so much as 4,000 acres more, but I don't object to the quantity at all. *Land* is going to be *land* in this country—that is my judgment; so now for the fire. You said you wanted to get a *cheerful* letter from me. This is, I think, on the whole, a pretty cheerful one, and a faithful copy of my thoughts while I have been writing it. Good-bye.

Affectionately, LINTON.

[From L. S. to A. H. S.]

SPARTA, October 14, 1864.

DEAR BROTHER—No letter from you yesterday. In my letter of yesterday, I forgot to say that one of yours, whose reception I acknowledged, was the one containing the sad news of the death of poor Dick Greer.* I am truly pained at this news. Poor Dick was characterized by a frankness and honesty that made me like him very much from a boy up; and then he seemed to have a relish for life, which renders his early death peculiarly sad. Poor Dick! Well do I remember the trip which he and his mother took with me from their house to Hamilton, when he was a baby in his mother's arms. Well do I remember, too, some of the incidents of that trip, which owed their origin to his state of babyhood. . . . . Dick was more closely associated with his mother, in my memory, than any other of her children, and death is a renewal to me of my sense of her loss. Poor Dick! Truly do I mourn his untimely fall.

Poor Catharine! Poor Catharine! How vividly do I remember her death-stricken face as we saw it in the coffin— reposing calm and pale amidst the framing of premature gray hair, which spoke of affliction and pain long endured before death's kind release! Oh, God! how sharp the pang that flashes through my breast from the memory of that mournful sight! . . . .

I am reminded to tell you of a talk which the children and I had on the way to Mr. Thomas' the last time we went there. It started from a sudden remark which Claude made about you. She said, "Papa, if uncle Ellic was a school-teacher, his scholars wouldn't learn any-thing." "Why not?" said I. "Because," said she, "he'd tell 'em everything." I thought it was a decidedly good

---

* A nephew killed in the battle near Winchester, Virginia.

hit on you. That remark led us into a talk about their school and their studies, and to some questions from me as to how each of them was getting on in each study. When I struck Becky on her arithmetic, Emm put in her oar. Said she, "Papa, sister Becky has got to be nearly as bad as ———. She most always *misses* her 'rithmetic lessons." Against this very pointed assertion, Becky entered a vehement protest. Without stopping to settle the dispute, I asked Emm how it was with ———? In answering this question, she went into a vein of humor almost as rich as I ever heard from Mr. Toombs, or your Bob, and very much of the same kind which I have often seen displayed by those two masters of the art. I can't give you much idea of it, because the best part of it consisted in her *mimicry* of poor ———'s actions while undergoing the torture of having a very bad recitation wrung out of her. I can only give you a point or two in words, leaving you to imagine the exquisite mimicry by which the words were accompanied. " ———," said she, "why, she *always misses*. When uncle Carlos gives her a question in 'rithmetic, she just goes to saying the question over, and over, and over, and counts on her fingers this way," (mimicking). "Then she stops saying over the question, but keeps on counting with her fingers, and goes to working her lips as hard as she can, this away; then uncle Carlos tells her, 'I don't hear you;' then she works her lips and counts her fingers faster than ever, but don't say a word. At last, uncle Carlos * tells her the answer; and then she *jumps* this away, (mimicking,) and says: 'Mr. Stevens, I was jest agoing to say that!'"

This will give you an idea. Poor L.——— would have been sorely mortified if she had seen herself as portrayed by Emm. There was not, however, the slightest tinge of bad nature in a single one of the many pungent strokes; it was all pure *fun*. Poor ———'s agonies could not possibly have a keener or more appreciative eye to observe them than Emm showed she had had, hanging over them like a bee over a flower to gather its sweets. The child

---

* Rev. Carlos W. Stevens, who taught a select school of girls and young ladies. He married the aunt of Linton's children; hence, they called him uncle.

gets this talent from her mother, who had it in a higher degree, I think, than anybody—certainly than any woman—I ever knew. . . . .

"The old man Anthony," to whom reference is made in the following letter, is the Rev. Samuel Anthony, of the Methodist Church, so well known in Georgia, and so much beloved and respected by a multitude of acquaintances throughout the State. He, Rev. Mr. Jackson, and Mr. Benjamin T. Harris, had spent an evening at Judge Stephens' house:

[From L. S. to A. H. S.]

SPARTA, February 7, 1860.

DEAR BROTHER— . . . . When the old man Anthony bade me good-bye, he kept my hand in his for a few moments, and said to me: "Don't you forget the one thing needful—you need religion to bring up these little ones right." I think I give his very words. The tears started in his eyes, and I confess they started in mine, too. I have always thought that he was a good man, and I have a very great respect for his old-fashioned, out-spoken piety. He used to be a prime favorite of uncle Jack's. . . . . You may be curious to know whether the old gentleman recognized me or not at sight. He did, but his memory had been refreshed by seeing me on two occasions since he used to see me at uncle Jack's—once at Liberty camp-meeting, (in Greene,) in 1847, and again in Macon last summer. He is a remarkable man in some particulars—remarkable for his simple piety, and being totally devoid of what is properly called ambition; but perhaps not least remarkable for his marvelous state of physical preservation. He looks just as he used to look a quarter of a century ago, when he must have then been at least thirty-five years old. He is sixty at least now, but scarcely seems to be forty. . . . .

[From L. S. to A. H. S.]

SPARTA, February 8, 1860.

DEAR BROTHER— . . . . You asked me in one of your late letters whether I had read Mrs.

Bryan's "Lovable Heroines." I have read it, and most heartily indorse it. Her criticism on Beulah expressed my sentiments exactly, so far as it went. She is an uncommonly sensible woman—a real woman—only more of a woman than most of her sex, and, therefore, a better specimen of it. I have thought more of her since I have heard that she inclines to *fat*, because that gives me assurance that she is a flesh and blood woman—none of your pining, poetical shadows that live upon moonbeams and dewdrops. . . . .

The gifted authoress above referred to is Mrs. Mary E. Bryan—now (1876) at the head of the literary department of *The Sunny South*.

[From L. S. to A. H. S.]

SPARTA, February 11, 1860.

DEAR BROTHER—To-day, I got your letter of yesterday, and yesterday evening, on my return from bringing Becky home, I got one of the day before. And this is another anniversary of the day of your birth. You were born forty-eight years ago. Oh! what crowds and floods of events that you can number, and what innumerable myriads more, of which you knew nothing, have transpired in that period of forty-eight years! Oh! it is a long, *long* time! but I am not in a moralizing mood to-day. The day has so far (and it is now four o'clock in the afternoon) been an unusually pleasant one to me. That part of it which has been most so was spent with my children. At this very moment, I hear their busy little feet pattering down the stair-steps that go up from the library door. They have been up stairs on some raid or other, I suppose. Becky's return home yesterday was quite an event to her and her little sisters, and, most of all, to the negroes. In coming home, she repeatedly urged me to make Charlie go faster, sometimes in a direct way, and at other times by insinuation. For instance: she asked me once, with a cunning smile, which was the best to make Charlie go fast—whipping or clucking. . . . . Have you seen Mr. Toombs' speech? It is one of great power. It is the worst drubbing that I have ever seen administered to the Republicans. . . . . I was much amused at your quarrel with the common mode of designating colds, pains, etc., as *my* cold, *my* headache, etc., but I hardly think you made good your point. I think, after all, there is a property in the things, though they may be, as you say, our decided enemies. It is an involuntary and disagreeable property, but still it is a property. The mode of speech which you criticise is carried so far, and properly carried so far, as to say—*my enemy*, *my trouble*, my grief, etc. The epithet "my" is not necessarily one of endearment, but it is one of property; it expresses a *peculium* you have in the pain, or in the enmity—a stock which is yours, etc. I have just got your letter of yesterday, your birthday. I am glad to know that your cold has got better—or rather, that you have got better of your cold—that you are gaining ground on your enemy. All well to-day. It is a bright, beautiful day, but rather cold. . . . .

[From L. S. to A. H. S.]

SPARTA, February 16, 1860.

DEAR BROTHER—My dinner is just over; and not feeling inclined to do any work this afternoon, I turn to you for a little pleasant occupation. No letter from you to-day. I missed the accustomed visitor a good deal. This morning, I sent you a long letter, written yesterday, with a postscript added this morning. It reinclosed to you the letter which you sent me from Mr. Toombs. While I think of it, let me mention several letters which I have written to you, but of which you have made no mention. It is possible that you have acknowledged some of them by their *dates*, for I don't keep much account of dates in the ordinary run of days; but you have not acknowledged all of them, either by dates or accounts, or other marks of identity. One is the letter in which I commented on your recently developed "abomination of this way of carrying pipes about," and also gave an analysis of the humor in a certain scene in Sterne's two Shandy brothers, and asked you if I had not given you an analysis of that same thing at some former time. Did you get that letter? Another is the letter enclosing Mr. Crittenden's letter to you and a

copy of your reply to it.   I made some remarks on your
reply, mostly in a laughing vein.   I remember I said your
speculations about "organ-issues" struck me very much as
Jenkinsons learning about the "Cosmogony of Creation"
struck the old vicar in jail.   It seemed to me I had heard
something very much like that before.   You have made
no allusion to that letter.   Did you get it?   When a fellow
writes a letter intended to produce a laugh, and never hears
from it, he feels about as flat as he does when he attempts
a joke in company, and gets no response from the company.
That is a very bad feeling; I don't know whether you ever
had it or not—I have.   Another letter, from which I have
never heard a word, was the one about the night spent with
me by Mr. Thomas, and the old crazy professor.   Besides
these, there are yet others, but I do not now remember
them.   I am inclined to think that you never received
them.   Silence from me on such matters would not mean
so much as your silence does, for you are usually very careful about acknowledging letters, while I am generally very
remiss.   Well, to change the subject: I have just turned a
beggar away from my door without a cent; I don't believe
I ever did so before.   He was a great big strapping fellow,
who came to me with a "paper."   I took it in my hand,
but read only enough of it to confirm me in my supposition that it was a begging paper, and then handed it back
to him, remarking that I had nothing to give him.   He
then drew out and offered to me a memorandum book and
pencil, and said, in pretty good broken English, that the
sum he asked of me "was but small."   I did not take the
book, but replied to him, "I do not wish to give you anything."   He bowed with an air that might have become an
offended prince, and retired without a word.   Isn't it a curious thing that such transparent scamps should be offended
at a refusal?   The offense certainly is on the other side, for
the presentation of one of their "papers" to a man is a
plain impeachment of his understanding.   The action put
into words means exactly this: "I take you to be fool
enough to give me something."   As I turned from the door,
after dismissing the beggar Claude and Emm came running out of the nursery to meet me, their little faces all
radiant with glee, and ready for a frolic.   Transparent and
certain as was the unworthiness of the application which I

had just refused, yet the sight of my children immediately suggested to me that the poor fellow, too, might have little ones, and that if so, they were probably in want and wretchedness, while mine were so bright and happy. What made the difference, except the accidents of life? All these thoughts passed through my mind like a flash, and for one instant I felt something like a pang of repentance. But reflection immediately corrected it, and I allowed the begging impostor to go on his empty way. . . . .

Hon. Iverson L. Harris, formerly one of the Justices of the Supreme Court of the State, in a letter from Milledgeville, dated 11th of November, 1873, in forwarding, under the published notice of the author of this memoir, some letters he had received from Judge Stephens, uses the following language:

"One of his letters, commenting on Bailey's Essay on Truth, and on the formation and publication of opinions, evinces such power of intellect in treating that difficult subject—belief in miracles—that I ever thought it ought to go before the public. So highly have I ever appreciated it, that I ventured to read it to distinguished churchmen, that they might learn to correct their answers to Hume. It impressed them favorably. In my poor judgment, it gives the only true answer to Hume which a great logical mind can give. I esteem it as an *original* answer, displaying a vigor and profundity of thought which placed, at a bound, Judge Stephens with the highest class of thinkers. . . . "I not only admired his high intellect and manly character, but really loved him. I would have gone to Sparta to have evinced my regard when he was committed to mother earth, but disease forbade the attempt. I desired very much to have been at Atlanta when General Toombs offered his report and resolutions, designed as some slight memorial. I could not have sat silently by." . . . . .

Here follows the letter alluded to:
20*

[L. S. to Hon. Iverson L. Harris.]

SPARTA, April 21, 1860.

MY DEAR SIR—On returning home last Saturday night, from court at Atlanta, I found your highly appreciated letter of the 31st ultimo. I was called home by the illness of one of my children, and have since been so weary and spiritless that I have not, until now, undertaken to bring up my correspondence, which had fallen in arrears during my absence. Instead of *one sick child*, I found all *three* of my children quite unwell, and two of them decidedly sick. I am glad to be able to say now that they are all on foot again, with a fair promise of complete restoration to their usual excellent health.

I will carry you the books, as you request, when I go over to court. My brother and I have both finished reading them, as you supposed; and for myself, I will say that the reading of them has been of decided advantage to me. The fairness, and candor, and courage which mark them cannot fail to exert a happy influence upon any mind whose vocation is the investigation of *truth*. The *spirit* of the work (for the two books are but parts of one work) is just such as ought to characterize every *judge*. And now, having said thus much of the work, I must say more to avoid a misunderstanding of my *opinion* concerning it. The *spirit* of it is fine, and its scaffolding of rules and preliminary reasoning, admirable; but the conclusion to which it mounts from these premises, I regard as almost inexcusably illogical. That conclusion, as you know, is that a miracle cannot be established by human testimony. The author takes Mr. Hume's definition of a miracle, to wit, a violation of the laws of nature, and then concludes that human testimony is inadequate to establish a violation, because the violation involves a departure from the *uniformity* of *causation*. The uniformity of causation he rightly assumes as a necessary truth which the mind cannot be made to doubt by any possible accumulation of human testimony. Now, I remark, in the first place, that if his argument is good, it proves much more than he claims it proves—not only that a miracle cannot be established by human testimony, but that a miracle is absolutely *incredible*, *impossible*, beyond the power of God. I do not say this consequence proves the argument unsound, but I state the consequence merely to aid a full conception of the argument itself.   There is no covert in which a fallacy is more apt to lurk than in a *definition*. So in this case, I think, the whole error lies in defining a miracle to be a violation of the laws of nature.   Nor do I perceive that the churchmen have helped the matter the least in the world by defining it to be, not a violation, but only a *suspension* of the laws of nature.   This is no nearer the truth than the other is, nor does it at all escape from the force of the argument; for a *suspension* of the laws of nature is a departure from the uniformity of causation just as certainly as a *violation* is such a departure.   The truth expressed by the term, "uniformity of causation," is that the same *cause*, or combination of causes, will *invariably*, *infallibly* and *necessarily* produce the *same effects*. Now, to say that the laws of nature are *suspended* is simply to say that the very same combination of causes, which heretofore invariably produced a given effect, is still *present*, but is no longer followed by its appropriate effect—that is to say, that causation has ceased to be uniform, and the uniformity of causation ceases to be a truth.   I think, there-fore, that a "suspension" affords no escape from the con-clusion to which. we are inevitably led, starting from Mr. Hume's definition.   I think the truth is that his defini-tion, as well as that of the churchmen, is both erroneous and *highly unphilosophical*.   The miracles to which these definitions relate are those recorded in the Scriptures. Now, these neither involve, nor *profess* to involve, either any violation or suspension of the uniformity of causation. They are only exhibitions of extraordinary and superhuman power, differing from the ten thousand other daily exhibi-tions of such superhuman power in nothing but this: they were given to man as a witness for the truths and teachings that accompanied them.   The miracles of the gospel imply no more *power* than we see exhibited by nature every day of our lives.   The *causes*, or *combination of causes*, which produce these results are in both classes of cases equally *hid from us*, the result being designed for a special object in the one case, and, in the other case, the object being often as obscure to us as the cause is.   To say of any event or phenomenon, that it violates the uniformity of causation, *assumes* that we knew with *certainty* the *exact combination of causes* operating in the case—an assumption which, so far from being true, would be absolutely false in almost, if not indeed in every case of a natural phenomenon.   Our author puts a case: He says that it would be an incredible thing if all the witnesses in the world should state that they had seen ice fail to melt when exposed to a white heat.   His argument is that any man, having once seen ice melt in a white heat, cannot afterwards be made to doubt that it will always melt under the same circumstances, because it is a necessary truth that the same cause will always produce the same effect.   He quietly *assumes* that the cause is the *same*—no more, no less—but the identical same cause which he has seen produce the effect of melting ice. Such an assumption seems to me to be highly unphilosophical.   It amounts to an assumption that there can be no causes at work in a given case, except such as are *patent to the human senses*.   For poor little mole-sighted man to declare that, in any given case, there is no single cause in operation, except such as he wots of, is just about as ridiculous and arrogant as if the ant from the top of his hill should deny that he was moving at an immensely rapid rate, upon the ground that no such motion was sensible to the very acute wisdom of his antship.   I remember reading a story once of an East Indian Chief, who was utterly incredulous when an English officer told him that he had often seen water in a solid state.   He thought the fact asserted involved a departure from the uniformity of causation, and he rejected it as spurious.   His error was in *assuming* that his own experience was sufficient to enable him to know all the causes in operation, and that it was *impossible* there could have been any cause unknown to him.   I have no idea that Jesus raised Lazarus from death, or fed the multitude, or himself arose from the dead, by either violating or suspending the law of causation, but he did all these things by using causes and agencies which were entirely beyond their comprehension.   The Godhead stood revealed, not by results without adequate cause, but by the use of agencies which defied human power to command them. The truly philosophic spirit is cautious about pronouncing an *impossibility*.   There is quite as much lack of philosophy in believing too reluctantly, or in refusing to believe at all, as there is in believing too easily.   True wisdom neither rejects as impossible nor adopts as true, except according to *evidence*. The range of real *impossibility* is exceedingly limited. I should not be at all surprised if you and I should live until the progress of science shall render the skepticism of our author concerning the melting of ice quite as ludicrous as we already know that the skepticism of the Indian Chief was concerning its existence. The chemist may yet be able to hold ice in a white heat without melting, by the use of some agency at present unknown to science, and also imperceptible to the human senses.

But I must stop and beg your pardon for having gone into the reasons why I dissent from the conclusion of the author of the work under consideration. After all, I have only given you an outline of my views; but all I set out to do was simply to express my dissent without any reasons at all. I must repeat, in conclusion of these remarks upon the work, that the *spirit* of it is very fine, and highly essential in every man engaged in the pursuit of truth.

I feel very much gratified that you concur with me in my views of drunkenness in accusations of crime. I never felt more confidence in the soundness of a conclusion, and in the soundness of a process of reasoning, by which I arrived at a conclusion. That men, who are opposed to drunkenness and in favor of good morals, and a wholesome administration of the laws, should abuse the decision, as many such men have done, can be explained only by their ignorance of what the decision really accomplishes. They are indignant because the decision declares that drunkenness may be considered in investigating whether an act has been done, or if done, with what intent it was done; but they utterly forget that the light which drunkenness casts is sometimes *against* the accused, and that the decision, therefore, declares a principle which not only protects the guiltless, but also uncovers the guilty. But most of all, they forget, or rather they do not perceive, that this decision puts the punishment of drunken men upon a ground perfectly consistent with reason and humanity, and, therefore, greatly breaks down the reluctance with which juries inflict the punishment. The decision explodes the idea prevalent, even among judges and law-writers, that a very drunk man has not mind enough to furnish the mental element in crime, and is punished by virtue of a constructive capacity

infused into him by law.   *The* best account which even Mr.
Bishop, the latest and most scientific writer on the subject,
has been able to give of the reasonableness of punishing a
drunken man is, that he has not sufficient mind to commit
the crime at the time when he does the act, yet his *intent
to get drunk* is an unlawful intent, and coalesces with the
act when done, and so gives it a criminal quality.   Would
not you shudder at hanging a man for a drunken action, if
you could not give any better justification than that for
your conduct?   If I had to say what was the greatest merit
of the decision, my answer would be, that it has rescued
the doctrine of punishing drunken men from the miserable
sophism by which it has been heretofore defended, and has
placed it on a *new* and *rational* ground, and so has greatly
contributed to the advancement of public justice.   But my
sheet is out.

Yours, most truly and respectfully,

LINTON STEPHENS.

P. S.—After the approbation of his own conscience, the
next dearest reward to a faithful public servant is the approbation of those to whom his service is rendered; and I
therefore do not consider it out of taste to tell you what I
have heard of *you*.   My brother told me that your charge
to the jury in the negro murder case in Greene was the
ablest he ever heard given to a jury on the law of homicide.   He said he sometimes differed with your rulings,
but he was delighted with your administration, and that
you had made great progress in the good opinions of your
bar.   DeGraffenreid (Wm. K.) told me, at Atlanta the
other day, that your bar—and he thought the people, too—
were greatly pleased with your administration.   One point
which they both selected for special praise was your *independence* and fairness.   There are few men to whom I would
write as I have written to you; but it is only your *due*, and
if a friend may not tell you of pleasant things, who may?

[From L. S. to A. H. S.]

SPARTA, February 19, 1860.

DEAR BROTHER—This is Sunday evening about 5 o'clock.
Mr. Thomas has just gone home.   He and I went to the

Methodist Church to-day to hear Bishop Pierce preach. It was a good sermon, and about as rich in language and illustration as any I ever heard from him. His text was the exhortation of Barnabas to the Church at Antioch to cleave unto God with purpose of heart. The purpose of heart was a *full* purpose, reserving nothing, but determined in *all* things to do the will of God. One of his figures was, that, as to himself, he had felt this purpose as a wall of adamant on the one side, and the other, the world, the flesh and the Devil, shutting them out, and shutting him in, in moral safety, etc. . . . .

When we, or rather when I returned home from church, I found your long letter of yesterday. This is the longest letter I ever got from you, or anybody else. I had read it almost half through when dinner was announced, but I finished it before I went to dinner. It touched many points, and they were all interesting to me. It was a deeply interesting letter to me. The theme in it, the *most* interesting, was my children. What you think of them was partly suspected before, if not fully comprehended, but I confess that its expression was to me a savor of exceeding sweetness. I think it will do me good all the days of my life, unless, indeed, my children should hereafter force me to abandon my own estimate of how well they merit the opinions you have expressed concerning them. It is one of the greatest pleasures I have to see them love and reverence you, and feel that they are worthy of your high estimate of them. There is one subject in your letter on which I will make a remark while it is in my mind. I allude to what you say about your *silence* as to some of my late pleasantries which you say were made at your expense, and therefore did not make you laugh. Now, I never expected you to acknowledge them by saying that you had *laughed* over them. I never expected you to do more than acknowledge "a touch," as the fencers do when touched by the foil—the foil that covers the sharp point that would make a wound but for the friendly covering. Now, the humor of my hits at you, if humor there was, was the point, and my playful motive the covering which disarmed it of its power to pierce. . . . .

[From L. S. to A. H. S.]

SPARTA, February 23, 1860.

DEAR BROTHER— . . . . In my last
letter, I intended to say a great many things which occurred
to me at the time, but which I was not in the mood to say
then.   I was in one of my states when nothing seems to be
worth the doing of it, and when I hastened, therefore, to
the end of my letter.   One of the omitted things was that
I had read the article in the *Westminster*, on "Social Or-
ganism," before I got your letter about it, and had formed
the distinct intention of calling your attention to it, as showing an almost marvelous coincidence with your views on
that subject.   I was very much struck with the coincidence,
but not half so much with the speculation itself, as I have
with *some* of your speculations in conversation and letters
on the same theme.   It was truly tedious, as you characterized it, and I did not read the whole of it.   I read
enough to perfectly get the run of it.   There are a great
many things which, in this day of *words*, WORDS, WORDS,
I read in the same way.   They are such things as I am not
willing to leave totally unread, and yet, which I cannot
afford to peruse through all of the platitudes, and common-
places, and repetitions which are employed to invest them.
I therefore pick out such of the real grains as are obvious
to inspection, and leave all the rest as chaff.   No doubt my
leavings of chaff often contain some grains of wheat. . .
Have you seen "A. B.'s" echo of the "Cato-like lamen-
tations" of "that virtuous magistrate," Judge Holt, over
the abomination of desolation that will result from the decision of the Supreme Court in poor Jones' case?   I saw
it in a very *conspicuous place in the Constitutionalist* yesterday.
"That virtuous magistrate!"   To say the least of it, that
is a very easy virtue which manifests itself in punishing the
crimes of other people, and that virtue is still more easy
which inflicts the punishment without troubling itself to investigate whether the crime has been committed or not.
To the practice of this virtue, nothing is requisite, but free
rein to a savage heart.   The natural gravitation of malice
and blood-thirstiness will accomplish the result.   "*Facilis
descensus Averni.*"   To the honor of mankind, this "species"
of "virtue" is rare, and when found is generally worked

up as the material for *executioners*. I am afraid I shall lose
my patience under demagogical censures of my public acts.
It is hard to remain peaceful under misrepresentation and
obloquy, when you are conscious of holding a rod which
could smite your assailant. It is hard to even bide your
time. I can do it, but I say it is *hard?* . . . .

[From L. S. to A. H. S.]

SPARTA, February 29, 1860.

DEAR BROTHER— . . . . I have
finished the opinion in Jones' case. I just concluded to
throw overboard my beautiful theory, indicating the con-
sistency of the law in punishing drunk men for murder.
It costs me a pang to do it; for I have got quite in love
with it. I think it would give me more reputation with intellectual people than anything else I have written; but it
makes the opinion too long. I think the sacrifice is needed,
and I shall make it. You can't know how much virtue I
am showing, unless you knew *what a good thing it is.* . .

There is a great clamor about this decision among the
people, I hear. Several men in this county say they are
against the court on account of it. I suppose it is so else-
where. Let it be so. I am rather glad of it; I know they
can't stand the argument. I think my day will come, but
I would rather have my day, *as it is*, than theirs. I am right
and know it, and have demonstrated it. All the clamors
of Bedlam—and the clamors of this world are Bedlam
clamors—can't make me regret it, or doubt it. I will not
say I have contempt for the opinions of mankind, for that
is not the feeling. I prefer to have their favorable opinions,
and do many things to obtain them. It is more pleasant
on many accounts to have their opinions on your side; but
I do have an utter *disregard* for them as an index of truth.
There are several men whose opinions against my own
would lead me to examine mine with great care—that is
all. I have often done so before, and changed my opinion
on re-examination; but even that has been in cases where
I had not before made much, if any, special examination.
The *clamors* of a *mob*, however large and respectable in the
general acceptance of the term, would scarcely have *that*
effect. They would not make me re-examine when I had

21 *

examined the case well before, but would, where the first examination had been slight, and the opinion formed on it not strong. . . . .

The decision referred to in the two foregoing letters was the celebrated one pronounced by him in the case of Jones *vs.* The State, noted so conspicuously in Judge Bleckley's paper, given on a preceding page.

[From L. S. to A. H. S.]

SPARTA, March 5, 1860.

DEAR BROTHER— . . . . I this evening finished the opinion in Jones' case, and turned it over to Charley to copy for me. I will send you a copy by Wednesday's mail, I hope. It is fourteen pages long, but I think the public will read it. I have put it in readable shape for the general reader. I had a much greater affection for the bantling several days ago than I have now. I still think I have cut the Gordian knot about punishing drunken men for their actions, consistently with general legal principles, and of yet allowing drunkenness to be used, as an instrument of evidence, to throw light wherever it can throw it, either on the physical or mental element of crime. In other words, it is a satisfactory solution to me of a problem not before solved to my satisfaction. I had intended to write a piece for the newspapers about the clamors against the court, but I have, for the present at least, lost my interest in the subject. . . . .

Who is "Fair Play" that writes in the Macon *Telegraph*, protesting against your name being mixed up with the Presidency? I am sure he expresses your sentiments, and I should like to know who he is. Did I tell you that Jack Lane is going to the Milledgeville convention, but not as a delegate? He said that, as he was one of the executive committee who called the convention, he preferred not to be a delegate. You might write him a letter giving him your wishes in regard to your name being kept entirely out of the convention. . . . .

[From L. S. to A. H. S.]

SPARTA, March 17, 1860.

DEAR BROTHER— . . . . Now, you needed
not to tell me that you would not speak to anybody else,
as you would to me, concerning your speeches; nor did you
need to make the least apology for speaking so to me. I
think it a legitimate pleasure that every man feels in a sense
of having done anything well, and in having others to entertain the same opinion of it. I don't think there is any
indelicacy in expressing one's true opinion of his own performance to another, who is interested in it, and who can
receive the opinion in the same spirit in which it was communicated—knowing full well that men often entertain good
opinions of their performances, whether they express them
or not. You need not hesitate to express to me the best
opinion you may have of anything you may have done, for
it gives me as much pleasure as it does you; and I know,
from experience, it is a pleasure which can never be fully
enjoyed, either on the part of the one or the other, unless
there is some one to share it and sympathize with it.
There is nothing truer, in all my experience, than that all
pleasures are doubled, and all sorrows divided, by being
truly shared with one true and sympathizing heart. I am
glad you like Harris as a judge, and that he is gaining in
the good opinion of his bar. He is a man I like. He has
his own peculiarities, as all *real* men have; and he has, besides, a bottom of sincerity and honor which very *few*
men do have. He is a favorite with me. . . . .

[From L. S. to A. H. S.]

SPARTA, May 1, 1860.

DEAR BROTHER— . . . . I begin to
believe the Charleston Convention will end in a row, and
that Black Republicanism will be triumphant. The Democratic party, instead of being concentrated against the public enemy, presents the spectacle of quarreling about the
ownership of the House, while the burglars are rifling it.

. . . .

[From L. S. to A. H. S.]

MILLEDGEVILLE, May 18, 1860.

DEAR BROTHER—I have been very busy, or I would have written you sooner. Thweatt will to-day send you a telegraphic dispatch which came here for you yesterday, and I inclose you another of the same import, and from the same person, and by one day, of earlier date. I opened them both, in order to see whether they ought to be sent by special messenger. You have, of course, seen Mr. Toombs' letter. You are right about him. His intimation that the Northern Democrats had attempted to interpolate into the party creed the doctrine that a Territorial Legislature has the power to abolish slavery is very extraordinary. *How* did they attempt it? All they wanted was the Cincinnati platform, and this is just the Kansas Bill of 1854 on *that point*—nothing more, nothing less. The platform adopts the bill. When that bill was on its passage, they said then—just what they say now—that the Territorial Legislature would have the power to regulate slavery as they might please. We said not. Each side was willing to trust its own version of the Constitution, out of which the difference of opinion grew; hence, provision was made in the bill for referring the question to the Supreme Court. Mr. Toombs liked that arrangement, and advocated it, when he had no decision of the court on the subject, and no expression of *opinion*. *Now*, he has got a *decision* in his favor so far as the power of the Territorial Legislature can be derived from a transfer by Congress, and the opinion of the court *obiter;* also, upon the power as derived from the principle of self-government. He was content to refer the question to the court in utter ignorance of their opinion, and he is not satisfied now for the reference to stand as it was made, when the court has declared their opinion in his favor. For my part, I like the arrangement none the less since finding that the judge is in my favor. True, Douglas denies that the court has decided his question, and he is right in the denial. But if not decided, it yet remains to be decided according to the original bargain and provisions of the Kansas Bill, and I have quite as much confidence *now* as I had at first in a decision in our favor. The *opinion in our favor* has not impaired my confidence; I am quite as ready now, as I was at first, to tolerate the contrary confidence of our allies. All we can require of them under the agreement is to stand by the decision already made in the one branch of the power, and by that which shall be made on the other branch of it. This they expressly reaffirmed their resolution to do. What more can we require of them without a violation of the understanding? I had a letter from Reese, (of Washington, Wm. M.) and he says your letter expresses his views *exactly*. I hear that Glenn (Cobb's brother-in-law) is against him. I think the letters of Mr. Cobb and Mr. Toombs will do *good* in a way not intended by them. They will break down the Richmond movement by opening the door to be represented at Baltimore. A *new delegation* from Georgia will not secede, and such a new delegation will now go as the representative of both branches of the party. Good-bye.

LINTON STEPHENS.

[From L. S. to A. H. S.]

SAVANNAH, June 15, 1860.

DEAR BROTHER— . . . . As to your request that I may so arrange my will as to provide against a separation of families among your negroes willed to me, I will certainly attend to it if I should outlive you. There is a provision in my present will, applicable to all the negroes I may own at my death, securing them from the separation of families. I intend to change my will in some particulars if I live in health long enough to do so after getting home once more, and I will look carefully to that point. I would like to talk to you about it, not only so far as your negroes are concerned, but as to the proper provision covering all my negroes. . . . . We broke through our new schedule this evening, and, after sitting until 3 o'clock, went back at five and heard arguments until seven. This we did to accommodate the Augusta bar, who had a case in which eight or ten of them were to make speeches, and which they were anxious to finish this evening, and assured us they would finish, if we would go back and hear them after dinner. When we were going back after dinner, Tom Miller said he did not like being brought back after dinner, for he wanted to go to Thunderbolt to get some *crabs*. I told him if he was so unreasonable as to complain of that which he had himself requested, he would be very apt to find crabs *in the court-house*, without going to Thunderbolt for them. This was said in a considerable crowd at the court-house door, just before going in, and the miserable pun raised a great laugh. The laugh subsided, and Judge Lumpkin added, "Yes, sir; and we promise you they shall not be *soft* crabs at that." Again the crowd exploded in a laugh. They really seemed to think all this was excellent wit. Well, the result of our effort to work off the case (which had already been largely argued) was, that we only worked off one speech from Judge Starnes. He spoke two solid hours, and five minutes over, after assuring us that he would not speak an hour, and that they would all get through in two hours. Any man makes a great mistake to speak longer than his promise when he is speaking before a court. After he passes his self-appointed limit, he makes the judges mad and impatient. They feel as if they had a grievance. . . . . And now, for the want of anything better to write, I will tell you of another saying of mine the other night at Judge Henry's. One of the Misses ―――― rather sets up for a wit and a woman of learning. She had on hand a piece of knitting, which she said was Penelope's web. I asked her if she was pursuing Penelope's plan of *unraveling* it as she went. She said, "Oh, no!" "Well, then," said I, "*so far*, you have shown only a *difference* between your web and Penelope's—hers having been constantly unraveled as it was made—yours going on to a rapid completion; I suppose its *likeness* must consist in having a *promised marriage* at the end of it." Her reply was, "I acknowledge you have r-a-t-h-e-r got me." . . . .

[From L. S. to A. H. S.]

MACON, June 28, 1860.

DEAR BROTHER— . . . . The first case we had here was a bank case. We have decided it against the bank directors, and all agree in opinion. It is Lyon's case, but I shall also give my views on it. This was a case against *directors* for an excessive indebtedness incurred under their administration. Mr. Toombs' cases were against *stockholders*, and were based upon a different clause in the charter. This case does not, therefore, decide his point; but I am against him on his point. Jim Johnson argued this case against the directors, and argued it far better than Dougherty did the case against stockholders. Jim Johnson argues a case upon the principles and philosophy of the law in a style not surpassed by any man in Georgia. But I must now go to consultation. This has been written in my smoking time just after dinner. . . .

P. S.—Just as I am closing, a storm is brewing. Charley has just come in, too, and told me that he has just learned, through a letter from his wife, that poor old General Sayre is dead. He died day before yesterday.

[From L. S. to A. H. S.]

MACON, June 29, 1860.

DEAR BROTHER—It is nearly 11 o'clock at night, and I have just returned from hearing Governor Johnson * speak in Concert Hall. . . . . The Governor spoke very well to-night, but he did not speak as effectively as usual. He had a house full, and I thought that about half the crowd, who demonstrated at all, seemed to be with him. But I thought he had as many with him at the beginning as he had at the end. I will give you the particulars when we meet, if we should think of it then, or perhaps in some letter, when I have more time. For the present, I will only add that he does not appreciate, as I do, the point of greatest strength in his position—that is, the danger of rendering slavery odious to our allies, and to the world, by making it *aggressive*—by forcing it upon any unwilling people upon the face of the earth. The ark of safety and progress is the doctrine of perfect and universal non-intervention, leaving all people to please themselves upon the subject, forcing it upon none, and securing it to all who desire it. If this principle becomes established as an inter-State doctrine, and would become established as an international doctrine, it will, of logical necessity, become afterwards the doctrine among individuals of the same State or

---

* Herschel V. Johnson was then a candidate for the Vice-Presidency.

nation, and every man, the world over, will have slaves if
he wants them, and is able to buy them. The whole battle
of slavery turns upon the single issue of its moral right or
moral wrong. If it is wrong, everybody ought to do all
that can be done, consistently with a prudent regard to circumstances, to abolish it; but if it is right, everybody ought
to have it who wants it and can get it—*States* or individuals.
All *legal prohibitions of it* would disappear from the face of
the earth if you once establish the doctrine that it is no
question of right or wrong, but is only a question of political economy. If it is a question of political economy, it
must be a matter of *free trade*, neither forced nor prohibited
anywhere, but left to the laws of free trade everywhere,
not going in point of fact to all places, but prohibited by
law in no place—free as the cotton-plant and sugar-cane
are to go anywhere, but, like them, taking root only where
it may be found profitable. Douglas is the great champion
of this great principle on which rest our hopes of the progress and salvation of slavery; and it is black ingratitude, as
well as suicidal folly, for the South to assail him or abandon him. But good-night.

Affectionately,   LINTON STEPHENS.

[From L. S. to A. H. S.]

MACON, SUNDAY MORNING, July 8, 1860.

DEAR BROTHER— . . . . The commencement
sermon is to be preached to-day by Dr. Joseph C. Stiles.
Have you ever heard him? I heard him once, about seven
years ago, and thought he was the greatest *orator* I had
ever seen in the pulpit. I must go and hear him again to-
day, and see how that impression may be sustained or
changed. I wish you could hear him with me; and I have
a distinct recollection of having wished, when I heard him,
that you and Emm could have heard him, too—so greatly
does any pleasure depend upon its being shared with others
who are near and dear to us! . . . .

[From L. S. to A. H. S.]

MACON, July 8, 1860.

DEAR BROTHER—I wrote you a letter this morning, and
mailed it on my way to church. Since then, I have re-

ceived yours of the 6th instant, saying that you were feeling much better, and that you had had a little rain and a great deal of cooling in the air. I am truly glad to hear it. So my notions about the rains, as expressed to you this morning, turn out to be correct. I think you have got still more rain by this time. . . . .

And now, a word as to Dr. Stiles' sermon to-day: His subject was the "Gospel as an instrument of education—the *sole* instrument of educating men out of their great aberrations, and leading them back to their first great estate of their likeness to God." It was a grand discourse. His soul seemed to be all on fire with his great theme, and to be throwing off, not scintillations nor corruscations, but masses of sheet-flame. After such a general account, it is perilous to give specimens; but I will try a few, begging you to imagine what infinite force was added to them by powerful language, which I do not remember, and still more by the noble and inspired aspect of the orator. He pointed out some of those great aberrations. One of them was a constant proneness in man to exalt the things of Time above the things of Eternity—to ignore Eternity and make Time all in all. The cry of his fallen nature is, What shall I eat, what shall I drink, and wherewithal shall I be clothed? He asked what a *great* aberration this was! The smallest imaginable fraction of the first breath of Methuselah bore a larger proportion to the rest of Methuselah's life than Time bears to Eternity. Time is but the egg-shell prison of the bird: he is formed and hatched there, but before you can have the *bird* in the glory of his creation, he must *peck out*, and soar, and sing, and flock in the forests, and through the grand empyrean. Man has his origin in Time, but before he achieves his true glory, or even enters upon his real existence, he must *burst* through these cerements of Time, which restrain the heaving of his immortal nature, and fly to his great possession at the throne of God, where he shall be a joint-heir with the Son of God. Another of these great aberrations was man's proneness to set himself up as independent of God. What stupendous folly! What alarming insanity! Man, without God, is a swift chariot without a reinsman—a storm-tossed ship without a rudder—an affrighted stag, plunging through the forest, *without an eye!*

22*

These are a few, out of a large number, of his striking
and glowing illustrations. To feel the force and beauty of
these as I did, you would not only have to imagine the language and action with which they were delivered, but also
the preceding parts which had prepared the audience for
the full effect of them. In my judgment, he is the prince
of preachers. I greatly wonder that his fame is not much
greater than it is. . . . .

[From L. S. to A. II. S.]

MACON, July 10, 1860.

DEAR BROTHER— . . . . I have just returned
from a ride out into the country to a beautiful pond, where
I took a swim. I went to the same place and took a bath
on the night of the 5th instant. Our landlord sends such
of us as wish to go in his carriage. The pond is at a place
of his about a mile out of town. It is fed by springs, and
is very clear. There never was a more beautiful place for
swimming. Judge Lumpkin went out the first night, and
went into the water, but didn't swim, for he don't know
how. The company had some sport out of my efforts to
teach him. He went into the frolic with the spirit of a
boy. . . . .

[From L. S. to A. II. S.]

MACON, July 12, 1860.

DEAR BROTHER—I take a few moments, before going to
the court-house, to drop you a line. Yesterday, we had no
court, but attended the commencement. I have no remarks
to make, except that it was a poor affair, with the exception of the commencement oration by Dr. Lipscomb,* of
Alabama. That was a very entertaining address; it was
highly poetical, in thought, in parts of it. It was not written. I will give you a specimen, which, I think, has the
true ring of beauty and poetry: he called the Gulf-stream
"The Wandering Summer of the Sea." I never heard the
idea before; nor has Judge Nisbet, or Lumpkin, or anybody else whom I have heard speak of it. . . . .

* Dr. Lipscomb was afterwards Chancellor of the University of Georgia.

[From L. S. to A. H. S.]

MACON, July 13, 1860.

DEAR BROTHER— . . . . . . I learn to-day, through Charley and Judge Lumpkin, that Ben Hill says that he has been consulted by the Bell and Everett men of the North to get his opinion whether a combination between them and the Douglas men at the North would hurt them at the South, and that he has answered them to make the combination. Ben talks against the seceders. The three parties—Douglas, Breckinridge and Bell men—are now stationed for a *triangular* fight, without any certainty, on the part of either, as to which of the other two will prove his real antagonist in the end, and with a rational disposition, therefore, on the part of each, to weaken that one which, for the time, gives most promise of final strength. It is a category very promising of combinations and bargains, and nobody can tell what may yet be effected by trading. The temptation and facility for trading is likely to produce it.

Charley* says he heard Judge Lumpkin break loose, the other night, upon the subject of my resignation. He said he had not a word to say in opposition to it, and had not tried to dissuade me from it, because my reasons for it were good; but he would say that there was no man in Georgia who could fill my place. He said he meant just what he said—that my equal in the position could not be found in Georgia; that he would rather have me as an associate on the bench than any man he had ever had; that I had an absolute and undeviating purpose to administer the law independently of all personal considerations; and that, from his experience, it was no easy matter to find such a man. He went on to say how great my ability was, etc. I write you this because I feel some gratification at it, and think you may feel some also. It did not surprise me to hear that he expressed such sentiments; for I had thought before that he entertained them, but was surprised to hear that he had said, in so public a manner, things which would be distasteful and disagreeable to a good many people of ambition and influence. He and I held court to-day without Judge Lyon, who has gone home while cases in which he has been of counsel are up. In our consultation, this even-

---

* Hon. Charles W. DuBose, then Clerk of the Supreme Court of Georgia.

ing, we had no trouble at all, and I do not think either one
of us yielded a conviction he had.   I am sure I did not,
and I don't think he did.   He told me the other day that
he agreed with an opinion I had expressed, to the effect
that judges who interchange views on a question, and are
all animated with a single desire to arrive at the truth, can
seldom differ in the end. . . . .

[From L. S. to A. H. S.]

MACON, July 15, 1860.

DEAR BROTHER—This is Sunday evening.   I have had no
letter from you to-day.   Your letter of the 12th, which I
got yesterday, telling me of the sickness of "the Parson," *
made me anxious to get another to-day that I might hear
how he had got. Poor old Parson! I do hope he is well
again. By the way, however, if he should be well, don't
let him know that I said "poor old Parson."   He would
possibly like that quite as little as he did Jesse Woodall's
recollection of having gone to school to him.

I had a good laugh at Judge Lumpkin last night at the
supper-table.   His wife and son, Miller, arrived here yesterday morning before breakfast, very unexpectedly to him;
so when he was about to deliver an opinion in a long case,
yesterday morning, he prefaced it with an apology for the
desultory manner in which he expected to do it—saying
that while he was engaged in preparing the opinion that
morning, *circumstances beyond his control had broke in upon
him.*   This manner of alluding to his wife's arrival created
quite a merriment among those who knew of her arrival,
for the old fellow said it with great humor.   So, last night
I told Mrs. Lumpkin, who sat right opposite to me at the
supper-table, that she ought to haul the Judge "over the
coals."   She, of course, wanted to know why, and I told
her because the Judge had called her "a circumstance." The
Judge's reply to me was, "Ain't you ashamed to report me
so? I said nothing about *a circumstance;* I said *circum-*

---

* Mr. O'Neal, a most estimable gentleman, who has long been one of
Mr. A. H. Stephens' household. The title of "Parson" was given him
from his general probity of character, by the boys about town, when he
was Ordinary of the county.

stances." "So you did," said I; "but you said circumstances had broken in upon you, and as I knew nothing had broken in upon you, except your wife and son, I took Mrs. Lumpkin to be *one circumstance* and Miller another." With a fine affectation of annoyance, he said: "Ain't you ashamed to do me so?" and the whole of our end of the table took a hearty laugh at this transpiration, in his wife's presence, of the manner in which her name had been handled behind her back. Mrs. Lumpkin said she thought my inference was a sound one, and indeed she didn't see how there could be any escape from it. Before this, the Judge, affecting the air of a man who was caught and had resigned himself to martyrdom, said to me, "I'll tell you now, she'll believe anything you tell her, for she has taken up a notion that you have got one of the honestest faces she ever saw." His quisical and complaining manner of saying she would believe anything I might tell her raised another roar. I then went on to tell Mrs. Lumpkin that I had not told her the *worst*, for he said "circumstances *beyond his control*" in a manner that indicated that he was well-nigh a *ruined man*, and that he would have controlled them if he could. "But," said I, "he didn't fool anybody at all, for through all his assumed air of martyrdom and ruin, his secret delight was plainly apparent to all, and the way everybody read the story was, that he was so tickled at the pleasant surprise he had had, he couldn't help telling right out in the court-house that his wife had come to see him— his joy had made him incontinent." This pleased her very evidently, and pleased him also, and was regarded by the company as a most just analysis and pleasant hit. I have not told you all that was said, but I have given you the thread on which you can string other such things as you may imagine to have been appropriate to the occasion. On the whole, it was a very pleasant supper-table passage, and a little play in which I suspect that the lady figured very much to her liking and to her husband's gratification. By the way, the reason of her coming here was the news she had got that the Judge was sick. He was quite unwell, a few days ago, but his wife found him quite well on her arrival. And now I will say that I have been "broken in" upon by two terrible bores since I commenced writing this letter. Before I had finished the first page,

————, of ————, came in and sat and talked for three solid hours. He sat until the supper-gong was sounded. Then, immediately after supper, in popped ————, and he sat until eleven o'clock. I gaped, and yawned, and told him I had some letters to write, but all to no effect. When he continued to sit after such hints, I concluded that he certainly meditated a *foray* upon me in some form or other, and I was at last quite as much surprised as relieved when he took his hat and bade me good night without asking me for anything. My solution of it now is, that his heart failed him for the time. I shall look out for him *in the morning*. The reporter's place will be vacant at the end of this term by the resignation of Martin, and I have a suspicion that ———— wants to put in. That was ————'s business. ———— is also an applicant, and ————, of and ———— of and ————, of ————. As I am to retire myself at so early a day, I shall not take much interest in the appointment of Martin's successor. The appointment is made, as you know, by the judges. The temperature here is pleasant, but no prospect of rain. What is to become of the country? Good-night. I intended to write you a *long* letter this evening.

Most affectionately,

LINTON STEPHENS.

[From L. S. to A. H. S.]

MACON, July 21, 1860.

DEAR BROTHER— . . . . What does Mr. Toombs say about politics, or does he refrain from the topic in your presence? What is the reason for your opinion that no combination can be effected between the Douglas and Bell men? You expressed such an opinion in one of your letters to me the other day. What do you think are the probable combinations, or antagonisms and results? It will be some weeks before I can see you, and I should like to know your general opinion of the field, and of the result of the battle. Mr. Thomas writes me that he is afraid he and I may differ, and then tells me that he favors a combination with the Bell men. He says Cosby is really for Douglas, but says he is going to vote for Breckinridge. I only mention that as a curious thing. Yesterday, I saw a

letter from Stewart, of our county, to Charley, saying that
the Hancock people were in a stir and in a curious condition of politics. He does not go into particulars, nor does
he state anything about it, but only drops remarks, from
which I can discover the tendency of things. One thing
is, he *wonders* if he shall at last vote for Douglas after swearing he never would. He then adds that Bill Hunt tells him
it is as easy to swear in as it is to swear out. Then again
he adds that Bill Hunt, however, is the *only* old-fashioned
Democrat who talks right about it; and then adds that
there is great swearing among them—some of the Douglas
men swearing that they will never vote for Bell, and some
of the Bell men swearing they will never vote for Douglas.
From all this, I infer that the proposition for a combination
is urged by some of each—the Douglas and the Bell men—
but strenuously resisted by others of each party. Was it
this sort of feeling which you foresaw as an obstacle in the
way of a combination? Is this obstacle greater than the
same sort of obstacle which stood in the way of the union
of Whigs and Democrats in the formation of the Constitutional Union party, and in the formation of the Anti-Know-
Nothing party? I don't see that the obstacle is greater
now than the same obstacle was in each of those cases; nor
indeed is it so great, for the disintegrations which have óc-
curred in party organizations within a few years have tended
to render the process of disintegration familiar to our people, and, therefore, less difficult. But while disintegration
may be more easy, it may yet be true that the reformation
of disjointed parts may not be so. In other words, that
our general progress has been towards anarchy, and away
from integrity and union. But enough of all this, too.
What now shall I write? I am unwilling to quit; and yet,
I have nothing more to say. . . . .

[From L. S. to A. H. S.]

MACON, July 23, 1860.

DEAR BROTHER—I have done the deed! I mean I have
sent my resignation to the Governor, to take effect, not at
the end, but at the *beginning* of the Atlanta term. When
I say *sent*, I mean I have it ready to send, and shall have
it mailed to-morrow morning along with this. The Gov-

ernor, if he should be at home, will have it in his hands
before you get this notice of it.   I feel better.   The place
has worn me out.   I should like it if I could be *sole* judge,
but I do not like a divided sceptre.   I do not think I have
the slightest relish for power for its own sake, but I like
what power I may have to be undivided, in order that its
exercise may be guided by system and symmetry, and not
be a "mighty maze without a plan."   I feel a great relief
in knowing that the word which is to cut me loose from
"this body of death" has already been spoken.   Charley
says tell you that he is "in *particular* hot water."   He
says he will be terribly lonesome. . . . .

    Affectionately,   LINTON STEPHENS.

At the meeting of the General Assembly, in November,
1859, the Executive appointment of Judge Stephens to the
Supreme Bench was gracefully indorsed.   He was elected,
without opposition, for the unexpired term.   The compliment therein implied loses nothing of its significance, or
gracefulness, when it is remembered how hotly some of the
preceding and succeeding canvasses, for the like office,
have been conducted.   Failing health induced him, however, to resign his commission, as has been seen, in July,
1860.   The regret felt and expressed at the event was
very general and very sincere, as was the necessity of it
deplored; nor was there any one more earnest and emphatic in giving utterance to that feeling of regret than
the late Chief Justice, Joseph Henry Lumpkin.

[From L. S. to A. H. S.]

SPARTA, September 8, 1860.

DEAR BROTHER— . . . . But let me
turn to a lighter theme; the other one is a painful one to
me.   I want to poke a little fun at you about a small point
in your speech.   There would be no fun in it if it were
not for your great character for exact accuracy in your
statements and *allusions*.   Now, you may open your eyes,
for I am going to peck a flaw in a scriptural allusion which

you made. You spoke of *those* who *held Stephen's* clothes while he was stoned to death. Now, I make a point on every one of three words which I have underscored—*those, held* and *Stephen's*. I shall take them up in their reverse order. In the first place, then, so far as the record shows, (Acts 7th chapter and 58th verse) there was nothing done to Stephen's clothes; the account is that the witnesses did something with their clothes—not Stephen's. In the next place, what they did was not to *hold* them, but to *lay them at the feet* of somebody. In the third and last place, the clothes were guarded (not held) by one person only, and not by several, as is implied in your word "those." The clothes-minder was no less a personage than Paul. Now, I want you to review the history, and either own up, or tell me why you won't. I should like for you to read this scriptural criticism of mine to "the Parson," and write me what he says about it. . . . .

After quitting the bench, Judge Stephens entered with unwonted zeal into the Presidential canvass of 1860. His speeches in advocacy of the election of the Douglas-Johnson ticket were the ablest he ever delivered on the hustings. No speeches of the campaign were better reasoned from his stand-point, and they were uttered with all the nervous eloquence *despair* only can inspire.

On the 15th of October, he wrote his friend Johnston:

MY DEAR DICK— . . . . And now, one word in relation to politics, in which I feel more interest than in anything else at this time—not the interest of an office-seeker, for I desire no office in the world, but the interest of a *citizen* who feels that he lives under the freest and best government on earth, and is utterly opposed to its destruction *without cause*. I am not fighting now to defeat Lincoln's election. To live under his administration will be a great calamity, and to avert that calamity is a sufficent aim to inspire the efforts of any man who loves his country. But I am afraid that we shall be reduced to the alternative of living under his administration, or resisting it by force of arms. The leaders are undoubtedly respon-

23*

sible for the result. Posterity will hold them so. I repeat, I am not fighting to defeat Lincoln; I am afraid that is impossible; but I fight now to prevent the "precipitation" of the revolution which is intended to follow his election. . . . . Nothing can defeat it but the defeat of Lincoln, (which is almost hopeless) or a clear break down of the Breckinridge cause in the South. It is of the last importance that the popular vote of the South, and especially the majority vote of Georgia, should be given against Breckinridge. If so, they may be discouraged from making the attempt. I am now working to that end. This is all so, but a great number of people cannot be made to believe it. They are as incredulous as those were who laughed at Noah when he preached the flood. I trust that a kind Providence may avert from their incredulity the like terrible retribution, which seems to me to be almost its necessary result. What a causeless catastrophe it will be! and how terrible its results! May the God of our great fathers preserve their degenerate sons in spite of themselves.

Most truly yours,

LINTON STEPHENS.

[From L. S. to A. H. S.]

SPARTA, October 16, 1860.

DEAR BROTHER—Yesterday, I got your letter of the day before, and the day before, I got the one written just on your return home. Both bore date of the 14th, but the first was, of course, written on the 13th. I will meet Mr. Douglas at Chattanooga if nothing unforeseen shall prevent. I trust that your apprehensions as to the treatment he may receive in Georgia may prove groundless. Mr. Toombs' remark about what will be done in Columbus, in case he repeats his Norfolk sentiments, looks ominous. I am sorry that the time for him to be in Columbus is not longer before the election; for any ill-usage he may receive will only do him good in the election if the news could have time for circulation among the people. We are on the verge of a precipice. May God preserve us! . . . .

JACKSON, TENN., SUNDAY, October 21, 1860.

DEAR BROTHER—You may be surprised to learn that I
am in Tennessee, but you have possibly heard already that
I had gone to Illinois. I got Judge Wright and Bob Sims
both to fill my place in Murray, and started from Atlanta
to Centralia last Friday morning. It had rained nearly all
the night before, and continued to rain until we got to
Chattanooga. Within a half mile of the depot, at Chattanooga, our engine ran off the track. We would have lost
the connection but for the Memphis train waiting for us.
They had, however, already waited so long that they could
not wait for us to get supper; and as I was quite hungry,
and didn't relish the prospect of riding all night without
eating, and as I furthermore didn't like to pass through the
region of *land-slides* and impending rocks in such a wet and
dark time, I staid all night in Chattanooga. Yesterday
morning, I started again and got to the "Grand Junction"
last night about 10 o'clock. There I had to stay all night
for a train. This morning, the train came and I took it at
8 o'clock, and arrived here about 11. This place is forty-
eight miles from the Grand Junction. It is now about 3½
o'clock in the afternoon. I am to leave here at 9:45 to-
night, and, with good luck, shall reach Centralia at 9½ in
the morning, in time for the grand gathering there to-morrow. You will readily conjecture that my present deten-
tion at this place is owing to its being Sunday. You will
readily imagine that it has been a weary, heavy day to me.
I am an utter stranger here, in face and in name. The
landlord at the Junction evidently knew me from reputation, but this one does not. I am all alone here; but I am
wearing through the day better than you would imagine.

I think Douglas is strong in this part of Tennessee, but
I have no doubt but that Bell will carry the State. Douglas is to speak at this place on Tuesday.

And now for the reason of this unexpected trip on my
part: When I got to Atlanta, Dr. Hambleton showed me
a dispatch, which he had just got from Mr. Douglas, inquiring *when you would meet him in Illinois*, and Hambleton
told me that it was published in the papers that you were
going to Illinois. Hambleton was afraid that the "when"

in Douglas' dispatch implied that he expected you with certainty at *sometime*, and he might wait for you, and so give up his Georgia appointments. The truth is, he seemed very uneasy, lest Douglas might not go to Georgia at all, unless you or I should meet him, as Hambleton had promised him one of us would do. He did not acknowledge to me in terms that he had made such a promise, but I became perfectly satisfied that he made some such promise. The only doubt I have is as to what the exact promise was. *I think* it was that *you* would meet Mr. Douglas; but it is possible that it was in the alternative—you or I. At all events, he begged me to come and I came. When I got to Atlanta, I found that Ben Hill had spoken to a very large crowd there the night before, and had got resolutions passed for a fusion of all parties in Georgia, so as to run a ticket which should be pledged to neither of the candidates, but pledged only to vote for that one who would have the best chance to beat Lincoln when the vote should be cast. The Douglas men and Bell men were all for it, and a number of the Breckinridge men also. I am inclined to think that if it is well managed, it may be a strong, wise and successful movement. I am afraid that it may be distasteful to Douglas men in some parts of the State, because it is inaugurated by Bell men; but I hope not. I find that there is great apprehension in the public mind from the prospect of Lincoln's election. The almost universal expectation seems to be that Carolina will secede; that the General Government will try to force her back, and that the whole South will make common cause with her. I say this seems to be the expectation, and it also seems to be the sentiment, of the people—Douglas men, Bell men and all. I really look upon that as the probable result. I do not know whether I shall speak to-morrow or not. I certainly shall not do so unless I am satisfied that Mr. Douglas really desires it. I feel, however, that, if circumstances should be favorable, I could give the Illinois men a talk which may do them good. My sheet is out. I have no envelope. Good-bye. You will not hear from me again until you see me in Atlanta. May God preserve us all! . . . .

[From L. S. to A. II. S.]

SPARTA, November 28, 1860.

DEAR BROTHER— . . . . I have often thought
it was a pity you did not—or rather, that you and I did
not—at once close in with Mr. Toombs' proposition to join
us in an address, recommending that neither any *immediate*
secession man nor any non-resistance man be sent to the
convention. That would have been a strong card for effect
upon the hot-headed States. Is it too late yet? . . . .

[From L. S. to A. II. S.]

SPARTA, SUNDAY, December 2, 1860.

DEAR BROTHER—One reason why my letters to you, since
you left here, have been so few and tardy is this: I sleep so
late in the morning that the mail-hour passes by before I
get my breakfast and finish my smoking thereafter. "Well,"
you may say, "admit all this to be so, and yet, why don't
you get up sooner, (which would be the best,) or write on
the preceding day for the mail of the next day?" My answer shall be an honest one, whether it is satisfactory or
not. It shall at least have that virtue which Mr. Thomas
proudly claimed for his report of his premium wheat, when
he reported that he made exactly two and a half bushels to
the acre, and concluded with the declaration that it was as
honest a report as ever was made. First, then, as to the
alternative of writing on the preceding day for the next
day's mail, (as I am now doing): I have not adopted that
plan, because it is not the *best*, and have each day concluded
that, on the next day, I would adopt the best by getting up
soon enough to write before the closing of the mail; and
the reason why I have each morning failed to carry out the
good resolution of the preceding day has been that, from
playing whist sometimes, and at others from a mere dread
of going to bed, I have sat up too late to be in a condition
to rise early. This is just the truth of the matter; but this
is not the whole truth, nor even the main part of it; for,
after all, the great reason of my failure to write has been a
general indisposition to write, or to do anything else. I
have been sunk into an inglorious gloom and idleness, which
found no other relief so congenial as a game of cards--whist

with the children, or even the poor game of *solitaire*. I
have not written one line of my judicial opinions. I shall
not begin until next week, and then I *will* begin, if nothing
unforeseen shall prevent, and continue without remission until
the work is ended. I mean to do it rapidly, yet hope to do
it well; and the ground for expecting to do it well, and yet
rapidly, is that I intend to make it *brief*. It is easier for
me to condense than it was when I first wrote opinions.
Some of my first opinions would be better if they were
shorter; and yet, I do not think that prolixity is a leading
fault in them. *Comparatively*, at least, brevity is their prevailing excellence; but that brevity cost me a great deal of
trouble and *time*. Some of my shortest opinions could have
been quicker written if they had been longer;[*] but now, I
can make short opinions with more ease, and, indeed, with
greater ease. . . . . I have just received
your letter of yesterday. I still do not agree with you as
to the result in this State. But ought not the State to be
canvassed? I feel so, and think so. I think it would have
been a good lick if you had promptly accepted and acted
on Mr. Toombs' suggestion to join him in an address to
the people. It does seem to me it would have been a great
blow for the right direction of sentiment in Georgia and the
whole South. Is it too late *now?* Think of it. Let me
say to you that I think you are too much disposed to *despair*. The feeling is the surest means of fulfilling its omen.
Your despair will be a *cause* of defeat—not an indication of
the coming inevitable defeat. I don't believe the dema
gogues yet have full possession of the people. On the
contrary, never was the confidence of the people in you so
strong and so pronounced as it is now. Don't disappoint
them. You can save the country. I do firmly believe it.
I see that Fitzpatrick is opposed to separate State action by
Alabama. . . . . I see that Mr. Yancey
is reported to have expressed himself at Columbus in favor
of a conference among the Southern States. Write to
Ewing and all that class, (substantially, though, of course,
not literally) that he is a fool, (as he is) and that the only

---

It is related of Sir Walter Scott that, when his " Life of Napoleon
Bonaparte " appeared, some friend asked him why he did not make it
shorter ? Scott's reply was: " *I didn't have time.*"

possible mode of accomplishing his darling object—the preservation of the Union—is by giving the more fiery Southern States such a programme as they will accept, and that it is the height of folly for Virginia, Tennessee and Kentucky to drive the others to their own chosen course from very despair of getting any co-operation which they can accept. If the more conservative States will step one pace forward, I do not doubt but the more extreme States will fall one step backward. These extreme States *want co-operation*—there is no mistake about it. They feel the need of it, and they are willing to do something to get it. I have no doubt that secession is the only remedy they will accept, but I also believe that they can be induced to accept it as an *ultimatum*, instead of a remedy to be applied at once, as they desire to apply it. I have more distrust of bringing Kentucky and Tennessee *up* to the proper mark than of drawing the others *back* to the proper mark. It occurs to me, with great force, that there is the point to strike the blow. You are the man, and the only man, who can do it successfully. The very fact that you have averted one immediate pressing danger causes the Union-loving States to regard you as their champion, and will make them *believe* what you may tell them. You may think that personal jealousies will interfere and prevent. These would arise at a later period beyond all doubt; but now their cry is, "Help me, Cassius, or I sink!" They will not reject your help. . .

I think that Providence has a great work for you to do; don't be discouraged by the demagogues. "He makes the wrath of man to praise him." There have been demagogues, and bad men, and selfish men, conspicuous in every great struggle for liberty and the right, and many such have been canonized in English history as heroes and patriots. They never would have brought good to their country, as they did do, if God had not made the "wrath of man to praise Him." Some of the most brilliant achievements on record have been wrought by the wicked in the hands of an overruling Providence. . . . .

[From L. S. to A. H. S.]

SPARTA, December 29, 1864.

DEAR BROTHER— . . . . Yesterday I saw the *Herald's* account of the proceedings which were the foundation for Toombs' telegram. I have no remark to add to what I said on the subject yesterday, before seeing the *Herald's* account. . . . . I am more impressed than ever with the truth of what I said in my letter to you yesterday, that the clamor for new *constitutional* guarantees is an artifice of men who are resolved to defeat all settlement, and is used only by them, and those who are influenced by an over-anxiety to conciliate them. Have you seen Mr. Yancey's letter, in which he says we don't need new constitutional guarantees—that the Constitution, as it is, is good enough, and that all we need is an obedience to it on the part of the North? I saw such a letter from him yesterday in the Columbus *Times*. That is the truth of the case, well stated. He makes one use of it, and we another. But his statement of the case can be and ought to be effectually used to silence the artful and deceptive clamor which his co-laborers are making for new constitutional guarantees. . . . .

[From L. S. to A. H. S.]

SPARTA, December 31, 1860.

DEAR BROTHER— . . . . The secessionists here have now got out Edge Bird in place of Mr. Harley, who resigned. To-morrow, Lewis is to speak here by way of getting up a sensation in favor of his ticket. I shall reply to him. South Carolina is his capital. He can't make anything out of the position I shall take on the subject. His object is to question Harris, Turner, and myself, before the people on that subject particularly. He wants to know what course we think Georgia ought to take in the event the Federal Government should attempt to coerce South Carolina back into the Union. I shall tell him that South Carolina having taken her own course for herself, without any consultation with us, we are under no obligation to *her* to defend her against the consequences of it; that the sole consideration of Georgia should be her own safety and honor; that when such an attempt may be made, the government will be at an end; for it is impossible that our system can be worked by *force* against so large a portion of the people as is represented by a whole State of the Confederacy. The application of force *to such a case* would end the whole system, and Georgia should then look for new safe-guards, and ought to look where she may be most likely to find them, under the circumstances as they may exist; while she would be under no obligations to South Carolina, she yet should treat her as she would treat all the rest of the sound States, North and South, and her course towards them all should be to propose to them to exclude the unsound ones, and then go right on under the old Constitution and the old flag, and with the Union purged and purified. If South Carolina would accede to that proposition, then we ought to make her cause our own; but if she should refuse, then we ought to leave her to work out her own destiny, while we should go on with such of the other States as would accede to our plan. In other words, we ought to make Carolina's cause our own, if she would join us in what we might consider the right course; otherwise, leave her alone. Let me know what you think of this. In great haste.

Yours, most affectionately,

LINTON STEPHENS.

Judge Stephens was chosen as a delegate to the State Convention of 1861, which passed the Ordinance of Secession. It was done on the 19th of January of that year. He earnestly opposed the movement in favor of immediate secession for then existing causes; but, after the ordinance was passed, he drew up the following preamble and resolution, which were presented by Judge Nisbet, and passed the convention by an overwhelming majority:

"WHEREAS, The lack of unanimity in the action of this convention, in the passage of the Ordinance of Secession, indicates a difference of opinion amongst the members of the convention—not so much as to the rights which Georgia claims, or the wrongs of which she complains, as to the remedy and its application before a resort to other means of redress;

"AND WHEREAS, It is desirable to give expression to that intention, which really exists among all the members of this convention, to sustain the State in the course of action which she has pronounced to be proper for the occasion: therefore—

"*Resolved*, That all members of this convention, including those who voted against the said ordinance, as well as those who voted for it, will sign the same as a pledge of the unanimous determination of this convention to sustain and defend the State, in this her chosen remedy, with all its responsibilities and consequences, without regard to individual approval or disapproval of its adoption."

The war came.

Judge Stephens enlisted in the military service of the Confederate States in June, 1861.

On the organization of the Fifteenth Regiment of Georgia Volunteers, he was elected lieutenant-colonel. His friend, the late Thomas W. Thomas, then judge of the Superior Courts of the Northern Circuit—recognizing, as he said, the force of the maxim, "*Inter arma, leges silent*"—doffed the ermine to take command of the regiment; it was composed of companies raised exclusively in that judicial circuit, and the muster-roll was illustrated with the flower—"the rose and expectancy"—of that section. Alas! how many of them heard their last *reveille* on the consecrated soil of Virginia!

Ill-health enforced the resignations of both Thomas and Stephens in the course of a few months: the former came home, as it proved, to die.

[From A. H. S. to L. S.]

CRAWFORDVILLE, June 29, 1861.

DEAR BROTHER— . . . . I was truly sorry to perceive from your two last letters, and particularly the one I got to-night, that you were suffering such a depression of spirits. I know what low spirits are—what intense and profound melancholy is—and have sympathized with those who feel them. Last week, I had a sad time myself in looking over and reading old letters that I was laying away and arranging; some of them brought tears to my eyes, and yet I can imagine that that almost sacred pile you opened must have induced much more intense feeling in your heart. These emotions, though painful, may do good; their tendency by nature is to chasten and improve the heart when their legitimate results follow. I always endeavor to make them produce such a result with me. The mysteries of life and existence with its multitudes of ills and sorrows often perplex and overwhelm me! What you say of your belief in causation is not far different from my own convictions: the creed with me, when run out, leads to this settled rule of action—patiently to bear all that befalls me after doing my own duty in all things as far as I can, believing and feeling assured that it is all right and all for the best, myself included as an atom of the great universal existence. This is my feeling when, upon reflection, I feel satisfied that I have done my duty as far as I knew; and if I discover, as is often the case, that by omission or commission some error has been perpetrated, then I feel like crying out, "God be merciful to me a sinner!" This is my only stay, prop and hope! The great mysteries that involve all things around us, and particularly the frailties as well as sufferings of this life, of good and evil, I cannot understand and shrink from inquiring into. Then life's active scenes and duties call my attention; and in these, I have long since found, consist all the happiness it is possible for me to attain. I have felt intensely for you in your position, in relation to entering the military service. I felt too much to talk to you freely about it, for fear that I might influence you improperly. Your situation was so peculiar every way, I could not myself judge for you—and now only rely upon the principle of my creed, that all is and will be right, let results be as they may, without murmuring or upbraiding that all-controlling Divinity that guides our fortunes. I trust I shall, with patience, fortitude and resignation, bear whatever may come, howsoever painful—hoping all the time that the result may be fortunate, propitious and agreeable. Of one thing I feel confident: where duty leads, we may never fear to tread.

I used to be melancholy. I am not so now. Perhaps it is because I am in better health: the health of the body has a great deal to do with the state of the mind. You are now suffering from dyspepsia; the coldness in the side is caused by that. I doubt not you will recover from it. . . . . I have thought of nights on my bed how could I sleep if I knew you were on the cold ground in camp, with nothing but a blanket under you and a tent-cloth to shut out the rain! This is exceedingly painful to me, and yet, I do trust in the providence of God, that if you go, and I now expect you will, it may all prove to be beneficial, instead of injurious, to you. It has been so with others. Mr. Crittenden once told me that, in the war of 1812, he slept often without any tent—on the ground in the rain—and slept soundly and healthily with the rain-water running under him; but it seems to me I should die if I knew that you were in such condition! May God protect you wherever you go, or whatever you do! . . . . . .

Affectionately, ALEXANDER H. STEPHENS.

To his friend, Colonel A. J. Lane, he writes:

CAMP, NEAR FAIRFAX C. H., September, 1861.

MY DEAR JACK— . . . . . . Our regiment has suffered greatly from sickness, and our Hancock companies, while faring better than any others, have not escaped. Three of them have died. . . . . As to the future movements of our army, nobody knows anything, except the generals in command. The brigadiers seem to be as much in the dark as any of the rest of us. I have a conjecture as to the object of moving our forces up to their present position at Fairfax; and for the want of anything better, I will give it to you for what it is worth.

The idea was probably to make gradual incroachments (as we have been doing) upon the lines of the enemy on this side of the river, and by at least getting possession of a number of points from which we could annoy them within their entrenchments, compel them to come out of their works and give us battle in order to rid themselves of the annoyance. This was probably the leading idea, with the superadded general intention to take advantage of any opportunity which might offer of pursuing a different programme. . . . . What I fear most is this naval expedition which has lately started out for some place unknown—the *denouement* of which may be known when you are reading these lines. I do not mean to say that I apprehend from it anything more than a harrassment of and plundering our coast; but I don't know what they will attempt, and it is useless to indulge in conjectures on the subject, except so far as to be prepared to meet them according to our ability. . . . .

At the reorganization of the regiment, in 1862, Judge Stephens was importuned to accept the coloneley; but continued ill-health, as well as regard for Major McIntosh,* who desired the office, constrained him to decline.

Judge Stephens opposed with his might the doctrine of conscription. He believed it to be hostile to the genius of our American institutions—false in theory and pernicious in practice; and, indeed, it would seem that the idea of *forcing* men to fight for their own liberty—and that, too, by means of a measure unauthorized in the fundamental compact of government—involves not merely a paradox, but an absurdity. The following letter sets forth some of the reasons of his opposition to it:

[From L. S. to J. A. Stewart, Esq.]

SPARTA, December 28, 1862.

MY DEAR SIR—I have always intended to send you my acknowledgments and thanks for your valued letter of the 29th of November, but have been prevented from doing so by the pressure of other matters, and by necessary absence from home.

I have never passed through any political struggle without bringing out of it a personal regard for those of my associates in it whom I had found to be actuated by love of country and genuine devotion to the principles of liberty and good government. The Douglas campaign left me just such an impression as to yourself; and hence, it is a source

---

* A gallant and accomplished officer, who fell at the head of his regiment, in the engagement at Garnett's farm, June 27, 1862, during the "Seven Days' Battles."

of personal gratification to me to find my subsequent political course receiving your approval. Our people do not appreciate the mischiefs of conscription. That it is a violation of
the Constitution is demonstrable in a few words. Nobody
has answered, nor attempted to answer, the real argument,
and nobody ever will. The conscriptionist, from the President down, including our Supreme Court and Ben Hill, all
dodge the argument, because they can't answer it. No man
can assign to the framers of the Constitution a rational purpose in the very remarkable *guards* which are thrown
around the power "to provide for calling forth the militia,"
unless that "militia" means the *arms-bearing people of the
States,* and not a mere organization which may itself be destroyed by the removal of the men who compose it. No
man can save these framers from being regarded as mere
babbling geese, except by construing these guards as covering the men, and not a mere worthless organization—the
kernel, and not the mere hull—the substance, and not the
mere shadow. No man has ever suggested a possible reason for throwing these guards around the organization, and
yet, leaving the men who may compose it without any
guards at all against the power of Congress. Unless, then,
the framers of our Constitution were a set of geese, they
meant to confine the power of Congress "to provide for
calling forth the arms-bearing or fighting men of the States"
to some one of the three purposes, of executing the laws,
suppressing insurrection, or repelling invasion, and to reserve to the States the *sole* and *exclusive* appointment of
officers for their men so "called forth." Now, my complaint against the Conscript Act is, not that it has "called
forth" our fighting men for an unconstitutional purpose—
for the purpose is the constitutional one of repelling invasion—but that it has called them forth in a manner which
has robbed the States of the appointment of the officers,
and has robbed the soldiers of their right, under State laws,
to elect their own officers. There can be no escape from
this reasoning. But the unconstitutionality of conscription,
palpable as it is, sinks into minor importance when compared with its monstrous impolicy. The effect and design
of it are to decitizenize the whole army—to reduce them
from the dignity of citizenship, and degrade them into mere
machines of unquestioning obedience—instruments for the

unquestioning execution of the designs and commands of their masters. These brave fellows may achieve independence indeed, but if the war lasts long under the degrading influences of conscription, they will come out of it utterly unfit for liberty. I do not intend to enlarge on this view; but it is a very alarming one when we consider the vast extent of our armies, and the consequent magnitude of the degrading influence. The whole tendency of conscription is to make armies which are fit for despots, and to unmake citizens who are fit to exercise and preserve liberty. I know there is a difference of opinion in the army itself as to the best mode of appointing officers; but those who object to elections take not only a wrong view, in my judgment, of the best mode to procure good officers, but they take a wofully *narrow* view. The great question is, not the best mode of procuring good officers for a war, but the best mode of preserving men who shall be fit for peace. For myself, I have no sort of doubt that *election* is at once the best mode of securing the best officers and keeping them good—the best mode of preserving the gallantry and effectiveness of the men, and the only mode of preserving in them the spirit of freemen and a fitness for their subsequent duties as citizens. This is a subject of the very highest importance; and I repeat that our people have not risen to its due appreciation. Large and long wars are always destructive in their tendency to the spirit of liberty; and we shall need all possible care and precautions to come out of this one with enough of that spirit left to save us from being drifted into irrevocable despotism. Our people would not believe this if it were told to them, but it is true, nevertheless. It is founded on the teachings of history, and, what is more, on the *nature of man*. It seems to be a fatality of men and nations that they cannot see their own future, nor believe it when it is truly foretold to them. Mankind, in all ages and in all countries, have ever been just as those were who laughed at Noah preaching the flood, and as Hazael was when he said, "Is thy servant a *dog* that he should do this great thing?" and yet, he turned around and did the very thing. Our people did not believe there would be any war, but war came. They did not believe, if any war occurred, it could be a big or a long war; but it has already lasted nearly two years on a scale of appalling magnitude. They would not believe me if I were to tell them now that they have not yet reaped its bitterest fruits in the devastation, and blood, and tears which it has brought to us; and yet, I do not hesitate to declare, that by far the most of all its horrors is the *dragon's teeth* which it is sowing as *seed* for a future but early crop.

But I must close. I have written you a very different letter from what I intended. I began with an intention to say that my judgment is decidedly against what is called "Reconstruction," and to give you my reasons for that opinion. I may yet do so on some leisure day. With good wishes for you personally, and for our unhappy country, I remain   Yours, truly,

LINTON STEPHENS.

[From L. S. to A. H. S.]

SPARTA, January 14, 1863.

DEAR BROTHER— . . . . Dr. Burkman came home with me day before yesterday evening from Dawson's, where I found him, and staid until bed-time. He and I played piquet a little—I beat him. He told me that you beat him also. He said he was professor of the game and was getting beaten by all of his pupils. He complained that he couldn't get good cards. He had a good deal of talk about you, and, among other things, said it was difficult to teach you a game, because you insisted on being taught your own way—or rather, you undertook to learn without teaching. Cosby and Evans soon came up after the doctor got here, by invitation, which I gave them as the doctor and I were passing through town, and piquet was then dropped for whist, he remarking that he supposed he was about to play with *professors* of the game. Evans and Cosby both very modestly, and, in my opinion, very insincerely, disclaimed such pretensions As for myself, I said nothing, but simply smiled at the *modest lies* which Cosby and Evans were telling. By the way, I have found out that there are a great many circumstances in which a fellow may avoid telling lies by simply remaining silent; this is quite a discovery, as much as you may be disposed to laugh at it; or, at all events, it is an act but little understood. There is a class of matter-of-fact things which,

when said, are generally expected to elicit a corresponding
matter-of-course answer, which answer, if given as expected,
is, in ninety-nine cases out of a hundred, a lie.   This con-
ventionalism gives rise to a pretty extensive class of lies
which the world has agreed to consider *necessary* and innocent.   Now, I am satisfied that the world is mistaken as to
the necessity, whether it is as to the innocence or not; for
while a certain set-answer is expected on such occasions,
yet, it is almost always considered as given, whether it *is*
given in point of fact or not.   There are very few persons
who ever notice the answers which are actually given on
such occasions.   For instance : I have no idea that Dr. Burkman discriminated between the response of Cosby and Evans
on the one part, and my *silence* on the other; and I doubt
not that, if he had occasion to report us, he would represent us all as having entered the usual disclaimer to his
compliments.   None but a keen observer will ever notice
that the expected answer is not given; and *with a keen observer* you never get any credit for the lie when it is told.
So my conclusion is that such lies, so far from being necessary, are *never* so, with proper management.   I think you
will scarcely read this without some disturbance of the
muscles of your face; but you may be assured, nevertheless, that my object is to enforce a truth no less than to
excite a smile.   You don't know *how* I secretly plumed myself on my superiority over Evans and Cosby in avoiding
that monstrous lie which they were entrapped into telling.
The old doctor does not play a good game of whist.   Piquet
he plays well, so far as I had an opportunity to judge.   He
knows how to play to make the most tricks with a given
hand; but how far his skill goes in forming his hand by
judicious *discards*, I could not tell by the little play I had
with him.   By the way, how do you spell *piquet?*   I notice
that Sir Walter Scott spelt it, as I have just done, without
a *c* before the *q;* but, until I saw his orthography, I never
hesitated to put in the *c*.   I have just read "St. Ronan's
Well," in which frequent mention is made of *piquet*.   That
was the game by which the false Earl of Etherington ruined
poor Mowbray.   The character which struck me most in
St. Ronan's is Peregrine Touchmond, *alias* Scrogie-Scrogie,
who was disinherited by his father because he refused to
follow his father's whim of merging Scrogie in the more

25 *

euphonious and aristocratic name of Mowbray-Scrogie, who wandered and grew rich; who lectured against innovations, and yet, turned every place he went to up-side down with improvements, and who was generally full of whims and full of sense. As I am fresh from the book, I will give you some of the points which you were trying to recall when you talked to me about the book not long ago. The name of the singular old hostess was *Margaret Dods*, and the name of the vehicle in which she made her remarkable visit to the town of Marchthorn was a *whisky*. I have a criticism to make on this book, and I wish to know what you think of it—I mean of the criticism. I think the tragical term-ination of it is a great blemish. The result, or *denouement*, is against the logic of the antecedents. The hero, Francis Tyrrel, is portrayed as a gentleman, and a man of *sense*, and yet, he is made to play the fool in the most important matters; but I insist that it is out of character for a sensi-ble gentleman—a man of sense and of good instincts and breeding—to play the fool on a point of sentiment. He made himself wretched, and brought the woman whom he loved, and who loved him, to the most tragical end by re-fusing to marry her, because she, by mistake of the man, had passed through a marriage ceremony with his treach-erous brother. She discovered the mistake immediately, and repudiated the marriage indignantly. All this was known to Tyrrel; and, besides, he had a clear idea that the marriage had no *legal* validity. It does seem to me that a *true gentleman* would have *felt* and *perceived* that it had just as little validity in a court of morals, or a court of propri-ety, or *taste*, if you please, as it had in a court of law. To allow his own happiness, and that of the woman he loved, to be wrecked on so miserable a *punctilio* was conduct to be expected from the crazy brain of Don Quixote, but not from the thoughtful, high-bred, sound-minded and well-regulated Mr. Tyrrel. The truth is, that Scott himself was not a gen-tleman, and he didn't know how to paint the character. His only good touches in that line were what Healy told us all his painting was—pure *copies* from actual existences. Healy told us he couldn't paint without a model before his eyes. So it is with Scott, I think, in drawing all his char-acters, but especially in all his portraitures which have any success in exhibiting the gentleman. If I were not so near the end of my sheet, I would give you more about Scott; and I may do so hereafter in relation to some points in his life, and the order in which his different works were written.

I will only add now that your *puppy* is here, and that I have named him *Bingo*, from Sir Bingo Binks, in "St. Ronan's Well." Bingo is a good-sounding name, in itself, for a dog, and then, Sir Bingo was a most suitable fellow for having dogs named for him. My observation of dogs teaches me that they make the best dogs when named for the meanest people. All the "Troups" whom I have known in the canine race would suck eggs and kill sheep, while the "Clarkes" have generally been good dogs. My observation of dogs inclines me to think there is something in old Sir Walter Shandy's philosophy of nomenclature.

By the way, I have a negro whose name of Bing has troubled my speculations a good deal. I am now satisfied that *Bing* is only an abbreviation of *Bingo*, and that my negro owes his name to the worthy who figures in St. Ronan's. I have not published the puppy's name, and, of course, it remains subject to your ratification. He is a fine, smart fellow. . . . .

[From L. S. to A. H. S.]

SPARTA, January 14, 1863.

DEAR BROTHER—I have just finished a pretty long letter to you, which will be received by you at the same time with this; and if you should chance to take up this first, why, lay it aside and take up the other. This is a sequel to that, and should come after it in the reading. About the close of the other, I made three or four remarks which I will now pursue. One was that Scott was not a gentleman, and, therefore, didn't know how to paint the character of a gentleman. By this, I don't mean to concur in Thomas' idea that he was a *scoundrel*. I think he was a *canny Scotchman*, with keen observation, a teeming memory, a fertile fancy, a stock of good, healthy common-sense, and had an easy flow of words—possessions which, according to the testimony of his contemporaries, made him a most entertaining companion, and which make him also a very entertaining author. These are his excellences: his faults are, a dash of pedantry, which is considerably subdued by his general good sense; a carelessness and hurry which indicate that he wrote for wages, and a *low breeding*, which frequently betrays itself in spite of that same general good sense. He was himself conscious of his low breeding, if I am not mistaken, and endeavored to hide it under a show of ease in portraying the characters of the great and the genteel. The cloven foot often peeps out, however, through all his affectation of ease—or rather, the ease is always affected, and, therefore, discloses the cloven-foot. The universal fault or pretenders is *excess* in the part they are performing; and excess is the precise fault of Scott in delineating a gentleman. He makes Tyrrel ruin himself and his beloved by a foolish, fastidious *punctilio*. A true gentleman would have been above such littleness. There are passages in Scott's life which directly prove what is so clearly inculcated by his works. He was a *sycophant*, as is shown by his letters— particularly by one letter to some duke—the Duke of Buccleuch, I believe it was. He evidently was quite proud of his servile intimacy in the duke's family. I can't now give you the particulars of that letter, but I know that it impressed me as containing language which, after making all allowances for the state of society in which he lived, could not be used by any independent, high-spirited man. Another remark was about the order in which Scott's different works were written. I do not propose to give you that order, but I propose only to tell you how you can get it. Lockhart, his son-in-law, gives it in his biography, and, in editing his works, arranged them in a series, according to the times when they were written. I have Lockhart's life and edition of the works. When you come over next time, you can satisfy your curiosity on this point. Why don't you come? Another remark was to the effect that old Sir Walter Shandy's philosophy of nomenclature had something in it—at least, when applied to dogs. The truth is, there is a good deal in it, whether it be applied to dogs or men. I have no doubt that there are cases where names have a decided influence upon the character of the men or dogs who happen to bear them. In a case which once came before me, from Coweta county, while I was judge, one of the parties bore the name of Napoleon Bonaparte Potts. Now, sir, I am ready to maintain, against all comers and goers, that a man with that name can never rise in the world. A union of the grandiloquent and the mean is a never-failing source of ridicule; and a fellow, whose appellation is Napoleon Bonaparte, topped off with Potts, is destined to be somewhat of a *butt* in his passage through this world. He feels the ridicule of his name, and cowers and sinks under it, or he takes the only other alternative, and glories in it. Either turn is fatal to true elevation and dignity of character.   I admit that Napoleon Bonaparte Potts' is a very extraordinary case, but it illustrates a principle, nevertheless. In the case of human beings, this influence which a name may have upon the bearer of it is of two kinds: one direct from the name itself, and the other reactionary from the world—one flowing from the inherent tendency of the name as perceived and appreciated by the bearer of it himself, and the other reflected from the world's appreciation of it. There is a curious tendency in men (and dogs, too) to conform to the estimate which the world has of them; in other words, a tendency to become what they are considered to be.   To give a dog a bad name (in this sense, name means character) is not only to hang him, but also to render him, to some extent, at least, deserving to be hanged.   The tendency is to conform to the imputed character.   Now, in the case of dogs, the only influence from the name is of the reactionary kind; for I do not suppose that a poor dog can have any appreciation of any quality or tendency in a name. The world, however, does have such an appreciation, and the dog feels the effects of it by reflection from them—he feels it in caresses or in kicks.   He knows not what procures him the one or the other; but who doubts that every caress and every kick has an influence upon character, and who doubts that a caress or a kick has often been administered on no better foundation than a name?   Names, then, have an influence upon the destinies of men and dogs; but it would be illogical to conclude from this that great names have a good influence and mean names a mean influence. I said there was something in old Sir Walter's philosophy; but I did not say there was *correctness* in it.   It always takes at least two generations of philosophers to develop one truth in its fullness; and what Shandy began remains to be completed by *me!* He found out that names had an influence; but his error consisted in supposing that the influence was happy or otherwise, as the name was good or bad in itself. On the contrary, the true rule is the inverse ratio, instead of the direct, and Tristram was lucky, instead of unfortunate, as his father supposed, in losing the great name of Trismegistus. The philosophy of the true rule is very obvious. Let it be borne in mind that the influence of a name lies in the tendency of men and dogs to become what they are thought to be; and then, let it further be borne in mind that the world does not form its opinions of men or dogs according to the direct import of the names they bear. A great name, when coupled with a man or dog who is not great, dwarfs him into absolute meanness in the eyes of the world, and, by contrast between the expectation and the performance, becomes a source of ridicule and disgust. Great names excite great expectations, which are soon converted into woful disappointments; and then comes the damaging contrast between the expectation and the performance; then come ridicule and contempt in the case of men, and kicks in the case of dogs. Within the sphere of my experience, the name of Troup was an honored one, while Clarke was supposed to embody all that was opposed to Troup. The consequence was that the Troup dogs all fell far below what was expected of them—got into disgrace and soon became as mean as they were thought to be— were kicked into sucking eggs within the first six months, and into killing sheep the first year; while the Clarkes reversed all this by rising above the expectations formed of them. I do not doubt that all this is reversed in families where Clarke was the favorite name. So that the true philosophy of naming men and dogs is to give them names which are *yet* to be made illustrious. It is all the better, of course, if the name is *odious*, and, therefore, I named your puppy *Bingo*. . . . .

[From L. S. to his niece, Mary Grier.]

MILLEDGEVILLE, March 28, 1863.

DEAR MOLLIE— . . . . Yesterday being fast-day, we had no meeting of either House of the Legislature; but we had instead two sermons—one in the forenoon from Bishop Pierce, and another in the afternoon from Dr. Palmer, a Presbyterian minister of great reputation, who is now a refugee from New Orleans. Both sermons were delivered to large audiences, and both were well received. Both orators came up to public expectation, and expectation ran high in both cases. Copies of both sermons will be asked for publication. If they are published, I will send you a copy of each, and leave you to settle for yourself the question, which has been often asked here and variously answered—which is the best? I shall want to know of you, not only which you think is the best, but also what parts of each you may think unsound or illogical—if, indeed, you shall find any errors in either. . . . .

[From L. S. to A. H. S.]

SPARTA, April 4, 1863.

DEAR BROTHER— . . . . On my arrival here, I found your long letter of Sunday. It has interested me more than you expected, if I may measure your expectation by the apparent hesitation with which it was written and the apology. I assure you no apology was needed. I have often sought to draw you out on religious subjects, but have never fully succeeded. I have always felt and known that you held something in reserve, and I have often suspected that the thing reserved was *skepticism*, instead of that never-failing and all-sustaining faith which you have now so simply and so nobly expressed.* I have been wondering who was the man that suspected you of infidelity or atheism, and I have rather concluded that he was Preston, of Virginia. Am I wrong? This letter of yours has a remarkable coincidence with some other things. It was written the same day on which I heard that noble sermon † of which I have written you, and which, in its tone, was so like your letter—not more difference than strictly different breezes would make in blowing over the same golden harp, or than the same breeze would make in blowing over different harps. On that same day, Dick Johnston wrote me a long religious letter—such a one as he never wrote me before, and such as was called forth by nothing but a casual statement which I had made to him in a part-

---

* It is a source of regret that I have not been able to find the letter alluded to.—ED.

† Dr. Palmer's sermon at Milledgeville.

ing note, as I was leaving home, about feeling sad and melancholy. Like your letter, his dealt in his personal experience, and was very cheering. It really looks as if the Holy and loving Spirit, of whom Dr. Palmer discoursed so beautifully, was, at that very moment, breathing upon many and distant harps, and bringing forth from them all harmonious melodies which lifted the soul from earth to heaven. This does not strike my mind as an unreasonable supposition, and it is a very pleasant and consoling one. No subject occupies more of my thoughts, or troubles me more, or interests me more, than what the world calls religion—calls it properly, too, and beautifully, too, if you will only strip it of the *cant* which has become polarized about it, and will view it simply as the chord which binds fallen man back again to the holy Author of his being. I shall take special care of your letter, and treasure it as a precious memorial of you, if it shall be my fortune to tarry behind you on this earthly stage.

I will meet you here at Hancock court. Don't fail to come, for I want to see you before you return to Richmond. I will now bid you good-bye.

Most affectionately,   LINTON STEPHENS.

The largest liberty of the citizen, compatible with protection to property and preservation of order, was the controlling principle of Judge Stephens' political creed; it was the *gravitating law*, so to speak, of his political philosophy. Government, he believed, had accomplished its purpose, its full, legitimate object, when the laws, justly enforced and administered, protected property and preserved good order; and that when government had compassed those things, its whole mission was done. Hence, he set his face like a flint against the proposition, made in the Confederate States Congress, to suspend the privileges of the writ of *habeas corpus*. He looked upon the slightest movement in that direction with alarm and horror. The first lesson he had learned in the science of American popular government was that the writ of *habeas corpus* is the chief corner-stone of personal liberty—hewn out of the mountain by our sturdy English ancestry at Runnymede.

[From L. S. to A. H. S.]

SPARTA, April 6, 1863.

DEAR BROTHER—As William Hidell returns to Crawford-ville to-morrow, I write another letter, in addition to the one of yesterday evening, with the view of getting him to carry them both. Some things which he tells me are news to me, and are of ominous significance. I refer particularly to the "political prisoners" at Salisbury, and the President's application to Congress for authority to suspend the writ of *habeas corpus* whenever and wherever *he may please*. I be-lieve that if this authority is granted to him, free govern-ment will be irretrievably gone. What can he want with it? It is a delusion to let our preconception of his charac-ter weigh down the tremendous significance of his present actions. He has inaugurated, and persistently and consist-ently pursued, a *system* of policy which seems to me to look to absolutism. He and the Lincoln government seem to me to be running a rapid race against each other in usurp-ation and madness. Each faithfully follows every pattern that is set by the other, upon the apparent conviction that what is borne in the one will be borne in the other, and each has shown a remarkable alacrity in furnishing its due proportion of examples to the common stock. We gave them "conscription," and now we have taken from them in exchange "political prisoners" and discretionary suspen-sion of *habeas corpus*—not such a suspension as comports with the constitutional restrictions upon it, but such as are *intended* to get rid of these very restrictions. It is not the least exaggeration to say that all the usurpations and tyr-annies of each are promptly and faithfully copied by the other; and what must be the possible result but the crush-ing out of constitutional liberty, and the establishment of absolutism in both countries? Their emissaries and bribed journals are engaged in the partially secret but certain and persistent work of decrying free government as a failure, and thus preparing the sickened and weary hearts of the people for the *coup d'etat*. If Congress yields to this last demand, I believe we shall be lost forever. I would intro-duce warning and rallying resolutions into the Legislature if I did not feel well assured that they would be overwhelm-ingly lost, and that their loss would encourage the enemies

26*

of liberty, and rivet the chains which they are preparing for
our submissive and pusillanimous limbs.   Our submission
to conscription was a woful mistake.   It ought to have been
resisted promptly, and utterly resisted.   Will mankind never
be able to appropriate the teachings of history without a
personal experience?   Must they wait to be enslaved before
they will learn that every usurpation which is accomplished
becomes a new fortress from which tyranny assails the ram-
parts of liberty; and that usurpation is never appeased, but
always whetted and strengthened by submission?   Are our
people only insensible to this truth, or have they, indeed,
become sick of their liberty, and resolved to take refuge
under the wings of an absolute ruler?   In either case, *decency* demands that we should cease to denounce the usurpations and tyrannies of Lincoln.   These rapidly accumulat-
ing and gigantic usurpations, with a *connecting thread* running through the whole of them and binding them together
as links in a chain, fill me with alarm, and the mean and
pusillanimous submission of our people fills me with despair.   One significant link in that chain is the scheme of
State indorsement of Confederate debts; and we have had
a foretaste of the operation of it in the insolent assumption
of sending a special agent to lecture the State Legislature
upon its duty to the central head.   I wish I could see you
before I go back to Milledgeville, but I cannot.   My impression is that the indorsement scheme will be *worked*
through, and that the conscription resolutions will either be
cut off by an early adjournment, or will be indefinitely postponed by a large vote.   A Legislature which can be be-
guiled and scared into an acquiescence in conscription, by
the plea of necessity and the bug-bear of reorganizing the
army in the face of the enemy, when the only reorganization dreamed of by anybody is just *such a one* as was effected
by conscription itself in the face of the enemy—a change in
the mode of appointing future officers—will submit to anything!   I have no hope from them.   My judgment of them
is that they are against a *fuss* under all circumstances, and
that they will, therefore, submit implicitly to whoever may
be in possession of that power which surrounds them at the
moment—to Mr. Davis now, and to Mr. Lincoln if he
should ever overrun the country.   They would not hesitate
to repeat the ignominy of the Kentucky Legislature with

the same surroundings. The personal pusillanimity of some of them is such that they would to-day sign and seal a bargain for the security of their victuals and clothes. God grant that I may be mistaken, but I believe we are lost! Congress could save us—the Georgia Legislature could save us—but neither of them has the courage or sense to do it; and I repeat that I believe we are lost! . . . .

Most affectionately, LINTON STEPHENS.

In the summer of 1863, Judge Stephens raised a troop of horse for State defense, and repaired to Atlanta. Rosecrans was threatening our northern border. The company was merged into a battalion, organized at Atlanta—Judge Stephens being elected to the command.

[From L. S. to A. H. S.]

SANDTOWN, GA., 5½ O'CLOCK P. M., Sept. 16, 1863.

DEAR BROTHER— . . . . General Cobb is as agreeable as I had expected. He thinks the State troops are likely to be out a good while; he didn't say the whole term of six months, but I think we are regularly *in*. I feel very much as if we had been tricked—indeed, I shared the general suspicion, from the beginning, that we were walking into a *trap*. I walked in with my mind made up to be trapped; but it is a deplorable state of things when the pledges of the government fail to inspire credence even in its blindest supporters. Nobody relishes the consciousness of being *fooled*; but I remain resolved to bear whatever may come. I have not lost my temper, on any occasion, from the beginning to this time. I am very much annoyed by many things, but I have kept cool. The men—especially the boys—run to me with their slightest accidents, even to the broken straps and strings about their saddles. I have, in every case, given them the best advice which occurred to me, and treated their little mishaps with sympathy and kindness.

We are all getting on harmoniously in the main—more so than I ever saw any company before. The sick man has become very sick. I have got him into a private house, and detailed Dr. Tom Andrews, his neighbor at home, to attend him. I am afraid he will have to go to the hospital; for the lady, whose house he is now in, said she could keep him only last night. Besides this case, there are two others of sickness—one of chills and the other rheumatism. They remain in camp as yet. We had a very sudden change of weather night before last, and this morning we had quite a frost. Everybody complains of the cold, and of having slept very cold last night. I got very cold, and thought once I should have a chill, but I escaped. The rations which I drew yesterday, as far as meat is concerned, consisted of 10½ pounds of bacon and 297 pounds of miserable beef for 47 men *one week*. The beef I take by installments. General Cobb says he thinks there will be considerable "billing and cooing" before the big fight begins, and that a big fight will then come off. He told me that Bragg was drawing rations for seventy thousand men. I am going in town to take dinner with Anderson, and must wash up and change my clothes. I am exceedingly dirty, as are all the rest. My company is the only one of the battalion that has arrived. General Cobb tells me, as I expected, that we will all have to form regiments, or be thrown into regiments by him. He still allows us the chance to form them ourselves and elect our own officers. He told me that General Toombs and his regiment would remain at Athens, where they now are. I am sorry that Mr. Conrad's visit is likely to prevent you from coming here. I would like very much to see you. You can get quarters at Mrs. Whitehead's, as I told you, and as you will see from the inclosed note from her. She handed it to me after you left Sparta. I intended to send it to you by Evans, but forgot it, in the hurry and stress of attention to other matters, in getting off. I must write Cosby a letter; and so good-bye. I am writing on my knee, with my back against a hickory sapling. Write to me often; it does me good to get letters from you, even when they are short.

Yours, most affectionately,
LINTON STEPHENS.

[From L. S. to A. H. S.]

ATLANTA, September 23, 1863.

DEAR BROTHER— . . . . Speaking of appointments, my old class-mate, Robert J. Henderson, of

Covington, desires promotion to a brigadiership. He has eighteen months' experience as a colonel, and he is a man of character and education. I have no doubt he would make a better brigadier than many we have. He and his regiment were among the Vicksburg captives. I told him what rule you had adopted in relation to military recommendations, but that I would lay his case before you, with a request that you would do for him what you could consistently with your views of right and propriety. . . . . General Cobb is *very* agreeable to me; but he has always been so towards me in a pretty marked degree. . . . . Our side seems to have had the decided advantage in the late fight, but I do not regard the *result* as yet decided. I can't help feeling great apprehension.* . . . .

[From L. S. to A. H. S.]

ATLANTA, October 3, 1863.

DEAR BROTHER—It has been several days since I have written to you, and several since I have received any letter from you. I suppose this will probably find you at home. I am still ignorant of the future probable movements of my battalion, farther than a slight inference that we will not be moved within the next four or five days. Last night, I recommended a furlough to a man on condition that the General should think the furlough would probably expire before the battalion would be moved. The furlough was granted; and, as it was for five days, I concluded the General thought that we would not be moved within that time. This is all I know beyond the General's intimation, of which I have before informed you, to the effect that we might be kept here to catch deserters. You see I have made a rise in the way of writing implements, and I hope the change from pencil to ink will be as pleasant to you as it is to me. I have a box for a writing-desk, and am altogether better prepared for writing than I have been before. I now have five companies in camp, and I understand that the captain and first lieutenant of the Baldwin company are in the city; the company is probably near at hand. On Monday, I

---

* The battle of Chickamauga had been fought on the 19th and 20th of September.

want to hold an election for an additional field-officer, and complete the organization of the battalion. Whether it will be run up to a regiment, I don't know, but General Cobb says he intends so. The cavalry material here present is exhausted, with the exception of a squadron of four companies, which the General has agreed may retain its separate organization for the present, and two other companies, one of which has boundaries not extending across the Chattahoochee River. I don't know how he will manage it, but he says he intends to run my battalion up to a full regiment. Night before last (the first), we had a terrible storm of wind and rain. Our tents blew down and leaked so that we all got very wet; some have taken cold from the exposure, but I have not. I put on my overcoat and saved my body from the wetting, though my legs got well soaked. After the storm abated, I took a nap of an hour's length in my wet clothes. . . . . I am standing up as well as anybody so far. . . . . . . The Baldwin company has come into camp since I have been writing. Two lads came here this morning, from Sparta, and told me that, on last Wednesday night, my smoke-house on the lot was broken open and all the meat taken out of it, and that quite a number of negroes had been taken up and were in jail on account of it. . . . . I feel very uneasy about the state of things at home, and in the country similarly situated. This war cannot be carried on successfully upon the present basis. If we are prepared to admit that we cannot continue the struggle without stripping the country of all its men, we might as well abandon the contest and accept our fate. There is a plan by which the contest can be successfully conducted without the present rapid and destructive consumption of all our resources, but will it ever be accepted? But enough of this. . . . . I saw General Forrest yesterday evening. He was just from the "front" (to use a phrase which has become a cant), and he said he didn't think there would be any more fighting in several days. He said he was going to LaGrange to rest himself a week. On the other hand, ammunition drays were running nearly all last night from the arsenal to the railroad, indicating preparation for another fight. It seems to **me** that the two armies have now settled down for a spell, and I have no doubt the State troops will be retained to guard Bragg's rear, or for some other purpose. Our negro population is going to give us great trouble. They are becoming extensively corrupted. The necessary pains to keep them on our side, and in order, have been unwisely and sadly neglected. The terms on which I told you I would be willing to *settle*, there is a great deal in. My mind has only been *confirmed* in the views then expressed. I believe that the institution of slavery is already so undermined and demoralized as never to be of much use to us, even if we had peace and independence to-day. The institution has received a terrible shock, which is tending to its disintegration and ruin! . . . .

Most affectionately,   LINTON STEPHENS.

[From L. S. to A. H. S.]

ATLANTA, October 17, 1863.

DEAR BROTHER—To-day, I got a letter from Cosby, saying that you had promised, and expected to return to Sparta next Monday to be present at the trials of the negroes; and I therefore have little hopes of these lines reaching you before you get off, and still less of seeing you up here. I have been very desirous to see you; and, as I cannot go to see you, I thought you would come to see me; but I have now given up that idea, and have made up my mind to get along on my own hook. This is Saturday night, not quite dark yet, and I am writing by a candle in my tent, and I am immersed in a hum of voices discussing such matters as men in camp can find to interest them. The weather is now charming. The clouds cleared off yesterday evening, and I walked out to the edge of the camp for the express purpose of getting a clear view of the new moon. My first sight of it was very clear. I dispensed with the usual drill this evening, and had all hands to clean up the camp, each company cleaning off its own ground, and all ventilating and cleaning out their tents. All the offices of the battalion are now filled, except ordnance-sergeant and chaplain. . . . . The ordnance-sergeant, though not ranking high, is a very important officer; for he has charge of all the ammunition. Mr. Akerman* fills this place for

---

* Mr. Akerman was, after the war, Attorney-General of the United States.

General Toombs.   I wish I had such a man to fill it for me.
. . . .   General Cobb is now gone to the
"front," and, in his absence to-day, I got a note from his
adjutant, saying that General Bragg had telegraphed to
General Cobb to send forty or fifty men to Meridian, Mississippi, to drive beeves from there to his army, and asking
me if I could furnish the men for the service.   I answered
him very promptly that I *would not*, and then rode up to
see him, and gave him my reasons for refusing much more
in full than I had done in the written answer to his note.
My reasons are these: In the first place, I think it very
doubtful whether there are any beeves at Meridian ; in the
next place, if there are any there, and it were proper to
bring them away, *we* are not the people to do it.   Where
are the Mississippi State troops, I wonder?   Cobb's adjutant informed me, in response to my question, that some of
them are at Meridian now.   Did you ever hear of more
patent folly?   It would be three weeks, with the best of
work, before my men could get there to start the cattle, to
say nothing of the hardship of asking us to go and do the
work which lies at the door of the Mississippians.   In the
next place, if I approved of the job, and as the selection of
us as the men, I still would not do it, because we are not
provided with the means.   The proposition was to start
forty or fifty men for Meridian on horseback, provided with
two days' rations and nothing else.   It is about a forty days'
job, and the men would have to support themselves and
horses.   I have not yet, nor has any captain, got back one
cent of the money we paid out in getting here, and in the
detached service in which my Greene county company was
sent after they got here. . . . .
Our battalion-quartermaster is a first-rate business man.
A few such men in the high places of the quartermaster's
department would soon produce magical changes in its affairs.
He is a Wilkes county boy, who went to New York as a
clerk, and soon worked himself up to a partnership in a
large mercantile house.   He never saw West Point in his
life, and only knows *business*.   Seven eighths of the work
of an army is *business*, and requires business talent.   The
other eighth is statesmanship, and requires a talent possessed by very few men in the country. . . .   Good-bye.

Affectionately,   LINTON STEPHENS.

[From L. S. to A. H. S.]

ATLANTA, October 29, 1863.

DEAR BROTHER—In great haste, I drop you a line to say
that we have received orders to go to Savannah to meet an
attack which General Beauregard apprehends at that point,
and to suggest that you do not come up here as you expected. I give you the earliest notice of this movement,
hoping it may be in time to stop you. We go by home in
separate companies, with orders to the several captains to
take up the line of march, from their respective court-
houses, for Savannah, fifteen days from to-morrow morning.
I like the movement very much. I shall send my horses
home by Cary, and go myself by railroad. I expect to get
to your house Thursday or Friday, day or night, I don't
know which. When I see you, I will explain all to you;
at present, I have not time.

Most affectionately yours,

LINTON STEPHENS.

[From L. S. to A. H. S.]

MILLEDGEVILLE, November 18, 1863.

DEAR BROTHER—I arrived here this morning, and went
into the session of the House without shaving or changing
the clothes which I wore away from here last Thursday.
With the dirt, and loss of sleep, and cold last night, I am
feeling to-day very much like a "stewed witch." On my
arrival here, I found three letters from you, of the 13th, 14th
and 15th. Of course, I am unable to tell you, as you desired to know, which of these came quickest. This is the
first I have heard from you since I left here. I also found
a long letter from General Cobb. The inference which I
draw from it is that he wishes to be senator. He says his
personal wishes are balanced by conflicting considerations;
but he also says he will *accept if elected.* Mr. Toombs is
absent, to my great regret. Shockly thinks there is a majority for him now, with an improving tendency in his favor.
I hope so. I think Mr. Toombs is mistaken as to Cobb's
true position, and, therefore, I am very doubtful of the esti-
mates of himself and friends. I feel very badly to-day, but

27

not low-spirited. . . . . . . I left everything quiet in
Savannah. . . . . . . I am to meet a committee now,
and must close.   Good-bye.

Most affectionately,   LINTON STEPHENS.

[From L. S. to A. H. S.]

MILLEDGEVILLE, November 20, 1863.

DEAR BROTHER—The adjournment of the House to-day,
in respect to the memory of a deceased member, gives me,
not leisure—for I have business enough—but a respite from
pressing duty; and I avail myself of it to tell you that I
have not heard from you since I wrote last, and to tell you
how gloomy and lonely I feel.   The deceased member was
Mr. Herrington, of Terrell county.   I did not know him
even by sight.   He had just gone through a successful contest for his seat, and then laid down and died.   Old man
Oslin, the well-known messenger of the House, is now about
to die—is considered hopeless.   Poor old man! I have
known him long, and have valued him for some sterling
qualities.   His industry, particularly, was a model.   His
kindness of heart and general accommodating spirit are also
very conspicuous traits in his character. . . . .
We had a fight in the House to-day over a bill to stop
interest on all contracts where payment in Confederate
money might be refused.   I opposed it on the constitutional
ground that it impaired the *obligation* of contracts.   There
was a considerable little debate between Wallace and Elam
and myself.   Mathews, of Oglethorpe, made a very sensible speech on my side.   I *walloped* them so badly that they
couldn't get enough to call the yeas and nays.   On the
policy of the bill, I expressed no opinion of my own, but
told them what Washington's contract was in refusing Con-
tinental money at par when it was only five to one.   ———
said he had never heard of *that* before, but did not doubt
its truth after my statement of it.   He then went on to say
that it was a disastrous day when Washington took that
position; the cry went out all over the country that the
"Father of his Country" had refused to take war-currency,
and then the fate of that currency was sealed forever.   I
asked him if he did not know that Washington had taken
that position, how could he know what sort of a "cry" was

raised about it? This raised quite a laugh on ———, and was a sort of settling stroke. I doubt which made the most votes—my argument, which, I think, was unanswerable, and which certainly was unanswered, or that little *hit*, which had nothing to do with the merits. I also caught ——— in as bad a trap—worse, really, for he did not escape under the cover of a laugh as ——— did. He referred to the law of 1845, changing interest from 8 to 7 per cent., as an authority to show that interest on existing, as well as future, contracts was under legislative control. He represented that law as operating on contracts which then existed, as well as on future ones. At first, he put it with some hesitation; but, finding that I did not correct him, he grew very confident, and spoke of having made settlements on that basis. He then said he knew he was right in his recollection of that law; and yet, he had never heard its constitutionality called into question. He had then got his foot properly into it, and I rose and read to him the first lines of the law—"On all bonds, notes, contracts, etc., made *after* the passage of this act." I laid down the book and took my seat without a word of comment. He looked badly, and soon subsided. It made a hole in him and let out all his steam. He collapsed and sunk like a bellows with a similar disaster. Then these gentlemen pitched into me, and not I into them.

But I must bring this letter to a close; for I have some others to write, and then a long and somewhat difficult bill to draw, to provide for the education of the children of indigent soldiers. . . . .

Yours, most affectionately,

LINTON STEPHENS.

[From L. S. to A. H. S.]

MILLEDGEVILLE, December 4, 1863.

DEAR BROTHER—I ought to have written to you yesterday, but I did not, because I was sick—quite sick—and confined to my room (but not to my bed) until the afternoon. I should have staid in doors during the afternoon also, but Mr. Bacon came to see me, and said the cotton-bill was coming to a vote, and begged me to go up and vote on it.   I went and made a speech—as good a one, *me ju-dice*, as ever I made—but it didn't succeed.   It had too much truth to be digested at a single meal.   The restriction-bill was carried by one majority.   There will be an effort to reconsider this morning, probably successful.   The House, yesterday, concurred in a Senate resolution to adjourn on the 12th.   I must hurry up to the House, and have no time to write as I wish.   I never was so oppressed with a parting, as I was last Tuesday, in taking leave of you and the children and Cosby.   I had a feeling of unutterable woe, and I have it now.   It seeks no utterance, because it is conscious of being able to find none.   I am much better this morning.   I have just got your letter, written as you were about to depart from my house, and it has helped me somewhat.   I wish I could bring myself to the point of being resigned to whatever may happen!   Sometimes, I have thought I had reached it, but poor human nature has broken down on the way.   God help us all!   And, O God, have mercy on poor, miserable sinners, of whom I am one!

Yours, most affectionately,

LINTON STEPHENS.

[From L. S. to A. H. S.]

MILLEDGEVILLE, December 11, 1863.

DEAR BROTHER—I have just read your two letters of the 9th and 10th; and, though I am not able to write, I have determined to drop you a few lines, because these letters, and the one of the 8th, which I got last night, have filled me and oppressed me with a sense of my injustice and negligence of our correspondence.   I got the Governor to write to you for me last Tuesday.   I see, and was surprised to see, that you had not got his letter when you wrote yesterday.   I have been very unwell ever since I left home—or rather, ever since I got here the last time. . . . . . .

Your account of "the Parson" is a most wonderful one to me, but beautiful in the extreme.   It looks as if all the landmarks, in this world, of my whilom acquaintance, are all passing rapidly away.   It is very painful and depressing to me; but the manner in which you speak of them shows that you feel them as deeply, if not as violently, as I do, and the calmness and quiet resignation which you display in speakin,; of them are beautiful to me, while it rebukes my own despair. . . . .

Yours, most affectionately,

LINTON STEPHENS.

The reader will see, from the last three preceding letters, that Judge Stephens was chosen a member of the House of Representatives in the autumn of 1863. The most important measures with which he was intimately and prominently identified were: An act of the Legislature, granting supplies of food, raiment, etc., to persons left destitute by the ravages of war, in sections of the State overrun by the Federal army; that measure he ardently supported. Another, which he opposed, was the measure to indorse, by the State, the Confederate debt. He introduced a series of resolutions declaring the suspension of the writ of *habeas corpus* to be unconstitutional. His speech in advocacy of the resolutions was regarded by those who heard it, and who had heard him on other occasions in deliberative bodies, as the ablest he ever made in a parliamentary assembly; it was worthy of the subject, the occasion, the time, and the man. It convinced the reason of the Legislature; for the resolutions were adopted. Here follow the resolutions entire—the text of the masterly plea he uttered in behalf of constitutional government and the liberty of the citizen:

RESOLUTIONS

INTRODUCED BY HON. LINTON STEPHENS ON THE SUSPENSION OF THE WRIT OF HABEAS CORPUS.

The General Assembly of the State of Georgia do resolve, 1. That, under the Constitution of the Confederate States, there is no power to suspend the privilege of the writ of *habeas corpus*, but in a manner and to an extent regulated and limited by the express, emphatic and unqualified constitutional prohibitions, that "no person shall be deprived of life, liberty or property without due process of law," and that "the right of the people to be secure in their persons, houses, papers and effects, against unreasonable searches and seizures, shall not be violated, and no warrants shall issue but upon probable cause, supported by oath or affirmation, and particularly describing the places to be searched and the persons or things to be seized." And this conclusion results from the two following reasons: *First*. Because the power to suspend the writ is derived not from express delegation, but only from implication, which must always yield to express, conflicting and restricting words. *Second*. Because this power, being found nowhere in the Constitution, but in words, which are copied from the original Constitution of the United States, as adopted in 1787, must yield, in all points of conflict, to the subsequent amendments of 1789, which are also copied into our present Constitution, and which contain the prohibitions above quoted, and were adopted with the declared purpose of adding further declaratory and restrictive clauses.

2. That "due process of law" for seizing the persons of the people, as defined by the Constitution itself, is a warrant issued upon probable cause, supported by oath or affirmation, and particularly describing the persons to be seized; and the issuing of such warrants, being the exertion of a judicial power, is, if done by any branch of the government except the judiciary, a plain violation of that provision of the Constitution which vests the judicial power in the courts alone; and, therefore, all seizures of the persons of the people, by any officer of the Confederate Government, without warrant, and all warrants for that purpose, from any but a judicial source, are, in the judgment of this General Assembly, unreasonable and unconstitutional.

3. That the recent act of Congress, to suspend the privilege of the writ of *habeas corpus* in cases of arrests, ordered by the President, Secretary of War, or general officer commanding the trans-Mississippi military department, is an attempt to sustain the military authority in the exercise of the constitutional, judicial function of issuing warrants, and to give validity to unconstitutional seizures of the persons of the people; and as the said act, by its express terms, confines its operations to the upholding of this class of unconstitutional seizures, the whole suspension attempted to

be authorized by it, and the whole act itself, in the judgment of this General Assembly, are unconstitutional.

4. That, in the judgment of this General Assembly, the said act is a dangerous assault upon the constitutional power of the courts, and upon the liberty of the people, and beyond the power of any possible necessity to justify it; and while our Senators and Representatives in Congress are earnestly urged to take the first possible opportunity to have it repealed, we refer the question of its validity to the courts, with the hope that the people and the military authorities will abide by the decision.

5. That, as constitutional liberty is the sole object which our people and our noble army have, in our present terrible struggle with the government of Mr. Lincoln, so also is a faithful adherence to it, on the part of our own government, through good fortune in arms, and through bad, one of the great elements of our strength and final success, because the constant contrast of constitutional government, on our part, with the usurpations and tyrannies which characterize the government of our enemy under the ever-recurring and ever-false plea of the necessities of war, will have the double effect of animating our people with an unconquerable zeal, and of inspiring the people of the North more and more with a desire and determination to put an end to a contest which is waged by their government openly against *our* liberty, and as truly, but more covertly, against their own.

THOMAS HARDEMAN,
Speaker House Representatives.

L. CARRINGTON, *Clerk.*

PETER CONE,
President pro tem. of Senate.

L. H. KENAN, *Secretary of Senate.*

Approved March 19, 1864:

JOSEPH E. BROWN, *Governor.*

He also introduced the following resolutions, "Declaring the ground on which the Confederate States stand in the war, and the terms on which peace ought to be offered to the enemy:"

The General Assembly of the State of Georgia do resolve, 1.
That, "to secure the rights of life, liberty and the pursuit of
happiness, governments were instituted among men, deriv-
ing their just powers from the consent of the governed;
that whenever any form of government becomes destructive
of these ends, it is the right of the people to alter or to
abolish it, and to institute a new government, laying its
foundations on such principles, and organizing its powers in
such a form, as shall seem to them most likely to effect
their safety and happiness."

2. That the best possible commentary upon this grand
text of our fathers of 1776 is their accompanying action,
which it was put forth to justify, and that action was the
immortal declaration that the former political connection
between the Colonies and the State of Great Britain was
dissolved, and the Thirteen Colonies were, and of right
ought to be, not one independent State, but thirteen independent States, each of them being such a "people" as had
the right, whenever they chose to exercise it, to separate
themselves from a political association and government of
their former choice, and institute a new government to suit
themselves.

3. That if Rhode Island, with her meager elements of
nationality, was such a "people" in 1776, when her separation from the government and people of Great Britain
took place, much more was Georgia, and each of the seceding States, with their large territories, populations and resources, such a "people," and entitled to exercise the same
right in 1861, when they decreed their separation from the
government and the people of the United States; and if the
separation was rightful in the first case, it was more clearly
so in the last—the right depending, as it does in the case
of every "people" for whom it is claimed, simply upon
their fitness and their will to constitute an independent
State.

4. That this right was perfect in each of the States, to be
exercised by her, or at her own pleasure, without challenge
or resistance from any other power whatever; and while
these Southern States had long had reason enough to justify
its assertion against some of their faithless associates, yet,
remembering the dictate of "prudence," that "governments long established should not be changed for light and

transient causes," they forbore a resort to its exercise until
numbers of the Northern States, State after State, through
a series of years, and by studied legislation, had arrayed
themselves in open hostility against an acknowledged provision of the Constitution, and had at last succeeded in the
election of a President who was the avowed exponent and
executioner of their faithless designs against the constitutional rights of their Southern sisters—rights which had
been often adjudicated by the courts, and which were never
denied by the abolitionists themselves, but upon the ground
that the Constitution itself was void whenever it came in conflict with a "higher law," which they could not find among
the laws of God, and which depended, for its exposition,
solely upon the elastic consciences of rancorous partisans.
The Constitution thus broken, and deliberately and persistently repudiated by several of the States who were parties
to it, ceased, according to universal law, to be binding on
any of the rest, and those States which had been wronged
by the breach were justified in using their rights to provide
"new guards for their future security."

5. That the reasons which justified the separation, when
it took place, have been vindicated and enhanced in force
by the subsequent course of the government of Mr. Lincoln—by his contemptuous rejection of the Confederate
commissioners, who were sent to Washington before the
war to settle all matters of difference without a resort to
arms, thus evincing his determination to have war—by his
armed occupation of the territory of the Confederate States,
and especially by his treacherous attempt to reinforce his
garrisons in their midst, after they had, in pursuance of
their right, withdrawn their people and territory from the
jurisdiction of his government, thus rendering war a necessity, and actually inaugurating the present lamentable war—
by his official denunciation of the Confederate States as
"rebel" and "disloyal" States for their rightful withdrawal
from their faithless associate States, while no word of censure has ever fallen from him against those faithless States
who were truly "disloyal" to the Union and the Constitution, which was the only cement of the Union, and who
were the true authors of all the wrong and all the mischief
of the separation, thus insulting the innocent by charging
upon them the crimes of his own guilty allies—and, finally,

by his monstrous usurpations of power and undisguised repudiation of the Constitution, and his mocking scheme of securing a republican form of government to sovereign States by putting nine-tenths of the people under the dominion of one-tenth, who may be abject enough to swear allegiance to his usurpation, thus betraying his design to subvert true constitutional republicanism in the North as well as in the South.

6. That, while we regard the present war between these Confederate States and the United States as a huge crime, whose beginning and continuance are justly chargeable to the government of our enemy, yet, we do not hesitate to affirm that, if our own government, and the people of both governments, would avoid all participation in the guilt of its continuance, it becomes all of them, on all proper occasions and in all proper ways—the people acting through their State organizations and popular assemblies, and our government through its appropriate departments—to use their earnest efforts to put an end to this unnatural, unchristian and savage work of carnage and havoc; and to this end, we earnestly recommend that our government, immediately after signal successes of our arms, and on other occasions, when none can impute its action to alarm, instead of a sincere desire for peace, shall make to the government of our enemy an official offer of peace, on the basis of the great principle declared by our common fathers in 1776, accompanied by the distinct expression of a willingness, on our part, to follow that principle, to its true logical consequences, by agreeing that any border State, whose preference for our association may be doubted, (doubts having been expressed as to the wishes of the border States,) shall settle the question for herself by a convention, to be elected for that purpose, after the withdrawal of all military forces, of both sides, from her limits.

7. That we believe this course, on the part of our government, would constantly weaken, and sooner or later break down, the war-power of our enemy by showing to his people the justice of our cause, our willingness to make peace on the principles of 1776, and the shoulders on which rests the responsibility for the continuance of the unnatural strife; that it would be hailed by our people and citizen-soldiery, who are bearing the brunt of the war, as an assur-

ance that peace will not be unnecessarily delayed, nor their sufferings unnecessarily prolonged; and that it would be regretted by nobody on either side, except men, whose importance, or whose gains, would be diminished by peace, and men whose ambitious designs would need cover under the ever-recurring plea of the necessities of war.

8. That while the foregoing is an expression of the sentiments of this General Assembly, respecting the manner in which peace should be sought, we renew our pledges of the resources and power of this State to the prosecution of the war, defensive on our part, until peace is obtained upon just and honorable terms, and until the independence and nationality of the Confederate States are established upon a permanent and enduring basis.

THOMAS HARDEMAN,
Speaker House Representatives.

L. CARRINGTON, *Clerk.*

PETER CONE,
President pro tem. of Senate.

L. H. KENAN, *Secretary of Senate.*

Approved March 19, 1864:

JOSEPH E. BROWN, *Governor.*

Judge Stephens always felt the liveliest interest in the fortunes of aspiring and ingenuous youth; and while he was the most undemonstrative of men, perhaps no man in the country could count a larger number of young men so warmly attached to him. He was ever ready to aid the deserving by his counsels or by his purse; nor was he the least obtrusive with the one, or the least stint with the other.

The following letter was written to the son of his old friend, Dr. Edward W. Alfriend. The boy, at the age of sixteen, had entered the military service of the Confederate States. He is now a member of the Georgia bar, of brilliant promise:

[From L. S. to Master Alfred Alfriend.]

SPARTA, May 30, 1864.

DEAR ALFRED— . . . . At all events, I took a thorough search for you, but did not find you. I

have never yet ascertained where you spent that night in
Augusta. Cousin Sally expressed her regret that you did
not go to her house with brother and myself, after she had
learned from us that you had gone along on the same train
with us, and had to spend the night somewhere in Augusta.
My regret on the occasion was not founded on my anxiety
for your comfort during the night, for I did not doubt that
you would find comfortable quarters somewhere; but on
the desire I had to have you spend the night with me, and,
at all events, to give you a parting grasp of the hand and a
hearty God-speed in the new and important career on which
you were entering. This letter is intended mainly to speak
that God-speed now for then, and to assure you of, at least,
one friend, outside your own immediate family, who will
always look with an anxious eye for your preservation amid
the dangers of many kinds which will surround you, and
for your restoration to friends, unscathed in body and soul,
with worthy laurels, wrung from rugged war, to be long
enjoyed and increased amid the charms of blessed peace.
I don't wish to render my letter disagreeable to you by ob-
truding upon you unwelcome advice; nor do I think that
you will take that view of a few words drawn from the experience of one who has been a pretty close, if not a very
long, observer of the world, and whose motive for speaking
them is a desire to serve a young friend treading an untried
path. I know the enemy well, and whether you have yet
found out the fact or not, I know that you will be exposed
there to peculiar and strong temptations. I do not mean
to flatter you when I say that I know no one of your age
on whom I should expect such temptations to produce less
impression; and yet, I must beg you not to be too self-con-
fident. I do not mean to guard you against vanity, but
against an over-confidence in your stability and firmness.
Some *distrust*, on that point, is far better than an undoubting
confidence. "Let him that *thinketh* he standeth, take heed
lest he fall." This is an admonition from God himself, and
no sensible man has ever reached my time of life without
having had occasion to apply it to himself. There are *two
things* which, united, can bring you safe through your present moral ordeal, and *nothing else can:* the cultivation of a
habit of careful *self-watching*, and a meek, but unflinching
resolution never to disregard the dictates of your judgment.

Never let any circumstance seduce you into the taking of even a single drink of liquor, unless it shall be in good faith prescribed for you by a physician; and never allow your lips to take the name of God in vain. The scenes of death and havoc, amid which you will have to move, will inevitably tend to render you *callous*, and to harden and blunt those gentle and noble sympathies which are so appropriate to youth, and which are an honor and ornament to all ages and conditions. I say this will be the tendency, and there is no man who can entirely escape its natural effects. Hence it is that long wars always tend to produce a relapse from civilization back into barbarism. Under these circumstances, there is, for the preservation of the moral nature, no expedient equal to the careful cultivation and habitual exercise of the *intellectual faculties*. I know there is no very favorable opportunity for this sort of cultivation in the midst of camps, but there is some. I was glad to know that you had sent home for a book. You will not have much opportunity to read, for you cannot procure the necessary books, but you will have ample opportunity to exercise your *reason* upon events passing around you. I don't mean to invite you to throw yourself into the invidious attitude of a young critic, but to cultivate a habit of exercising your reason and drawing conclusions from the great events and scenes in which you will be moving; and, by all means, cultivate the habit of reducing your thoughts (whatever course they may take) to writing and sending them home to your friends. After all, there is no process, for training and developing the intellect, equal to writing. Lord Bacon said, "Reading makes a full man, conversation a ready man, and writing an *accurate* man." I shall always be glad to get letters from you myself; but I need not assure you that my motive in advising you to write is not a selfish one. Form the habit of trying to understand all you hear, all you read, and all you see, not excepting the plans and military movements of your great leader in arms. There is nothing presumptuous in your endeavoring to understand them all, and the cultivation of the habit, and the comparison of your antecedent conclusions with subsequent events, will soon render the study both pleasant and profitable to you. Better occupy your thoughts in this way than let them dwindle and dry up. A well-occupied intellect is

the best security for a sound and happy heart. I shall not
undertake to give you a word of news, for Ben can tell you
more in an hour than I would with you in a day. I think
of you very often, and never without a fervent-aspiration to
God to preserve you through all your dangers, and to
lighten all your privations and toils with a good conscience
and cheerful spirit. I commend you to some verses which
I take from Burns' epistle to a young friend. The sentiments are noble, and expressed with much force and beauty.
. . . . Good-bye, and may God bless you.

  Your friend,   LINTON STEPHENS.

> "The fear o' hell's a hangman's whip,
> To haud the wretch in order,
> But where you feel your *honour* grip,
> Let that aye be your border—
> Its slightest touches, instant pause,
> Debar a' side pretenses,
> And resolutely keep its laws,
> Uncaring consequences.
>
> "The great *Creator* to revere
> Must sure become the *creature*;
> But still the preaching cant forbear,
> And ev'n the rigid feature;
> Yet, ne'er with wits profane to range,
> Be complaisance extended,
> An Atheist's laugh's a poor exchange
> For Deity offended.
>
> "When ranting round in pleasure's ring,
> Religion may be blinded,
> Or if she gie a *random sting*,
> It may be little minded;
> But when on life we're tempest-driv'n,
> A conscience but a canker,
> A correspondence fix'd wi' heav'n
> Is sure a noble anchor."

[From L. S. to A. H. S.]

        ATLANTA, June 4, 1864.

DEAR BROTHER—Joe Myers told me, yesterday morning,
that he left you better the night before, and I hope you are
as well as usual by this time. I am writing now in the
Governor's office. It is a rainy, muddy morning. I am
told that it rained nearly all night last night. I slept in a

room so remote from the outer world that I had no idea
what the elements were doing until daylight gave me a view
through the window. I then found things very much in
the same state as they now are at 8½ o'clock A. M. Charley DuBose and I slept in the same bed in the printing-
room of his brother-in-law, Richards. We have a mattress
on a bedstead, and do very well. The night before last,
the Governor and I slept in the same bed, out at General
Foster's, two miles in the country. The Governor's head-
quarters, or his lodgings, are at Colonel Erskine's. He invited me to go and share his bed with him there last night,
but I declined. After this, Dick Johnston and I will occupy the bed in the printing-office, and Charley will sleep
with Richards in the back room of Richards' book-store.
You may infer, from all this piling up in sleeping, going,
as it does, to the extent of causing even the Governor to
sleep double, that this city is very much crowded. Not so,
however. Its quietness, on the contrary, is a striking feature in comparison with its condition last fall during the excitement of the Chickamauga fight. I judge, from appear-
ances in the city, that General Johnston has very few idlers
and dodgers in the rear. The newspaper accounts of the
multitudes of refugees crowded here are monstrous exag-
gerations. I want no better evidence than a walk through
the streets here. I can't help suspecting that the representations which have been made on this point were a trick
to get people to send provisions into this place. This has
been the effect. Our Hancock people sent up a lot of provisions for refugees. John T. Martin and John Little arrived here with the Hancock cargo yesterday morning. In
the lot brought by them were fifty pounds of flour contributed by me. After seeing the state of things here, I felt
as if I had been *sold*. I am *messing* with the Governor's
staff. Dick Johnston, Charley DuBose, Hidell, Colonel
Fulton, Colonel Mobley (of Harris) and myself comprise
our mess. We draw rations from the State and turn them
over to an old gentleman in town by the name of Mitchell.
He takes our rations and charges us four dollars a day
apiece for board at his table. He gives us very good plain
fare, and we all like the arrangement very well. I do not
expect to take up quarters at the camp here ; but when the
troops move forward to the front, I shall go with them as a

private in the ranks.   I had every reason to believe that, if I would only permit the use of my name, I would be elected brigadier-general without opposition.   Colonel Carswell, of Jefferson, who has been elected in the first brigade, sent me special word that if I would say I would serve, he would not be a candidate.   Soon after my arrival here, I became convinced, and I have not doubted since, that I could have been elected with great ease; but I have not doubted that I have done right in declining.   I have kept pretty well since I have been here.   Did you find a letter which I left on your table for you?   It is a letter which I had mailed to you at Richmond, and got back out of the post-office after getting your announcement that you had got back home.   I pulled it out of my pocket and laid it on the table while we were talking.   I intended, at the time, to tell you of it, but forgot it.   I see there has been further and heavier fighting between Lee and Grant.   I am very sorry to hear of Doles' death.   I reckon poor Dick Greene had to run the gauntlet once more; or, was he not in the hospital when he wrote to you?   I believe he was; but, whether or not, I trust that he is still safe.   I have just this moment received and read your letter of yesterday. I am very much relieved at hearing that you were better, and that your pains were rheumatic.   Rheumatism in the bowels, proper, is itself a dangerous affection, but I think, by some remarks dropped by you, that yours is in the abdominal muscles, and not in the bowels.   Your little *shower* that you received with apparent gratification sinks into insignificance when compared with our rains here. Rain, rain, rain—it still rains!   Dick has somewhere picked up the last volume of " Les Miserables," and I have been reading it.   It is now at my bed-room, but I shall go and get it, rain or no rain, as soon as I finish my letter; for I am very much in want of something to do.   I should like very much to be at home; but I am not discontented. . . I am not in a complaining mood this morning, nor in a particularly unhappy state, but I see about as little light under the political clouds as I do under the murky, physical ones that envelop us.   I know the latter will in time give way to renewed sunshine; will the former ever have a like blessed sequel?   Not in my day, at least.   General Smith is expected here to-day to take charge of the State troops, and the Governor has telegraphed General Johnston that they will be ready for him in a few days. I believe he said "two or three days." Now, my own opinion is that they will not be ready to move as soon as the Governor thinks, for I have seen enough of *organizing* to know that there is always more delay than anybody expects; but I have no doubt but that they will be sent to the front pretty soon. I doubt, from all I hear, whether there will be any early engagement between Johnston and Sherman; but they are having fighting there every day—sometimes pretty heavy. . . . .

[From L. S. to A. H. S.]

SPARTA, September 15, 1864.

DEAR BROTHER— . . . . Strange, strange, passing strange that the rulers and wise men of the world should be so inattentive, if not so profoundly ignorant, concerning a history which, in my judgment, teaches the profoundest wisdom in a light which, from its very clearness, is at once splendid and fascinating. What a splendid illustration Mr. Calhoun could have drawn from this history for his theory of concurrent majorities and nullification as a peaceful remedy! By the way, I think Mr. Calhoun, while he was the soundest and most philosophical expounder of our system, was exceedingly unfortunate in his *nomenclature*. The phrase "concurrent majorities" fails to convey a clear idea of what he meant by it; but, worst of all, it loses a great element of popularity which would have been found in the true and accurate statement. A government of the people—that is to say, of the whole people, or a liberal approximation of the whole, in opposition to a government of a fragment of the people, even though that fragment might reach a majority of the whole— a government wherein every State, each State constituting, in the main, a homogeneous people, with identical interests, should have security for life, liberty and property, dependent not upon the will of any one man, or number of men, on the face of the earth, but solely upon its fidelity to itself—a government without power to oppress any interest, because every interest would have the power of self-protection—a government, therefore, disarmed of all inter-

28

nal aggressive power, and fulfilling the requisites of a model government by being confined to the sole legitimate office of government—that is, affording security to its members by restraining aggressions upon their rights. But church time has come, and ¶I must suspend. . . . .

I think the term "nullification" equally unfortunate, or more so, for it conveys a *false* idea of its real meaning—or rather, of the sense in which Mr. Calhoun used it—and that false idea was the greatest obstruction to its acceptance among the people. There is a real difference, and a still greater popular difference between annulling a law which has passed through all the forms of the law-making power, and interfering to prevent the final passage of a law. One house of the Legislature rejects a bill which has passed the other, or the President rejects it after it has passed both, and it never becomes a law. So after it has passed all three of these, it may be rejected by the interposition of any one of the sovereign States; and such a rejection as this is not so much a departure from popular government as the rejection, which we have confessedly in our system is—the rejection by one man. It ought to have been called the *veto power of the States*, and never the right of nullification—a veto not provided for expressly in the Constitution, it is true, but resulting necessarily from the fact that sovereign States are the parties to it, and forming, therefore, a part of our system of government, and being no more *revolutionary* in its exercise than in the exercise of the veto power on the part of the President, and intended, like that, to be an additional check upon legislation; that is to say, an additional security in the hands of every State against aggression from the rest. When you go further and draw the very clear distinction which there is (but which Mr. Calhoun failed to make sufficiently plain) between one State governing all the rest, and preventing them simply from governing her, you would, I think, go a great way in relieving this much-abused theory from the demagogical misrepresentations which make it odious by making it misunderstood. All fair-minded men will desire a government which, while it withholds their own hands from aggressions upon others, secures them also from aggressions by others. Wise men will see still further that there can be no reliable protection to any without protection to all; or, in other words, that any system whose protection does not extend to all interests cannot be reliable and steadfast for any. I could write page after page on this subject, but the brief outline which I have given will be sufficient to give you a full understanding of my ideas, and that is all I wish. Before I pass entirely away, however, I will say that I consider all the talk which speakers and writers (including Mr. Calhoun) have held on the subject of the "social compact" is sheer *fiction*. There is no such thing as "social compact"—never was, and never can be. It is as pure a fiction as the common law doctrine of a superse-assumpsit is, and a much more useless one. Indeed, I think it has been the source of serious mischiefs. The common law supposes every man to promise to do certain duties, and there is no harm in this, since the fiction is used merely to furnish the form of a remedy for the breach of those duties; but what possible use can there be in supposing that mankind, or any part of them, ever agreed to form society?

Mr. Calhoun himself says, very justly, that society is the natural state of man—that all men are born into it. How, then, can he talk, as he does talk in his debate with Mr. Webster, about the social compact being the foundation of society? My idea of it is that all things, including man, are under an obligation, imposed upon them by the Creator for their own good, to live according to their own nature; that is to say, to live so as to attain the greatest possible development of their natural gifts. Society is the natural state of man; he can do nothing in any other situation, and this is the ground of his obligation to maintain society— not any promise or agreement to do so, for none such was ever made. Society cannot be maintained without government, and, therefore, the maintenance of government, of some sort, rests on the same foundation of natural obligation, and not on any fictitious compact. There is no compact, no agreement among men in relation either to society or to government, until you come to what is properly called the *constitution* of government. This is indeed a compact which creates obligations correspondent to its provisions; but it is not a compact to support either society or government in general; it is a compact to support the particular government established by it. Society and government are

ordained by God, as is shown by their manifest necessity
to the nature with which He has formed mankind; but the
particular forms of either are a very different affair.   There
is no room for difference of opinion on the first proposition,
and accordingly, we find that all mankind, in all ages, and
under all circumstances, have had society and government,
but not so as to the form of either, best suited to different por-
tions of the human family.   I think, however, it is easy to
prove that, for a people who are sufficiently enlightened to
understand it, the best possible form of government is that
which arms every interest in the society with the power of
self-protection.   The very reason which renders government a necessity is the *selfishness* of men, leading them to
aggrandize themselves at the expense of others, and this
reason requires the remedy to go to the extent of having
every part of the society protected against all the rest.
How can this possibly be so well effected as by giving every
interest the power of self-protection?   With an *enlightened*
people, this would be the perfection of the science of government. . . . .

[From L. S. to A. H. S.]

SPARTA, October 13, 1864.

. . . .
I have seen Burke's review of your letter.   The answer
which you make to him, in a letter which I got from you
the other day, is not the right one, as it seems to me.   The
consent of the two governments does not relieve your proposed convention of States from the objection of unconstitutionality.   I don't mean to say that I think your plan is
really obnoxious to that objection, but I don't think the
consent of the two governments has any bearing on that
point.   The prohibition against compacts or agreements
between States is not at all applicable to your plan.   You
don't propose to form any compact or agreements between
States; you simply propose to interchange views, and, if
possible, to unite, not in a compact, but in a plan to be
submitted to the States for ratification, or rather for adoption.   You expressly negative any binding authority in
the convention, confining its action to simple conference
and recommendation.   So much for the convention.   When

you get one step further, and propose to the States a scheme of peace which may involve the termination of the existing government, as the convention might do, the case assumes a new aspect; but the proposed action would not be unconstitutional unless secession was so. I don't believe that secession was unconstitutional, nor do I believe it would be unconstitutional to take the proposed action. If the scheme of peace proposed should contemplate a subversion of the existing government, its adoption by any State would, it is true, terminate the operation of the Constitution in that State; but the right of each State to do this whenever she pleases is the foundation-stone of our government. It would not be a question of carrying on the government, consistently with the Constitution, but it would be a putting of the new government upon trial, as we have already put the old one on trial and decided against its continuance. To carry on the government according to the Constitution is one thing—to decide whether the government shall be continued or not is a very different thing. The *consent* of the government doesn't seem to me to touch this question of *constitutionality*. The consent of the two governments is very desirable, but not at all necessary to cure any unconstitutionality. There is no unconstitutionality; and if there was any, their consent couldn't cure it. This reminds me to remark upon a new idea which is passing current without a challenge from any quarter, so far as I have seen, but which is full of error and mischief: I mean the idea that all the States of our Confederacy are forbidden, by *good faith*, to secede from it during the war. Whence comes this obligation of faith? Where is the pledge that would be broken by secession? How can the question be affected by the state of war? Shall it be said there is an *implied* understanding on the part of all to abide the common fortune? To abide it how long? Forever? Then secession has ceased forever as a rightful resort. During the war? Then our rulers may defeat the right as long as they choose by prolonging the war. There can be but one sound view on this subject. It is gratuitous to be implying obligations when the Constitution was intended as the expression of all that were assumed. Those people who prate about the *bad faith* of breaking pledges, which can nowhere be found, are the

same who defend the government in breaking its most specific and formal promises.   It is a cant invented to serve
the purpose of usurpation and consolidation.   It is an artifice of power to perpetuate itself, and to deny all principles
which can imperil its existence.   It is a lie, a cheat, and a
delusion.   It is the right of all States to quit associations,
and form new ones whenever they please.   It is a right
which is truly inalienable, which cannot be surrendered
even by the most solemn constitutional compact, for the
power to bargain it away involves the power to alter the
rights of mankind.   To admit that any generation can be
barred from this right by the action of predecessors is to
deny the right itself *in toto*.   The essence of the right consists in making the change whenever the people please.
Such is the right.   Its exercise can be justified only by considerations of national interest, and is always proper when
interest justifies it.   In other words, there can be no such
thing as power or good faith in conflict with the *true* interest of either nations or individuals.   True interest and
power always pull in the same direction. . . . .

When the Federal army, under General Sherman, ap-
proached the capitol at Milledgeville, in 1864, the General
Assembly was in session.   The panic the intelligence produced was very great ; nor was it confined exclusively to
the citizens of the city.   A large number of members of
the Legislature shared it with them.   Vehicles of every
description were in urgent demand ; the most fabulous
prices were paid for every sort, from the gentleman's coach
down to the clumsiest and most unsightly ox-cart.   Governor Brown, in view of the near approach of the Federal
army, and consequent dispersion of the Legislature, sent a
message to the General Assembly, officially communicating
the intelligence already so appallingly known to the members individually, wherein he submitted to their judgment
the necessity, or propriety, of adopting some measure which
would authorize him to exercise extra constitutional or discretionary powers in certain emergencies, until the Legislature should re-convene.   The message was immediately

taken up in the Senate, and the recommendation, or suggestion therein contained, adopted by that body, *nem. con.*,
or nearly so. It was forthwith transmitted to the House,
and immediately taken up for action. Judge Stephens at
once rose and opposed its adoption in a thirty minutes'
speech of superlative power and eloquence. Its effect was
electrical and crushing. After making a noble plea for "a
government of laws and not of men," he concluded by saying, in substance:

"I, sir, have been denounced by some mistaken, but
doubtless well-meaning men, as an enemy to the administration of the Confederate government, because I opposed those of its measures, which, in my judgment, involved unconstitutional stretches of power, dangerous
alike to the success of our common cause and to popular
liberty. Time will determine whether they or I are the
better friends to the administration—I, who warn it of the
rocks and breakers ahead that will wreck it, or they, who,
if they have eyes to see, see not, or tongues to speak, speak
only to flatter or deceive. It has been said that I am a foe
to President Davis. That is not true. It has been said I
am the friend of Governor Brown. That is true. It is also
true that I warmly espoused his side of the controversy with
the President on the subjects of conscription, impressment,
etc. Why? Because, Governor Brown was right. President Davis was wrong, in my humble judgment—no personal feeling, one way or the other, lent bias to that judgment. Governor Brown was right in that controversy: in
the measure now before the House, he is wrong. *I want
no master!* I am the political friend of no man, *of no man—*
FREEMAN! *alack!* who is ready to accept a *master!* be he
Abe Lincoln, or Jeff. Davis, or Joe Brown, or anybody
else! I am the friend of citizen-liberty,, of rational, constitutional liberty, *to-day*, to-morrow and forever! And before I support any measure authorizing, by any possibility,

the exercise of powers so monstrous and so dangerous to that liberty as those contemplated in the resolutions on your table ; or before I stand by any man who would, if he could, by any semblance of authority, exercise such powers, may my right hand forget her cunning and my tongue cleave to the roof of my mouth! No, sir—never! I would perish sooner. If I am to have a master, HE must forge the chains; I will never hold out my hands to take on the accursed manacles!"

The Hon. L. N. Trammell, who was a member of the House, and to whom I am indebted for the incident, pronounced that speech the grandest outburst of fervid, patriotic, pent-up, *indignant* eloquence he ever heard uttered. The resolution was tabled without a division.

When the awful curtain fell upon the scene of surrender at Appomattox, the last hope of the Confederacy was lost. Nothing was left to the Confederates but to secure the best terms they could with their successful adversary. Of course, it was a question, of a few days only, how long the small but heroic army of General Johnston could continue the struggle against the combined forces of Grant and Sherman. The stipulations of Johnston's surrender, as set forth in the Sherman-Johnston convention, were alike honorable to the patriotism and magnanimity of both, and reflect credit alike upon the spirit of the warrior and the sagacity of the statesman. The work of that convention was, after the surrender of the army, with all its appointments and equipments, ignored and repudiated by Andrew Johnson, who had just acceded to the presidency of the United States, in consequence of the ever-to-be-lamented assassination of Mr. Lincoln. Mr. Johnson lived long enough to regret—if his subsequent political course may be regarded as testimony— that he put his foot upon that basis of settlement—not the *reconstruction*, but the *reconciliation* of the States. The effects of that rejection—or rather, of that *ignorition*, (if I may be

allowed to coin a word,) are felt now; and happy it will be
if all their traces shall be wiped out ere many years yet to
come "be numbered with those before the flood."

For several years, Judge Stephens was a member of the
Presbyterian Church; he, however, dissolved his connection therewith—not because his faith in the truth of Christianity had in any degree abated, but because he had lost
faith in so many who called themselves Christian men. The
contrast between their practice and their profession was too
marked and too wide for his charity to cover; for this reason, coupled with the additional one, that he did not entirely subscribe to all the tenets, rites and ordinances of any
of the denominations, he quit the fellowship. In February,
1866, he gives this partial epitome of his religious faith, in
a letter to a female friend:

. . . . I think I am very nearly, if not
quite, devoid of religious prejudices. . . . . . I believe
in Christ as the Son of God and the Saviour of men. I believe He was made man for our Teacher and Pattern, and
that His teachings and life should receive implicit obedience and imitation, so far as God may, with propriety and
without offense, be imitated by men. While I believe all
this, yet I confess to you frankly, that I have never been
able to believe that any one of the many organizations,
claiming each for itself to be His peculiar and exclusive
representative on earth, is either altogether bad or altogether good. I can but regard them all as partaking of the
infirmities of the poor human beings who compose them.
. . . .

Judge Stephens suffered intensely at times from dyspepsia. It was his physical demon—his thorn in the flesh.
His occasional fits of depression—of melancholy—sometimes augmented into moroseness, which none but those
who knew him with some degree of intimacy could well account for—are attributable to that cause.

To the same friend, he writes:

SPARTA, February 12, 1866.

. . . . You were perfectly right, my friend, in saying that I ought to be back in ———. I have never been so well off since I left there as I was while there; and this leads me to incur the horrible risk of boring you (this idea of being a bore at all, particularly of being a bore to *you*, is intolerable) by giving you some account of my *health*. Do you know what dyspepsia is? I hope you do not. I really think it is the worst bodily (ah! and mental) affliction I ever endured. About five years ago, I was an intense sufferer from it. The horror of it must be felt to be understood. The deep melancholy; the constant *feeling* of being on the verge of paralysis, and of consequent imbecility; the profound disgust with life, petulance which constantly disgusts one with his own littleness; the waking up twenty times in a night with a sense of deadness in your limbs, and with a sense that if you had waked one moment later, you must have died instantly—can you begin to conceive of it, my friend? I believe a dyspeptic must have written these lines:

> "But, ah! life's beauty and its pride,
> Its freshness and its light,
> Have fled, and little left beside
> But weariness and blight."

By the way, do you know these lines? You must have *seen* them, but I trust and believe that you have never *known* them. I have. I will only mention one other very distressing peculiarity of this horrible visitation: the utter incapacity for any prolonged mental exertion. Well, I recovered; I never felt, however, that I was in possession of good health again until last fall, during my sojourn in the glorious climate of ———, and at a distance from cares, and in the midst of friends who made the time pass so delightfully. Then I regained my health fully, and "Richard" felt that he was "himself again." Now, what I have to tell you farther is, that I have, to a very considerable extent, relapsed into that old "slough of despond." This attack is not so decided as the old one; and then there are now many mitigating surroundings; for you must remember that the great horror consists in the effect upon the *mind*—upon its fears and affections, and upon its natural clinging to life. In the first place, it is no mean advantage to have the experience of having passed through all this before. In the next place, a man who has lost a country, lost thousands of warm friends in the mismanagement of a holy cause; who has seen human blood poured out like great rivers, yet poured in vain—such a man *must* have a very diminished appreciation of the value of any one poor life, even if that one happens to be his own. Such an experience necessarily reduces a man's capacity for misery. I do not say this in a spirit of sardonic defiance, but in the sober spirit of comforting philosophy—that same old philosophy which discovered that a fellow at the bottom of fortune's wheel has at least one advantage from the situation—the sense of security against anything worse. Well, the "murder is out" now. I have never written so much as this at any one time before in my life, to any one person, on the subject of my own ailments. I have talked it sometimes during the days of my horrors, but then I could regulate the quantity by my observations on the patience of the listener. I have thrown myself utterly upon your mercy, trusting somewhat to your generosity, as well as to the warmth and truth of your friendship. But, my friend, don't you believe but what I shall get well again. I should get over it very soon if I could control my own time, as I hope to do soon, but that I have not been able to do for a long time past. You have no idea how I am constantly pressed and annoyed by people who come to me for advice and assistance in these terrible times; but be assured that I am preserving a reasonable patience, even under the tortures of a disease which tries one's patience in a peculiar degree. They are my fellow-sufferers in a noble cause, and that memory invests them with a respect which is not always due to their personal worth. I hope to be able to take a little recreation soon, and run away from trouble for a while and get well again. . . . .

To another female friend, he writes:

SPARTA, March 18, 1866.

. . . . After finishing and sealing up my letter of last night, I have remembered to return to you

brother's letter which ———— sent me.   I cannot let it pass
by without telling you how profoundly I am gratified at the
good understanding and cordial relations which now seem
to be established between those whom I love best.   There
is between you and dear brother a great deal more in common than you have even yet suspected.   With a very
marked simplicity of character in most respects, he still has
a peculiar reserve which has never been entirely penetrated
by anybody but me, and perhaps not entirely even by me.
He has been an extraordinary sufferer—mental as well as
physical—and I am sure he has never confided the nature
of his keenest mental sufferings to anybody but me.   I
would tell you all about it if I could do so without a breach
of confidence.   I will only add that he has come out conqueror over all his sufferings, and has at last ceased to suffer
from the one great cause.   He has a deep, intense nature,
but long, and patient, and watchful self-discipline has obtained the mastery over it.   He now moves along—for
years has moved along—in peace and contentment, with
eye, and heart, and soul fixed steadily on the things which
lie beyond the dark, cold river.   His earthly affections are
warm and pure, and, in one instance, very strong; but they
are all subordinated to duty and to Heaven.   His religion
is very beautiful, and forms a large part of the present man.
It is exceedingly modest, almost shrinking from all human
observation; but it is very deep and very constant.   He
does not know that I am aware of this; and if I were to tell
him of it, it would be like the sudden dropping of a great
stone into a deep, quiet, shady pool.   He has never talked
much to me about religion, and still less to other people;
what I know of his religion has been gathered chiefly from
my habit of putting things together in connections, which
sometimes brings true light out of them—*sed satis*.   .   .   .

After the election of Mr. A. H. Stephens to the United
States Senatorship by the General Assembly of 1865–66, he
was *granted permission* to visit the federal capital.   His Fort
Warren parole had previously restricted the theater of his
movements to the State of Georgia.   From Washington
City, he wrote his brother:

[From A. H. S. to L. S.]

WASHINGTON, D. C., April 8, 1866.

DEAR BROTHER— . . . . The President received me with frankness, and I may say cordiality. The cabinet received me as cordially as any cabinet ever did. All sides—Democrats and Republicans, Conservatives and Radicals—seemed glad to see me. General Grant seems to be very marked in his regards for me. He is a most extraordinary man in some respects. The invitation given me to spend the evening with him, to which I alluded in my other letter, I did not understand exactly at first. It was the evening of one of his receptions. There was a very large company. President Johnson was there—the first instance of a President of the United States ever going out into society, as it may be termed, or accepting an invitation to join a party of friends on such an occasion as this. I was much entertained at two things I witnessed there—or rather, one thing and two reflections on it: that was that General Grant and the President seemed a little awkward, or not at ease, in the characters they were acting. They both seemed to be out of their element. This, in Grant, I was pleased at; but somehow I would have preferred to see the President more graceful and elegant—or rather, more at ease in his manners. Everything, however, passed off very well and very agreeably. There was a perfect jam and a great array of fashion and court-style. I send you two slips— one from the *Herald* and one from the *Times* correspondents—giving an account of it. The longest one is from the *Herald*. My own opinion is that I was *more looked at* than any man present, and more talked to, though I did endeavor to keep in the back-ground. Sir Frederick Bruce sought an introduction to me. I give this as an illustration of the state of things. He is a gentleman of fine personal appearance, and talks well. I declined to see him on his visit to Fort Warren. Mr. Burlingame told me Sir Frederick wished to see me when he was there, and Major Livermore said if I would signify a request to see him, under his orders, he would allow it. I told Mr. Burlingame that it might not be approved at Washington, as I was a State-prisoner and he a foreign minister, etc., and no such interview had been anticipated or thought of when he had been permitted to

visit the fort, or when I had been permitted to see such
friends as I might desire.   Sir Frederick alluded, the other
night, to his visit to Fort Warren, and his desire then to
see me, etc., but did not disclose any knowledge, on his
part, of my agency in his not succeeding.

But I find my letter becoming too long.   You wish,
doubtless, to know what I think of things here.   Well, I
think of them just about as I did before I got here.   Nothing will be done towards the admission of Southern members this session.   This question will most probably be decided by the next fall elections.   The most radical men in
Congress—the most *rabid*—talk with me heartily, freely and
fully, and I think I may say, almost unanimously, would
prefer to see me in the Senate to any other man from the
South—or, at least, they say so.   So my election has certainly done the State no harm in this particular.   The point
on which they are going to rally is a proposition to amend
the Constitution on the suffrage question—to allow admission to those States which will agree to an amendment allowing representation on the *ratio* of votes.   This will be, I
think, the Radical platform for the next fall elections, and
I need not say that I think it will be rather a dangerous
platform for us before the Northern people.   How easily
this might have been avoided by the Southern people in
allowing a wisely-restricted suffrage to the black race in
their new Constitutions!   This proposition, however, ema-
nates from no real philanthropic sentiment for the negro.
It is, when sifted to the bottom, founded upon nothing but
a desire for power.   It is not believed that the Southern
States will grant suffrage under it to the black race, even if
it should be adopted.   The object is to deprive the South
of political power, and to leave the poor, unfortunate sons
of Africa, as our fellow-citizens, to their fate.

I called to see Senator Wilson yesterday.   This was in
discharge of an act of duty for his personal kindness to me
while in prison.   He introduced Mrs. Wilson to me at General Grant's party; I, therefore, called to see both of them.
We had a long, pleasant talk, differing widely on many
points, but agreeably.   I got a letter, a day or two ago,
from Mrs. S———.   She is in Baltimore, and I shall go
over to see her in a few days.   She will continue or remain
there next, or rather this week.   I shall try and prevail on

her to go on with me to Georgia.   I now think I shall start
home the latter part of the week.   That, though, is uncertain.   Many urge me to remain here, and if I see any prospect of doing good by it, I may do so; but, really, I do
not now see that I can do more good than I shall do by the
latter part of this week.   By that time, my views will be
very generally known.   The loss of the Civil Rights bill—
or rather, the passage of that bill, in the Senate, over the
veto—might have been prevented.   I cannot go into particulars now—one more vote would have sustained the veto.
The vote stood 33 to 15—48 voting.   The whole Senate
now is 50; but Stockton having been turned out leaves a
full Senate—49.   Dixon, of Connecticut, was sick in his
room, and would have voted, making the vote 33 to 16.
That would have sustained the veto, under the understanding of the Senate.   By that understanding, it required 17
votes when the whole vote was 49; but I think differently.
If Dixon had voted, as he would have done if he had
thought that his vote would have prevented the passage of
the bill, the vote would have stood, 33 yeas to 16 nays,
making 49 in all; 33 is not two-thirds of 49.   The general
opinion was that it would take 17 votes to sustain the veto,
and he did not go to the Senate.   But I think 16 would
have done it.   The bill, I have no doubt, will pass the
House.   I don't attach any great importance to this measure.   It will not affect Georgia, I think, or any other State
that has done as she has.   I have not read the bill carefully; but this is my understanding of it: the great error of
the bill is the principle assumed in its passage, the jurisdiction claimed by Congress, etc. . . . .

To his intimate friend, Samuel Barnett, Judge Stephens
writes, May 25, 1866:

[From L. S. to Samuel Barnett, Esq.]

DEAR SAM—You are, of course, aware of what decision
Judge Reese has made in our insurance case.   Mr. Hull
acquiesces in it, and has sent me the money—three thousand and sixty dollars—which I have paid over to Mrs.
Stanford, reserving five hundred as counsel-fees.   Is this
enough?   I am sure it is not too much; and yet, I felt

equally sure that, in taking a fee from a poor widow, you
would trust our joint interest to my sense of proper charity.
That is really my only apology for not consulting you before fixing the fee.   In a similar case, I should expect you
to do just as I have done.   The money was in hand and
the woman wanted it—not only desired it, but needed it.
If you had been at hand, I certainly should have consulted
you before paying it over, and fixing our fees; but as you
were not present, and sometime required to hear from you,
why, I just did as I would have you do in such a case—I
acted for both of us; and, as I have begun to play dictator,
I believe I will run the part through, and tell you that your
half of it is in my hands, subject to your order.   What shall
I do with it?   We are all well as usual, and I hope you and
yours are so, too.   I saw your two boys, the other day, out
at Dick's school.   The eldest is a very close copy of you.
I was pleased to make their acquaintance, and pleased at
the air with which they greeted me.   It plainly told that
they knew they were grasping the hand of their father's
friend, and that they had no doubt of a cordial reception
for his sake.

Most truly yours,

LINTON STEPHENS.

P. S.—Did I tell you I had found Underwood's answer?
I am awfully afraid we shall never get any fee in that case
beyond the tobacco which I have already got out of him.
You don't smoke?   Well, then, you will get no "half" in
this business.   L. S.

The next extract from one of his letters not only discloses
his method of reading an author, but illustrates a prominent
feature of his intellectual character:

[From L. S. to a female friend.]

JUNE 6, 1866.

. . . .   You say you know I love study;
and so I do in my own way; but I have a horror of details
and minutiae.   I love to group facts into large generaliza-
tions, but the plodding after small facts, which have no significance, save in the brains of heated enthusiasts, is irk-

some and impossible to me beyond conception. I scarcely
ever read any book entire, except those I read purely for
entertainment. When I am studying to master a subject,
I wouldn't read all that any one man in the world ever
wrote on it, if he wrote *much*. When I am studying, I am
a terrible fellow to skip pages, and often chapters. I want,
first, the grand outlines, and then I will call for such fillings
up as I need; and a great deal of the filling up, which is
almost always considered essential by those who write
books, I never do heed, and, therefore, cannot very patiently tolerate. . . . .

[From L. S. to A. H. S.]

JULY, 1866.

DEAR BROTHER—We got home yesterday, before sunset,
all right. As we were entering the yard-gate, I remarked
to Becky, who was in the buggy with me, that it seemed
that she and her little sisters ought to be running to meet
me, and that a return home without a welcome or joyous
greeting from somebody or other was a sad thing. Little
did I then know how complete the lack of a welcome would
be when we drove up in front of the door. Cosby was sitting on the colonnade, reading Shakspeare. The little
ones cried out, "How d'ye, Mr. Connel?" before they got
out of the carriage, and then hurried to shake hands with
him. He slowly laid aside his book and spectacles, and
gave them a very hearty greeting. He and they were soon
deeply immersed in the exchange of news, and he gave no
indication of being at all aware of my being out in the yard.
None of the servants came to meet us. As Henry was
with us to take the horses, my thoughts turned on Pompey,
whose habit was to rarely fail in giving his welcome on my
return home, and my eye went in search of him, but found
him not. I felt uneasy, but said not a word to anybody.
Presently, the little ones, who got the news from Cosby,
came running out, and told me that Pompey was dead. I
almost reeled, as if somebody had struck me a blow. Poor
old Pompey, then, would never welcome me any more!
Dead! and buried out of my sight forever! The first thought
was for the poor old dog himself—the next for myself; the
realization of how rapidly the things which love me were
passing away shot through my heart with a keen and sud-

den pang! There are very few people in this world who would believe how much I was affected by the fate of a dog— a mere dog—nothing but a dog! He was, nevertheless, a great deal to me. I do almost mourn and grieve for the poor old fellow! . . . . I never was so much affected by any death outside of my own race— not even in the warm and tender-hearted days of my childhood. My poor old dog! my poor old dog! If he was a spirit still existing, and cognizant of the scene from which his body has departed, he feels to-day a grateful pleasure in the tears which his beloved master is shedding over his grave. I could have better spared many more valuable things.*

[From A. H. S. to L. S.]

CRAWFORDVILLE, July 24, 1866.

DEAR BROTHER— . . . . I am now reading Napoleon's "Julius Cæsar." The book is a very different one from what I expected. It is in two volumes. The first one I have not quite got through with yet. It is taken up with an epitome of the History of Rome up to the time of Cæsar's figuring in it. I like it very much. It is connected and clear, and, above all, what is agreeable to me, it gives the dates, as it goes along, from the founding of the city. It exhibits more learning than I should have supposed Napoleon to possess; the citation of authorities is more numerous than in any history I ever read, and a good portion of the pages is filled in this way. The paper upon which it is published is thick and heavy, making the volumes cumbrous and inconvenient to handle; besides, the leaves are not cut, which annoys me some; but, upon the

---

* Judge Stephens had a peculiar fondness for dogs and for horses. No one could be more kind to them, or more considerate of their comfort. He loved to feed them from his own hand, and took delight in seeing them eat. He prepared for the historic dog, *Rio*, so long the pet of " Liberty Hall," this epitaph:

RIO:
" Here rest the Remains
Of what, in Life, was a Satire on the Human Race,
And an Honor to his own—
A Faithful Dog,"

whole, I am tolerably well pleased. I suppose the cream of the work is in the last, or second volume. He has this philosophy—that *men* first make, or found, or form, institutions, and then these institutions form, or mold, the characters of men. These, in their time, react on the institutions, etc. He is a man of ideas. I see, clearly, that he is about to make Cæsar the great man of Rome. He was the advocate of popular rights against the incroachments of an insolent, corrupt aristocracy. I always had kindness of feeling towards Cæsar until I read Cicero last summer. Whether Napoleon will win back my generous sympathy for him, I don't know yet. I got my first ideas of Cæsar from Dr. Foster.* . . . .

[From A. H. S. to L. S.]

CRAWFORDVILLE, July 25, 1866.

DEAR BROTHER— . . . . I am still on "Julius Cæsar." I need hardly say, I suppose, that Napoleon is winning back, in some degree, my old regard for the great man. . . . .

[From A. H. S. to L. S.]

CRAWFORDVILLE, July 31, 1866.

DEAR BROTHER—I got nothing from you this morning. I am anxious to hear from you about the convention, whether you will go or not. I see that the great Ocean Telegraph has succeeded at last. America and Europe are put in immediate communication through the wonderful and mysterious agency of magnetic electricity! What next? I have got through with the second volume of "Julius Cæsar," by Napoleon, but was sadly disappointed at the end. It closed with the crossing of the Rubicon by Cæsar, the beginning of the civil war. I had expected the volume to

---

* The Dr. Foster alluded to was the late Dr. Thomas Foster, of Walker county. He was a bold, original thinker, and a gentleman of learning and culture. To him, as much as to any one else, is the State indebted for the construction of the Western & Atlantic Railroad. Mr. Stephens' speech carried the measure in the Legislature. Dr. Foster supplied him with much of his *data*, both of fact and argument.

finish a full history of his whole life, closing with the *Et tu, Brute!* which, in the fore part of the work, Napoleon says were his last words. He says that Cæsar spoke and wrote Greek nearly as well as he did Latin. Of course, there is to be another volume—perhaps more, I don't know. Napoleon is a great man himself. In drawing the character of Cæsar, he is evidently drawing the character of one whom he would like to be considered himself. The book shows mind of a high order, and sentiments which ought to do honor to any rational mind. Some points are cleared up in this book which were always unexplained to me: one is, What was the exact point of difference between Cæsar and the Senate, which led to civil war? I can but think, with Dr. Foster, that Cæsar was not *so much* to blame for the sad results as others. His enemies, at first, passed a resolution in the Senate that he should disband his army. This he had before said he would do if Pompey would do the same. The time was not out for which they both held their commissions; his lacked a year or more. After the Senate passed the resolution ordering him to disband his army, very much to the surprise of Marcellus, the Consul at the time, who had taken the lead in the matter, Cicero offered a resolution that Pompey also disband his army, and this resolution likewise passed by over two hundred majority. But Marcellus would not obey the last resolution. He and others (a few) declared the commonwealth in danger; and, without any legal authority, called upon Pompey to protect Rome—to levy troops, etc. Pompey consented, and assumed the powers thus usurped. Upon this news reaching Cæsar, he crossed the Rubicon. The reason of the opposition to Cæsar in the Senate was his known hostility to the Aristocratic party and their policy, which had been carried out by Sylla. He was the representative man of the people of that party; while the Gracchi and Marius were the representatives of the Democratic party. Cæsar, on the paternal line, had descended from plebeian stock.

. . . .

The following extracts from letters addressed to a female friend evince a strong and beautiful religious element of his nature—never ostentatiously displayed, but always felt, and on befitting occasions acknowledged:

JUNE 3, 1867.

. . . . There is not, in all the beauty of the plan for man's salvation, a more beautiful picture than the provision of a Priest after the order of Melchisedek. "Touched with a sense of our infirmities," His sympathy, His suffering with and for those He came to save, His very suffering is, in a certain limited sense, incompatible with a *totality of perfection*. The *human* nature, touched with a *sense* of our infirmities, partaking, not at all of our sin, but still in our *weakness*, is the very thing which renders Him a *Mediator* between God and man, which brings the Son into the closest and sweetest relations with the hearts of men.

. . . .

[From same to same.]

JANUARY 6, 1867.

. . . . The very same sentiment has different phases, and finds vent in different expressions, without suffering any change of nature or force. God is above all change in *Himself*, and yet He is ever presenting Himself to His creatures in endless changes of manifestation and expression—the necessary result of His fullness and infinitude of glory. Of course, I do not mean a *comparison;* I only mean to illustrate, by the highest example, an idea which struck me as likely to need illustration. Speculations concerning the Divine character (I know no better word) are always dangerous ground, and should be cautiously and reverently restrained within proper limits; but there are limits, after all, within which our conceptions of God are not speculations at all, *but knowledge*—more certain, by far, than that which we can possibly have of any other being in the universe. To dwell on his known attributes and character, and from these, as our starting point, to learn the Unknown—so far as poor human reason can draw sure conclusions from sure premises—is not irreverence, but the study of the profoundest wisdom, reverence, fear, love, and worship. My thoughts turn, very often, upon the contemplation and reverent study of the Supreme Intelligence which fashioned the universe, and filled it with beauty; and of the Infinite love which provided redemption for man, who had fallen from the high estate of his creation.

I am prone—perhaps too prone—to draw from that high and holy source illustrations for even the tritest ideas of every-day life. What, after all, *is* religion but the knowledge of God, applied to all the affairs of life? The knowledge involves and carries with it the love and adoration; and the deepest knowledge brings love and adoration of the highest type. . . . .

After the lapse of twenty-nine years, he thus recalls a half-dreamy revery of his orphaned childhood:

[From same to same.]

MAY 8, 1867.

This is a bright and beautiful morning—a bright and beautiful morning in May; a bright and beautiful morning, bursting upon my little sense with a brilliance which is a glorious contrast with the clouds, and rain, and gloom of yesterday and the day before. Yes, the morning is bright and beautiful, but it is cool—quite cool. We have had a narrow escape from frost. The green glories, which are so radiant with life and sunlight, have had a narrow escape from death and darkness. But they have escaped; and if they had human thoughts and feelings, they might now be rejoicing in the new joy of a great peril safely passed. I remember, there was a frost just twenty-nine years ago this very day—the 8th of May, 1838. Ah! how far back my memory runs! How well I remember that day, twenty-nine years ago! I was a little school-boy then, boarding in the country, and walking to the village school, a distance of two miles. That morning, I mastered a lesson before breakfast, sitting in a *swing* that hung out in the large, white, sandy, shady yard—sitting, swinging to and fro, with a slight, gentle motion, and conning my lesson, yet listening all the while to the low, soft music of the young poultry crying for their morning meal. I was a little dreamer, even then; strangely enough, too—strangely for so young a dreamer, my thoughts turned to the past, not the future. The lesson finished, the book was laid in my lap, my arms were clasped around the poles which formed the swing, one foot keeping up the gentle swaying motion, by a regular, recurring, mechanical, and almost unconscious touch upon the ground; my head drooped upon my breast, and thought floated upon the sweet, plaintive sounds around me, away to the spot where reposed the ashes of my loved but *unremembered dead*. I was in the past, and yet not in the land of memory. Imagination was picturing out the scenes of the old homestead, as best it could from the treasured materials of imperfect tradition. There was the log-house in which I was born, the garden, the orchard, the immense wild grape-vine, amid the great rocks, at a little distance; and the spring—the glorious spring, bursting from a rock under a great bluff, and dashing and dancing down the valley in a bright stream, that sang as merrily as it danced. And I strayed back up the hill again, in search of the living forms that moved amid the scene. Father, brothers, and sisters rose up before my eager eyes, but my deepest interest was centered in the tall form of a *woman*, still young and handsome, moving with a sedate grace, which bespoke the very sweetness of dignity, and selecting for her walk the very sweetest spots, with an unerring instinct, that told of a heart at once deeply loving and deeply *hallowed*. She seemed to cast bright and hopeful glances towards the "new house" rising unfinished from a clump of trees on the brow of a gentle slope. She had laid away some of her darlings among the cedars in the garden; but she was now beginning to emerge from the darker shades of poverty, and was about to secure a *better house*, a sweeter home, for the dear ones who were left to her love. But, ah! the "new house" was destined to remain unfinished forever! The cedars in the garden! The lovely form pointed me to the cedars in the garden, and then faded from my view. I followed her pointing, and stood solitary and desolate among the cedars in the garden! Amid their deep, dark shade was a grave—*her* grave, already grass-grown from age! Lilies—sweet, white lilies—were bending over it, and dropping their fragrance upon the sacred dust. The boy in the swing uttered a low, deep moan, and burst into tears—tears of intense yearning for the unknown blessing of a mother's love! . .

. . . .

In May, 1865, Mr. A. H. Stephens, ex-Vice-President of the Confederate States, was arrested at his home by a de-

tachment of United States soldiers. He was carried to
Boston harbor, and imprisoned in Fort Warren. After
months of confinement, friends from the South, and else-
where, were permitted to visit him. This was accomplished
mainly through the personal and persistent exertions of the
late Henry Wilson, afterwards Vice-President of the United
States. It was by his efforts, too, that Mr. Stephens was
granted more comfortable quarters, after weeks of exposure
and suffering in a damp, unwholesome dungeon. As soon
as intelligence reached Judge Stephens that he would be
allowed to see his brother, he left his business, his home,
his children, to visit and stay with the captive—thus voluntarily accepting the privations of prison-life, and sharing
with him the hardships of a common cell. It is a noble
exemplification of unselfish devotion, recalling and excel-
ling the beautiful, fraternal affection which makes the fame
of the Cicero brothers "*whiter* than it is brilliant." The
incident proved to be one of the fortunate felicities in the
life of Judge Stephens—a "blessing in disguise." Among
the almost daily visitors to Fort Warren, after permission
granted, were Dr. Salter and family. They were residents
of Boston. Of the members of the family, was one whom
Judge Stephens had met five years before, in Washington
City—a bright and beautiful girl, then not past her teens.
Memories, doubtless, of those earlier and better days were
revived; a mutual attachment sprang up between them; it
ripened into a warmer passion, and she—Mary W. Salter—
became his wife in June, 1867. This excellent lady is still
in life—*serus in cælum redeat;* but still, it is hardly doing
violence to this necrological office to record, that, in all respects, she was to him a help-meet indeed, and that the testimonials he has left of her worth and her virtues, and of
his high appreciation of her in the relations of wife and
mother, shed an aromatic redolence around their wedded
life. I well remember the last time I saw Judge Stephens.

It was the afternoon he left Atlanta—to return no more—
in the first days of July, 1872. He had been engaged by
the Governor, as counsel in behalf of the State, to assist in
investigating the alleged frauds of the preceding State administration; and some weeks had been occupied in making
the investigation. We took a long walk together. The
thought of going home was uppermost in his mind, and the
pleasure it gave him lit up his features with an unwonted
glow of sunshine and joy. He spoke of the sweet attractions of his home; of his wife and children, so affectionately and so fondly; and then—a tear standing in his large,
deep-set, blue eye—he said, "How I wish I were through
with this business! I would not give *one* day at home for
a lifetime of the toil and turmoil of public or professional
life." His manner lent emphasis to the words, and deep-
ened the impression they made.

[From A. H. S. to L. S.]

PHILADELPHIA, 415 NORTH FOURTH STREET,
February 13, 1868.

DEAR BROTHER—Your two letters, or rather, coverings,
with contents, of the 7th instant, were received last night.
I regret very much indeed the fatality, or bad luck, which
caused the delay of my letter to you, inclosing the introduction. Your suggestions have produced a very deep impression upon me. The impression is not unlike that which
I supposed was produced upon Myers, the painter, by a
view of Healy's picture, according to the account you gave
me of it. I was myself very much pleased with the introduction—indeed, better pleased with it than with any part
of the work; but when I read your remarks upon it, and
saw your suggestions for improvement, I changed my mind
about the whole concern. I became disgusted, not only
with the introduction, but with the whole work. If matters
had not gone so far, I should have pitched the whole into
the fire and retired to my den, there to live out my days,
few or many, in perfect seclusion.

I am now fully convinced that writing is not my *forte*.

The truth is, I have no *forte*. I am fit for nothing, and ought never to have attempted to do what nature never designed me to do. Had I got your letter a few days ago, the introduction would have been thoroughly remodeled. But it is now all over the country—in the mails and in the hands of the newspaper men in this city, and all the leading presses in New York and Boston, to appear simultaneously to-morrow morning—so Mr. Jones informs me. It is too late to touch it now, before its full appearance before the public. The first impression will be that which will ever accompany it. For the book, I might do with it as Foster's boy proposed to his father to do with the beef—throw it away, and try my hand upon another; but that would do no essential good. I now feel about the whole book—the whole undertaking—as John Dyson did when his rusticity and ill-breeding exposed him to the laugh of genteel company—"*I wish I was to home;*" but when I shall get there, I do not know. . . . . I have lost all interest I had to see the book out: I now feel as if it would be a fortunate thing for me and my reputation, that something should occur to arrest its further progress, and prevent its ever seeing the light. I hardly think I can be at our Taliaferro court.

If you can go over there, I wish you would; and if you can be at Columbia court, I wish you would attend to a case in equity in that court for me; my client is Crawford, a brother to George W.; Charles, I believe, his name is. If you cannot go conveniently, it will make no great difference—I shall write to Shockley, and ask him to continue it; but I should like for you to go, if you can, without inconvenience. I don't know if you have any court to attend that week: it is the first Monday in March, I believe. My love to all.

Yours, most affectionately,

ALEXANDER H. STEPHENS.

The book alluded to in the foregoing letter is "The History of the War between the States." How well founded Mr. Stephens' misgivings were as to its merits and popularity, may be judged of by the fact that his receipts from sales amounted to the sum of forty thousand dollars.

SPRINGFIELD, MASS., February 25, 1868.

DEAR BROTHER— . . . . I see the House has passed a resolution, directing articles of impeachment to be brought in against the President: this I have been looking for for sometime. The President's letter to the Senate, in answer to their resolution on the subject, is an able paper, and will forever justify his acts in the minds of rightly-thinking men, whatever may be the result of the impeachment question. I have said nothing to you on politics, lately—nothing since I left home. The reason has been, I take very little interest in the subject. I feel like a passenger who has no control in the direction of the ship; and hence, it is just as well to be silent, and not busy myself about matters over which I cannot exercise any control, and not to permit myself to vex my mind, or think about public affairs. . . . .

Judge Stephens felt the most anxious solicitude in the result of the Presidential election of 1868; but he took no active part in the contest. The ashes left by the fires of the sectional war were yet too warm to be stirred. The expression of any choice for the presidency, by any Southern leader who had been prominently identified with the fortunes of his section, in the struggle, would, he believed, hurt, rather than help, the cause he had at heart; and therefore, conforming his conduct to the principle of the mathematical axiom, " the addition of a negative quantity is equivalent to the subtraction of a positive one," he held himself aloof from active participation in the contest.

———, June 1, 1868.

DEAR BROTHER— . . . . I have just written to her in relation, or in answer, to what she asks about Judge Chase, that, in my opinion, Pendleton is the man for the Democratic party to nominate. In my opinion, he is the strongest man that can be nominated, and, upon the

whole, is the best, all things considered.   I stated that I
would be willing to take Hancock, Thomas Seymour, Governor Parker, or Adams, or any one that the Democracy
may likely nominate, not excepting Judge Chase.   In the
present state of things, if the Democracy should nominate
him, he would be preferred by the South as a choice of
evils.   This I gave as my own opinion ; but I stated that I
did not think that the Western Democracy would nominate
Chase.   I stated that I thought that Hancock and Adams
would make a ticket that would take well in Georgia.   But
can Hancock run well in the West?   I added, wouldn't his
compulsory connection with Mrs. Surratt's condemnation
lose him many votes at the West?   The letter, I told her,
was for herself only, but I concluded by saying that, in my
opinion, Pendleton was, or ought to be, the man. . . . . .

[L. S. to Hon. Iverson L. Harris.]

SPARTA, July 21, 1868.

MY DEAR JUDGE—Great is my regret that I cannot be at
home when you propose to spend the day with me on your
way to commencement.   I start, to-morrow morning, for
the Virginia Springs ; and the state of my health requires
that there should be no failure in the trip.   I do not expect
to return before the middle of September.   I hope you
will avail yourself of some other early occasion to make me
a visit.   By the way, why don't you come to our courts ?
Come to our next, and spend your time with me ; and let
me know beforehand whether you will come or not.

I have long intended to tell you how much I admire your
dissenting opinion in the case where the majority of the
court decided against the validity of a contract for a substitute in the Confederate armies.   Your opinion, for the luminous, philosophical, and sound views which it presents
on a subject of profound interest to mankind, is entitled to
immortality.   If I were not very busy in preparing to leave
home, I would go into particulars.   As it is, I must content
myself with the general expression, which means all it says,
Most truly, your friend,

LINTON STEPHENS.

A proposition was made that Mr. A. H. Stephens should
move his residence from Crawfordville to Sparta, and that

the brothers should form a copartnership in the practice of law. The letter following relates to that subject. They had never been of counsel on opposing sides. If the proposition of partnership was ever seriously entertained, the consummation of it was frustrated by the terrible mishap which befell the elder brother in February, 1869, and from the physical effects of which he never sufficiently recovered, during Linton's lifetime, to be able to leave his home.

[From A. H. S. to L. S.]

CRAWFORDVILLE, November 8, 1868.

DEAR BROTHER—. . . . . I fully reciprocate your feelings and wishes as to our being together, as much as possible, during the remnant of my days, or our joint lives. I am the more and more, every day, impressed with the conviction of the truth of the great uncertainty of human affairs, and especially of the uncertainty of human life. I know I am approaching that period at which, or beyond which, a few years, at best, can be reasonably expected. This thought, or reflection, however, does not bring with it any feelings of regret or sadness; it only more fully awakens a desire to have all things in order, and to be ready to depart when the time comes; and also quickens a wish, while I am here, to enjoy, to the best advantage, and as fully as possible, those pleasures which contribute what of happiness is allowed to this form of existence. To me, amongst those, none are greater than such as spring from association and communion with you, especially when we are entirely to ourselves. I have often thought of the many, many associations of this sort—such as our travels to the western part of the State, in 1847, as well as our repeated travels to Washington and other places, to say nothing of our short drives from here to Sparta, and from court to court. . . . .

[From A. H. S. to L. S.]

CRAWFORDVILLE, December 31, 1868.

DEAR BROTHER— . . . . I never heard the inquiry made before about the origin of *ism*, in our language. I have thought about it since, and have solved the puzzle quite satisfactorily to myself. I think it is a sort of contraction of *them* into *em*, and *then* into *ism*. I will take catechism to illustrate by: First, it was catechise, then catechise 'em, then "catechism." The noun catechism came to be used to express the process of "catechising 'em." So incivism, from "incivise them;" so radicalism, from "radicalizing them," and so on. When once the form of making a noun from a previous proceeding, or process, was instituted, it was adopted, without reference to its origin. But I can say no more: you have my solution. It will do to account for it, if no better be pointed out. Radicalism is the process of "radicalizing them." I rather suspect catechism was the first of the words. It was the one I began with, in solving the problem. . . . .

The above was in answer to an inquiry of Judge Stephens. They frequently, in their correspondence, discussed the meaning of the like terminations; *e. g.*, God-head, Godship, etc.; as, see the following:

[From A. H. S. to L. S.]

CRAWFORDVILLE, January 2, 1869.

DEAR BROTHER— . . . . What is the origin of ship, at the end of English words; such as, worship, authorship, etc.? Also, what is the origin of ness, at the end of certain other words; such as, greatness, highness, manliness, etc.? . . . .

[From L. S. to A. H. S.]

SPARTA, January 6, 1869.

DEAR BROTHER— . . . . With a big and troublesome day's work before me, I begin by writing you a line to let you hear from us all. I am quite unwell—annoyed to death, besides being sick—made sick chiefly, perhaps, by annoyances. Land sold here, yesterday, at prices considerably higher than any recently obtained: one large place of thirteen hundred acres, at four dollars per acre, and one of one thousand acres at seven dollars.

Your account of the origin of "ism" is certainly very

ingenious; but I don't think it is correct. When you said you thought that the habit of forming words with the termination "ism," began with the word "*catechism*," the thing became rich in humor. The fact is, I laughed over your theory heartily. It certainly never could have started with any other word. How do you account for the termination "ise," in verbs; such as, advertise, catechise, harmonise, etc.? The "ise," in verbs, and the "ism," in nouns, are from the same root. What that root is cannot be told by my poor skill in the old English roots; but the *meaning* of that root is, to do, or *make*. Take advertise, for instance: advert and "*ise*" are its three distinct roots. To advertise a thing is to *make* it adverted to; you see my idea. The termination, "ship," means a *state*, or *situation*; and I strongly suspect that it comes from—no, I am wrong; it don't mean state. State is *passive*, but ship is *active*. It means something very nearly akin to process, or *practice*, or acting. For instance, authorship, author, practice, author-acting; heirship, heir-practice, or heir-acting. Sometimes, the meaning becomes more obvious by reversing the positions of the parts; as, author-acting, heir-acting, means acting-author or acting-heir. The termination, "ness," means *being*, existence, or *essence*; and I suspect "esse," in Latin, and essence and ness, are all from the same root, which probably pervades many languages, if it is, indeed, absent from any. The word to express "being" is irregular in all languages; and irregularity is in proportion to universality.

But enough. I have no time now. The fact is, I am harrassed, annoyed and worn almost to despair and prostration. I intend to go and see you in a few days.

Most affectionately,   LINTON STEPHENS.

[From L. S. to A. H. S.]

SPARTA, February 13, 1870.

DEAR BROTHER— . . . . By the way, the adjournment of the Richmond court may have a contagious influence on our courts generally; and I shall not be at all surprised if your court is also adjourned. I suppose you noticed an account of the adjournment in August—that it was put on the ground of doubt as to the validity of any proceedings which might be had.   I think the adjournment, on that ground, was a mistake, and a mistake which, from its contagious nature, may produce annoying delays in business.   If the courts would only go along and attend to their business, I have very little doubt that the validity of their proceedings would be sustained without even serious question.   Any government that is likely to be put on us will *treat* all its predecessors as *de facto* governments, whatever it may say about them.   The fact is, no Radical can believe more strongly than I do, that all the government which we have had since the war ended has been utterly illegal; but I am not prepared, nor do I believe the Radicals are prepared, to pronounce it all *null and void*.   They hold that all the government, under secession, was illegal; and yet, in their new Constitution, they affirmed every bit of it, except such parts as were in conflict with their own subsequent action.   So it will be again.   This is the necessity of society, and cannot be ignored in action, however much it may be denied in speech. . . . .

[From L. S. to A. II. S.]

SPARTA, May 31, 1870.

DEAR BROTHER— . . . . Alfriend himself had a decided attack of the same disease, and laid up on account of it yesterday and the day before.   I got quite a laugh on him, last night, by dragging out of him a confession that he had not used, for himself, the remedies which he was prescribing for his patients.   He made an explanation; but it was so lame that it did not make impression enough to be even remembered.   The explanation is— his reluctance to take medicine.   I don't think it would be quite just to go so far as to say that it is his lack of faith in the virtue of the medicine; and yet, there is undoubtedly a general tendency in mankind to appreciate the virtue of medicine more highly for *others* than for one's self.   I hope we shall all be well again in a few days. . . . . .

I have been reading "Bledsoe" with great entertainment and some profit.   He is a very peculiar man.   He is quite a thinker—and logical, too; but the light of his understanding seems to be always *refracted* by its passage through the medium of his passions.   It will always lead to error, instead of truth, unless it is subjected to the correcting guidance of some other mind that understands the laws of refraction. Still, he is a *luminous* body, and emits light in great profusion. Even his article on the "Theory of Reasoning," while it is freer from the blurs and errors of zeal and passion than any other which I have ever read from him, is still not entirely free. I think that is a grand article; and yet, I do not think it goes to the bottom of the subject. It is far in advance of anything else ever seen on the same subject, but does not go to the full extent of the ideas which I have long entertained on that subject. He has gone far ahead of me in the power and beauty of his illustrations, without going so far as I have gone with the main idea. The idea that deductive reasoning leads to new truth, and so becomes worthy of the name of *reasoning*, only when it is employed upon the relations of things, instead of their properties, etc. . . . . . . Sam. Barnett came over Wednesday and staid with us until Saturday morning. His visit was a very pleasant one to all of us, and apparently to him also. . . . .

Judge Stephens' norms of political action were fixed, pronounced and stable, as those he prescribed for the government of his personal conduct were "without variableness or shadow of turning." Truth—simple, naked, rugged—was the divinity he worshipped; he bowed before no other altar: *there* he knelt "with an almost Eastern idolatry." He scorned any "*policy*" in political tactics, as in anything else, which compromised, in the least, any cardinal doctrine of his creed. He spurned triumph when achieved at the sacrifice of one jot or tittle of the truth, as he understood it. He regarded "the coalition" between the Democrats and the Liberal Republicans, proposed about this time, as little less than a surrender, on the part of the former, of the most cherished principles of their faith. Hence, he repudiated "the coalition." His counsels did not prevail ultimately; and the movement culminated, two years afterwards, in the nomination of Mr. Greeley for the Presidency

30

by the Liberal Republicans, and the ratification of their nomination by the Democrats. Posterity will determine who was the more sagacious—he, and the minority with whom he acted, or the large majority of the Democratic party. Two facts are historic: the one that Mr. Greeley was defeated—the other is that Governor Smith was elected to the gubernatorial chair without regular opposition, first, and re-elected by the largest popular majority ever received by any candidate before for any office in the State. The platform upon which Smith was elected was framed by Linton Stephens.

On the 28th of July, he writes to his brother:

SPARTA, July 28, 1870.

DEAR BROTHER— . . . . I have just written a letter to Andy Dawson, on politics, pouring hot shot into the *Chase* movement, and into all people who want to abandon principle and go into coalitions for public plunder. I have talked with several leading Democrats in this county, and found them all right. They all said they wanted me to go to the convention. I told them I would go if chosen. I do believe that even one powerful battery would be sufficient to break up coalition and drive the hosts into the support of sound principles. The strong power to use on them is to convince them that a sound man, on sound principles, will be run *anyhow*, and that coalition will, therefore, be a necessary *failure*. Coalition flees from failure, as purity flees from pollution. They would pull down their own banner, and take chances for the *good luck* which falls pretty liberally to even the rogues who help honest men into power.

Yours, most affectionately,

LINTON STEPHENS.

[From L. S. to A. H. S.]

SPARTA, August 7, 1870.

DEAR BROTHER— . . . . The delegates from this county to the Democratic convention are—Ben

Harris, John Culver, T. J. Adams, and myself. I doubt whether any of them will go to the convention, except Ben Harris and myself. I shall go with very little hope of doing any good. The men of luck, all over the world, have been against the cause of good government ever since secession; and it is still unbroken. It is just as perverse and persistent as the run of cards. I believe that the Prussians will beat Napoleon, and accomplish Bismarck's scheme of a consolidated German Empire. I believe so, only because the run of luck is that way—*against liberty, everywhere*. The ideas now moving the world are, for the most part, morbid and crazy ideas, which are the legitimate fruit of hot-bed and universal education. I am beginning to believe that many things, usually accounted as unmixed blessings to mankind are more curses than blessings. Education is one of them, and religion is another. I speak of education and religion, *so-called*, and such as pass current in the world. Speaking of education reminds me to tell you that I expect to have your protege, Harris, for the teacher of our little school. I wrote to Professor Waddell to send me a teacher. He offered Harris, with a *very* high commendation of his talents, attainments, and character; and I have just written my acceptance of the offer. He is to remain at Athens, perfecting himself in the *pronunciation* of French, under Professor Charbonnier, until the 1st of October, and is then to come and open the school. So the children have quite a vacation still before them. . . . .

He was of the committee on the business of the State Democratic convention, and here follows the platform, as drafted by him, whereon the party so triumphantly swept the State:

Resolved, 1. That the Democratic party of the State of Georgia stand upon the principles of the Democratic party of the Union—bringing into special prominence, as applicable to the present extraordinary condition of the country, the unchangeable doctrine that: This is a Union of States, and of the indestructibility of the States, and of their rights, and of their equality with each other, as an indispensable part of our political system.

Resolved, 2. That, in the approaching State election, the Democratic party cordially invite everybody to co-operate with them in a zealous determination to change, as far as the several elections to be held can do so, the present usurping and corrupt administration of the State government, by placing in power men who are true to the principles of constitutional government, and to a faithful and economical administation of public affairs.

Resolved, 3. That the president of this convention be instructed to appoint an executive committee, composed of two from each Congressional district, who shall choose a chairman from outside their own number, with power on their part to call a future convention of the Democratic party, and with such other powers as have been usually exercised by Democratic executive committees; and that their appointment last until the assemblage of the next Democratic convention.

Judge Stephens was selected chairman of the State Democratic Executive Committee. In his letter of acceptance, he avowed so strongly his unalterable adhesion to the old faith, that some of the new-departurists, so-called, condemned his letter as impolitic. He resigned in consequence thereof. A meeting of the committee was called at Macon to fill the vacancy thereby created. The following letter to his friend, Hon. Martin J. Crawford, a member of the committee, evoked by the occasion, explains itself:

SPARTA, September 19, 1870.

DEAR JUDGE—Your letter, forwarded to me from home while I was at Greene court, was received last week. I had no opportunity to answer it then, nor was my mind then made up as to *all* I might have to say in answer. I did not need a moment's reflection to say that it gratified me very much, and made me laugh very heartily; but I needed both further developments and further reflection to determine my course; and I at once foresaw that, if my course should be what I have now determined it shall be, I should have to ask your *assistance*. Don't be alarmed, for I am not going to ask anything that involves martyrdom, or even heroism, or that requires you to incur any personal hazard whatever. Don't understand me as intimating the least doubt that you are capable of winning the hero's chaplet, or the martyr's crown, in a *proper case:* I only mean that, in the present instance, there is no *need* for the sacrifice.

The assistance I want involves a confidence, and although a confidence like a bargain, requires *two* to make it; yet, I do not feel that I am presuming too far on your friendship, in assuming that it will be accepted by you for me, as it would be accepted by me for you, in a like case. The executive committee, when it meets at Macon, on the 27th instant, may, or may not, elect me chairman. If I am *not* elected, why, there is an end of it, and there is nothing further to be done on *my part;* but if I am elected, then I wish to *decline* the appointment; and I wish you to express this determination for me *after the event,* and on the spot, and at the moment. Of course, I cannot allow the completion of the committee to be longer delayed by any action of mine; and, therefore, it shall not be prevented, by me, from *securing* a chairman before it disperses.

The confidence which I commit to you, is to keep my intention sacredly *secret* until the election is *over.* Don't communicate it to anybody at all, but keep it in your own breast until the election is over. I should despise myself if I were capable of holding out my intended declension as an *inducement* to bestow on me an empty personal compliment; but I am not weak enough to place the least value in it, if it should come in a way to deprive it of all *meaning.*

Therefore, it is essential that my intention shall not be made known before the proper time. If the question shall be raised, as it may be, whether I would accept or not, you are authorized to say I *would;* and then, if I should be elected, you are further authorized, and specially requested, to say that I *do accept,* and do also *resign.* There is a great deal in the way of putting a thing, and the way to put this thing is, not that I decline the position, but that I *accept it,* and *resign it.* There is a substantial and wide difference between the two things, and my form of statement is the proper one to develop the difference. The language which I have myself used in the preceding part of this letter, about "declining" and "declension," is inaccurate, and should not be repeated. The proper language, if the position be tendered to me, would be that I accept it, and resign it; and, therefore, the proper response beforehand, if the question should be asked, is, that I *would accept it*.   I ask you to act for me, because the action which I propose to take must be taken on the spot before the committee disperses, and I can't afford to be present myself at the meeting which is to make the election   I can't afford to be even in the city of Macon at the time; for I *will not* assume the appearance of seeking the place.   I am not seeking it, and I don't mean to incur the appearance of seeking it; and now, a few words for you, and for you alone, as to my course after the organization of the committee: It will depend on the action they may take in making that organization.   If they tender the chairmanship to me, and pass a resolution leaving the subject of selecting candidates with reference to so-called disabilities just where the convention left it, I shall be "harmonious;" but if they undertake to put any condemnation on my course or views, I shall make the *terrapin crawl*.   I know that I hold in my hands the necessary *coals of fire*, and I shall not withhold them from the back of the animal.   I don't intend to be thrown into disgrace, because I am unwilling to join in betraying the Democratic party by hauling down its colors, silencing its guns, and surrendering it bodily into the hands of the enemy; or, what is the same thing, by hauling down its colors and silencing its guns, and thus leaving it to become the inevitable prey of the enemy.   The men who want to haul down the colors and silence the guns want it as a means to an end, and that end is *surrender*.   Some of them, who are working on that line, and talking largely about ruling me out of the Democratic party, have just now, for the first time, come into the Democratic party themselves, and have come only to betray it, and to secure its defeat and destruction; and they are, at this moment, carrying B————'s money in their pockets as a price of their treachery.   If I were with you in person, I would tell you things which I am not yet ready to write, even to you; for I am not yet willing to commit them to the chances of the mail.   When men talk about "accepting our government as it is," as the convention in the ————th district talked the other day, and about putting away "dead issues," as ———— and ———— habitually talk, I know what they mean—they mean *treason*; and they take an inside position only to surrender the fortress. If the "issues" which the Democratic party made at New York, in 1868, against the validity of Radical usurpations and warfare on the States, are indeed "dead," then the Democratic party is dead also—dead already—although, like the dead stage-horse, it may not find out the fact until it gets to the next station. To abandon these issues, and accept the government as it is, means to form a *coalition* on the basis of giving some of the offices to so-called Democrats, and conducting the government on Radical principles, and all who join the coalition will become followers of ———— at a long distance behind. The fact is, they will be out of *smelling* distance at the start, and will need infinite self-abasement to bring them within range of it. They will have to acknowledge ————'s superior sagacity in foreseeing the necessity three years in advance of themselves, and they will also have to confess, with great openness and contrition, their mortal sin in having withheld from him their aid during the very period when their aid might have enabled him to accomplish still greater ameliorations of a necessary bad thing.

This question, as to paying any regard to so-called disabilities in soliciting candidates for Congress, can be placed in a practical light that is exceedingly plain. It may be, as Judge Hook, in his recent letter, said with great force, that the Radical Congress will be *compelled*, by public opinion, to recede from its proscriptive policy, and by act remove all the so-called disabilities. If so, of course, it is all useless and foolish to pay any regard to those so-called disabilities in selecting candidates, or choosing members of Congress. But suppose Judge Hook is mistaken, and the Radical Congress shall *not* recede: then the removal of so-called disabilities will *remain*—as it heretofore has been—a matter of *grace*, in favor of particular persons; and no man of sense can doubt that the grace will be granted to none but such as will agree to accept the government as it is— usurpations and all—and *conduct* it on *that basis* without even a pledge against unlimited usurpation in the future. Why, ———— and ———— actually favored and advised the ratification of the so-called XVth amendment. This is the crucial test: Does the proposed candidate accept the government as it is—confessed usurpations and all—or does he, as the National Democratic party, in its late utterance at

New York, declared it would do, wage war upon the usurpations, and insist upon the Constitution in its purity, and
upon the rights of the States, which have been trampled
in the dust by these usurpations? To vote for a man holding the first of these positions is simply to kill the Democratic party by the action of its own members. If Radicalism is to be fought at all, I suppose it ought to be fought
for some reason ; and when a man tells me either that he
does not intend to attack it, or that he intends to attack it
without weapons, or with the weakest weapons in his armory, I know his course will never *whip it ;* and when he
pretends that it will, he is either a fool or a traitor. The
cry of "revolution" and "revolutionary," which is now applied, in unison, by the *Era* and the *True Georgian,* the
Constitution and the *Telegraph,* to any "issue" which is
made against the validity of the so-called XIVth and XVth
amendments, is as useless as it is treacherous. The *turn*
which its vociferators endeavor to give to it is, that any denial of the validity of these so-called amendments is an attack on our present *established form* of government. Established? How? By Congressional enactment and Presidential proclamation! *I* say these pretended additions to
the Constitution could be "established" only in the mode
prescribed by the Constitution itself; and that, not having
been so established, they are *nullities,* and ought to be
treated, and by the Democratic party *will* be treated, as
nullities, whenever that party comes into the administration
of the government. They are just as much nullities as if
they had been enacted and proclaimed by a mob in the
street. They are not established, nor never will be, until
the *country* shall accept, as a finality, the doctrine that the
Constitution can be changed by Congressional enactment
and Presidential proclamation. The Alien and Sedition
acts raised the question as to what *powers* were conferred in
the Constitution, and the XIVth and XVth (so-called)
amendments raise the question as to what *papers,* or *scrips,*
or *words,* if you please, are in the Constitution, and form
a part of it. How is the one issue any more revolutionary
than the other? Nobody proposes to resist the present
government with arms, but only to turn out the usurpers
by *votes,* and then administer the government according to
the *true* Constitution, leaving the usurpers to submit, as we

have done, or inaugurate a revolution of violence and blood-shed, if they shall so choose. But enough. The importance of the subject is my excuse for the length of this letter.

Yours, very truly,

LINTON STEPHENS.

P. S.—I take it for granted that you will attend the meeting of the committee. I beg you to do so. L. S.

[From L. S. to Hon. Martin J. Crawford.]

SPARTA, September 21, 1870.

DEAR JUDGE—Since writing to you the other day, reflection has changed my mind, and I now hasten to say that I do not wish to have the chairmanship, even if tendered to me; and, of course, my position *now* is, that I would not accept it, if it should be tendered. If you find yourself inclined, on this announcement, to revert to the fable of the fox and the *sour grapes*, I beg you to make an accurate analysis of the two cases. I persuade myself that such an analysis cannot fail to disclose a *difference*. The fox made repeated attempts to get the grapes, and, after finding that they were beyond his reach, he said they were *sour*, and then he walked away. It has always seemed to me that he had no reason for the change of opinion which he expressed in relation to the quality of the grapes, and I have, accordingly, always believed that the change was feigned, and not real. My belief has always been, that the fox had just as good an opinion of the grapes when he was walking away from them, as when he was *jumping at 'em*, and that he would have quickly retraced his retreating steps, if some friendly hand had bent down the bough for him. The real points in his case are reducible to two: the first is, that he undoubtedly committed the *crimen falsi*; and the other is, that his motive was to preserve his dignity under ridiculous circumstances. My case presents very different features. I have never tried to get the chairmanship, and, therefore, I have no failure which needs to be covered. On the contrary, I let it go when I might have held it by virtue of the proxies, after it had been put into my hands, *unsought*. In the next and last place, I have really changed my opinion about the quality of the fruit. At first, it was fair to the

eye, and promised to be pleasant to the taste; and I would
have taken it, if I could have carried off the prize without
raising the whole neighborhood at my heels. The fox evidently entered upon his enterprise with a determination to
snatch the spoil, if possible, and then flee from the wrath
to come. For my part, I never had a fancy for carrying
even my own property in a *running attitude*. I don't think
the situation a *graceful* one. I was remarkably good at the
game of "deer," when I was a boy, and I was famous at
"wrap-jacket;" but now I would surrender my own hat
rather than run for it or scramble for it. I have arrived at
a time of life when a man may lose his dignity in trying to
preserve his property. I don't want anything that I can't
hold without a "fuss;" not that I am opposed to a fuss,
per se, and on proper principles; but I haven't the heart to
keep up a clamor when I can stop it by *dropping something*
I happen to have. The sensation of being pursued for
"*some'um you've got*," is an unpleasant one. I'd drop it *at
the start*, even if it were a thing of the greatest value. But,
as I have said, I have changed my opinion about the fruit,
and I now regard it as a thing of no value at all. The fact
is, the Democratic party in Georgia, and in the United
States, is rapidly becoming a mere *tail* to the reconstruc-
tionists, and my idea is, that neither honor nor profit can
be found in identifying one's self with its fortunes. The
tail is the least respectable member, even of a noble animal;
and my compassion is excited for the agony of degradation
which awaits the Democrats who are struggling for the *tail-
ship* of Radicalism. I shall not cease to point out to them
the self-abasement which they are about to perpetrate, so
long as I can see the least prospect of preserving a sound *nu-
cleus* for the basis of a subsequent reorganization; but I shall
take no part or lot in the present concern. It is *rotten*—
ruined by the infernal *lust for office*. Defeat, disastrous and
disgraceful, is alike its doom and its due. The first fruits
are already seen in the Maine election. The Connecticut
Legislature refused to conform to the so-called XVth amendment; the Democracy of Pennsylvania and California, and
perhaps other States, have declared against its validity, and
we are ingloriously abandoning the fight which our friends
are making for us. And we are doing it for the *greed of
office*, and at the dictation of a Congressional committee!

The chairman of it, ———, does not have the confidence of his own constituency, as I am informed. Their foolishness even exceeds their want of principle. But enough. Mark the prediction!

Yours, truly,

LINTON STEPHENS.

Judge Stephens, although he declined the chairmanship, felt anxious concern, and took an active part in the gubernatorial contest. So far as his heavy professional engagements permitted, all his energies were given to the success of the ticket. Take, as a specimen, the letter below, addressed to his client, friend, and kinsman:

[From L. S. to Hon. T. J. Smith.]

SPARTA, October 2, 1870.

DEAR JACK—Your letter was handed to me yesterday. The interest it manifested in me and my fortunes is very gratifying to me. I knew before, just as I know now, that you have a great regard for me; but I am not superior to the human weakness which finds pleasure in repeated expressions of an already known regard, even when I also know that the expression called out in any particular instance is not equal to the regard in general.

And now I am very sorry to be compelled to tell you, that you must not depend on me to represent you in your defense against the suit of Wilkinson & Wilkinson. I don't see how it is possible for me to do so, if Judge Andrews goes on with our Hancock court until Saturday night, as he must do, unless he leaves a large amount of unfinished business. It will be *impossible* for me to be at Washington court on Saturday, or on any other day of that week. The Judge has *usually* adjourned our court on Friday night, and gone home Saturday morning; but the probabilities are, that Friday night, this time, will find the business in a state which will oblige him to go on Saturday with the court. We have a number of criminal cases, several of them capital, and Friday night is very apt to find us right in the *midst* of one of these. But, however this may be, I know that, by Friday night, I shall be *worn out* with these criminal trials. This class of cases always *wears* me far more than civil business; and I shall be incapable of discharging my duties at Oglethorpe the following week, unless I can get a *little* intervening *rest*. If I go to Washington, I shall have to take a night drive, and get no day of rest; but if I do not go, I shall at least have Sunday. The fact is, I firmly believe that, after toiling through the criminal trials here, and riding the greater part of the night afterwards to reach your court, I should be incapable of doing justice to your case the next day, and should do you an injury, instead of a service, by keeping the lead out of fresher, and therefore safer, hands. My idea of your defense is briefly, but clearly, embodied in the plea which I drew up and sent down by John Traywick; and I think it would be wielded by Governor Johnson and Judge Harris with more power and *effect* than it could be by me—especially in a jaded and worn-out condition. It is my deliberate judgment that my attempt to serve you, if made under the circumstances that *must* attend it, would *hurt*, instead of help, your case. I have as much confidence, perhaps, as I ought to have in my legal ability; but experience leaves me no doubt of the great extent to which my capacity for any particular business is impaired by preceding *wear and tear*. If I should appear in your case, under the disadvantageous circumstances which would necessarily attend me, I should, in all probability, have the mortification of disappointing you, and of being obliged to believe that my friend's cause had only suffered from my incompetent effort to serve it. This is my sincere feeling and judgment. If the case goes to the Supreme Court, my services would be as valuable to you *then* as anybody else's, perhaps; and I will render them with the greatest pleasure.

I am much gratified, but not at all surprised, to find that you approve my recent course in relation to so-called "eligibility." It is approved most heartily by brother, General Toombs, Governor Johnson, and by almost *everybody* in old Hancock. The fact is, it is approved by all *sensible* men, who have not made up their minds to abandon *principle* for *office*. The number of these, as shown by recent developments, is alarmingly large. They have made up their minds to *accept* and *abide* by all the usurpation and malignant oppression perpetrated by the Radical party, for the gracious *privilege* of being *allowed* to hold office, if they can get it. In my judgment, this class of so-called Democrats are just as guilty as the Radicals, and still more contemptible. They pledge themselves not to disturb, but to *accept*, and *abide by*, and *carry out* what they themselves have been loudest in denouncing as enormously criminal and destructive. This constitutes their guilt. The contempt comes from the baseness of their motive, as well as the ignominious failure which will inevitably mark their treachery. They are followers of ———, at a long distance behind; and they will soon discover that they can remove the intervening land between him and them only by *vigorous dirt-eating*. They will have to acknowledge his superior forecast, and, like the dog returning to his vomit, gulp down again all the dirty denunciations which they have poured out upon his head. The depths of self-abasement to which they will descend are unfathomable; and then their failure will be as ignominious as their motives are base. It may turn out that the Radical party will be compelled, by the force of public opinion, to recede from their proscriptive policy altogether, and pass an act of Congress removing the so-called disabilities from *everybody;* but so long as the removal continues to be as it has heretofore been—a *grace* extended to particular persons—the grace will never be—as it never has been—extended to anybody without an *assurance*, either from himself or somebody else who *vouches* for him, that he will sustain and carry out the reconstruction scheme—including the XIVth and XVth so-called amendments of the Constitution. You may rely upon this proposition as true, *without any exception*. It is possible that they may occasionally "catch a Tartar" in some fellow who will refuse to stand up to the assurance given for him by his vouchers; but I have yet to find a single instance of this kind. Of all the men who have had their so-called disabilities removed, I do no know *one* who is not obliged to answer, if the direct question is asked him, that he intends to abide by and carry out the reconstruction scheme. I need not point out to you the vast difference between abiding by and carrying out these measures, on the one hand, and on the other, the mere yielding to them, or not resisting them, so long as they are enforced by the bayonet. To resist them, under present circumstances, would only fasten them on us by our own folly: to abide by them and carry them out would be to fasten them upon us by our own baseness. The true course of wisdom and patriotism is, neither to resist them nor accept them, but to hold them as they truly are—*nullities*—which are to be utterly disregarded and wiped out, whenever sound men are put into power. The vital principle of the Democratic party is, devotion to the *true* Constitution, and opposition to these monstrous usurpations; and whenever this issue is allowed to die, the Democratic party will, and ought, to die with it. Their mission is, not by force, but by the peaceful ballot, to put into power sound men, who are pledged to wipe out all the usurpations, and re-establish the true Constitution in its purity. The first thing to be done for the Democratic party is to purge it of its rotten element. If it were purified, it would soon become as strong as it would immediately be glorious. My hope now is that the ignominious defeat which awaits its present desertion of principle, will teach it the much-needed lesson, that its success depends on its fidelity to truth. But enough. All in usual health, and all join me in love and good wishes to you all.　　　　　　　Your friend,

LINTON STEPHENS.

[From L. S. to Colonel Herbert Fielder.]

OCTOBER 8, 1870.

MY DEAR SIR—My acknowledgment of your letter, expressing your approval of my recent course, was postponed, in the hope of having leisure to write you somewhat at length; but I am at last obliged to confine myself to a brief expression of the pleasure I received from your approbation, and of my high appreciation of the views presented by you on the same line. I am particularly gratified to find, as I have found, that I am completely sustained by the very first intellects in the Democratic party. I believe I am sustained by all sensible men who have not made up their minds to abandon principle for the chances of office. I am just in the midst of my principal courts; otherwise, I should take great pleasure in giving you some additional views connected with those so strongly expressed by you. I am truly obliged to you for your letter.

Yours, very truly,　　　　　　　LINTON STEPHENS.

[From L. S. to A. H. S.]

SPARTA, October 10, 1870.

DEAR BROTHER— . . . . I imagine,
however, that it is just as well I have no time to write anything at all; for I am satisfied that the so-called Democracy
are bent on destruction for the present. I know that the
only idea of those who are manipulating the Democratic
party, just now, is to get a *thing that will win*, and my hope
is that the disastrous beating that awaits them, on their
present line, may knock some *sense* into them. *Want of
sense* is their greatest trouble; for, great as their baseness
is, it is exceeded by their folly. I know they will quit their
present folly as soon as it gets its inevitable threshing.
They always quit a thing that *fails to win* at the first trial,
just as they have already run away from the New York
platform, and from every vestige of Democratic principle;
but my fear is that, in dropping their present folly, they
will take up with something else that will be no better. It
is almost impossible for corrupt men to have faith in the
power of *truth*. Naturally enough, they cannot expect it to
exert over others an influence of which they themselves
have no perception. They will never find out that the battles of truth, when they are lost at all, as in 1868, are lost,
not by the fidelity and candor of her supporters, but by the
treachery of her pretended friends.

My last and surest hope is that the *people* will find out,
from bitter experience, that their present leaders are even
bigger fools than knaves, and will at last commit their fortunes to the counsels of sensible and honest men. . . .

The Constitution of the State requires a poll-tax to be
assessed, which shall be exclusively appropriated for educational purposes. A large number, of the colored people
especially, failed to pay that tax in 1869. The Radical
Legislature of the following year ignored that provision of
the Constitution by passing an act instructing the several
collectors to "desist" from collecting the poll-tax for the
years 1868, 1869 and 1870. The manifest aim of the proceeding was to secure the benefit of the colored vote in the

coming election of Governor and members of the General
Assembly. In the county of Judge Stephens' residence,
that population largely preponderated; and, standing by
the Constitution, he made issue with the action of the
Legislature, on the day of the election, by challenging the
votes of such as had not paid poll-tax for the preceding
year; and, when overruled by a majority of the managers
of election—three out of five—on his own affidavit, he had
the refractory majority immediately arrested, carried before
a magistrate, tried, committed, and they, refusing to give
bail, imprisoned. Their places were at once supplied, and
the election proceeded. The affair created prodigious excitement. It was an episode in the life of Judge Stephens,
in that it brought on a personal collision with an old friend.
He was the only person Judge Stephens, since the date of
his majority, ever struck in anger, and the only man he ever
knocked down in his life. The affront was very gross.
The unfortunate matter was, however, soon amicably adjusted in a manner honorable alike to each, as the following
correspondence discloses:

[From Dr. A. S. Brown to L. S.]

SPARTA, December 24, 1870.

HON. LINTON STEPHENS—From a misapprehension of
facts, I did a very foolish thing on Tuesday. I heard that
the managers of election were arrested, the ballot-box
seized, and an armed party were in line, near the court-
house. I hastened to town. On the way, I met many
persons, white and black; all I could get to stop said they
were going for arms.

On reaching the street, I inquired of several gentlemen
about the disturbance; had no intelligible answer, and,
without due reflection, came to the conclusion that it was a
plan previously arranged, and that a collision with the negroes was inevitable and speedy. I selected you as the presumed author of the revolutionary procedure.

I am satisfied that the arrest of the managers was right
and lawful; that the ballot-box was properly cared for, and

that the appearance of an armed force of citizens on the scene was a mistake, and that you had nothing to do with this armed party whatever.

Therefore, I make the most ample *amende* in my power; withdraw, with pleasure, my language and my action towards you; and I now respectfully request the re-establishment of our former friendly relations.

Yours, respectfully,   A. S. BROWN.

[Reply.]

SPARTA, December 24, 1870.

DR. A. S. BROWN—*Sir:* Your note, by Eddie, is just received, and is entirely satisfactory. I was utterly surprised at the time; and now, the misapprehension under which you acted, as you inform me, explains it all. I can and do truly say that the explanation restores us to our former relations, and leaves no grudge in my mind.

Yours, respectfully,   LINTON STEPHENS.

Although Dr. Brown was satisfied of the prudence and propriety of Judge Stephens' course in arresting the three managers, Governor Bullock pretended not to be. At his instance, Judge Stephens was arrested, by a United States marshal, on the ground stated in the following letter:

[From L. S. to A. H. S.]

SPARTA, January 18, 1871.

DEAR BROTHER— . . . . Soon after I got home, I was arrested by a United States marshal, under a warrant issued by United States Commissioner Swayze, founded on affidavits of the two negro managers of election in this county, charging me with divers violations of the Enforcement act—"intimidation," "hindering," etc., under the sixth section—and interfering with managers of election in the discharge of their duties, etc., under the nineteenth section. The marshal called himself Seaford. He was very polite—took my word for my appearance at Macon next Friday, the 20th instant, and took his leave. I asked him to take me before Judge Erskine,

31

instead of Commissioner Swayze. This he would not do. I expected him to decline it, as he did; but I wanted the benefit of his refusal.

The people here are in pretty much of a stir. George Pierce is to go with me to Macon, and carry a power of attorney, which was signed by a large number yesterday, and will be signed by more to-day, authorizing him to sign their names to any bond that may be required of me; besides George, who knows all the facts of the prosecution of the managers, Clarence Simmons and John Culver (one of the two dissenting managers) will go over as witnesses, in case I shall need them. I don't expect to need them; for I think I shall draw everything out of the two negroes, and thus get the concluding argument on the commitment trial. If I am not deprived of my voice by a horrible cold, which has been developed, or caught, perhaps, since I left you, I think I shall make the infernal rascals sorry that they ever molested me. I have got thunder in me: I only pray for a happy vent. . . . .

Judge Stephens, as has been seen, opposed, with his might, every new departure from the old landmarks of the Constitution. He believed the XIVth and XVth amendments of the Constitution to be nullities, and that they ought to be treated as nullities by the courts. The reconstruction acts of Congress, and all the monstrous outrages upon popular liberty and local self-government, which were germinated of the same spirit and spawn, he loathed and spat upon. The following speech, which he made in his own defense, in January, 1871, at Macon, when arraigned before the United States commissioner on a charge of having violated the Enforcement act, so-called, avouches the accuracy of this statement. The reader will concede that the wealth of all forensic literature may be searched in vain for a performance that surpasses it in point of genuine manliness, civil courage, nervous English, the eloquence of patriotic fervor, or cogent, compact, red-hot logic. It is a demonstration of his whole proposition, "if there be one in Euclid:"

SPEECH OF HON. LINTON STEPHENS, IN MACON, GEORGIA, ON THE "RECONSTRUCTION MEASURES," AND THE "ENFORCEMENT ACT" OF 1870, DELIVERED 23D OF JANUARY, 1871.

May it please the Court: I know full well that, if your Honor is not superior to the average of poor human nature, you will find it difficult, if not impossible, to give my defense in this case an impartial consideration, and an honest decision. The prosecution against me is founded on the course which I took in the recent political election, which resulted in a victory for my party and a defeat for yours. It is also directly in the line of an assault which was lately made against me in the newspapers, by the official head of your party in this State. I, therefore, recognize in this case a *political prosecution*, just as distinctly as I recognize in my judge a most zealous and determined political opponent. Yet, sir, there are other considerations which encourage me to hope that I may obtain, even from *you*, that decision which is demanded by justice and by the laws. From the personal knowledge of you which I have acquired since the beginning of this trial, I have discovered that you are a man of decided intelligence; and I am told that you are a man of courage. I am also told that you, yourself, have been, in some instances, a victim of political persecution, and an object of unjust obloquy. Surely, such a man, with such an experience, *ought* to give a fair hearing to one whose only fault is *not* any wrong which he has committed against the laws, but the damage which he has inflicted upon a political party. My *greatest* encouragement, however, is derived from my confidence in the lawfulness of my conduct and the power of truth. To truth, bravely upheld, belongs a triumph which cannot be defeated, nor long delayed, not even by the intensest prejudices of partisan strife. I am strengthened, too, in the advocacy of truth, on this occasion, by the consciousness that, in defending myself, I shall be but defending principles which are dear to every American, because they lie at the foundation of the whole fabric of American constitutional liberty. Now, sir, unless I am much mistaken in the estimate which I have formed of your character, will you listen to my defense any the less favorably because of the frankness and boldness with which I shall present it.

I am accused under the Enforcement act of Congress.

My first proposition is, that this whole act is not a law, but a mere legal nullity.

It was passed with the professed object of carrying into effect what are called the XIVth and XVth amendments of the Constitution of the United States, and depends on their validity for its own.

These so-called amendments are, as I shall now proceed to show, not *true* amendments of the Constitution, and do not form any part of that sacred instrument. They are nothing but usurpations and nullities, having no validity themselves, and therefore incapable of imparting any to the Enforcement act, or to any other act whatsoever.

I take occasion to say, that I regard the XIIIth amendment, abolishing slavery, as clearly distinguishable from the XIVth and XVth so-called amendments, in the manner both of its proposal and of its ratification. The contrast between it and them will contribute to make their invalidity all the more apparent. It is true, that when the XIIIth amendment was proposed, ten States of the Union were absent from Congress; but their absence was *voluntary*, and therefore did not affect the validity of their proposal. It is true, also, that the Legislatures which ratified it for these ten States had their initiation in a palpable usurpation of power on the part of the President of the United States; yet, it is also unquestionably true, that they were elected and sustained by overwhelming majorities of the true constitutional constituencies of the States for which they acted; they rested on the consent of the people, or constitutional constituencies of the States, and were therefore truly "Legislatures of the States." This amendment was ratified by these Legislatures of the States in good faith, and in conformity with the almost unanimous wish of the constitutional "Peoples."

How different is the case of the XIVth and XVth so-called amendments! If these are parts of the Constitution, I ask, How did they become so? Were they proposed by Congress in a constitutional manner?

In framing and proposing them, every State in the Union was entitled, by the express terms of the Constitution, to be represented in speech and vote by "two Senators" and "at least one Representative." But ten States of the Union were absent. This time their absence was not voluntary, but compulsory: when they were claiming a hearing, through their constitutional representatives, they were driven away, and denied all participation in framing and proposing these amendments! Was this a constitutional mode of proposal? I say, it was an unconstitutional mode, and that the proposal was, *ab initio*, null and void.

But how stands the *ratification* of these so-called amendments? To say nothing about the duress of bayonets and Congressional dictation, under which the ratification was forced through the ratifying bodies in the ten Southern States, the great question is, Who were these ratifying bodies? Were they Legislatures of the States? They were *not*. They were the creatures of notorious and avowed Congressional usurpation. They were elected, not by the constitutional constituencies of the States, but by constituencies created by Congress, not only outside of the Constitution, but in palpable violation of one of its express provisions. The suffrage, or political power, of the States is not delegated to the General Government by the Constitution; but, on the contrary, its reservation, by the States, is rendered exceedingly emphatic by that provision of the Constitution which, instead of creating a constituency to elect its own officers—President, Vice-President, and members of Congress—adopts the constituencies of the States, as regulated by the States themselves, for the election of the most numerous branch of their own Legislatures.

Ten of the ratifications, which were falsely counted in favor of these miscalled amendments as ratifications by Legislatures, were only ratifications by bodies which had their origin in Congressional usurpation, were elected by illegal constituencies, unknown to the Constitution of the United States, or the Constitutions of the States, and were organized and manipulated under the control of military commanders who claimed and exercised the jurisdiction of passing upon the election and qualification of their members. Can these joint products of usurpation, fraud, and force be palmed off as Legislatures of States? Can ratifications by them be accepted as ratifications by Legislatures of States? Can falsehood thus be converted into truth by the thimble-rigging of Presidential proclamations? These bodies were, indeed, set up by their usurping creators as Legislatures *for* and *over* States; but until the known truth of recent his-

tory can be blotted out by the mere power of shameless assertion, they cannot be recognized as Legislatures of States.
The Parliament of Great Britain is a Legislature *for* and *over*
poor, down-trodden Ireland; but what Irishman will ever
recognize it as the Legislature of Ireland!

The false, spurious, and revolutionary character of these
ratifying bodies is rendered still more glaring by the fact
that, supported by the bayonet, they subverted, or rather
repressed, the true, legitimate Legislatures of all the States
where reconstruction was applied. That such Legislatures
existed in these States, and are indeed still existing, is demonstrable from the facts, viewed in the light of either of
the two theories of secession—that of its validity or invalidity. On either theory, the seceding States remained
States. On the one theory, they were States of the Union;
on the other, they have remained all the while States in the
Union. The Supreme Court of the United States, in the
recent case of White *vs*. Texas, speaking through Mr. Chief
Justice Chase, held that secession was invalid, and that the
States which had attempted it remained, and still are, *States
in the Union*.

A State is not a disorganized mass of people: it is an organized political body. It must have a constitution of some
sort, written or traditional. Being an organized body, it
must have a law of organization, or composition, or constitution, defining the depositary of its political power. Where
there is no such constitutional, or constituting, or organizing, or fundamental law, there can be no organization—
no *State*. These ten States, then, which seceded, or attempted to secede (as the one theory or the other may be
held), have all the while had *Constitutions*. In point of fact,
each of these has ever been a written Constitution, giving
the ballot to defined classes of citizens who are known as
the constitutional constituency of the State. This constitutional constituency is entrusted by each of these constitutions with power over the constitution itself, in modifying
or changing it, and, of course, in modifying or changing the
organization or composition of the constitutional constituency. This constitutional constituency is the depositary of
the highest political power of the State. Any change made
in the Constitution or organization of the State, or in the
composition of the constitutional constituency, as it may ex-

ist at any time, without the concurrent action of the constitutional constituency itself, is *revolution :* it is disorganization; it is the subversion or suppression (as it may prove permanent or temporary) of one organization, and the substitution of any other; it is the abolition (permanent or temporary) of the old State, and the introduction of a new one.

Each of these ten States, in 1865, at the close of the war, being then a *State*, had a Constitution and a constitutional constituency linked back by unbroken succession to the Constitution and constitutional constituency as they existed before secession. Secession made no break in the chain. The provision which was put in the Constitution at the time of secession, connecting the State with the Confederate States, instead of with the United States, as its Federal head, is wholly immaterial to the present purpose. On the one theory, it was simply void, and left the organization of the *State*, the Constitution, and the constitutional constituency *intact*. On the other theory, being valid, it modified, but did not impair, the integrity of the State organization. All this follows from, or rather is comprehended in, the one proposition that these ten States have never lost their character as *States*.

Each of these ten States, being a State at the close of the war, in 1865, stands now *de jure*, just as it stood then, unless it has, since that time, been changed by the action of its constitutional constituency. I think each of them *was* so changed in the latter part of that same year. In each of them, a convention was elected by a large and unquestionable majority of the constitutional constituency (although a portion of them were excluded from voting) for the purpose of modifying the Constitution. These conventions repealed the ordinance of secession, abolished slavery, and made some other changes in the several Constitutions, but, in most of the States, left the constitutional constituencies just as they stood before. In conformity with the Constitutions, as last modified by those conventions, each of the States was speedily provided with a complete government, consisting of a legislative, executive, and judicial department. It was by the Legislatures thus formed that the XIIIth amendment of the Constitution of the United States, abolishing slavery, was ratified.

Since that time, no change has been made in the organization of any of these States, with the co-operation or con-currence of the constitutional constituencies.   Only very small minorities of the constitutional constituencies have co-operated in the work of reconstruction.   It is a notori-ous and unquestionable fact, that an overwhelming majority of them, in each of the States, have been steadily and un-swervingly opposed to it, and have voted against it, when-ever they have voted at all.

The clear result, in my judgment, is that each of these States now stands *de jure*, just as she was left by the action of her convention in 1865, with a complete government, formed under the Constitution of that year, including a Legislature which still constitutionally exists, and is capa-ble of assembling any day, if it were only allowed to do so by the withdrawal of the bayonet.   But she stands *de facto*, *suppressed* by a government originated and imposed on her by an external power, and supported alone by the bayonet. Such a government is the embodiment of anti-republican-ism and despotism.   Under just such a government, Ire-land is writhing and Poland is crushed.

Is it not now demonstrated that the bodies which ratified the so-called XIVth and XVth amendments, in the name of these ten States, were the revolutionary products of ex-ternal force and fraud, displacing the *true* Legislatures which alone could have given a constitutional ratification?

The so-called amendments, then, have been neither con-stitutionally proposed nor constitutionally ratified.   How can they form parts of the Constitution?

A successful answer to this question would long ago have brought that peace and harmony which can never come from might overbearing right.   Instead of giving such an answer, the authors of these measures have sought to drown reason and argument in clamorous charges of vio-lence and revolution against the victims, not the perpetra-tors, of those crimes.

But an answer has at last been attempted from an unex-pected quarter.   Strangely enough, it comes from one who has greatly distinguished himself by the vigor and ability with which he has denounced the whole scheme of reconstruction as a revolutionary usurpation and nullity; and, still more strangely, he adheres to that denunciation, while now arguing that these so-called amendments—the creatures and culminating points of that reconstruction scheme—are valid parts of the Constitution. Such a conclusion from such a beginning! And yet, he is hailed by his new allies as a very Daniel come unto judgment. They were in a sore strait for an argument.

He says these so-called amendments have become parts of the Constitution, because they have been proclaimed as such by the power which, under the Constitution, has the "jurisdiction" to proclaim amendments.

There has been much said, sir, about issues which are "dead:" surely here is one which is not only alive, but *very lively*. Let Americans hear and mark it: The Constitution of the United States can be changed—can be subverted—by Presidential proclamation! I once knew a man whose motto was, that a lie, well told, was better than the truth, because, he said, truth was a stubborn, unmanageable thing; but a lie, in the hands of a genius, could be fitted exactly to the exigencies of the case; but even he admitted that the lie must be *well told*, or it would not serve. If it should *appear* to be a lie, it would be turned from a thing of power into a thing for contempt. There has been progress, sir, since that man taught. It is now discovered that a *known*, *proven* lie is as good as the truth, provided it can only get "proclaimed" by a power having "jurisdiction" to proclaim it! I, sir, know of no power—either on the earth, or above it, or under it—that has "jurisdiction" to "proclaim" *lies*! Nay, sir, I know of no power which has jurisdiction to proclaim amendments to the Constitution. According to my reading of that instrument, amendments constitutionally proposed "shall be valid, to all intents and purposes, as part of the Constitution, when ratified by the Legislatures of three-fourths of the several States, or by conventions in three-fourths thereof, as the one or the other mode of ratification may be proposed by the Congress." The ratification by three-fourths of the *States*, acting through their Legislatures or their conventions, sets the seal of validity on the amendment and makes it a part of the Constitution. Nothing else can do it. It must be a *true* ratification by a *true* Legislature, or a *true* convention of the State. A false ratification by a true Legislature of the State will not do. A true ratification by a spurious Legislature will not do. The va-

lidity of the amendment, and its authority as a part of the
Constitution, are made to depend upon the *historic truth* of
its ratification as required by the Constitution.   Proclamations of falsehoods from Presidents, or from anybody else,
have nothing to do with the subject.   This is plain doctrine,
drawn from the Constitution itself.   The validity of the
Constitution, in all its parts, depends upon the facts of their
history.

But, according to this new discovery, the President of the
United States can subvert the whole Constitution, and make
himself a legal and valid autocrat, by simply " proclaiming "
that an amendment of the Constitution to that effect has
been proposed by two-thirds of each house of Congress, and
ratified by the Legislatures of three-fourths of the States,
although it may be known of all men that there is not one
word of truth in the proclamation.   The President of the
United States can legally convert himself into an autocrat
by his own proclamation.   Theories are quickly put into
practice in these days.   Let the country beware!

We are also told by this new Daniel, not only that the
usurpation has become obligatory by its success, but there
is no hope of getting rid of it; for he says it cannot be
changed without another amendment, ratified by three-
fourths of the States, and that there is no prospect of getting these three-fourths.   Wonderful!   Why, he himself
has taught us that the whole thing may be accomplished by
a Presidential proclamation.   We have only to elect a Democratic President, and let him " proclaim " that a new amendment, abolishing the XIVth and XVth, has been duly proposed and duly ratified, and the thing is done.   That, sir,
would be the way taught by this new light; but it would
never be my way.   I do not propose to walk in the ways of
falsehood: I prefer truth, because it is nobler and grander.
I believe, also, that, when it is supported by true and bold
men, it is always more powerful.   My way would be to elect
a Democratic President, and let him treat the usurpation as
a usurpation and a nullity, and let him withdraw the bayonet
and " proclaim " that the revolutionary governments in
these ten States would not be supported by him, but that
the constitutional republican governments which now exist
here would be left free to rise from their state of forcible
repression, and do their natural and legitimate work of true

restoration, real peace, sincere and cordial fraternity. The whole problem is solved by the simple withdrawal of the bayonet.

I have now shown that the XIVth and XVth amendments do not form any part of the Constitution, and thus have made good my first position, that the whole Enforcement act, which depends solely upon them for its validity, is not a law, but merely a legal nullity.

My second position is that, even if the so-called XIVth and XVth amendments were valid, yet all those parts of the Enforcement act, claimed as applicable to my case, are utterly "outside" of them, and (being confessedly outside of the Constitution, apart from them) are unconstitutional, and not binding as *law*.

The XIVth amendment, and the small part of the Enforcement act relating to it, have no relevancy to this prosecution, and I shall say nothing further about them.

Those parts of the act, claimed as applicable to my case, rest solely upon the XVth for their validity; and, in order to see whether they are outside of it or not, it becomes necessary to know what are the terms and extent of the amendment.

The effect of its terms is strangely misapprehended. It seems to be regarded as a thing which, by its terms, secures the right of suffrage to the negro, and empowers Congress to enforce that right. This is a total and most dangerous mistake. Here is the amendment; it is not longer than the first joint of my little finger:

"SECTION 1. The right of citizens of the United States to vote shall not be denied or abridged by the United States, or by any State, on account of race, color, or previous condition of servitude.

"SEC. 2. The Congress shall have power to enforce this article by appropriate legislation."

This is the whole of it. Now, sir, I defy refutation, when I affirm that, by these terms, the right of suffrage is not conferred upon, nor secured to, any person or class of persons whomsoever. The whole is simply a prohibition on the United States, and the several States. The United States, in legislating for the District of Columbia or a Territory, and the several States, in regulating their suffrage, each for herself, are prohibited from denying it to anybody, or abridging its exercise on either one of the three grounds—race, color, or previous condition of servitude—but are left perfectly free to abridge it or deny it on any *other* ground whatsoever—sex, female or male, ignorance or intelligence, poverty or wealth, crime or virtue, or any other of an innumerable multitude of *other* grounds. In point of fact, the right is denied, both by the United States and by each one of the several States, on many of these *other* grounds, and the denial is enforced under heavy penalties, not only by the laws of the States, but by this very Enforcement act itself. To say that the right is conferred on or secured to anybody, because it cannot be denied for any one or all of three reasons out of an indefinite number of possible and usual reasons, is simply absurd. As well say that a plat of ground is fenced or secured from intrusion by putting a wall on one of its many sides, leaving all the *other* sides perfectly open. A right is not conferred or secured by a law when it can be denied without a violation of that law.

This brings me to the crucial test of my second position. Whether I have violated any provisions of the Enforcement act or not, it is at least certain that I have *not* violated the XVth amendment. It is affirmatively proven, by the testimony of the two prosecutors in this case—the two negro managers of election—that I did not object to, or in any manner interfere with, any vote on the ground of either race, color, or previous condition of servitude. It is manifest, then, that if I have violated any part or parts of the Enforcement act, such part or parts are "outside" of the amendment, and unauthorized by it, since I have *not* violated the amendment itself. I have not violated the amendment, even if its prohibition reached private citizens, instead of being confined, as it plainly is, to the United States and the States severally.

The truth is, that *far the greater part* of the Enforcement act is "outside" of the amendments which it professes to enforce. This act presents another live and very lively issue to the people of this country; and already are the thunders of opposition heard from Republican as well as from Democratic quarters. Under the pretense of restraining the United States and the several States from denying or abridg-

ing the right of suffrage on account of race, color, or previous condition of servitude, this act takes control of the
general and local elections in all the States—seizing the
whole political power of the country, and wielding it by the
bayonet; and fills up pages of the statute-book with new
offenses and heavy penalties leveled, not against the United
States or the several States, or their officers, by whom alone
the XVth amendment can *possibly* be violated, but against
private citizens.   The Alien and Sedition acts, which, by
the power of their recoil, exterminated their authors, were
not equal to this act, either in the nakedness or the danger
of their usurpation.   If this act shall prevail and abide as
law, then our heritage of local self-government, lost to us,
will pass into history, and there stand out forever a glory
to the noble sires who wrung it from one tyranny, and a
shame to the degenerate sons who surrendered it to another.

My third and last position is, that even if the Enforcement act were valid in all its parts, yet I have not violated
any one of them.   I am accused under its fifth and nineteenth sections.

The fifth provides a penalty against "preventing, hindering, controlling, or intimidating, or attempting to prevent,
hinder, control, or intimidate," any person from voting, "to
whom the right of suffrage is secured or guaranteed by the
XVth amendment."   I have already demonstrated that the
XVth amendment secures or guarantees the right of suffrage
to nobody whomsoever.   It is impossible, therefore, that I
am, or that anybody ever can be, guilty under *that* section.

But again: The testimony utterly fails to show that I interfered in any way with the voting of any person legally
entitled to vote, or, indeed, with the voting of any person
whomsoever.   It was incumbent upon the prosecution to
show *what* persons, if any, and that they were persons entitled to vote.   The Enforcement act itself inflicts a penalty
on all persons who vote illegally, and, of course, cannot intend to punish the prevention or hindrance of *illegal* voting.
The attempted proof, as to my interference with voters, relates to four persons only.   It fails to show that either one
of the four was a person entitled to vote; it fails to show
that three of them did not actually vote; it fails to show
that any one of them offered to vote or even desired to do

so; it fails to show that any one of them heard me make a single remark, saw me do a single act, or was even in my presence from the beginning to the end of the three days' election.

As to the remark which I made to a small crowd, about prosecuting all who should vote without having paid their taxes, I have this to say: In the first place, it is not shown who composed that crowd, nor that a single one of them was a person entitled to vote. In the next place, the remark was a lawful one; for it was simply the declaration of an intention, not to interfere with legal voters, but to prosecute *criminals;* and, therefore, cannot be tortured into a threat in any legal or criminal sense of that word. A threat, to be criminal, must be the declaration of an intention to do some unlawful act; and it never can be unlawful to appeal to the laws.

I pass to the charge, under the nineteenth section, that I interfered with the managers of election in the discharge of their duties, by causing their arrest under judicial warrant. That part of the nineteenth section which is invoked against me is in these words: "Or interfere in any manner with any officer of said elections in the discharge of his duties."

My first answer to this charge is, that the managers were arrested, not in the discharge of their duties, but in the violation of one of the most important of them—one prescribed, not only by the Constitution of the State, but by this very Enforcement act itself: for the act made it their duty to reject all illegal votes, and provided a penalty for receiving them. These managers had received, and were still receiving, the votes of persons who had not paid their taxes of the year next preceding the election, as required by the Constitution of this State. The testimony shows that this fact was fully proven, and not denied by them, on the commitment trial before the magistrate. The reply to it then was, and now is, not a denial, but a justification, on two grounds: one of these grounds was, that the oath which they had taken, under the Akerman Election act, required them to let every person vote who was of apparent full age, was a resident of the county, and had not previously voted in that election. They said then, and it is now said again here, that they could not inquire into the non-payment of taxes, or any other Constitutional qualification for voting,

except only non-age, non-residence, and previous voting in
that election; and yet, a man who was of full age, and a
resident of the county, and who had not previously voted,
was excluded by these same managers on the ground that
he was a convicted felon. Their own action in excluding
the felon is utterly inconsistent with their construction of
the obligation of their oath. The oath, as construed by
them, and now construed here by the prosecuting attorney,
is in plain conflict with the Constitution, and is, therefore,
void, and could not relieve them from their Constitutional
duty to exclude all who had not paid their taxes. The first
ground of the managers' justification, therefore, fails.

Their other ground was, that the unpaid tax of those
whom they had allowed to vote without payment of taxes
was only poll-tax, and that the poll-tax had been declared
by the Legislature to be illegal and unwarranted by the Constitution, and its further collection suspended.

The fact that it was only poll-tax does not appear from
the evidence before your honor, but I admit it to be true.
I did not come here to quibble: I am here to justify my
conduct under the *law*, on the truth as it exists, whether
proven here or not. My answer is, that this declaratory
act of the Legislature is false, unconstitutional, null and
void. The act is but the opinion of the Legislature, concerning the constitutionality of a previous act of 1869, imposing the poll-tax of that year. That act is before me,
imposing a poll-tax of one dollar per head "for educational
purposes," using the very words which are used by the Constitution itself in defining the purpose for which poll-taxes
may be imposed. Now, sir, the question which I ask is,
What is it that makes *this* act "illegal" or unwarranted by
the Constitution? Surely it is not made so by the subsequent declaration of the Legislature, put forth just before
the election, to serve a palpable, fraudulent, party purpose.

The Legislature is not a court; but, on the contrary, it
is expressly prohibited by the Constitution from exercising
judicial functions, and its declarations concerning the constitutionality of legislative acts have no more authority
than those of private citizens. The single question, then,
is whether the declaration in this case is *true*. The Legislature assigned its reason for the opinion it gave. What is
that reason? It is, that the Constitution limits the imposi-

tion of poll-taxes to educational purposes; and that when the poll-tax in question was imposed, there was no system of common schools or educational purpose to which it could be applied. Therefore, they said its imposition was "illegal and unwarranted by the Constitution." They said it was unwarranted by the Constitution to provide the money before organizing the schools to which the money was to be applied; that is to say, the only constitutional way to organize the schools was to go in debt for them! I lack words, sir, to properly characterize the *silliness* of this reason.

But, curiously enough, the Constitution itself took the very course which these sapient legislators declared to be illegal and unwarranted by the Constitution. It provided money and devoted it to these very common schools, which were still in the womb of the future at the time of its adoption. It dedicated to that purpose the whole educational fund which was then on hand. Therefore, I say, this declaratory act is not only false, but is in the very teeth of the Constitution itself. Mark you, sir: it did not *repeal*, nor attempt to repeal, the poll-tax: it only suspended its collection. But, I say, if it had been a repeal in terms, instead of a mere suspension, it could not change the case as to the right of a person to vote without having paid the tax. The constitutional requirement is, that "he shall have paid all taxes which may have been required of him, and which he may have had an opportunity of paying agreeably to law for the year next preceding the election." The poll-tax was required in April, 1869, and continued to be required up to the passage of the aforesaid false declaratory act in October, 1870—a year and a half. During all that period, tax-payers had "opportunity" to pay it. On the day of election, then, any man who had not paid his poll-tax for 1869 stood in the position of not having paid a tax which had been required of him, and which he had had very many opportunities of paying agreeably to law. He stood clearly within the *letter* of the constitutional disqualification for voting. He stood also within its reason and spirit, for its true intention was to discriminate against the citizen who should not have discharged a public duty for the year next preceding the election. Nothing but *payment* could remove from him the character of a public delinquent. Legislative remission of the tax cannot serve the purpose, for he still

stands, after that, as a man who *has failed in a public duty.*
The most that can be said for him is, that after the repeal,
the tax *ceased* to be required of him; but the only material
facts—that *it had been* required, and could have been paid,
but had *not* been paid—remain unaltered.

The managers, then, in receiving the votes of persons who
had not paid their poll-tax were not in "the discharge of
their duties." Whether they *thought* so is not the question.
If they were really wrong, then I was *right;* and surely I
am not to be punished for *being right.* There was no interference with them in the discharge of their *duties.*

But again: even if I were wrong in the opinion which I
entertained of their duty, yet I did not interfere with them
unlawfully. The whole context of that clause, in the nineteenth section, under which I am accused, shows that the
interference contemplated is an *unlawful* interference—especially the words which come immediately after it: "Or
by any of such means or *other* unlawful means," etc. This
word "other" shows, conclusively, that all the means contemplated were only such as were of an *unlawful* character.
This would be implied in construing any penal statute, even
if it were not expressed; for the universal rule of construction for penal statutes is to construe strictly against the
prosecution, and liberally in favor of the accused. Is it possible that any judge can have the hardihood to hold that it
was the intention of this Enforcement act to impart to managers of election the sacred character of Eastern Brahmins,
making them too holy to be touched even for their crimes?
Surely it was not intended to give them greater sanctity
than belongs to peers of the British Parliament, or to legislators in our own country, while engaged in legislation.
Notwithstanding all the high privileges accorded to them,
all of *these* are subject to arrest in any place, at any moment, under a warrant charging breach of the peace or felony. Was it intended to protect these managers from immediate accountability for all felonies which they might
commit during three whole days? Until *this* shall be held
as the intention of the Enforcement act, it is impossible to
maintain that I have violated it in any particular whatever.

The Constitution declares that "the right of the citizen
to appeal to the courts shall never be impaired." My whole
offense, sir, is this—*that I appealed to a court of competent*

32

jurisdiction! I devoutly believed that I was right in my opinion of the law. I believe so now; but, whether I was right or wrong in my *opinion*, who will dare to say that I was wrong in testing that opinion—not by the strong hand, but by appealing to a court appointed by the Constitution for the very purpose of deciding the question? That court decided that I was right; and the "interference" which followed, sir, was the interference, not of myself, but of the *law*, as expounded and administered by a judicial tribunal. Moreover, sir, the decision of that tribunal stands as the law of the case until it shall be reversed according to law. These managers were charged with felony under the laws of this State. Was it a crime for me to seek a judicial inquiry into the truth or probability of such a charge? I suspect, sir, that my real crime, in the estimation of my prosecutors, is, that the judicial interposition invoked by me had the effect of preventing numerous repetitions of a crime which would have done signal service to their *political party*.

If angry power demands a sacrifice from those who have thwarted its fraudulent purposes, I feel honored, sir, in being selected as the victim. If my suffering could arouse my countrymen to a just and lofty indignation against the despotism which, in attacking me, is but assailing law, order, and constitutional government, I would not shrink from the sacrifice, though my *blood* should be required instead of my liberty!

The doctrine of constitutional popular liberty, so truly and so boldly set forth in the foregoing speech, has, since its delivery, been indorsed in an exhaustive decision of the Supreme Court of the United States. That decision is but the commentary whereof this speech is the text.

It is a proof of the stupidity of the commissioner, and the madness of the times, to add that Judge Stephens was committed to answer the alleged charge before the United States District Court, at Savannah. He gave bond and security, voluntarily and eagerly tendered to an hundred fold over the amount nominated in the bond. The grand jury, in the Federal court, ignored the charge, and there the infamous prosecution was dropped.

[From A. H. S. to L. S.]

CRAWFORDVILLE, January 27, 1871.

DEAR BROTHER—I have just received, by the express,
your letter of yesterday. I was exceedingly interested in
reading it, and was highly gratified at the whole. Your
reporter must have been my friend McGuire. I was, as I
told you before, not disappointed at the result at all; and
I repeat, I think the ultimate result will not only add *vastly*
to your already high reputation, but do an immense deal of
good for the cause of truth, right, and the sound principles
of government. The popular mind needs an awakening
up. Particular *cases* have always been the immediate occasion of all past similar awakenings, and, perhaps, ever will
be. Most fortunate it is for any man, so far as it relates to
his fame and distinction, to be the one prominent in the
case of the awakening. . . . .
The people everywhere look upon it, I think, as the
greatest thing you ever did. As to the newspapers, they
really do not understand it; they measure the merits of a
production of this sort by the extravagance of opprobrious
words and epithets it contains. I speak of our editors in
the main. There are some exceptions, but many of them
don't know where they stand. Their instincts are right,
but they need an awakening up. It is fortunate you made
the speech when and where you did—in Macon. . . . .
I do hope you will, just as soon as you get through with
your speech, bring it over. You can go back the same
night if you wish, but I shall expect you to stay one night,
at least. Make the preparation of this speech your first
business, and get through with it as soon as you can without hurrying the mind: let that act, at all times, in free
play. I have some ideas of my own about the case, which,
I suppose, you have presented; but, lest you may not have
done so, I wish to give them to you to use in your note, or
otherwise, as you may think proper, if you approve. I
have no apprehensions whatever of a conviction; but if that
should take place, so much the better for you in respect to
present, as well as future, true honor, fame, and glory.
Love to all. . . . .

Judge Stephens rarely appeared for the prosecution of
any case in the courts affecting life. "Blood-money," as

it has been not inaptly called, he did not covet; but in the case referred to in the succeeding letter, he would have taken a fee, if it had been offered him *before* he was retained for the defense. Although the slain, in this instance, was his friend, no rule of professional ethics would allow him to refuse his services, previously applied for, to the slayer, who was likewise his friend:

SPARTA, July 28, 1871.

DR. S. G. WHITE—*My Dear Sir:* When I got home from the North, on the 16th instant, I found your letter of the 4th, in behalf of the mother, sisters, and brother of Captain Lewis H. Kenan, asking me to represent the prosecution for his homicide against J. R. Strother. I had to go right off, next morning, to Wilkes court to defend a man charged with murder; and when I got back from there, I had to go into an adjourned court, which is still sitting here.

I have the opportunity to answer you to-day only because I am too sick to be in the court-house. Indeed, I am so sick that I am availing myself, as you see, of an amanuensis. I got a telegram at Boston, on the 5th instant, from Obadiah Arnold, requesting me to appear in the defense of this same prosecution. Acting on my uniform rule of defending any accused person who applied to me, to the extent, at least, of seeing that he had a *legal trial*—provided he secures me a reasonable fee, looking to the nature of the case and his ability to pay—I responded to Arnold that I would appear for the defense. Such was my engagement eleven days before I got your message.

I take this occasion to say, that I presume the mother, sisters, and brother of Lewis know, as you do, that he was my friend, and that I was his. I was greatly pained at the news of his death, and do most deeply lament the event and the manner of it. I assure you and them that I shall do nothing in the defense beyond my convictions of duty; and the extent to which I may be carried by my views of duty will depend upon the developments in the case.

I trust that my position in this case will not, as it ought not to do, cause the slightest interruption of cordial relations between myself and those most attached to my lamented friend. Yours, very truly,

LINTON STEPHENS.

[From L. S. to Colonel Herbert Fielder.]

SPARTA, July 29, 1871.

MY DEAR SIR—The night after receiving your very suggestive letter, in relation to the proper course to be pursued by the South, I was suddenly seized with bilious dysentery. I am now getting better, and, therefore, will not delay my answer; but I am not yet at all well, and, therefore, my answer must be brief.

There is great force in your views, and they are on the *line* of wisdom, in my judgment, as they certainly are on the line of honor and courage, in the judgment of all honorable and brave men. There is a great deal, however, in the *name* which is given to a thing—in the mode of putting a case. Mr. Calhoun, for instance, killed the most salutary doctrine of nullification by calling it *nullification*. That *name* gave rise to the great popular outcry against the arrogance of a single State *nullifying* a *law* passed by all the rest. The popular voice might have been secured in its *favor*, if he had only called it the *State veto :* then the idea would have impinged upon the popular brain and heart in *this* form : The vice of all governments is *excess ;* the whole philosophy of good government consists in *checks*, which render the passage of laws difficult. Hence the beauty and utility of dividing the powers of government among *three* co-ordinate and co-equal departments. A logical adherence to the *reason* of this division, or to the division as it is actually made in the Constitution of the United States, would lead inevitably to the true and sound conclusion that nothing can acquire the force of *law*, and be *executed* as such, unless the legislative and executive departments, in *all* cases, and the legislative, executive, and judicial departments, in most cases, shall *concur* in the *constitutionality* of the measure. Each department must be governed by *its own* convictions of the *law*, and dares not to subordinate its own views of the Constitution, which is the highest law, to the views of any other department, nor to the concurrent views of the other two departments. Whenever occasion comes for either department to *act* on the *law*, it must necessarily act on its *own constructions* of the law. This is a very familiar doctrine when applied to the *courts ;* but it is equally *sound* and *important* when applied to the *legislative*, the executive, and to the *citizen*. The right and the duty to judge of the law belong to all alike, and, in the case of all, rest upon the very same foundation—the *necessity of the case*: it cannot be otherwise. The rule of conduct for *everybody* is the *law*, and nobody can pursue the rule until he first determines what the *law* is. There is, to be sure, a marked peculiarity in the instance of the *citizen*: while he, like all the departments of the government, must act on his own convictions of the law, when he acts at all, yet he takes the *risk* of having his views of the law *overruled* by the tribunal appointed to determine and *administer* the law between him and anybody else with whom he may have an *issue*. So he may suffer in his person, as well as in his property, for views which the appointed *tribunal* may hold to be *wrong*. The departments of government are subject to this risk in an essentially modified and much more limited degree. The individuals who fill them are subject, *politically only*, to the high court of *impeachment*; and there, the *punishment* extends only to removal from office and disqualification for office. This idea of equality and independence of the three departments of government is not well understood; but it is, nevertheless, *true*, and *fundamentally* important. It is a great error to suppose, as is supposed by the small party leaders of this day, that the Supreme Court is appointed as an expounder of the Constitution for the other departments: there is nothing like this in the Constitution. The Supreme Court decides *cases* in *law* and *equity*; and even its judgments in particular "cases," like those of *all other courts*, are *void*, if outside of its *jurisdiction*. If the Supreme Court were to adjudge a man to be hung for killing another in a private quarrel, *nobody* would think of respecting the judgment. It was on this idea that Mr. Jefferson was fully justified in turning out the prisoners who were *under sentence* for violating the infamous Alien and Sedition acts. The courts which pronounced the sentences had no jurisdiction. The acts conferred it in *terms*; but they were *null* in effect. Nor is there any *mischief*, or *rebellion*, or *revolution* in this doctrine: on the contrary, there is nothing but the *great blessedness* of *triple security* against the vice of all governments—*excess*. If I seem to have wandered from my subject, the wandering is only seeming—not real: I have only been developing one very important branch of a very large and important idea—the idea of checks on government. A people who are content, that the veto of *one man* shall prevent a measure from becoming a *law*, certainly could not be greatly shocked if the veto of a *great sovereign State* should have the *same effect*—the effect of not nullifying law, but of preventing measures from having *the validity of law*.

My illustration of the importance of nomenclature, and the mode of *putting* things, has run into great length; but I beg you to excuse its length for the sake of its importance. Now, allow me to throw your idea into a different form—to put it in a new mode: *I* should say the South ought to take an immovable stand against all "new departures" from the true principles of the Constitution, as seen in the time-honored creeds of ALL STATE-RIGHT parties, and as embodied and applied *to the facts of the situation*, in the New York platform of the Democratic party. One of the fundamental principles is, that all *usurpations*, all assumptions of powers not delegated, all *frauds*, are NULLITIES, *not laws;* and •when such acts assail and suppress, or repress, constitutional governments in the States, they are also "*revolutionary*" and literally *treasonable*, if enforced by *arms*. This is literally "levying war against the United States"—just as much so as if the British army were to attack the State of Massachusetts; and when war is levied against *any part* of the United States, by a citizen of any State, he is a literal *traitor* against the *United States*. The South should not co-operate with any party which refuses to stand by the State-rights creed, which is *now* to be found embodied and organized nowhere but in the time-honored and unchanged creed of the Democratic party. The departurists themselves have taken a *name* which ought to *damn them*, and will damn them, if skillfully used by the true and bold men. *Theirs is the blunder of secession* over again. We want no secessions—no *departures*—but we want, in a superlative degree, not a division, but a concentration, of all the constitutional forces in a grand effort to prevent the war which was waged for the *preservation* of our system of government from being converted into a false and fraudulent pretext for overthrowing it. Whether I have worried you or not, I have at least wearied out myself, and must close. I would be very glad to hear from you again, and to see your pen enlisted in the grand fight. With high appreciation and kindest regards,

Yours, very truly, LINTON STEPHENS.

The hint given in the following letter to his young friend, who had just commenced the practice of the law, may be useful to older members of the profession. The prisoner, whom he defended, and who was acquitted, was charged with the crime of murder:

[From L. S. to Zeno I. Fitzpatrick, Esq.]

SPARTA, October 29, 1871.

. . . " . . . . Of course, I am gratified at your account of the estimate which is put upon my speech in behalf of Sandy Luther. Let me, however, tell you a secret which may not be useless to you as a lawyer.

While the speech was the thing which struck the crowd, and which was also certainly needful to the end in view, yet it was the examination of witnesses which laid the indispensable *foundation* for the speech, and for the acquittal, without striking the spectators as being at all remarkable. I made the State's own witnesses show (as the truth was) that it was really a case of great forbearance and magnanimity, instead of either malice, or hasty, unlawful resentment.

But enough. With kind regards to Colonel Lawson, and best wishes to you and the "firm," I am truly

Your friend,   LINTON STEPHENS.

The following letter is in answer to one written him by his life-long friend and college class-mate, Judge Pottle (now, 1876, presiding so ably and acceptably over the Superior Courts of the Northern circuit), wherein he urged Judge Stephens to allow his name to be presented to the General Assembly for the United States Senatorship:

[From L. S. to Hon. Edward H. Pottle.]

SPARTA, October 30, 1871.

DEAR NED—Your letter was received Saturday night. The spirit of friendship which it shows towards your country, and towards me personally, is appreciated not one whit the less because it was no surprise to me. On the contrary, I value it the more highly for the very reason that it is in exact conformity with what I expected of you. It is a pleasure, as great as it is rare, not to be disappointed in people of whom we think well. I am not a candidate for the United States Senate, nor for any office in the world; nor do I see that any crisis has arisen, or believe that any will arise, which can require me to accept office. On the contrary, I believe that the great cause, which should now command the unselfish devotion of every good man, can, just at this juncture, be better served by another, than by me, in the position of Senator-elect. I think Herschel V. Johnson is the man. He is no candidate, and knows nothing of my thoughts on the subject; but he is *all right*, and has a *power* peculiar to himself—from the very fact that our State was defrauded of her constitutional representation when applying therefor, through *him*, as one of her chosen Senators. The other one chosen with him is, of course, now out of the question—put so by his physical "disability."[*] Johnson, if elected, will not, like poor ———, and ———, and ———, go whining to Washington, and begging the removal of fraudulent "disabilities," but will demand his seat as a *constitutional right*—claim and *get* a hearing on that question, and then make a speech which would ring through the whole country, and secure the election of a Democratic President. He would do *that* magnificently, and *that* is the thing which just now most needs to be done. I know, too, that *I* should be much more effective in putting him forward than I could be in asking anything for myself. It is pre-eminently a time which demands unselfish and devoted effort for the *cause*, regardless of all personal considerations. . . . .

Truly, your friend,   LINTON STEPHENS.

P. S.—As you say, it is no time for dead-heads: we need men. I would prefer to be *unrepresented* rather than *misrepresented* at all times; and, just at this time, I would prefer to be unrepresented rather than represented feebly. If you can go to Atlanta, do so. Let us all do whatever we can, and I believe you can do much.   L. S.

---

[*] Hon. A. H. Stephens was elected United States Senator in 1866.

[From L. S. to Samuel Barnett, Esq.]

SPARTA, November 28, 1871.

DEAR SAM—Just a line in behalf of a young friend whom I believe to be as capable and deserving as he is needy. Malcolm Johnston wishes to retain his position as assistant secretary of the Agricultural Society. Please use your influence for him, if you can do so consistently with your views and obligations. I suggest that you might secure the object, by getting a promise beforehand to retain him, from the person for whom you may vote as principal secretary. If Malcolm retains his place, I shall be very, very much gratified. In great haste,

Your friend,   LINTON STEPHENS.

[From L. S. to A. H. S.]

SPARTA, March 4, 1872.

DEAR BROTHER— . . . . We got home the first night after poor Ben Harris was buried. I do miss him profoundly. His death is a heavy blow to me. He retained his perfect senses and speech to almost the last breath. Just before the last, he said, with marked calmness and distinctness, that he "trusted in the mercy of God, and was not afraid to die." It was said in response to a question put to him by some friend. It was a great saying, made, as it was, right in the face of death. He was a man of very uncommon virtues and worth. I shall always miss him. * . . . .

[From L. S. to Dr. R. H. Salter.]

SPARTA, March 9, 1872.

MY DEAR DOCTOR—My delay in answering your letter of the 22d ultimo has been caused by continued ill-health. Mary and I got home from Atlanta on the 28th—last Wed-

---

* The gentleman, whose death is noted in the preceding letter, was the Hon. Benjamin T. Harris, of Hancock—a leading citizen of the county, repeatedly elected to offices of trust and honor, and whose virtues and worth will keep his memory green and fragrant in the hearts of those who knew him.

nesday a week ago—about 10 o'clock at night, and in the midst of a rain. Our carriage failed to meet us at the depot, nor was the usual public hack there; nor, indeed, did we find there a single human being—neither the railroad agent nor anybody else. The night was remarkably dark. I never saw a darker one. I got the conductor of our train to lock up our baggage in a freight-car, which was standing at the depot, and a fellow-passenger, who got off with us, stumbled about through the darkness, and found a negro-house, and brought out, in great triumph, a lamp—not a lantern, mark you, but a naked, feeble *lamp*. This had to be carefully guarded from wind and rain to keep it alive through our journey—his destination being the hotel, distant about half a mile, and ours, of course, our own house, distant a good, or rather a bad, solid mile. Mr. Lewis (our fellow-sufferer) had his hands full of his own baggage, and Mary, as being the stronger of us two, volunteered to carry the remnant of ours (consisting of her bag and a bundle or two), leaving me, the invalid, to do the *lightest* duty; that is to say, the duty of nursing and carrying the light. Well, I found this same office of carrying the light, just as many better men have found it before me, to be the most difficult of all. I had to make a screen for the lamp, first out of one hand and then out of the other, and then out of my hat, according to the changing drifts of wind and rain. By the time we got home, I was wet, chilled, and most thoroughly *worried*. I was truly angry because the carriage had not met us in accordance with the timely notice which we had given of our coming. When we got in the house, we found it lighted up, and all the family awaiting our coming. This was *too* bad! Evidently expecting us, and yet they had left us to trudge home, as best we might, through darkness and rain! I met the girls with a cold kiss, and without a word of greeting. We soon, however, had the satisfaction of finding that Brad had not met us with the carriage because he had, in the darkness of the night, run it off from a bridge into a ditch, and *had turned it over* and *broken the harness all to pieces*.

The upshot of the whole matter was, that I got a cold, and quite a backset in my recovery. Yesterday was the first day I have really felt like getting well. To-day I feel still better; and now I expect to return to Atlanta day after to-morrow (Monday), and resume my work there. My sickness has greatly deranged the plan I had formed for avoiding conflict in my business at *different points*. If I had kept well, I should now have my Atlanta business at a point where I could leave it until the second week of April, and could therefore attend to other business which is now pressing at other places, and which I shall have to abandon, unless I can get it postponed. This I hope to do, but it is doubtful; so my employment for the State may not improbably turn out a losing business to me, in point of money, at least; for the business which conflicts with it is in my regular circuit of practice, and, if abandoned, may seriously diminish my future engagements. But this conflict is distressing to me for higher reasons than my own interests; for some of the business which I have to abandon involves the life of one man, and almost the whole fortune of another— both of whom are begging me to stand by them, and one of whom is my dear friend, Colonel Jack Smith. He has lately had the misfortune to have his house burned up, with all it contained; and he now has two law-suits, which, if they go against him, will almost, if not quite, ruin him. I am truly distressed. You will doubtless be surprised that I do not stand by my friend, and leave the State to get other counsel. The public considerations which forbid this course are almost absolutely imperative. To explain them would require much space, and might not interest you at all. I can only say, generally, that there has been much gallant volunteering in favor of the State, followed, in every instance, by a mysterious and very *ungallant* backing out, or, at least, by a silence which looks like backing out; and it is so construed by the people. When the matter was at last put into my hands by the Governor, the general feeling and expression was, that it would *now* be put through, without fear, affection, or favor. To disappoint this general and confident expectation would not only damage me personally, but, what is much worse, it would destroy public confidence, and contribute largely to increase the public demoralization. I have made my decision, after taking counsel with, not only my own heart and head, but with ———, and, through her, with St. Joseph, and all her numerous other saints, whose very names are unknown to me. . . . . . "We all" send love to "you all."

Yours, affectionately,   LINTON STEPHENS.

[From L. S. to A. H. S.]

ATLANTA, March 15, 1872.

DEAR BROTHER— . . . . This allusion to politics reminds me to tell you that I think our Governor and General Colquitt, and the great bulk of our Georgia leaders, are decidedly inclined to the policy of opposing Grant with anybody who is most likely to beat him, and are also decidedly inclined to believe that he can be most easily beaten by a liberal Republican. I believe, also, that General Toombs is the same way. I just give you these points in order that you may know how matters are in our own midst. I am opposed to running anybody who will not stand on a sound Democratic platform; but I am in despair. Our host is panic-stricken, and wofully demoralized—much more so than the Radicals, and cannot be rallied for *this campaign.* My fear and belief are, that the demoralization will be fastened upon it for *years to come*, if the policy of running a liberal Republican be adopted; hence, I prefer to run a sound man. In one case, it is defeat, without the loss of honor or our *army;* in the other case, it is defeat, with a routed army, and the panic made chronic. . . . .

[From L. S. to A. H. S.]

ATLANTA, March 16, 1872.

DEAR BROTHER— . . . . I have received, since my return here, an invitation to make the next commencement oration for Mercer University. I am inclined to accept, and give them a discourse on this theme: "The Uniformity of Causation—The only Basis of Harmony between True Science and Rational Religion." What do you think of it? I could give the intellectual world some new and striking ideas on that subject. Does the *theme* strike you at all? If it does not, why, then, I should doubt whether my treatment of it would make any real impression on thinkers. The uniformity of causation is the very bottom of the whole system of inductive philosophy; but it has not been made to *appear as such* to the world. The proposition that causation is uniform has so many corollaries, etc. . . . . M—— was quite entertained by Martin Crawford while she was here. He called, one night, to see me, and sat in our bed-room until bed-time. He was in a good vein. She asked him if Governor Smith would get back to Atlanta Monday night. He said, in his slow, *jesting* way: "I don't think he will—he has got off into the country, with nobody but his wife. *She* don't want any "*appintment*," you know, and I think Smith is just now very fond of that kind of company." . . . .

Affectionately,   LINTON STEPHENS.

[From L. S. to A. H. S.]

ATLANTA, April 7, 1872.

DEAR BROTHER— . . . . I was very much pleased with your remarks on your editorial life. You made it the occasion to strike some very powerful blows. By the way, have you seen the late speech of Voorhees? It is *tremendous*—blasting the fraudulent amendments and *all* the frauds and usurpations, and denouncing the whole Radical rule in terms not inferior to Demosthenes against Philip. It is *grand!* That speech, as a platform, would be like fire in a sedge-field. Do publish it, entire, in the *Sun*, and praise it in the high terms, which it so richly deserves. His groupings are powerful and thrilling. It was a Titan hurling mountains. I had no idea the man had so much *power* in him. If the Democratic party want to *succeed* in saving the country, or in the low purpose of even *getting office*, let them rally to Voorhees' speech. . . . .

SPARTA, April 19, 1872.

DEAR BROTHER— . . . . I suppose Billy told you of Croley's acquittal here last week. That was very gratifying to me: the case had given me great anxiety. I don't think it will ever bring me a dollar in the way of a fee; but I have the satisfaction of having got off a good fellow—one of "our kin," as we used to call all the *Paddies* we saw on our journey through Pennsylvania, in 1848. By the way, I have heard of a very sensible remark, made by Bishop Pierce, in relation to my speech—the first one of mine he ever heard. The remark was in reply to a question, on the part of young Tom Pierce—a preacher, and nephew of the bishop—as to how my speech could be reconciled with the teachings of the New Testament? The answer was, "The court-house is a place to hear *law* rather than *gospel.*" . . . .

The following communication from Samuel Lumpkin, Esq., the present (1876) accomplished solicitor-general for the Ninth Judicial District of Georgia, gives some account of the speech referred to in the preceding letter, and his impressions of LINTON STEPHENS AS AN ADVOCATE:

DEAR SIR—A compliance with your request to give you a statement of the impressions made upon me by the late Judge Linton Stephens, as an advocate, involves the performance of a task at once delicate and responsible. While I accede to your wish, it must be understood that what I shall say does not pretend to be exhaustive of Judge Stephens' great power in this respect. Indeed, to do him full justice would require a much longer and more intimate acquaintance with him, and a much closer study of the habits and peculiarities of his mind than my years and opportunities have allowed.

As an advocate, he had few peers. His whole soul was always in the matter of his discourse, and, whether his ultimate purpose was to please the fancy or convince the judgment, he rarely failed. As Professor Goodrich observes of Sir John Eliot, "His fervor, acting on a clear and powerful understanding, gave him a simplicity, directness, and continuity of thought, a rapidity of progress, and a vehemence of appeal, which reminded one of the style of Demosthenes." At times, he exhibited a wonderful power of persuasion. It has been written, "Words are things, and in the mouth of one who knows what words are, what potent things they are!" Judge Stephens knew well what they were, and how to use them. When he chose to call into action the better emotions of human nature, he was never at a loss; and, as results of this exercise, courts and juries have been held spell-bound, and strong men made to weep by the winning tones and touching pathos of his speech. A distinguished Georgian once said of him, that, though almost rugged in his manly face and form, he had in his manner all the gentleness and tenderness of a woman; but this does not constitute his chief characteristic as an orator. He possessed, in a far greater degree, the power of compelling the convictions of men by the *force* of argument. He invariably impressed his listeners with the sincerity of his own belief in the truth of what he said, and then, in spite of opposition, carried like convictions to their minds.

> " As rushing down, when winter reigns,
> Resistless to the shaking plains,
> The torrent tears its way,
> And all that bars its onward course
> Sweeps to the sea with headlong force,"

so did the power of this man's eloquence sweep away all obstacles that stood before him.

His reasoning was close and strictly analytical. It has been said of Lord Chatham that he had no power "to divide a speech into distinct copartments—one designed to convince the understanding, and another to move the passions or the will—but that all went together, conviction and persuasion, intellect and feeling, like chain-shot." Not so with our distinguished friend. He had a great faculty for exercising the " intrinsic, incommunicable power " of stern logic. His mind was capable of arranging and classifying the most complicated questions, and then presenting them with such simplicity that the most unlearned and unskillful readily comprehended them. He seldom made a mistake in properly dividing the propositions growing out of his subject, and he could argue abstractly upon their merits without resorting to the employment of passionate appeals to make his remarks impressive. When he did unite the two elements of logic and persuasion, he achieved the crowning glory of his eloquence; and the leading characteristic of that eloquence, in any view, was its *force*. Whether he reasoned, or appealed to the sympathies, or denounced, it was always done *forcibly*.

Again: few men had greater power to make a proposition appear ridiculous. There is a passage in the speech he made in his own defense, at Macon, in January, 1871, before the United States commissioner, under the charge of violating the Enforcement act (so-called) of Congress, which, you remember, splendidly illustrates his almost unequaled power and skill to use the weapon of *ridicule*. I shall not transcribe it; for sure I am that the speech will be published entire in your volume.

Words cannot describe the influence he exerted over the minds of others. It is certain that many, who held opinions contrary to his, declined to express them in his presence—not in anticipation of uncourteous treatment, but of certain and overwhelming defeat in the argument. He compelled them to see things from his stand-point; and it not unfrequently happened, in his practice, that opposing counsel, thoroughly satisfied by his reasoning, vouchsafed no reply.

No man excelled Judge Stephens in remembering facts. His mind grasped every detail of the evidence so thoroughly and so accurately that he was never involved in anything like self-contradiction, or doubt, in stating what had been proven, or in drawing his conclusions therefrom. He comprehended, without difficulty, the most complicated testimony, seeing instantly what most men arrived at by slow processes. He could, at pleasure, recall any particular part of the evidence he required, every fact being apparently prominent in his mind at the same moment; and he never failed to mention all that went to strengthen his side. He seemed peculiarly gifted in seizing upon the strong points of his case, in giving every circumstance its most favorable significance, and in making available to his client's interest every possible view of the entire transaction under consideration. Nothing was ever left for associate counsel after Judge Stephens had presented the facts of a case.

One of the finest addresses I ever heard before a jury was made by him in behalf of Timothy J. Croley, an Irishman, charged with murder, and tried in the Superior Court of Hancock county, at April term, 1872. While the defendant was beating a colored man with a pistol, for provocation by words, given some two hours before, the pistol fired and killed him. It was a case in which the jury might well have found a verdict of guilty, upon the idea that the accused had exhibited "a disregard of human life," amounting to criminal negligence.

. . . . The defense was, "Homicide by misadventure." To avoid conviction for murder, it was argued that there was no intention to kill; nor yet,

33

criminal negligence, because the beating was not such a one as would ordinarily result in death—the shooting, it was claimed, being accidental. It was conceded by both sides that the offense could not be voluntary man-slaughter. To escape a verdict for involuntary man-slaughter, and secure an acquittal, the defendant sought to justify the battery on account of the provocation given, which may be done under our statute, the jury having the right to determine whether or not the opprobrious words used shall constitute a justification. The deceased had called Croley a "d—d Irish dog," and used language to the effect that his mother before him was no better than a dog. In commenting upon it, Judge Stephens, in substance, said:

"Gentlemen of the Jury: Let us analyze this insult. In the first place, he called this man a *dog!* Think of the degradation imputed to a man when he is placed on a level with the brute creation! A man having feelings, sensibilities, and pride of character—a man made in the image of his God, with a heart, brain, and soul—*to be called a d-o-g!* But this is not all: he said *Croley's mother* was no better than a dog—that mother who had nursed and watched over him in his infancy—his best and earliest friend, whose prayers had ascended to Heaven in his behalf ere he was conscious of their meaning, and whose love had followed him, in all the fullness of its devotion, until her latest breath! Ah! gentlemen, this was more than *human* nature could stand. It is not wonderful, then, if this man's blood boiled under such a provocation, even if it had been no worse. But it *was* worse: he called him an *I-r-i-s-h* dog! This was a reproach to his patriotism—an insult to the green shores of Erin. Would it not be worse to call a man a *Georgia* scoundrel than simply to call him a scoundrel? Would not the insult to a colored man be made more offensive by calling him a *n-i-g-g-e-r* thief? Then, why was it not worse to call Croley an *I-r-i-s-h* dog? And this insult was *still* worse: he called him a *d—n* Irish dog! Not content with degrading Croley and his mother to the condition of brutes, and reproaching them for their nativity, he uses profanity to make his abuse even more emphatic and unendurable. What did it matter if two hours *had* elapsed between the provocation and the resentment? The State's counsel had spoken of *cooling* time: this was an insult about which, the longer a man thought, the hotter he got. If he was 'red-hot' at the time it was given, in two hours he must have become 'white-hot.' Croley was called upon to resent it, not o : y by every impulse of pride and manhood within him, but by his love for the land that gave him birth. He had been an unworthy son of the Emerald Isle, had he done less. The beating given the deceased was what he deserved; it was *his;* he had earned it, and he might have expected it. What else could he, or any rational man, have expected under the circumstances?"

The solicitor-general, invoking the decisions of the Supreme Court, in the cases of Brown *vs.* The State (40 Ga., 689), and Kitchens *vs.* The State (41 Ga., 217), had insisted, before the court and jury, that, while the jury are made the judges of the law, in criminal cases, they must take that law from the court. Here, .the great power of Judge Stephens was expended to its fullest extent. His idea was, that the jury were a part of the court, and, as such, had legal and constitutional rights, as distinct and as well defined as those of the judge; and that it was the duty of each branch of the court to earnestly maintain its respective rights, just as each of the three co-ordinate departments or our government, while co-operating with the other two, preserves its independence of them. In defense of what he regarded as one of these great rights of juries—one which had been purchased and perpetuated by the blood of heroes—he proclaimed that the decisions cited were *not law,* and *never could be law,* binding upon a *free* people, though repeated by a thousand judges through a thousand years. He told the jurors that they were judges of the law, in criminal cases, by a right older even than Magna Charta, and that they were the last conservators of that right, and could preserve it inviolate in spite of all the decisions of all the courts on earth. In thus addressing these sworn jurors, Judge Stephens was battling, not only for Croley, but for the establishment of a principle in which he believed with all his heart. It has never been my lot to hear a better speech. Not Erskine, in behalf of Hardy, could have been more grandly impressive. For three hours he commanded the attention of every man in the crowded court-room, and none were weary when he closed.

The jury very soon returned a verdict of *not guilty!*

Judge Stephens sometimes exhibited great tact and great power in another way: he would make his view of the law and facts so convincingly clear that opposition seemed unreasonable, and then defy the tribunal addressed to adjudge against him. It was not often he resorted to this style of argument, but instances did occur when he used it most effectually.

He was greater, as a lawyer, in civil than in criminal cases. The reason was this: from the nature of his mind, he was accustomed to regard criminal law as something not to be determined by what was written in statute-books and commentaries, but as a system of natural justice, written by the finger of God upon the hearts of all men. He very often rested the defense of persons charged with crimes upon the validity of principles that I have heard the distinguished Georgian, already referred to, speak of as "laws which no Legislature made, and which, thank God! no Legislature can repeal." Hence, he did not devote to the study of criminal jurisprudence so much time and attention as he thought it necessary to bestow upon the profounder and more intricate depths of the law regulating "the rights of things." While, therefore, he was more impassioned in the conduct of criminal causes, he was more learned and more logical in the management and argument of civil cases. . .

. . . .

I have attempted no eulogy of Judge Stephens; nor shall I, in this connection, attempt any expression of my gratitude for his many kind acts to me, or of that profound sorrow with which, in common with every Georgian, I lament his untimely death. I feel sure that his countrymen will hold in grateful remembrance his truthfulness, his courage, his patriotism, and his fidelity to every trust.

Most truly, yours,   SAMUEL LUMPKIN.

[From L. S. to A. H. S.]

ATLANTA, April 29, 1872.

DEAR BROTHER—This morning I got two letters from you—one of the 27th and the other of last night. I am truly glad that the latest news from poor Pluck leaves room for his recovery. By the way, I take this occasion to make a *confession* in relation to Pluck: when I first knew he was dangerously sick, I rather *think* a wish arose in my secret breast—scarcely acknowledged to myself—that his sickness should end in death. While I knew that result would give you some sadness, yet I thought it would, on the whole, be a real relief both to you and the poor dog. I did not comprehend how much you were attached to him, nor how deeply you would be pained by his death. Since I have learned the real state of the case, I truly hope that he may get well, and that the parting between master and dog may long be deferred. I feel a new and tenderer interest than ever before in the fortunes of poor Pluck. "Oh, long may he wave!" etc. The mutual tie which you have disclosed, as existing between you and your dog, gives me a new glimpse into the interior of your present life. M—— has frequently said that you seemed to possess a charm against *loneliness*, and I have felt a concurrence in that opinion to a greater extent than I allowed myself to express. During the last two or three years, while you have seemed to enjoy company, and to be quite cheerful, yet you have seemed to me to be less *dependent* on company for your enjoyment than you ever were before, and your cheerfulness has seemed to be less determinate and less dependent on your surroundings. You have seemed to be *absorbed* in your own currents of thought, and to live very much in a world of your own, where your purely intellectual nature predominated over your emotional, in a degree very unusual with you in former days. *Now* I see, or think I see, that, to some extent, I have been mistaken.

The General is resolute in his purpose to attack the constitutionality of the legislation passed after the expiration of the forty days. He has talked to me about it several times—the last time having been about two hours ago. He seems to have pretty calmly *studied* the views I presented to him as to what would probably be claimed by the enemy as to the logical consequences of the decision, if it should be made as he desires it; and, really, he presents some very strong *counter* views as to the probable course of the enemy. I will give you the strongest one—not precisely as he gave it to me, but in the clearer and stronger form (as I conceive it) which has been worked out by my own reflection. Mark you, the foundation of the whole trouble from that decision would be in the material it would furnish for attacking the

validity of the election in December, 1870.   If we can save
that election, *it* upholds everything else, and there is no
danger.   Well, Congress is fully committed to the validity
of that election.   The House has received our members,
chosen in that election, and the Senate has received our
Senator, elected by the Legislature which was chosen in
that election.   Grant also refused to back Conley in his intended resistance to the claims of Governor Smith.   Grant
must have held Smith to be the true Governor, and, of
course, the present Legislature to be the true Legislature.
Grant also would have to carry a very heavy load in bringing back into power the crowd of exposed thieves, who
bowed and retired, at his own bidding, in favor of what he
recognized as the legitimate government.   True, *he* might*
say his recognition was founded on the decision of the highest judicial tribunal in the State, and that he changes his
course with the change of that decision.   But Congress
could not say this—at least, the House could not—for they
received our members *before* any judicial decision had been
made.   To change front on the question would certainly be
embarrassing, even to such upholders and perpetrators of
usurpation.   They could easily *avoid* doing so, either by
saying the first judicial decision was the *right one*, or by taking the true ground, for once, and saying that the election
does not, by any means, fall within the act under which it
was held, since the lawful time for the election, having
passed, the election had to be held at *some* subsequent time ;
and this election was undoubtedly the true *expression* of the
constitutional constituency.   What do you think of this?   I
shall adhere, *I think*, to my determination not to raise the
question in the cases where it would benefit me ; but I shall
certainly not oppose the General's argument in the case
where he raises the question against me.   I shall not argue
against my convictions, and I shall give that explanation of
my silence.   But it is nearly night.

Yours, most affectionately,

LINTON STEPHENS.

Judge Stephens' health, never robust, began to fail, per-
ceptibly, in 1868.   Any imprudence in diet, or exposure
to inclement weather, or severe physical exertion, affected

him more or less seriously; still, he rallied so speedily that
the increasing frequency and violence of his attacks of illness
occasioned little of uneasy apprehension even in the minds
of those most intimately apprised of the fact.   His recu-
perative energies seemed indeed marvelous; and when dyspepsia—his lifetime demon—relaxed its grasp and gave respite to jubilant and playful spirits for a spell, they believed
it could not otherwise be than that many years of life remained to him.   But the heavy, incessant strain upon all
his faculties, physical and mental, in the spring of 1872,
required a power of endurance which his enfeebled constitution could not supply.   Outside of professional business—
large, onerous, exacting, in his own immediate circuit of
practice—he was retained, as counsel, by Governor Smith
to investigate the enormous frauds perpetrated against the
State during the preceding administration, and to prosecute
the offenders.   Never unmindful of the business of his life,
nor indolent in the profession of his choice—a profession
which is said to be "ancient as magistracy, noble as virtue,
necessary as justice"—he brought to his aid all his resources
of zeal, fidelity, assiduity, and candor.   How well he performed that difficult office—with what ability, fidelity, and
conscientiousness—is known to the people of Georgia; for
his services then and there rendered—alas! cut short too
soon—are among the diamonds that sparkle in the diadem
of the State.

It was whilst he was prosecuting these cases in the courts
that he was invited to address the people on the political
situation at the capitol.   The Presidential election was approaching; no Democratic candidate had been nominated.
Public sentiment was in its formative period—its crysalis
state.   It was his last appearance upon the politcal platform.
Weary and forworn with the professional work of the day,
the words he uttered were words of admonition and warning.   Some present then disputed the history he recited;

others derided the prophecy he made: but all since agree that the *admonition and the warning* came from a political seer; and what was prophecy then has ripened into history now.   Here follows his speech:

LADIES AND GENTLEMEN—It is a source of real regret that bodily weariness and mental lassitude, resulting from close confinement, for several consecutive days, in the court-room, will subtract so much from the small power which I might otherwise have to address you in a manner worthy of the great cause and of this intelligent audience.   As I must husband my strength and resources, I shall not attempt, even if I could do so, to entertain your imagination, or to amuse you.   I come to address the arguments of reason to your understanding, and to your hearts, the appeals of courage and honor.

There are two great questions which demand immediate answers from the Democratic State-rights people of this country: the first of these is, Shall the struggle for the establishment of Democratic State-rights principles be maintained; or, shall we abandon that struggle and accept the antagonistic principle of unlimited power in the central government, and its inevitable logical sequence—despotism?

There are now two candidates before this country for the Presidency—General Grant and Mr. Greeley.   What will either of these do for the advancement of Democratic State-rights principles?   And when any many asks me to contemplate and ponder the policy of supporting either, the question recurs, and I cannot refrain from putting it: Is the struggle for the restoration of these principles to be maintained?

What are these two antagonistic principles?   State-rights on the one hand—Democratic; and on the other, centralism.

My friends, have you contemplated the difference between the two?   What is State-rights?   What is the essence of it in a nut-shell?   It is, that while we recognize in the general government all the powers that have been delegated to it by the true Constitution, it is none but those that have been thus delegated by the *true Constitution*.   All other rights are reserved to the States, and the States hold these; that is, all reserved rights, subordinate to no body nor com-

bination of men: they are subordinate only to God, who
gave them.

Rights are not dependent upon the pleasures of men—
they are not matters of grace; and when a man talks to me
about State-rights that are *subordinate*—which they can exercise, *subject* to the central government, in the exercise of
its solemn constitutional obligation to maintain the equal
rights of citizens—then he is talking of one thing and I of
another; he is talking of State-rights that are *subordinate:*
I know of no State-rights that are not *absolute.*

What is this antagonistic principle—centralism—unlimited power in the central government? I care not whether
that unlimited power is to be exercised by one man, or by
one thousand: it is no better in one case than in the other.

The curse of the principle is the *unlimited nature of the
power!* What does it do? Take its works: the tree is to
be judged by its fruits. It sets aside the government of
our States at will, and erects in their places others of its
own creation. It legislates, not for the whole country, but
for particular States, whenever it chooses to do so; it
makes a law for the "*Rebel*" States—no such law for the
loyal; it makes a law for Virginia, by name, another for
Alabama, and one then for Georgia, by name.

Our fathers fought the Revolution on the principle that
there could be no taxation without representation. That
was but one small branch of a larger and a grander principle, and that is, that there is no security for good government, unless the men who make the laws, whether they be
few or many, are subjected to the operations of the laws
that they themselves make; and whenever a power, external to Georgia, makes laws for her, to which the law-making power itself is not subject, you have the completion of
despotism; you have the same sort of government that
poor Poland enjoys from Russia: you have the same sort
of government that gallant Ireland disdains to accept from
England, and struggles under to-night.

The Democratic State-rights principle is the only divine
right of government that I recognize on this earth. [Ap-
plause.] I pray God that I may ever be true to His holy
throne, and to all His good gifts to men; and I recognize
among His good gifts, as one of the brightest, the right of
self-government in every people who are fit to exercise it.

Where are the champions who will stand for this God given right of self-government? Who will stand with me, for one, upon the determination to struggle for its restoration—for it is now in the dust—and to struggle on this line, not only through the whole "summer," but through the whole of lifetime? I pray that I may die, and be buried out of sight, rather than that I should ever live to see the day when my own brethren, who have fought with me under this glorious banner, shall ever make up their minds to abandon it. [Applause.] Which side are you on, and are you in earnest?

Fellow-citizens, you are all for the maintenance of the true principle—the God-given principle—the divine right. You are for State-rights—for the supremacy of Democratic principles, which, in this crisis, means State-rights, nothing else; Democratic principles mean nothing but State-rights, for which Democrats and old Whigs used to fight, until the old Whig party received its death-wound, in 1852, when General Scott was run by such men as Sumner, Greeley, and Morton, and they gave it a weight it could not carry, and made it stagger and fall into its grave forever. Mr. Greeley is one of the men who killed the old Whig party by abolitionism.

I say Democratic principles now are just simply State-rights principles, for which Democrats and old Whigs, up to that time, stood shoulder to shoulder; and for which Democrats—it may be now only Southern Democrats—they say, we are going to lose our Northern allies; and if we lose them, I never intend to run after them [applause]; it may be, Southern Democrats only are now, and hereafter, to contend for these principles; but whether we have been Whigs or Democrats, let all men, who have drank from this cup of centralism, reconstruction, ku-kluxism and suspension of *habeas corpus*—drank to the dregs and found it exceedingly bitter—let all those make up their minds now, for a lifetime, never to bow down to the power that oppresses us.

How do these two candidates for President stand in reference to these two antagonistic principles—State-rights and centralism? I believe that everybody admits that Grant is a centralist; and how anybody can doubt that Greeley is just as intense a one, and more able, is a matter of amazement to me. [Applause.] He has advocated every one of these radical, despotic, centralizing measures—every one. He has been the *leader*.

Ah! some tell me we must ignore the past and stand upon the present. I am willing to ignore any man's past and stand upon his present, if I believe that his present is right, and that he is sincerely and honestly repentant for his past, and intends himself to stand upon his present. I won't stand upon any man's present when I have no confidence in the man himself. But what is Mr. Greeley's present? Is it any better than his past? Why, in his very letter of acceptance, giving his own interpretation of the platform on which he is running, he takes it upon himself to group all the things that we hold most dear—State-rights, which he does not even deign to designate by that name— he says "local government"—the supremacy of the civil over the military power, sacredness of *habeas corpus*, local government as against centralism—he groups all these to tell us, and he does tell us, that he holds them *all subordinate* to what he calls the central government's solemn constitutional obligation to maintain the equal rights of citizens— subordinate to the very power, the very duty, which he claims as the authority for the passage of every abomination which has disgraced our statute-books, and oppressed liberty and liberty's sons. [Applause.]

Do you want to know where the enforcement acts came from—the ku-klux acts, the suspension of *habeas corpus?* They came from this very same cry. Mr. Greeley led the race—he sounded the key-note. Has he ever taken one word of it back? Not one. Don't be deceived, my countrymen; for I tell you that your liberties are dependent upon your decision of this question. Don't let people deceive you; *he has never taken back one word of it;* but, on the contrary, he takes pains, in his last letter, to *re-assert* the very *quintessence of the principle* which was invoked for their passage, and on which he justified and demanded them. Is not this the truth?

What was the ground on which the enforcement of all those odious measures was demanded by Butler, by Morton, by Grant, by Greeley, by Trumbull, by the whole Radical crew? It was this very same plea of solemn constitutional obligation to maintain the equal rights of citizens. That was the party slogan under which they rode over you and your rights; and when I hear the same music now, I expect to see the same dance follow it. [Applause and laughter.]

Talk to me about Greeley doing anything to advance Democratic principles! Some folks say that his friends in Congress voted against the renewal of the suspension of *habeas corpus.* That is very good. I give them credit for that; but I never stopped to count his friends, or learn what they did; my principle of action is, when two men avow, equally, the right to oppress me, I shall never stop to count the chances whether one or the other shall find it to his interest to exercise that right of oppression or not. If he avows the right, I know he will exercise it whenever he finds it to his interest. [Applause.]

Our fathers declared their independence of Great Britain *after* the Stamp act had been *repealed*, and they declared it because, in the repeal, the right to tax without representation was claimed and reserved. After the blow had been withdrawn, your fathers fought the Revolution against the right of the tyrant to repeat the blow. Mr. Webster truly and grandly said: "The Revolution of '76 was fought on a preamble." That was just equivalent to saying that it was fought on a principle; and nothing was worth either the blood or the money that was spent in the conflict, unless the fight was one on principle. Give me principle, and I will fight on and fight ever, and die fighting! But when you take away principle, I have no longer any contest; and I say to you, "O Israel, to your tents!"

Some people say, "Anybody to beat Grant!" "Down with Grant!" I don't say "Down with Grant!" nor down with Greeley, nor down with Sumner, nor down with anybody! What I say is, down with radicalism, and everybody who supports it, whether it be Grant, or Greeley, or anybody else! I say down with Grant, because he supports *radicalism.* I say up with the true Democratic candidate that will be true to that banner, because under it I am willing to fight; and Democrats and State-rights men everywhere will fight with pride, and with honor and enthusiasm, and these are the greatest elements I know of success. [Applause.]

General Grant had quite a respectable set of principles when the war closed. Talk about Greeley going on a bond for our President, Davis! So he did; that was one good thing he did; I give him credit for it; and I thank God that I am capable of giving even the *devil* his due. When Stanton, that arch-fiend, was about to arrest Generals Lee, Gordon, and Cobb, and that noble band that surrendered to him—*overwhelmed*, as they said then—not conquered—and I hope to God they may never be conquered—General Grant said: "If it is done, I will resign;" and "resign," in this case, meant throwing up thirty thousand dollars a year; a tolerably handsome thing, even in the estimation of people here, in Atlanta, who are accustomed to seeing and hearing of very large operations. Not, fellow-citizens, that I mean to intimate that *the people* of Atlanta have been responsible for these large operations. You have gone through the ordeal of Bullock's radical, corrupt administration, and, even when the bait was held out to you, you have refused it— yes, in establishing in your city this very house, where you are now assembled. You stood true to honor—you passed through the fire. I have found the smell of fire on the garments of *some;* but, thank God! the great bulk of your citizens have shown themselves to be firm adherents of honest principles: they have gone through this ordeal, and come out purified gold. I don't know a body of sounder Democrats than the Democrats of Atlanta. When I spoke or large operations here, I meant it as no reproach. God forbid.

The man that preserves his virtue under temptation will do to be trusted always: the man that preserves it up to the time when temptation comes, we simply don't know what he will do when it does come.

General Grant said he would throw up his commission if Lee and his brave comrades were arrested. That's a good thing; I give him credit for it. President Johnson sent him down here to take a survey of the South, and report on our condition. He came; he was in this city; he was in divers central points of our country. He went back and reported that we were all right; that we ought to be restored to our places in the Union immediately, without any XIVth or XVth miscalled amendments (for that was before they were enacted); without any reconstruction and Radicalism; without any Enforcement act; without any ku-klux laws; without any suspension of *habeas corpus.*

And why was it not done? Why were we not restored? *The Radical cry was raised against it,* and again the same old arch-fiend, Horace Greeley, *headed that cry.* Grant quit his good principles, and went over, and became the *exponent* of Greeley's bad ones. This is the greatest objection that I have to Grant: that he quit his own principles and went over to Greeley's; and as long as reason maintains her throne in me, and the pulsations of my heart permit me to live, so help me God, I never intend to follow that man's example! [Applause.]

Democratic principles *restored* by supporting Grant or Greeley! I would just as soon think of advancing the principles of Christianity by hauling down the banner of Christ, and hoisting the colors of Mahomet! [Applause.]

The combination, or coalition, if you please, made by Democrats and Liberals, in Missouri and Tennessee, is quoted, and we are urged to follow the example. The proposition that was made by good Democrats and true, to accept Judge Davis as a candidate, is quoted. There was something in each of these cases to be gained for the advancement of Democratic principles in Missouri and in Tennessee. The combination, with Gratz Brown in the one and Senter in the other, *stood pledged* in each State to strike loose the fetters of about forty thousand Democratic voters, who were then under the iron heel of proscription; and when that was done, these States were in the possession of the Democracy. There was some sense in that. Judge Davis, on the Supreme Bench, conceived that his solemn constitutional obligation required him to pronounce sentence of unconstitutionality on some of the acts which had been passed by Greeley, Grant, and Sumner, to carry out *their* ideas of constitutional obligation. He pronounced these acts *null and void.* Judge Davis, under his solemn sense of duty, held those acts to be revolutionary, unconstitutional, null and void. He turned loose Milligan after he had been condemned by a military tribunal to be shot. He was about to turn loose McArdle, but Greeley again came to the rescue, and Congress, at the crack of his lash, passed a law to prevent Judge Davis from turning loose any other victim of tyranny.

Judge Davis, God knows, is not all I would have him to be; indeed, I never expect to find any human being who is up to the standard of perfection—not even those who were made last, and therefore made best, of whom the poet said:

"Auld Nature swears the lovely dears,
Her noblest work she classes, O!
Her 'prentice hand she tried on man,
And then she made the lassies, O!"

Not even these, far above the 'prentice work, can claim perfection; but to compare Judge Davis with Horace Greeley, and say that one was no better than the other—well, it is ungrateful, to say the least of it; and whenever we speak thus disparagingly of our friends in the North, and say that those there who are battling for our rights are no better than those who are helping to oppress us, shall we be surprised if our friends in the North continue to fall away from us? No people can long retain friends who do not treat them right when they do have them. Even the gallant Voorhees, who has always fought the fight, kept the faith—always been true to the flag of Democratic principles—is maligned and misrepresented; and papers and men, calling themselves Democrats, charge that he has been bought up by Grant, only because he is not willing to take a Radical that is just as much a Radical as Grant or anybody else. [Applause.]

What are you going to get by it? Why, I am told, if the Democratic party elects Greeley, he will be good to us. Give us something! [Laughter.] What is he going to give us? Give us any principles? Where is the principle he is going to give? He has not even said that he is going to give us *anything;* but the hope is that he is going to give some of us, who are willing to take it, a little share of the plunder. [Laughter.] Was there ever a more proper application of the motto, "Fear the Greeks when they are bringing gifts?" Fear the Radicals when they are bringing gifts; and I tell you that Radicals will never, never give you any gifts—only to persuade you away from your principles. Greeley wants you to swap your principles for a few pitiful little offices for *some people* [laughter]; and I don't know whether *some people* will ever get the offices or not; and I would not care.

But you say the Democratic party is so much bigger than Greeley's little segment, that has to do this great work of electing him—and that is not done yet [laughter]—that it will swallow up the little Greeley concern; and it has been wittily put: "Can a minnow swallow a whale?" No! A minnow cannot swallow a whale! but even a whale, if he be passive and float upon the water, without putting forth his fin-power, could be floated by a set of little minnows into any convenient harbor.   And this coalition is never to be formed, except upon the condition that all the Democracy that has influence is to become *passive*—to become dormant. We are to quit struggling to secure Democratic principles, and to go to fighting to secure the election of a Radical.

Well, I have seen little steam-tugs move great men-of-war on the deep; I have seen them pull them into the harbor: if the man-of-war will only let off its steam and become passive, the little tug can take it safely in.   And just so, if this great Democratic mass will turn off all the Democratic steam—Greeley for one tug—one great big tug—Gratz Brown a little one over in Missouri—Sumner a tug, too—and I have no doubt you will find a tug in Georgia, too. These tugs will be perfectly able to land this great Democratic leviathan safely on the Radical shore; and that is just where you are going, if you go with Greeley.

There is nothing in that but a new phase of the "new departure." That was a proposition to sanction all the usurpations—to quit being Democrats—to radicalize the Democratic party, and accept the new principle of centralism—unlimited power; and Greeleyism is nothing but a more virulent type of that same disease.   God forbid that anybody should understand me as intimating that the great number of people who have been, like my friend, who so eloquently addressed you just now (General Garlington), debating the question whether to go for Greeley or not, should be held by me as tainted by the Radical party! Not at all! I beg you not to take the step; because, if you do, they will radicalize you.   There cannot be any other result.

General Grant said, "Let us have peace;" the new departure and Greeleyism mean the same thing; it is addressed to *your fears;* it is addressed to your sense of personal comfort.   Buy your peace by grounding the arms of your opposition to Radicalism, and acknowledge our right to rule you, without limitation, in all things! That is a peace I never mean to accept! When they give me *right*, I will give them peace and co-operation; when they give me *wrong*, I will give them undying resistance. [Applause.] I know no way to maintain right but by fighting wrong.   All men,

who are in favor of maintaining their r'ghts, are called upon
to rally—to fight against the foul wrongs that have trodden
the right in the dust. Wherever you can find it, strike a
blow, if it is inscribed on the banner carried by Grant, by
Sumner, or by Greeley.

I understand the policy of not pressing all your principles upon a man at one time, if he will accept *some vital
one*; I can understand the policy—though by no means a
favorite with me—of taking Judge Davis on account of his
position on these reconstruction measures, because he held
that the central government was limited, and when it exceeded its powers, its acts were null and void—and this is a
great point. I can understand that; but I don't understand
any policy that can ever justify true men in giving support
to a Radical who does not hold a single principle in common with you, and in opposition to the other Radicals.
Why, say some, Greeley is quarreling with Grant. Sumner
is quarreling with Grant; Sumner made a great speech
against Grant the other day; and what do you reckon his
objections were? He charged Grant with usurpation, but
it was only that he had usurped a power which he said the
Senate should have exercised. It was not the usurpation,
but the person who perpetrated it, that Sumner complained
of. He has quarreled with Grant, but his only quarrel with
him was that Grant had robbed him of his rights. He
complained, too, that Grant had violated the laws of nations, and committed a great outrage upon a foreign black
republic; but did he say one word about any usurpation
that Grant had ever perpetrated upon us—upon folks at
home, either white or black?

Greeley says Grant is corrupt: he takes gifts; stands up
to his friends; is guilty of excessive nepotism; but what
does he say when it comes to this grand central question—
the solemn constitutional obligation of the central government to maintain the equal rights of citizens, which, they
say, not only justifies but requires them to pass all these
odious measures under which we have groaned, and under
which the gallant State of South Carolina is groaning to-
night? My God! how can a South Carolinian hesitate on
Greeley? I put it to my friend (turning to General Garlington), the only way to get out of these tangles is to stand
by your principles and by your guns. [Applause.]

34

It is a prime rule in whist, when you don't know what to play, to play "trumps;" and if you don't know who to vote for, play trumps; for trumps are always principles. I know something about Grant and Greeley's common principles: they put the Enforcement act upon us. I met them with argument; I whipped the fight. I well remember the words of cheer which were given me in that contest by the people, and their rejoicing in my triumph. I was proud, and it made my heart glad to see your devotion to principle. But I did not whip the fight by running away from it, but by fighting it with all the strength that God had given me. It is only by fighting Radicalism that you can do anything. Democrats can't succeed by yielding their principles, or ceasing to fight their enemies. The Atlanta Democrats never acted on that idea. I have known the Democrats of Fulton county when they were in the minority; they have made it a glorious majority by fighting. Georgia didn't act that way—cease to fight.

The Democratic convention, which assembled in this city last August a year ago, had principles in it. It was absolutely a Bourbon platform; it was actually written by a Bourbon, who is one of the strictest of the sect; and under that Bourbon platform you tore Bullock and his foul confederates from the throne, and put a Legislature and a Governor there of whom you are proud to-day. A Bourbon! They say a Bourbon never forgets and never learns. Well, I tell you, I can never learn the new lesson they want to teach me until I forget all I know and knew before; and as long as life shall last, and I preserve the principles with which I was born, I shall refuse to learn the new lesson. They would teach me to advance my principles by supporting my worst enemy.

But it is said we can't do anything! They say the Democracy was whipped in '68, and there's an end of the argument. Well, the Democrats were very badly whipped in 1840; they were about as badly whipped a set of fellows as I ever saw. They did not think it was the end; they fought on; they whipped the Whigs, in 1844, almost as badly as they got whipped in 1840. In 1848 they were whipped again; they did not quit the fight. In 1852 they were again successful; they elected Pierce. In 1856 they elected Buchanan; and those are the only two consecutive triumphs of

the Democratic party, in a presidential contest, since my recollection. The next time they lost again. When people
tell me that, because they lost in 1868, they can't succeed
now, I know they don't understand these American people,
or else they want to deceive me—one or the other. No man
comprehends the people of these States, unless he understands that there is a vast mass of the people who don't owe
any party allegiance, and that they go in each campaign
according to the issues of the times.

Whipped in 1868! How could it have been otherwise?
That platform said the reconstruction acts were revolutionary,
unconstitutional, null and void; and the doctrine of that
platform was, that the bayonet ought to be withdrawn, and
the people left free to resume State-rights, form their own
State Constitutions and organizations. That was the doctrine of that platform. Well, Seymour would never get up
on it; he never would say that the reconstruction acts were
revolutionary, unconstitutional, null and void; and Frank
Blair—he wrote his Broadhead letter, and said that the bayonet ought to undo what it had wrongfully done. Frank
jumped clean over the platform. And this is the way the
platform stood: one-half on one side, afraid to get up; the
other half jumped clean over, and on the other side, and
the two held together by nothing but the ligature of a common nomination. The two candidates were like a pair of
saddle-bags. And then the New York *World* refused to
support the candidates, and said that even these saddle-bags
should be taken down.

Yes, we were whipped in 1868; but remember that, in
1870, the elections in the Northern States went vastly in
favor of the Democrats, with substantial gains in Congress.
The new departure was sprung to stop the mischief; the
Democratic work was going on too well; it had to be stopped, and the new departure was put forward to stop it; and
now Greeley comes. The first gun that fires under them is
Oregon—gone Radical now. It is true—and I thank God
it is—that the best way to gain victory is to deserve it.
There is more power in the truth than there is in falsehood.
There is more in right than there is in wrong; and if you
have got but true men, whether few or many, relatively,
that is the road of success as well as of honor.

There is another great question—I began by saying there

were two—and the other is, Shall the Democratic party govern the Baltimore convention, or shall the Baltimore convention govern the Democratic party? Shall the principal govern the agent, or the agent the principal? Shall the servant obey the master, or the master the servant? There is a cry now, "Let us all go to Baltimore; we won't discuss it; we won't decide anything here—go to Baltimore;" and this when the proposition to be discussed at Baltimore is, whether or not Democratic principles are to be advanced by trusting them to the keeping of one of the chiefs of the Radicals?

If I were in the church, I would as soon think of abiding by the decision of the church, if the question debated was whether Christ should be repudiated, and Mahomet or Juggernaut substituted instead. I abide by the Democratic party as long as it remains a Democratic party, and no longer; I abide by the Democratic party so long as it maintains Democratic principles—*or some vital one, at least, of the Democratic principles*—and no longer. I don't mean anything harsh, but simply to tell you a plain truth—that I regard any body of men, associated politically for any purpose other than to maintain principles, as no better than a band of spoilsmen, bound together for plunder. The only cause of allegiance that binds a *true man* to any party, is the faith that it teaches. Suppose the Baltimore convention nominates Grant, will you take him? [A voice—"No!"] Suppose it nominates Greeley, why take him in preference to Grant? He is no better.

They say he is an honest man—a good man. They talk about his old white hat, and make jokes about his old white coat, to put people in a good humor. May be it is like a Bourbon to have a memory, and I have not lost mine. I remember he was the man that raised his voice in the North, and said we had the right to secede, and that if the North made war upon us, it would be a crime. Yes, he said "let the wayward sisters go in peace." After the war began he, too, raised the cry of war; and, to show how malignant he was, he said that, when the war was over, the rebels should not go free, but should have a punishment. Hear it! hear it! Southrons, hear it! Georgians, hear it! Georgia men and Georgia women, he said they should have a punishment that could be read in the anxious faces of our mothers, and

the rags of our children! That's what he said. Save me
from all such honesty as that. I believe I would rather
trust the honesty of Bullock himself than such honesty as
that. *Treachery* is what I call it; *malignity* is what I call
it—not benevolence. I don't want to "shake hands over
such a chasm." I will tell you when I will "shake hands over
the bloody chasm:" when he comes and offers me his hand
over these enforcement acts, and the ku-klux act—under
which South Carolina is groaning this night—and offers to
shake hands with me, and swears on these locked hands that
he gives up his principles, and that these so-called laws shall
be repealed, and never be repeated, and gives up the principle that our rights are subject to the obligation of the central power to maintain the equal rights of citizens, then I
will shake hands with him, and not before. [Applause.]

I want no Judas' kisses nor Judas' shaking of the hand;
and I will kiss no man, and I would not kiss even any woman [applause], much as I love them—and God knows I
love to live to love them [applause]—I would not even accept a woman's lips that came to offer Delilah's kiss. Talk
to me about abiding the Baltimore convention! I will abide
by it in all questions of policy, but I will not abide by that
convention, nor any other convention that bids me depart
from principle; and I want to know if these gentlemen who
say stand by the Baltimore convention, whatever they do,
will stand by it if they adopt the Philadelphia platform and
nominate Grant? The Cincinnati platform is no better in
principle than the Philadelphia platform.

But the office-rot has got among them; yes, and that is
what's the matter. They are like Esau—some of them:
they would sell their birthright for a mess of pottage. I
don't speak of the people; but there are men who are pining for pottage. They have been ineligible; they could
not get a crumb for lo, these seven years. [Laughter.]
The office-rot is what is the matter; they seek plunder.
There are some who are even willing to change their position from the plundered to the plunderers. As for me, let
me abide by the oppression. I would rather support principle than secure profit by committing the deed. Trust,
then, in the wisdom and justice of God. I do verily believe
that He, not as a speculative being, but as a natural Being,
rules every movement of this whole earth. It is my com-

fort and my consolation that there is a God who rules the
world, and that if I do not prove untrue to Him, I need fear
no human oppression now nor hereafter.   Stand by His
good gifts; He gave us this great right to govern ourselves;
let us not abandon it; let us honor, and not dishonor Him.

These, fellow-citizens, are my views of the political situation; these are my resolves as to my duty.   I will go for
the maintenance of Democratic principles; and if I can't
get the man who goes for all, I will take the one who goes
for some of the *vital* principles of the Democracy; I will
take no *subordinate* rights, but *absolute* State-rights.   The
way to win is to hoist your colors.   I do not mean any new
departurists—I don't mean any radicalized colors, but the
true Democratic State-rights colors that hold reconstruction
and all its triumphs to be revolutionary, unconstitutional,
null, and void.   We may not succeed in electing a President in this campaign, but we can put the party on this sort
of a platform, and give it standard-bearers worthy to carry
its colors.   We will be in condition to carry the next election; but, at all events, it will keep the *truth* for future use.

I see some say it takes a very nice calculation to tell
whether Greeley has the strength to succeed.   Well, my
God! if there is any doubt, then, will you hesitate?   I have
been sincere, and am warm, because my whole soul is in
this business.   I do not intend to die a slave myself, and I
do not intend peacefully to submit to slavery as an inheritance for my children; and, if we cannot do anything else,
we can, at least, maintain the glorious party we have inaugurated in old Georgia; and I would rather to-day have the
Georgia Democracy go forth into another canvass, true to
their principles, with true standard-bearers, than to have all
the spoils the office-seekers will ever get out of Greeley.
All the favors Greeley would give Democrats would be to
such Democrats as would never do honor to their party.
You could get all that out of Grant if you would go over to
him.   They say he is scared—he is badly scared at the
prospect before him.   Well, if you go over to him, he is
fond of his friends.   If you want peace, and will take it on
his terms; if you will acknowledge his right to lick you
whenever he wants to, he will take off all those enforcement
acts; but they won't stay off long; for as long as the principle is acknowledged, it has got to bear its fruits.   The

thistle will bear the same fruits again, plant it in whatever soil you may. You might stop Vesuvius by plunging Stone Mountain into it, but the fires would break out at some new crater. The vital force may stop, for a season, its operation in one direction, but it will break out somewhere else. If you take off the ku-klux bill, they will give you an educational bill next; then a religious bill, after awhile, to establish your religion.

Now, this constitutional obligation they talk about, to maintain the rights of citizens—the XIVth and XVth miscalled amendments, the XIVth and XVth frauds, the XIVth and XVth falsehoods, because the XIVth and XVth usurpations come last—they say they override everything else—the provision that *habeas corpus* shall not be suspended in time of peace—everything—these frauds which are not in the Constitution at all, and, if they were, never could be rightly construed, as they construe them—they say they override everything that was ever in the Constitution before. As long as this principle is held; as long as men are in power, who acknowledge it; as long as a party cannot be found in the country to war against that principle: that principle will live and flourish. The thorn-tree will bear thorns, and the American people will have plucked the last fig from the tree of liberty. [Great applause.]

A few days after the delivery of that speech—days of unremitting toil in the court-room and in the closet—he went home, in an exhausted condition of health, to meet his engagements in Hancock Superior Court. Employed on one side or the other of every important cause, the labor it imposed quite overcame him. When the excitement of the week—the *gaudia certaminis*—had abated, he was left in a state of complete nervous prostration. On Friday, he was confined to his room; Saturday, he was worse; and, although no alarm was felt, a physician was called in.

During the night, his condition became critical. At 5 o'clock P. M., Sunday, the 14th of July, 1872, he ceased to breathe.

Retaining perfect consciousness to the last moment, and

fully appreciating his situation, with all its relations—past, present, and future—he took his way into the Great Darkness undismayed—dying, as he had lived, "fearing God and knowing no other fear."

His obsequies are thus described by Frank L. Little, Esq., at that time editor of the *Southern Times and Planter:*

JUDGE STEPHENS' BURIAL.

This event occurred on Tuesday morning, at 10 o'clock. By general consent, all the places of business had been closed since his death, and every house was draped in mourning. Many sympathizing friends visited his residence on Monday; but, on Tuesday, the throng of people poured in from all sides, until hundreds were here to look, for the last time, upon the remains of the deceased, and to assist in the sad ceremony of his burial. Every man, and woman, and child seemed to be bowing under the consciousness of individual loss, and the general gloom was deeper than we have ever seen it before. The few words spoken were in a suppressed tone, and were all about the great loss to his family and country.

When the appointed hour for the burial had arrived, the plate was adjusted over the glass, and the pall-bearers, in the following order, bore him from the library, where his remains had been lying, to the open grave:

WM. W. SIMPSON and CAPTAIN L. L. LAMAR.
L. PIERCE, Jr., and J. CLARENCE SIMMONS.
HENRY H. CULVER and DR. E. D. ALFRIEND.
HENRY HARRIS and F. L. LITTLE.

The grave is just in front of his residence, beautifully surrounded with shrubbery and embowered with shade-trees. Under the reading of the impressive words of the burial-service, by his life-long friend, Colonel C. W. DuBose, whose voice was tremulous with his own deep emotions, not many eyes remained dry. This ended, the grave was soon filled, and all that was mortal of this distinguished man hid away forever from the sight of friends and loved ones. His body "was committed to the dust, his soul to the God who gave it."

Not least of the significant and affecting circumstances of his funeral rites was the large number of colored people who were present to testify their sense of sorrow at the common loss and pay respect to his memory. Their houses, too, were "draped in mourning," and they wept over the grave of their *real* benefactor and friend, whose counsels, in the early days of emancipation, they did not heed, but which later and riper experience had taught them were salutary and wise: for, to all men, at all times, he spoke *true* things rather than *pleasing* things—"*vera pro gratis.*"

In stature, Judge Stephens stood six feet, with more bone and muscle than flesh. All the features of his face were distinctly marked. His forehead, broad at the base, broadened as it ascended to the region of what phrenologists denominate Causality, Comparison, and Ideality. In youth, he had a thick suit of dark-brown hair, inclined to curl and crisp, which time somewhat whitened, but scarcely thinned. His was a deep-set, clear, blue eye, which, in repose, wore an expression of thoughtfulness and almost unworldly sadness; in moments of hilarity, it laughed with rich, soft light, betraying an almost feminine tenderness and gentleness; whilst, on occasions which called into exercise the heroic virtues, or excited the sterner passions of anger or indignation, it flashed forth a flame that was terrible to the trembling transgressor. His nose, fashioned rather after the Roman than the Grecian mould, was large and prominent; his chin, more broad than sharp, lent a Spartan resolution to the whole expression of his face; his head, like Napoleon's and Franklin's, grew larger after he had passed his third decade. His dress, never sloven, was sometimes negligent; he cared little for the fit of a garment, if it sat easy and was unsoiled.

The handwriting of Judge Stephens was remarkably legible, and somewhat feminine in type; it was formed upon no model, and resembled none I ever saw. With abundant indications to show that he used the pen with ease and rapidity, there are seldom to be discovered any signs of hurry—none of carelessness. In the large number of letters which I have had occasion to examine, there are to be found very few interlineations, and not more than one or two erasures. In this respect, his manuscript was as unblemished as one of Mr. John Quincy Adams', of whom it has been related that he never made an alteration on the written page during the last fifty years of his busy life.

In social life, he avoided the crowd. The circle of his intimate friends was not a large one; but of that "charmed circle" he was the idol; and, perhaps, it is not extravagant to record that, while the death of many Georgians has created a sorrow more extensive in its range, the death of none ever penetrated the hearts of so large a number with an anguish so personal, so near, so keen, so bitter as that occasioned by the death of Linton Stephens. How many felt as did the large-hearted, stalwart man feel when, standing by the open grave of Daniel Webster, he said: "How LONESOME THE WORLD SEEMS!"

Judge Stephens was an earnest student throughout his life. He had studied men, and knew them well; his judgments of character, sometimes almost intuitively formed, were rarely erroneous. It was in books, however, that he found the chiefest source of intellectual enjoyment; they were his passion and delight—*præsidium et dulce decus.*

He did not cultivate, with any great degree of assiduity, the knowledge of Greek, imperfectly acquired at college; but his knowledge of the Latin language and literature was extensive, accurate, and intimate. Tacitus, Cicero, and Horace were special favorites—each of his kind. His knowledge of the best English authors, both of prose and verse, was comprehensive, various, and wonderfully exact, for one whose vocation was the study and mastery of the "jealous science of the law." Bacon and Burke, "*welded together,*" he said, would have made the grandest character in history. It is safe to say, he had no superior in the State in a profound and philosophical knowledge of English and American history—political, ecclesiastical, or literary. He regarded Hume, in style, as the Prince of British historians—neat, perspicuous, nervous, condensed—far surpassing, for that sort of writing, the elaborate finish of Gibbon—*maternam superabat opus*—the stately elegance of Robertson, or the studied, breathless antitheses of Macaulay.

Of American historians, he esteemed Motley before Bancroft or Prescott. Prescott was too precise as to little matters; Bancroft had more words than ideas. Addison, among all the English fine writers of prose, he admired most, in sentiment as well as style. He has been heard to say, that "Washington Irving was the Addison of America." "Dean Swift," he said, "was a dirty dog, but no man ever wrote or uttered the Saxon of our tongue so vigorously as Dean Swift." Shakspeare and the English Bible he knew almost by heart. Pope, he said, was the greatest didactic poet of any language; Burns, Byron, Dryden, Goldsmith—all of different vein—were his companions—each of whom he had studied, and thoroughly appreciated.

Milton he did not very greatly admire, for the same reason that he little affected Gibbon: it required too much or palpable, ostensible effort to "*manufacture the Miltonic grandeur.*" The quiet, quaint, half-hid humor of Tristram Shandy he could read and laugh over by the hour, all day long; and he said "Sterne mistook his calling when he put on the sacerdotal robes." He never could detect any wit in Rabelais; and he said, "I have searched for it in vain; Toombs or Tom Thomas can, and frequently do, speak more witticisms in one night than Rabelais, in a lifetime, wrote." Bulwer was his *beau-ideal* of a monarch in the realms of fiction—greater than Thackeray, or Dickens, or Scott, because he had a deeper and more philosophic insight into human nature—especially in its nob'er manifestations; and *his* greatest merit was the beauty, and fidelity, and delicacy with which he portrayed the excellence of female character, in its best exhibitions. He once said: "There is no grammar, and hardly a dictionary, in our language. Webster is the best definer; but his orthography, in so many instances, is not akin to the etymology; for example, thea*ter* is only the step-daughter of theat*ron*, etc. Horne Tooke was the greatest of English philologists. He knew the power of words, and made them things; the shortest cut to a knowledge of our mother-tongue is through the "Diversions of Purley." He had peculiar aptitude and fondness for metaphysical study and inquiry; and, in the line of speculative philosophy, he ranked Sir William Hamilton above Reid or Stewart—even alongside his great prototype, Aristotle.

He was passionately fond of biography—"the philosophy which teaches by example" more aptly and specifically than history; and he gave full indulgence to his taste for that sort of reading. "Kennedy's Life of Wirt" he considered the best specimen of American biography, whether regarded in point of style, the skillful handling of his material, the delicacy and elegance of the portraiture, or the attractive light in which he presents his subject, as an example for the emulation of youth.

His colloquial talents were of the first rate. Like Burke, he talked because "his mind was full;" he never opened his mouth without having something to say. His conversation was alike instructive and entertaining—at times, adorned with classical allusion, enlivened with apt anecdote, enriched with prompt and sparkling wit, and illustrated by serious or comic incident. No man had a keener appreciation of the ludicrous, either in incident or in character; and none more exquisitely enjoyed a well-told story, or better relished a good joke; when the humor was on him, and the occasion to his liking, few knew so well how "to set the table on a roar."

All men of mark have their special theaters whereon their peculiar talents and abilities show to greatest advantage. There are those who shine most brilliantly in the forum, addressing the bench—like Toombs or Hull—or addressing the Twelve, like Wright or Lumpkin; others there are, whose Titanic strength is best displayed before deliberative assemblies, like Johnson or the elder Stephens; others, again, are in their element and in their glory on the hustings, like Hill and Yancey; others, yet again, in the lecture-room, like McCay or LeConte. I believe the greatest exhibitions of intellectual resource and power ever made by Linton Stephens were in familiar conversation, when, inspired by the topic under discussion, and conscious of no effort on his own part, he poured forth a wealth of learning and wisdom, wit, logic, and eloquence, that was marvelous to the auditor. He was one of the few men I have known, whose mental bulk and stature aggrandized on approach— possibly some frailty may have been, at the same time, more fully disclosed to view—but his real greatness enlarged—it did not diminish.

Other and abler pens have, in the preceding pages, portrayed him in the character of statesman, jurist, orator, friend: one, especially, has befittingly complemented— what his own letters do not entirely reveal—the excellence and beauty of the endearing and nobler parts of his nature, as daily exemplified in social and domestic life, and which, lending a mild and sweet expression to the sterner features of great mental endowment—severely cultured—masculine will, unquailing courage, complete the picture of MAN.

The affluence of just, discriminate, appreciative eulogy, which was heaped upon his tomb through channels of the public press, the courts, political conventions, primary assemblies of the people, epistolary correspondence, private conversation, is unequaled, perhaps, in the history of any citizen of the commonwealth—certainly, in that of any one who never occupied the highest political station.   He, himself, was unconscious of the space he filled in the general eye, and of the hold he had upon the popular heart.   His manly modesty would have crimsoned at suggestion of the fact; still, the sorrow—deep, boding, awful—so keenly felt, so eloquently uttered, when "tidings of his death came like wailing over the land," avouches the truth that he was the foremost citizen of the State when the awful curtain dropped.

When few of the many testimonials, in my possession, of the estimation wherein he was held, and of the sharp grief the news of his death shot to the hearts of great and good men, who knew, appreciated, admired him, are transcribed, my "labor of love" will have been imperfectly performed.

I am under obligations to Hon. Miles W. Lewis for the following admirable estimate of Judge Stephens' character as a legislator:

WOODLAWN, GREENE COUNTY, GEORGIA,
September 24, 1873.

MY DEAR SIR—Yours of the 18th instant is before me. You state that you are preparing a biographical memoir of the late Judge Stephens, and that, from the frequent and respectful mention made of me in his correspondence with his brother, Alexander, you infer that we often interchanged letters, and ask a loan of them.   It would afford me great pleasure to comply with your request; but, although Judge Stephens and myself were very intimate, I remember no letter he ever wrote me, except such as were entirely on professional business.   This I consider a strange misfortune, considering our social relations; for I claim no more honor than is due to truth when I tell you that, although the number of those who partook of his kindness and enjoyed his friendship was little less extensive than the circle of his acquaintance, yet those with whom he was intimate, and to whom he freely unlocked the arcana of his great heart, were comparatively very few, and that I was one of the favored few.

You also state truly that I served with him in the General Assembly, and ask me to aid your labor by giving you my reminiscences of him as a legislator, to be incorporated in the volume over my own name. I greatly regret that the imperfections of memory, the want of *data* at my command, and press of business, will render the contribution unsatisfactory to both of us, and unworthy of the character and talents of our deceased friend; but if I can chisel out even an humble and unsightly block to fill up an interstice in the literary monument you are erecting to his memory, it shall be at your free disposal. You are engaged in a noble enterprise—no less a one than enshrining in the annals of biographical literature, as it is already in the hearts of his countrymen, the memory of one of Georgia's noblest and greatest dead. His State could have but ill spared his services at any crisis in her history; but at the particular and peculiar time of his death, I hesitate not to say that Georgia—yea, the whole Republic—could have sustained no greater loss in the death of any one of her distinguished sons. Who, that knew his power and influence, can estimate the depth and extent of the wound inflicted on constitutional liberty by the fatal shaft which death aimed at this shining mark? Might not the administration of our State government, in all its departments (improved as it has been in the recent past), have been still purer, less selfish, more patriotic, more statesman-like, and more glorious? Might not the circle of this improvement, as the ripple on the agitated surface of the recently placid lake, have enlarged until its influence would have been felt throughout the whole extent of this mighty confederation? Who can say nay?

But to the duty assigned me of sketching, as best I may, his characteristics as a legislator. This I can do only in general terms, being unable to particularize and illustrate each trait, by striking incidents in his legislative career, coming under my own observation, from the fact that we served together in but one General Assembly—he in the House and I in the Senate—each attending closely to the business and debates transpiring in his own branch; but whenever I heard his familiar voice in debate, unless personally engaged in important business in the Senate, I always repaired to the Representative hall. He never spoke

merely to be talking, and for notoriety; and never, except
on matters of grave importance, and, usually, such as vi-
tally affected the interests of the (then) Southern Confederacy—such as the conscript acts, the indorsement by the
State of the Confederate bonds, the principles on which,
and for which, the war should be carried on, and when and
how it should be terminated; for the discussion of these
important subjects, which, at that time, absorbed the interest and attention of the whole South, he marshaled all his
intellectual forces. These were neither few nor feeble, but
formidable to opponents, and such as gave to allies assurance of victory.

His speeches were characterized by practical—or, as it is
generally termed *common*—sense, sound logic, animation,
zeal (not "without knowledge"), withering sarcasm, fine
discrimination, and fervid eloquence; in short, he held in
his intellectual armory, and used as occasion demanded, all
the weapons whose skillful handling constitutes the able debater and eloquent orator. He accomplished his purposes
by no maneuvering or indirect means, but marched boldly
up to his work, strong in his consciousness of right, fearless
of consequences to himself, "asking no favors and shrinking from no responsibility." Even his opponents honored
him for the purity of his motives, and admired his great
ability. He was always the champion of the liberty of the
people; and if there was any subject in the whole range of
political science, which he thoroughly comprehended, and
which was the idol of his patriotic affections, that subject
was CONSTITUTIONAL LIBERTY. In its defense, he fought
his most celebrated battles, and achieved his most brilliant
victories.

In the ordinary routine of legislation, and in his daily intercourse with his fellow-members, he was distinguished by
the same traits of character which so signally marked his
conduct in social life. He was truthful, candid, guileless,
generous, and brave. In each and all these qualities, if he
ever had a superior, the writer never saw him. This judgment is pronounced with no fear of its being criticized or
questioned by those who knew him.

Pardon a short paragraph on one of his prominent traits
as a lawyer. His rare legal attainments will doubtless form
the subject of a leading chapter in your memoir; but he

was as magnanimous and generous as he was able and eloquent.   An instance in point I not only witnessed, but ex-
perienced, and gratefully remember.   I was engaged in the
defense of some negro prisoners, indicted for a crime which
rendered them so odious that they were threatened with
Lynch-law, if acquitted in the court, which placed their
counsel in a position by no means enviable.   Friends warned
me of the danger of a loss of popularity, and the forfeiture
of the friendship and patronage of the most influential class
of society.   In my jury-speech, I spoke of the seductive
whisperings of ambition and vain warnings of pretended or
real friends that had been breathed into my ear—treated
them all (I trust) with becoming contempt, and made the
best defense I could, under the circumstances.   Judge Stephens followed me in the prosecution.   Never shall I forget
his look of approval, as advancing to me, when I sat down,
he said: "Miles, who has been talking in that way about
you?"   After informing him, he opened one of his most
masterly efforts by paying me a high compliment for the
force of the argument, and the honor I had reflected on the
profession, by what he termed my manly and independent
bearing in the case.   Then followed a withering rebuke to
my *would-be friends* for endeavoring to turn me aside from
the path of professional duty.   I then felt, and still feel,
richly compensated for any danger I was in from the malev-
olence of enemies or the desertion of friends.   But lest I
transcend the limits assigned me, I will close this imperfect
sketch of our departed friend with a familiar, but appropriate, couplet from the ancient classics:

"Clarum et venerabile nomen,
    Gentibus, et multum nostæ quod proderat urbi."

Yours, truly,   MILES W. LEWIS.

The Hon. Richard H. Clark thus graphically and elegantly
describes the effect of one of Judge Stephens' speeches in
the General Assembly in 1854:

The State capitol was located in Milledgeville in (I believe) the year 1807, because it was the nearest practical

35

geographical center of the State.   This was before the day
of railroads, and before there were settlements beyond the
Ocmulgee.   When Cherokee, Western, and Southwestern
Georgia became settled, the lands of the Creeks and Chero-
kees occupied, and the railroad system of the State established, Milledgeville was left rather out of the way for the
great majority of the white, or business, population.   The
removal of the capitol to Macon or Atlanta began to be
mooted, and, at the session of 1847, took shape in the effort
to pass a law to that effect.   Then, and after, the move
would have succeeded, if all the friends of removal could
have agreed on the site; but the contest between Macon
and Atlanta operated to keep the capitol at Milledgeville.
The removal feeling, nevertheless, continued to grow until
the sessions of 1853-'4.   An act passed "the House" to
move the capitol to Macon.   By a count of the Senate,
it was ascertained that the same act would pass that body.
This knowledge created intense interest among the people
of Milledgeville.   They *felt* that all their real estate would,
by the removal, become as ashes on their hands, and this,
with many, was absolute poverty.   Every man, and, indeed, woman, and even children, turned out to "stem the
tide" in the Senate.   I have never witnessed any excitement,
of the kind, so intense, deep, and pervading.   The bill was
made the special order for a day in (I think) February, 1854.
On that day, before the hour for the special order had arrived, the gallery, the lobby, the aisles, the windows—everywhere that sitting or standing-room could be had—was filled
with the population of Milledgeville.   The oldest citizens—
such as the eldest McComb—were furnished with the most
comfortable and most conspicuous seats.   If all of them
had been on trial for their lives, they could not have looked
more serious, more anxious, or more troubled.   We, who
were *fixed* for the removal, were moved with compassion at
the sight; yet, we felt it a public duty that must be discharged, and the people of Milledgeville had our deepest
sympathy in *our* realization that nothing that could be done
would prevent the enactment of the law for the removal.
They had always been the kindest of people—all, even to
the negro servants, who were the best collection in the State.
There is no man, with both sense and soul, who has ever
passed a session at Milledgeville, but must have formed an

attachment for the place and people, and one that must be a dear memory, even down to the latest period of the longest liver. Especially so it must be with those who passed there those long biennial sessions of some ninety days, and remained all the while as the guests of the very aged Mrs. Huson, or of (as he was familiarly called) "Old Bob McComb." When the time came and the special order was taken up, there was the most profound silence. It was of a kind that reminded one of a funeral occasion, when men and women were gathered to pay the last sad rites to a dear friend, just preceding the burial. Now, this simile is appropriate; for a majority of the Senate then proposed to bury forever dear old Milledgeville, the capital of Georgia; and her whole population had come out as mourners. My memory fails me, if any effort was made in the way for or against the bill, before the speech of Judge Stephens. I think not; but if so, the efforts were not marked by any length or power. I *know* that several of the most effective speakers on the removal side were reserved for closing the debate. The Milledgeville people had made a strong friend of Judge Stephens. His friendship was not merely political—it was personal, and *feelingly* personal. He was their champion—indeed, all their hopes were centered in him—to check the current that was fast and forcibly running against them. It was an occasion where everything conspired to a successful effort. There was the subject—the people, the interests, the affections, the time, the audience, THE ORATOR. It is useless—indeed, it is impossible—to describe the oration. It lasted for an hour and a half, and as much was said as was possible for man to embrace in that much time. For logic, for pathos, for humor, for ingenuity, it was grand; and, if judged by its *effects*, it was unsurpassed. The silence that prevailed at the beginning became, if possible, deeper, as the orator proceeded. The Milledgeville men and women wept tears of joy, and the most inveterate removal man looked ashamed of the deed he was about to commit; and, before Judge Stephens concluded, we regarded "Old Bob McComb," and his sort, as bearing "a charmed life," and that it was sacrilege to touch their person or property, either indirectly or directly, with or without the forms of law. I do not remember, except on one occasion, that all the feeling I had was one of enthusiastic admiration *for the genius of the speaker.* This feeling so took possession of me that, in casting my eyes to the gallery to see the effect of the oratory there, I discovered Judge Stephens' wife, and the thought that, with lightning rapidity came to me, was, "How proud she must be of her husband!" for if I, who was no kinsman, nor intimate, and, for the occasion, his antagonist, was *proud,* what must be her admiration? The speaker not only excited the admiration of both friend and foe, but did what is seldom done— *never,* in my knowledge—that is, capture *all* of them. It is as true as truth itself, that, without a demand, we laid down our arms and surrendered at discretion. When Judge Stephens concluded, it needed no vote to tell the fate of the bill. Every man felt it stronger than language or vote could express. The Senator from Bibb, Mr. Dean, seeing the effect, endeavored to rally his voters; but it was of no use. He appealed to me to answer Judge Stephens—a feat we occasionally did for each other—and I told him if I *then* spoke, it would be *against his bill,* for it would take time to get over the spell of Stephens' eloquence. But the vote had to be taken on (I believe) Judge Stephens' motion to indefinitely postpone, and there was no one who said "nay," and that *feebly,* but the "old guard" of the removal army— they who, through defeat, tears, and disasters, yet had the courage to stand by their colors—myself among the rest. It remains to be added, that the effect of that speech was not merely to defeat removal *then,* but killed it so dead that it never *kicked* again until after a four-years' bloody war. To prevent misconstruction, it seems necessary to state that, from the first, I was in favor of removal. I have often, in the times alluded to, told my Milledgeville friends that the "fates were against them," and, at no very distant day, removal would be accomplished. When it came, it came in a way I dreamed not of.

RICHARD H. CLARK.

Hon. Herbert Fielder wrote of him:

CUTHBERT, July 24, 1873.

. . . .

For close, severe, persistent, aggressive, and irresistible logic—upon fair, and open, and manly statement of facts—

I know of no man, among all my acquaintances, who was his superior; and, I can say, barely any who was, in every respect, his equal. His eloquence was like his logic. His voice was musical, his manner was so earnest, and his voice so in harmony with his manner, and both so true an index to the great thoughts that agitated his brain and stirred up his passionate nature, that he commanded the attention of all grades of mind, from his equals down to the masses.

When he argued a question, he not only was understood, but *felt* by every auditor; and when he was done, the question was exhausted; yet, he was neither prolix nor tedious. He followed wherever his convictions of truth led him, and the thoughts he uttered came from his great mind clothed in the habiliments of sentiment, affection, hatred, or contempt, that such thoughts would naturally produce in his great and fearless heart.

He was only a few years my senior, and I can't remember the time, since I came to manhood, that I have not been accustomed to hear Linton Stephens spoken of as a model of personal integrity and honor.

But his most distinguished characteristic was, that he had an iron nerve, a firmness and inflexible adherence to his convictions of right, and a fixed belief in the imperious necessity for doing what principle dictated in every case.

Other men whom we know, and love to honor, have talents equal, perhaps, to his, in some, and possibly superior, in other respects; still, in others, fall below his level; but I know of no man who surpassed, if, possibly, any who equaled, Judge Stephens in the firmness and inflexibility of his mind, when once made up on any subject. Foes could not intimidate, nor friends persuade, him to abandon any position, the correctness of which was dictated to him by his expanding powers of conception and analysis. . . .

I am truly, etc., HERBERT FIELDER.

The following, from ex-Governor Herschel V. Johnson, will be read with interest:

SANDY GROVE, BARTOW POST-OFFICE,
July 4, 1873.

. . . .

I knew Judge Stephens well, and I had many interesting conversations with him upon almost every subject that in-

terests intelligent men.   I estimated him highly as a man
of strong and original thought, extensive learning—especially in his profession—and of marked independence and
fearlessness in the embracement and advocacy of what he
believed to be true; indeed, I regard his devotion to truth
and principle as the prominent element of his character.
He was candid, patient, astute, and thorough in the investigation of all questions which duty required him to consider.   In his personal intercourse, he was amiable, unas-
suming, candid, and sincere.   It is difficult to measure the
loss of such a man, with such intellectual and moral endowments as he possessed; it was a great public calamity.

His name and career are worthy of commemoration; they
should not be permitted to perish; and I am truly gratified
that you are crystalizing them into permanent and enduring
form.   I wish you all possible success.

I am, dear sir, sincerely

Your obedient servant and friend,

HERSCHEL V. JOHNSON.

The following tribute to his memory, from the pen of
Hon. Edward H. Pottle, appeared in the Sparta *Times and
Planter:*

WARRENTON, July 27, 1872.

MR. EDITOR—Permit me, through the columns of your
paper, to offer my tribute to the memory of your distinguished citizen, Judge Linton Stephens.

There is a positive pleasure in grief, and I cannot refrain
from giving expression to some of the emotions which his
death has inspired in my own breast.   It is a real pleasure
to me to con over the numerous incidents in his life, and in
them to note how true manhood may be illustrated.   Perhaps there are few living, outside his own family circle, who
knew him so long and so well as myself, and who have had
so many opportunities for knowing the excellencies of his
character.   Just thirty-two years ago, I made his acquaintance, when we both were boys, in the State University.
He was then entering the Sophomore class.   His staid and
regular habits were marked, as well as that vivacity which

followed him through life; and now, after the lapse of so many years, no changes were observable in him, except developments. His manhood never lost the type of his boyhood.

He had the best-trained mind I ever knew: its caste was metaphysical and logical; and hence the disposition, patent to every one, to disregard authority or books, and rest his conclusions on his own mental resources. In early life, he was a student: he read, he studied, he thought; and what he learned, he learned well—learned to treasure up in the store-house of his own wonderful memory. He never studied to get ideas, but to compare them. Ideas he had of his own; and if, in search of truth, he found ideas of others antagonizing with his own, he rejected them, unless, tried in the crucible of his own severe logic, they were found to be *the truth*. He was a man of convictions; and the peculiar emphasis with which he always gave the word *truth*, in his addresses, was a sure mark of his devotion to it. There was a maturity in his mind, while in college, which few young men possess—a hardness which gave promise of a useful and illustrious future. I well remember an incident while he was in the Senior class. The subject of the lecture and recitation was, taxation, direct and indirect, on the department of political economy. In answer to a question growing out of the text, he dissented from the author, and the current opinions on that subject, and the hour was spent in earnest discussion between him and the president, who, at its close, paid him a compliment which proved to be a prophecy. The ease with which he mastered his lesson was a marvel to us all. He always had time for recreation, and the lecture-room always found him ready for exercise. Unlike the most of students, he had no specialties in his studies; he excelled in mathematics, as well as in other branches; and in debate, he showed the powers of analysis which characterized him in after life.

At his graduation—where the first honor was awarded him—no one doubted the merited distinction. His social qualities imparted a charm; and hence his popularity with his companions at college. There was a stream of humor and pleasantry which never ran dry, and a raciness in conversation which has kept alive many of his sayings to this day. His friendship was warm and real, and his attachments strong. To dissolve them without a struggle was hard for him to do with a cause.

I have heard it said of him, during his life, that he was inclined to skepticism. This was a great mistake. I never knew one who, in theory, had a more sacred regard for the truth of religion and its divine origin. It is true, he had views which were not in harmony with the teachings of some books; but the teachings of the Bible he cordially received. Not long before his death, he proposed to write a treatise on one of the topics of moral science, in which he intended to combat errors of some good men, which, in his judgment, tended to encourage unbelief, and obscure the real beauties of the Christian system as revelation unfolds them.

After a long and intimate acquaintance with him, I can say that I never knew a man of a warmer heart; with him it was a luxury to love; and some of the most pleasant moments of my life have been spent with him in recounting the happy scenes of the home-circle.

As a lawyer, he has left an example worthy of universal imitation: honorable in his relations, faithful to his clients, and devoted to truth. On the bench, he has left an enduring monument to his fame as a lawyer and his honesty as a judge. In the case of Hill (colored) vs. The State, reported in volume 28, Ga. R., he dissented from a majority of the court on a question of great interest to the bar, and one affecting liberty and right. Though the accused was a slave, he gave him the benefit of a lofty principle of constitutional law, which was unanimously declared to be law, subsequently, in Washington vs. The State, 36 Ga. R., and that, too, upon the able dissenting opinion which Judge Stephens had delivered in the former case. Of this reversal, he was ever afterwards justly proud, because the decision had settled a great right which every human being enjoyed under the laws and Constitution of the State. We all remember his grand orations in defense of outraged liberty and law. These utterances of his will live in history along with the best-prepared orations of men who have been made immortal.

In common with your bereaved community, I, too, mourn the loss of a friend. His warm hand I have clasped from boyhood to the closing of your last court.

"Friend after friend departs,"

And the heart-stricken and sad can only find relief in the memories of the past and the hopes of the future. Death comes, and the arm of affection cannot stay the stroke. In the midst of life it comes—invades the family-circle and bears away its victim to the tomb. It comes in ghastly form, as well as in sudden and resistless strokes; it comes to warn, and to remind us that we are mortal; it comes to teach us, "So to number our days that we may apply our hearts unto wisdom." Beneath its touch man's proud intellect is dethroned; and how low he lies! The speaking eye is dimmed of its luster, and the warm heart stops its throbs. Let us, in this affliction, heed the note of warning as it comes from the new-made grave of our honored friend, "Be ye also ready!"

I am yours, truly,   E. H. POTTLE.

ATLANTA, July 29, 1872.

HON. A. H. STEPHENS—*My Dear Sir:* During the many days which have passed since your bereavement, thoughts of your great sorrow have been ever before me. May I be allowed to express the sympathy I so deeply feel? To realize how great the loss is to you, I have but to recall your hours of sleepless watching at the bedside of your brother when he was prostrated with measles at Manassas, and the privations to which you subjected yourself, when you were illy able to bear them, that you might minister to his comfort.

Let it solace you now, my friend, to remember how faithfully you have discharged fraternal obligations; and, although I know the kind offices were rendered by you in the spirit of love, not duty, yet that must have made them more grateful to him, and should make the memory of them the more comforting to you. You have another element of consolation in the knowledge that he was loved and revered by all who knew him personally, and by many who knew him only as the talented and distinguished statesman and the pure patriot. The great heart of Georgia sends forth to-day one universal throb of regret at the loss which she, as a commonwealth, has sustained in his death. The good and true cannot help but admire the fealty with which he clung to his principles, while so many are bowing to the

high priest of radicalism; and all feel that he has left us at
a time "when our need was the sorest," of such wise counsels as he was in the habit of imparting, and the example
of such unflinching integrity, as he ever exhibited. When
the pure and excellent of earth pass through the silent halls
of death, they find them but the entrance to heaven's efful-
gent glory. Can we wish our loved and lost back amid
the turmoil and strifes of this world, when we remember
that they dwell with God, and that the Lamb, who is in the
midst of the throne, shall feed them, and shall lead them to
living fountains of water, and God shall wipe all tears from
their eyes?

Hoping that the rich consolation of the gospel may sustain you under your heavy trial, and commending you to
Him who alone can speak comfort to your sorrowing heart,
I remain, with the highest admiration and most profound
respect,

Your friend,   MRS. JAMES HINE.

SANDY GROVE, July 18, 1872.

HON. A. H. STEPHENS—

> " Friend after friend departs —
>   Who has not lost a friend?
> There is union here of hearts
>   That finds not here an end."

This stanza comes to me, unbidden, upon the announcement of the departure of your brother to the spirit-world;
and I hasten to give utterance, as far as language is adequate, to my unfeigned grief and sympathy. I sympathize
with you, with his widowed wife and orphaned children,
with his many friends and admirers, and with the State at
large. There are but few hearts, within this numerous
circle, that will not heave a sigh that Linton Stephens has
passed from the scenes and activities of earth. He was so
noble in his nature, so stern and inflexible in his devotion
to truth and principle, so able and eloquent in their advocacy, so energetic and constant in his labor for the public
welfare, that he had impressed himself so deeply and
broadly upon the general mind, that he had already, though
comparatively young, won the conviction in the popular
heart, that he was ubiquitous, not in a personal sense, but

in the sense that his fame occupied a field commensurate with the vast interests of the country.

But words of praise from me are nothing: they are emptiness to you, who filled for him alike the place of father and brother, and cherished both affections with the deepest intensity; they are less than emptiness to him who is beyond their reach; but I utter them, most sincerely, for what they may be worth for your consolation. Oh, how mysterious are the ways of Providence! What lessons of profound humility are inculcated by the majesty of His footsteps! How uncertain is our probation here! How the path of life is bestrewed by monuments of sorrow and disappointed hopes! What is called death is always sad and unwelcome to survivors. Even when infancy is cut down, like a bud, by the wintry blast, or old age is arrested in its tottering steps, tender affections are severed, and anguish exudes from every wound until the heart overflows with bitter grief; but when manhood, in his prime—in the meridian of intellectual maturity, and in the midst of usefulness, surrounded by all that makes the present happy, and the future bright, in its promise of fame and distinction— is stricken down, the blow is crushing. But

> " Leaves have their time to fall,
> And flowers to wither in the North wind's breath,
> And stars to set; but all—
> Thou hast all seasons for thine, O death!"

Calm resignation to the will of God is our duty, and its performance is sweet, however mournful, when we recognize that He is our Father—"too wise to err and too good to be unkind." To him I commend you, and all the dear ones clad in weeds of woe by reason of this heavy bereavement. Take comfort in these reflections: that he lived a useful life, and leaves to his family the heritage of unsullied honor; that, in our view of the mercy and wisdom of the Lord, he has been summoned at the very best time for him, and for those who loved him so fondly; that he is not dead, but lives in the eternal world, the same identical man that he was here; that he has gone *home*, just a little in advance of you and all of us, where, under the tutelage of angelic spirits, his intellectual and moral faculties will rise, and grow, and expand forever.

I had a brief interview with him, last January, in Atlanta; but the last time I had an opportunity for protracted conversation with him was in Savannah, whilst we were attending the Federal court, as counsel for Garsed. We talked frequently, and nearly always on religious topics, in which, I thought, he took pleasure. He listened to my views with deep interest; he argued with me in many of them, and, as to others, he expressed no opinions; because, he said, "whilst he could not combat them, he did not rationally perceive their truth." But he bought two or three new church works, intending to read them. I never learned, however, whether he read them, nor, if he did, what impression they made upon his mind. He was a lover of truth; his mind was always open to its reception, and I have rarely met a man freer from prejudice and educational bias. He was a strong and original thinker. Few equaled him in force and perspicuity of language, and in the power of condensed, logical thought. I never conversed with him without pleasure and profit. I regret that the occasions of our meeting were so seldom. If he had remained here to the usual limit of man's appointed time, he would have had no superior, as he had few peers. He would have been a conspicuous figure among the greatest actors of his day, and wielded tremendous influence in public affairs. His love of country was animated with the courage of martyrdom; and constitutional liberty had no more able and eloquent defender. His removal is a public calamity. But I will say no more. His eulogy is the place which he filled in the admiration, confidence, and affections of the people. May he rest in peace, and perennial laurel cluster around his memory!

Mrs. Johnson, Gertrude, and Winder unite with me in these expressions of sympathy. The rest of my children are scattered.

May the Lord bless, and console, and shield Linton's widow and orphans, and may He be the great Rock under whose shade you may retire, in this heavy tempest of sorrow, is the heart-felt prayer of

Yours, most sincerely and faithfully,

HERSCHEL V. JOHNSON.

BOSTON, MASS., July 26, 1872.

MY DEAR MR. STEPHENS—How my heart yearned towards you, and for you, when the telegram announced to us the death of Linton—and such a brother! Not one in a million so tender, so kind, so generous, so brave as he. In one point of view, it did seem to me that the agony of sorrow might extinguish your life. On second thought, it came to my mind, "According to thy day, so shall thy strength be." Yes, our dear Mr. Stephens has schooled himself not to rely too much on exterior comforts—not to confide altogether in human affections; but he cherishes entirely such a strong sense of divine love, that he will exclaim, at the weight and fullness of his grief, in most humble submission and Christian cheerfulness, "Not my will, but thine be done!"

When I first became acquainted with Linton, I entertained a very high respect and esteem for him. As I knew him better and more intimately, I began to love him; and this love grew stronger and stronger every day; it was more like the affection of a dutiful son towards a loving father than anything else. I cannot tell you how terrible was the blow when it came upon us. I cannot at all realize, now, that I shall see his face no more in the flesh. Poor wife and poor children! But Almighty God is good and merciful, and will have them in His holy keeping, and will be more than husband, father, and all, if they put their trust in Him.

I have taken up my pen several times to say a word to you, but hesitated, and laid it down again. To-day, I have made the venture. My feeling was rather, if it could have been, to act somewhat like the friends of Job, who "sat down with him on the ground seven days and seven nights, and spake not a word to him; for they saw that his grief was very great;" and I thought I ought to keep silence, and hesitated about expressing my deep sympathy for you; but you might reply, like Job to his friends, "Miserable comforters are ye all!" Still, I cannot, under the circumstances, be entirely silent. I must at least tell you what I feel it is my part to do: I would kneel beside you, and the other dear ones Linton has left behind, in silent, earnest prayer, press you all to my heart, sustain the drooping heads, take the hands in loving pressure and sympathy, but *speak not.* . . . .

Ever faithfully yours,

R. H. SALTER.

I am obliged to Pope Barrow, Esq., for the following excellent portraiture of some of the capital features in Judge Stephens' character:

> " Vex not his ghost: O, let him pass! he hates him
> That would upon the rock of this tough world
> Stretch him out longer."

Linton Stephens was one of the few—the very few—of whom it may be truly said, " None *knew* him but to love him." But to the thousands to whom his name and fame were familiar, and to many of those—perhaps a large majority—who were numbered among his personal acquaintances, his real character was, in many of its best features, completely unknown. He cared not to reveal himself—indeed, he seldom ever did, except to those who belonged to what I might call the inner-circle of his friends. The outside world honored him, respected and trusted him; for, however little they might know of him, that little was enough always to command confidence; but his intimate friends, whilst they also entertained these same sentiments of admiration of his talents, and implicit faith in him as a man, felt for him that affection which the beautiful story of David and Jonathan has handed down to us as "passing the love of woman." Those who knew him best loved him best. There was no danger, in becoming better acquainted with him, of having any illusions destroyed which are so often the creatures of first acquaintance with men of fascinating minds. In his case, every impression he made upon an acquaintance, from first to last, was genuine and true. Nothing was done for effect. He was, at all times, natural and *naïve*. As his real character and the generous proportions of his mind unfolded themselves more and more to his associates, it was hard to decide which to admire most, the pure and unsullied nature of the man, or the splendid intellectual powers with which he was endowed.

My acquaintance with him dates back to my boyhood; and I remember quite well the first impressions he made upon me; they have never been erased nor altered. They were perfectly correct interpretations of his character, and have been strengthened and confirmed as years passed on; and the slight acquaintance, then begun, ripened into a warm friendship, which continued, uninterruptedly, until his death. Judge Stephens possessed so many sterling attributes of mind and character, that it would be impossible to speak of them all in the brief limits of a memoir like this, which is not purposed to inform the reader in regard to his character or his achievements, but to remind him of some of his traits, and thereby serve, perhaps, to call up, in his own mind, many another familiar recollection of this great man. There are thousands in Georgia who, when they read these brief reminiscences, will each recall some half-forgotten experience of his own that is linked to the memory of Linton Stephens, which, for the time, perhaps, will carry his thoughts back with a softened heart, to freshen and deepen his recollections of him, and serve to keep his memory green among those whom he loved so well in life. I have found that all with whom I have spoken of him, since his death, who knew him as well as I did, had formed the same impressions of his character, had cherished the same kind of incidental recollections of intercourse with him in life—all of them illustrative of his warm, generous, faithful, and affectionate nature—and have mourned his loss in their hearts almost as one dropped from the circle of their own hearth-stone. Few men have ever lived who were so true to themselves as to stamp themselves thus upon thousands of different men with the same identical impression.

The influence which he exerted over his fellow-men was such as any man might well be proud of; and he well deserved it. It has been said by a very profound thinker, that there are two kinds of men who control and wield power over masses of their fellows: one is of that class to which great orators and poets belong; they persuade and reason men into acquiescence; they present arguments and utter appeals to their hearers and readers, and produce, sometimes, great results. But it is the great questions they discuss, around which the interest gathers, and not the man himself. The other class of men, according to this same philosopher, who make great leaders, are those who, without giving reasons, without striving in argument, and who, not turning aside from their line to examine the movements of others, are followed, and trusted, and appealed to in all emergencies. They inspire confidence; they commit no blunders; and, better than that, they are true to their faith, whatever it may be, even if it takes them to the stake.

It has frequently occurred to me, in reading this analysis of great men, by Emerson—as he has classified them—that Judge Stephens united, in an extraordinary degree, some of the best attributes of both classes. He possessed, in a large degree, the argumentative and persuasive powers of the orator; and, at the same time, he exerted an insensible influence independent of these, and which, in one sense, was more powerful. There was great force in him; no one could fail to realize it and feel it, who came in contact with him. Men followed him and trusted him, not doubting or fearing, because they knew he had no doubts nor fears himself. Such men are rare; they are more valuable to their generation than it ever gives them credit for; they do more good than is ever known, and prevent more harm; their presence in a community or a State is a repressive on fraud and wrong.

One of the most striking attributes, to the common eye, that Judge Stephens assumed, was in his profession as a lawyer, when engaged in the *certamina* of the court-house. The Northern circuit was, during the whole of his career, renowned for the high rank of its bar, as gentlemen who united, in many instances, the highest accomplishments of legal learning to the most powerful and effective oratorical powers. Younger than most of the lawyers with whom he came in actual contact in his circuit, he was trained, from the beginning, to put forth his best energies and tax his great powers to the uttermost. Like a young gladiator just alighted in the arena, he had to measure swords with veterans whose sinews were toughened by a hundred conflicts. The name he has built for himself in that circuit best attests how, in all those years of arduous practice, his demeanor as a man, and his success as a lawyer, have endeared him to the hearts of the people, and elevated him to the highest rank of the profession.

In his manner and his methods of conducting an important case, it was easy to see that he was no imitator. He reminded you of nobody else. His success was very great. If he was satisfied that justice and right were all on his side, it was impossible for him to lose the case; he was irresistible in such cases; he had the large faculty, in addressing juries, of giving them a clear insight into the case in his very opening sentences. To this one gift he owed many a triumph.

There were things in the practice of law, however, that always exasperated him to the last degree. One of these was a lying witness. If he found out that a witness was falsely swearing away his client's rights, his eyes, his features, and his whole form would show unmistakably that he was a dangerous man to trifle with. At such times, no ordinary man could encounter his eye and utter a falsehood on the stand.

But Linton Stephens was made for better times than these degenerate days. He would chafe himself to death at the corruption which, in the last years of his life, he saw, but could not prevent. Bound to earth by as many ties, both of affection and duty, as any one of us who is left, it is yet better for him as it is; but as for us, who knew him, and loved him, and who now mourn for him, when we chance to revisit scenes that are intimately associated with him, we cannot repress a sigh

> " For the touch of a vanished hand,
> The sound of a voice that is still."

. . . .

Yours, very truly,

POPE BARROW.

SUPREME COURT OF GEORGIA,

SATURDAY, October 5, 1872.

The honorable court met pursuant to adjournment.

Present—their Honors Hiram Warner and H. K. McCay and W. W. Montgomery, Judges.

Upon motion of Hon. Robert Toombs, it is ordered that the following memorial and accompanying resolutions, commemorative of Hon. Linton Stephens, be spread upon the minutes.

The committee appointed by the Supreme Court of Georgia, during this term, to report "suitable resolutions commemorative of Judge Stephens," submit the following

REPORT:

The bench and bar of this court are again called upon to hold a meeting of sorrow, commemorative of another of their most distinguished, valued, and beloved professional brethren. The hand of death, which has recently stricken the name of Linton Stephens from the roll of the living, leaves not upon our record a more perfect model of a pure, able, learned, and upright magistrate; of a just, profound, brilliant, and successful lawyer; of an earnest, self-sacrificing, devoted patriot; of a great-hearted, true man, whose life was spent in the practice of virtue, the pursuit and vindication of truth, and in the service of his fellow-men.

Linton Stephens was born in what was then Wilkes county—now the county of Taliaferro—in this State, on the first day of July, 1823. His father, of Scotch-Irish descent, was a gentleman of unusual education and intellectual attainments, in the day and among the people with whom his lot was cast, and his family ranked with the first-class of the early settlers of our commonwealth. He was left an orphan in childhood, with a slender patrimony; but he had great advantages in his youth, of which he availed himself to an extent rare among the youth of our country.

The providence which deprived him of a father's fostering protection committed him to the care of one pre-eminently qualified to discharge the duties of a father, brother, protector, and friend. Deep, fervent, unbounded fraternal affection molded that grand development of his moral and intellectual character, which won the confidence, the affection, and admiration of all who knew him. Having been thoroughly prepared under this training, he entered the Freshman class of Franklin College, the University of Georgia, in 1839, when sixteen years of age. He was immediately recognized as the head of a large class of Georgia's chosen sons—which position he maintained throughout his collegiate course—and graduated with the first honor of his *Alma Mater* without a competitor and without a rival. After leaving college, he was placed in the office of one of your committee to study law, and was soon afterwards sent to the University of Virginia, where he graduated at the head of the law-class under Judge Tucker, who foresaw and foretold his great professional success. After graduating in law, at the University of Virginia, he went to Harvard, in Massachusetts, to attend the lectures of Judge Story, of the Supreme Court of the United States, and remained there until Judge Story's death, when he came to Washington City and spent a winter in attending the Supreme Court of the United States and the debates in Congress. He returned to Georgia in 1846, having given three years to preparation for his profession—thoroughly prepared to bear the armor which he put on—and was admitted to the bar, in his native county, in 1846.

He located at Crawfordville, in his native county, and became a leader of causes in the court-house before he was scarcely known out of it. In 1849, he was elected to represent Taliaferro county in the Legislature, and re-elected in 1850 and 1851.

Thoroughly versed in the principles of constitutional government, his compatriots immediately recognized his merit and genius, and placed him at the post of labor and of honor.

In 1852, he married the daughter of Judge James Thomas, of Sparta, and removed to Hancock county; and the next year, the people of Hancock again called him into the public service as their representative in the Legislature, and continued to re-elect him until 1855, when he was a candidate for Congress in a district opposed to his political opinions by a large majority, to which his power and influence reduced to an extent which made his defeat a triumph of his principles. In 1857, he contested the same district with the same honorable result. In 1859, Judge Stephens was appointed to the Supreme Court of the State, and was unanimously confirmed by the Legislature to this honorable post, and, after thirteen months' service in that position, resigned it on account of ill-health.

We pass over his judicial record; it will pass down to future ages in our reports. His judgments were clear, concise, exhaustive expositions of the law and facts of the cases decided by him, and contain no word which his friends would wish to blot.

In 1860, he was elected to the Secession convention of the State of Georgia, and voted against the resolution. He acknowledged the right, but opposed the policy; but after the resolution was passed, and that grand, historic act was accomplished, true to his principles and allegiance to his State, he put his whole strength, and power, and soul into the cause of his country. He immediately returned to his home, raised a company for the vindication of the right, and joined the Fifteenth Regiment of Georgia Volunteers, and was elected lieutenant-colonel of that regiment; went to Virginia to meet the foe, and continued in the Army of Northern Virginia until 1862, when his health compelled him to retire from military service.   Upon his return home, he was again called into public service by the people of his county, who again elected him to the Legislature in 1862, and continued him in that capacity until the end of the war; but when his State was invaded in 1863, he raised a battalion of cavalry and again entered into military service for the defense of his native land, and served until the spring of 1864.   When the invader was devastating our land, he again put on his sword, and stood in the front until compelled to retire, from ill-health, to the duties of a legislator.

Having lost his first wife before the war, in 1867 Judge Stephens married Miss Mary W. Salter, of Boston, Massachusetts.

From the surrender of our armies, in 1865, to the time of his death, on the 14th of July, 1872, Judge Stephens was actively engaged in a very large and lucrative practice of his profession; and his last grand and successful effort was made in the vindication of public justice, and in the advocacy of the rights of the people.

His mind was peculiarly adapted to the profession which he had selected, elevated and adorned, clear, vigorous, analytical, and comprehensive; it seized truth, facts, and law with an iron grasp, and stripped sophistry and error naked to the mortal gaze of all beholders; while his stern integrity and devotion to truth gave irresistible power to his lofty intellect.

Judge Stephens was a husband—a father; and here his genial, kind, and affectionate nature shone with peculiar brilliancy, shedding happiness and joy over a household in which he was peculiarly blessed.   But we forbear to enter those sacred precincts in which there is no human consolation.

The committee offer the following resolutions:

Resolved, 1. That, in the death of Linton Stephens, the bench and bar of Georgia have lost an eminent jurist, and the country one of the best, ablest, and truest sons, whose memory we should perpetuate for the benefit of future generations.

Resolved, 2. That we respectfully tender to his bereaved widow and children the heart-felt sympathy of the bench and bar, and the officers of this court, whose warm friendship and affection he so well deserved and so fully possessed.

Resolved, 3. That, in token of this, we will wear the usual badge of mourning during thirty days.

Resolved, 4. That a copy of this report and resolutions be transmitted to Mrs. Stephens, for the family, and that this court be requested to have them entered on its minutes, and that the gazettes of the State be requested to publish them.

> ROBERT TOOMBS,
> CHARLES J. JENKINS,
> R. F. LYON,
> IVERSON L. HARRIS,
> HENRY L. BENNING.

[From the Atlanta Constitution.]

JUDGE LINTON STEPHENS.

Quis desiderio sit pudor aut modus
Tam cari capitis?

" What shame or limit can there be
In yearning for so loved a form ? "

In our private grief for our friend, it is difficult to realize the extent of the public loss which has befallen Georgia in the death of this her distinguished and trusted son. Nor can its proportions be fully appreciated until we get further from it. As one who feels it deeply, in both its public and private aspects, I am constrained, in advance of this full realization, to pay the partial tribute called for at once by affection and admiration. If the portraiture be at all life-like, it will receive many a response from saddened hearts throughout the length and breadth of the State.

Three great qualities fitted him for eminent public usefulness: great capacity, great honesty, and great fidelity. These properties inspired their proper counterpart, and gave him (what was no less necessary to usefulness) the entire, deserved, and familiar confidence of the people of his native State.

His capacity was great, not only of *thought*, extending over a very wide range, but also of *expression*, and that not limited to thinkers only, like himself, but embracing the common mind as well.

He did not live and reason apart from other men, but was one of their number, in accord with their modes and habits, understood them, and conveyed his own thoughts to them in strong, vigorous Anglo-Saxon, like Bullion, with a plain stamp.

His honesty was not less great and varied than his intellectual endowments. It pervaded his public and private life—his heart, head, and tongue. He was an honest seeker after truth. Falsehood, in all its forms, he detested and despised. He loved the truth in his heart. His intellectual appetite craved truth as its proper nutriment, and his tongue was equally candid and sincere. His manners exactly expressed him. He was, in fact, just what he seemed to be.

Such qualities justly commanded the public confidence, resting on a strong foundation of tried merit. That slow growth had become, after long and varied tests, deeply rooted and vigorous in the public mind, and it met no checks or drawbacks on his part; for he was honest with himself, and his gold had been first tried in the fire, for his own use, before it was offered for currency among others.

And so he was a bulwark of public virtue. Dishonesty shrank from his presence; tolerant in all else, for this he had little tolerance. Honesty rested fearlessly upon his strong championship, and felt safe in his hands.

A powerful intellect, of extraordinary breadth and scope, yet as acute as it was comprehensive—capable of vigorous action upon subtle and delicate points—a grasp of a subject perfectly vise-like—a nervous, direct energy of expression, which cut through all vapors—were at his command. These faculties equally fitted him for the investigation of law or of fact. A clear, general view of the entire subject, in all its relations, and in its just proportions, enabled him to systematize his thoughts and adjust himself to a case with wonderful rapidity. He never rested in investigation until he touched bottom, and, from the rock, once found, he could hardly be dislodged by any form of sophistry. If he had any difficulty, it was in his hearers—in their want of discrimination to perceive *real*, not fanciful, distinctions. But this very infirmity was incorporated in his scheme of presenting his case, so that he could show nice points even to dull eyes.

But it was, after all, the honest heart behind all this—of
which the intellect and will were the mere executive officers
and agents—which secured the public confidence that, with
all these faculties, he would do good, and not harm; that
he was not easily deceived himself, and would not willingly
deceive others. Of his powers in that direction, we cannot
speak; for they were not put to the test.

The warmth and sincerity of his personal friendships explain something of the grief, as well as sense, of public loss
which his death has occasioned. His public and private
character were all of a piece; only, in his private intercourse,
there was incomparably more of tenderness and marked
kindness than the severely logical character of his intellect
would have led those to suppose who only knew him in argument. Not comparatively alone, but positively, he was
considerate and kind in an eminent degree, in his intercourse
with others, and never gave willful or intentional offense to
any honest man, to any dull man, to the weak or to the
helpless.

All these traits were big, plain, and distinct—no mistake
about them, nor about the man; and the people knew that
they understood him. He had been tested until they were
satisfied; he had been seen weighed in the balance again
and again, under very varying conditions, and not found
wanting. We do not mean that he was without faults, for
he was a man; but they were not secret or disguised. He
wore no mask, and his faults were better known than their
palliations and his struggles against them. Suffice it to say,
they were not those of a selfish nature. Let none judge of
them harshly—only sorrowfully—for they injured himself
more than others, and deceived no one.

His death occurred in his full intellectual prime. His sun
went down at the high noon of his faculties. These were
very remarkable, and very reliable. He was grown in a
great school, accustomed to emergencies, full of resources,
and ready with them—a trained intellectual athlete, belonging to himself. His self-reliance was great and well-founded,
and inspired the full confidence of his hearers. Few men
had so thorough possession of their own faculties.

As a judge, his decisions were founded on principle—
not authority. He made authority—he was authority—for
he found a solid basis ever before he began to build. His

decisions needed little bolstering; they could stand alone.

But he exemplified a most rare combination of gifts—being great, not only as a judge, but as an advocate, before court or jury, or on the hustings, in cases civil or criminal, upon questions of law or fact, in the preparation or at the trial, or in the examination of witnesses.

Indeed, a measured estimate of his faculties would be regarded extravagant. Such power did a high intellect acquire, under the guidance of honesty. He grappled with great problems with a singular mixture of abstract and practical power, and subtlety and common sense, in his perceptions of truth; and, strange to say, where he went himself into the very heart of these problems, he was usually able to carry others along with him.

This brief notice would be incomplete, if I failed to say he was a firm believer in Christianity. I remember the marked emphasis with which he once expressed this conviction, with that characteristic clearness and boldness which admitted of no misconception, in the words, "I believe Christ is God." His further remark was, substantially, that, with this great intervention of Deity, all lesser and ancillary miracles, introducing the Christian system to mankind, followed on proper evidence, as matters of course. As his manner was, the great, huge fact stood out first, unmistakable, and its qualifications and modes were superadded afterwards.

The public loss is indeed great—the gap left, wide and yawning. Such capacities, so handled, lost at any time, to any State, would be a calamity. By Georgia, and just now, it is peculiarly felt; and yet, to say farewell to the man is harder than to say it to the statesman, the jurist, the public servant. That respect for his character which delighted to do him public honor, and to speak his praise as the peer of the first statesmen of the country, is lost in that deeper feeling of affection which found familiar expression in simply calling him "Linton"—a name which, in the wide limits of Georgia, and in many a circle beyond, is full of meaning, and needs no appendages and no tribute. "Linton!" It calls up the whole, at once, of that noble nature in which was garnered so much of public and private worth, of intellectual treasure and training, of friendship, honesty, and truth.

If such the loss to the public and his friends, what is it to the nearer circle? We cannot intrude here. We can but commend them, in this hour, to a consolation and sympathy above what humanity can give. There is an awful Power to which all must bow. This Power, alone, has the balm to heal the wounds which it has made, and bind up the hearts it has broken.

Mercifully, each day draws us closer to the future—leaves a veil betwixt us and the past. The earth of our State now teems with the loved and lost, who went to her bosom before the lapse of three score years and ten. Another name, worthy of Westminster Abbey, is added to the honored dead of Georgia.

SAMUEL BARNETT.

PROCEEDINGS OF THE STATE CONVENTION.

DEATH OF JUDGE STEPHENS.

Hon. George F. Pierce, of Hancock, introduced the following resolutions:

1. *Resolved by the Democratic party of Georgia in convention assembled,* That, in the recent death of Hon. Linton Stephens, an elected delegate to this convention, the cause of constitutional liberty has lost one of its ablest and noblest defenders.

2. *Resolved,* That Georgia has lost a son whose intellect, cultivation, fidelity, integrity, pure private character, and devotion to principle, illustrated on the bench, at the bar, in the forum, in legislative halls, and in social life, reflected honor upon his native State; and, at this time, when his noble qualities of mind and heart are peculiarly needed, she mourns his death as a mother a beloved son on whom she could depend under the sternest trials and in the darkest hours.

3. *Resolved,* That his well-earned fame is the heritage of all true Georgians, and it shall be our pleasure to cherish and emulate it.

4. *Resolved,* That we tender to his distinguished brother, the Hon. A. H. Stephens, our heart-felt sympathy; and,

commending his wife and children to the tender care of the God of the widow and the fatherless, we beg to assure them that, in every Georgian, they have a friend who will deem it a privilege to serve them.

After submitting the resolutions, Mr. Pierce said:

MR. CHAIRMAN AND GENTLEMEN OF THE CONVENTION—For myself and associate delegates from the county of Hancock, and for the stricken and bereaved county which we have the honor to represent in this convention, I move the adoption of the resolutions which have just been read. I conceive it to be eminently proper that the Democratic party of Georgia should deplore the untimely death of the distinguished gentleman to whom the resolutions relate; for, in all the length and breadth of the land, none could be found more steadfastly attached to its principles, and none more valiant always to battle for their defense. I think it extremely becoming that Georgia should mourn the loss of her illustrious son; for, among all her children—those who yet live to do her honor, and those whose dust is now mingling with his in her honored soil—there was none whose heart pulsated to the common mother with stronger and more earnest love. It is well that the voice of angry contention should be hushed to silence to-day, and that all the lovers of constitutional liberty, who are assembled here, should join in common love to do him honor; for, since the days when Hampden and Sydney died, none have lived who loved liberty more dearly than did he.'

I do not propose to-day, Mr. Chairman, to undertake to pronounce any eulogium upon the illustrious dead. Let this be done—not by those who loved him more, for there were none, but by those abler to do it well; for, sir, only a master's hand should strike the chords which make the music to sing his praise. It is my purpose, in the name of my county, simply to submit the resolutions which have been read, and to commit to Georgia's keeping the priceless memories of his public life.

When this duty shall have been discharged, Hancock's delegation will return to their people and his—to those who knew him best and loved him most—and, joined together, we shall keep, in hallowed remembrance, his local service and his private worth.

And, standing here to-day, sir, in the midst of Georgia's distinguished living, and in presence of her honored dead, remembering all the glories which cluster along the line of her history, it is my privilege, for my county, to say that we proudly feel that if we have contributed nothing more to the greatness of our mother-State, the gift of the distinguished ability and distinguished virtue of Linton Stephens makes as bright a jewel as sparkles in the gathered treasures of her glorious past!

Mr. Pierce was followed by Hon. Julian Hartridge, who said:

MR. CHAIRMAN AND GENTLEMEN OF THE CONVENTION—I beg leave to second the gentleman's motion. While I recognize the ability of the gentleman to do justice to his honored and illustrious colleague—now, alas! numbered with the dead—I ask the privilege to render my tribute to the memory of the noble deceased. True, he was the honored citizen of a single county, yet he belonged to the whole State, which, aside from the ties of family and relations, he loved better than all the world—better than the emoluments of wealth, honors, distinction, and power combined. Wherever the State's interest, principles, honor, and integrity were concerned, there his heart beat, and beat warmly.

I beg the privilege of seconding the motion of the gentleman from Hancock, the home of the distinguished dead. Though he lived in a community remote from my portion of the State, yet, in spirit, he was ever near, and our hearts ever beat in true accord in the desire to improve, uphold, and maintain the honor and integrity of our common State, and promote the welfare of the noble old commonwealth that gave us birth; and, therefore, we feel that he belonged to us as well as to others; for, as it is in a private family, when a loved child dies, a chord is touched, a sympathy is excited, and a tear is to be shed over the last and lamented remains, so it is when a man, distinguished by virtue, intellect, and devotion to State—a champion of her honor and liberties—is cut off by an all-wise Providence, then every citizen feels as if one of his family has died.

Therefore, I lay the humble tribute to the memory of an honored and beloved fellow-citizen, and to the dead brother of one whose hearth-stone is draped in sorrow and desolation; and, though one brother is mouldering in the grave—sacred sepulchre of a departed patriot—there is another still left, who has, is now, and will ever be dear to Georgia, whose heart, clothed in sackcloth, is bowed in humility to his God, and whose head, venerable with wisdom and age, is covered with ashes.

Hon. Warren Akin said:

Mr. Chairman—I beg to bring some tribute to the memory of the noble and distinguished dead. The gentleman from Hancock, when he spoke of his stricken and bereaved community, would have been more correct to state that Georgia had been stricken and bereaved.

I have known the deceased long and well. I have seen him at the bar of justice, in the forum, in the assembly, on the bench—everywhere, and I have ever found him a man of truth, honor, and principle, and of all the ennobling virtues becoming a man and a patriot—always reliable, honest, and avowed in everything that pertained to his associations with his fellow-man, and his doctrines regarding National or State policy.

If opposed, he was ever honorable and liberal. He loved the truth, and despised all that was low and mean. Ever ready to co-operate with the good and patriotic, he made no compromise with the wicked. He was a hero among the fearless, and a terror to the dishonest and the evil-doer.

I hope the resolutions of the gentleman from Hancock will be adopted by a rising vote. Linton Stephens—that loved name—he sleeps the sleep of death! yet, while Georgia has patriots, though she should lie groveling in the dust under a conqueror's heel, subdued to despair with the melancholy music of the victor's clanking chains, or should she mount higher and assert triumphantly her liberties and her honor; while there are women who love free government—and, thank God! they do love it with the warmest pulsations of their patriotic hearts—there will be a hallowed remembrance of Linton Stephens, the champion of his State's and country's honor, and the valiant defender of his beloved people.

Hon. Albert R. Lamar said:

MR. PRESIDENT—I trust I shall not weary the patience of this convention if I ask a moment in which to lay an offering upon the grave of my friend—a friend whose devotion and fidelity outlived political vicissitudes, and yielded only to a common conqueror. It is meet that Georgia should pay funeral rites to one of her noblest sons.

It is proper that we, his friends and companions, should send words of condolence and sympathy to his stricken household; and I may safely say that there is not a heart in this assembly that does not cherish a tender feeling for him whose hearth-stone has been made dark and desolate by this terrible affliction.

The time and the occasion will not permit me to pass an eulogium upon the character and services of Linton Stephens; but the future historian may find, in his name and fame, much with which to adorn and ennoble the annals of these troublous times.

He was a Spartan in all the sterner virtues of manhood— a Bayard in courage, integrity, and accomplishments. We, who have seen him face fearful odds in vindication and defense of the rights of his people, have had cause to say:

"How high a pitch his resolution soars!"

I can recall a recent incident which illustrates the salient point in his character: At the late convention which preceded this, he stood almost unaided and alone in a contest, upon the other side of which were arrayed many of the most cherished friends of his life.

There are gentlemen here who can bear testimony as to how he bore himself in that contest.

You and I, Mr. President, will remember how a gentleman, returning from the room of the Committee on Business, with voice and face aglow with admiration, remarked to me, "Is not Linton Stephens a man of iron soul!"

He was, indeed, sir; and if mortals are permitted to take into another world the temperaments of this, we may feel assured that our departed friend is steering his barque on eternity's ocean, with a sublime and unfaltering faith that he will reach a haven of rest in the sunlight of Mercy and Love on the other shore.

Mr. President, the mute faces* that look down upon us

* The walls of the Representative hall, at Atlanta, are adorned with large, life-size portraits of James Jackson, Andrew Jackson, Franklin, Crawford, Troup, Clarke, Howell Cobb, Jefferson, and others.

from these walls to-day are fitting reminders that broad acres, crowded marts, beautiful temples, and hoarded millions are the least of the great elements which constitute a State. They tell us that brave and virtuous men are the greatest glories of the commonwealth; and in the heroic mold in which these men were cast was cast Linton Stephens, body and soul.

But one moon has waxed since he sat here in the prime and plenitude of vigorous health and intellectual prowess. In the night that shall follow this day, that same moon will shed her waning sheen upon the spot where he sleeps in the embrace of his honored mother!

In time, we, too, sir, shall cease our strifes, and our pride, our ambition, and our hopes will follow us to the grave! In view, then, of this sudden and startling blow, which has fallen in our midst, may we not, with bowed heads and burdened hearts, exclaim:

"What shadows we are, and what shadows we pursue!"

JUDGE LINTON STEPHENS.

Obiit 14th July, 1872.

[The following tribute to the memory of the Hon. Linton Stephens is from the pen of a niece of Henry W. Longfellow, the American poet, who has attained so much distinction in the Eastern as well as the Western continent. We feel that our readers will, as we do, highly appreciate this tribute, not only from the tone of its touching sympathy, but from the source from which it comes.—EDITORS SUN.]

Another noble name is added
To the list of shrined dead;
Another strong, grand form departed
To his lowly, narrow bed!

Another guiding hand is taken—
One more heart is calm and still;
O my God! 'tis now in anguish—
Bow me to Thy higher will!

Gone, in all his prime and vigor,
Passed from out the field of life;
But he bore himself as conqueror,
Nobly in that weary strife!

To Thy feet, O Holy Jesus,
Now we bring this crushing load;
Only by Thy help and guidance
Can we tread this thorny road.

In Thy hands, we then, confiding,
Leave the one to us so dear—
Leave until a spirit risen
In Thy glory shall appear!

Boston, August 11. 1872.   MARIAN ADELE LONGFELLOW.

(From the Atlanta Sun.)

LINTON STEPHENS.

BY A. R. WATSON.

I.

Oh, Eagle of our gentle Georgia clime,
  Eyried so near the sky !
Whose sturdy wings beat strong against our time—
  Of never-flinching eye !

II.

Of sternest pulse, and eager, bounding flight,
  Touching the sun-tipped brow
That domes the top of fame's imperial height,
  Where eyrie such as thou !

III.

Oh, Eagle ! stricken from our Georgia skies,
  And stretched upon the plain,
With the full blaze of morning in thine eyes,
  Ours is the awful pain !

IV.

Oh, Archer ! that, amid the quivering strife,
  Winged swift thy truest darts,
And, through the core of his majestic life,
  Smit deep into our hearts !

V.

Oh, conqueror—Death ! thrice victor, pass along,
  Trophied above the past !
Our pulse of greatness, erewhile brave and strong,
  Is at its ebb at last !

VI.

A little room is all that's needed now—
  Oh, mother earth, be kind !
Methinks your breast should feel a newer glow
  With dust like his enshrined.

ANALYTICAL INDEX.

www.ingramcontent.com/pod-product-compliance
Lightning Source LLC
Chambersburg PA
CBHW030941110726
47900CB00004B/1079